A CHRISTMAS WEDDING IN THE COTSWOLDS

LUCY COLEMAN

Boldwood

First published in Great Britain in 2021 by Boldwood Books Ltd.

Cover Design by Alice Moore Design

Cover Photography: Shutterstock

A CIP catalogue record for this book is available from the British Library.

Paperback ISBN 978-1-83889-071-1

Large Print ISBN 978-1-80280-645-8

Hardback ISBN 978-1-80280-855-1

Ebook ISBN 978-1-83889-073-5

Kindle ISBN 978-1-83889-072-8

Audio CD ISBN 978-1-83889-069-8

MP3 CD ISBN 978-1-80280-272-6

Digital audio download ISBN 978-1-83889-070-4

Boldwood Books Ltd
23 Bowerdean Street
London SW6 3TN
www.boldwoodbooks.com

To all the wonderful people who so generously devote their time to fundraising, especially at Christmas. This one is for you! x

JUNE

PROLOGUE

My name is Immi Tolliman. When I was fourteen years old, I moved to Lock Keeper's Cottage in Aysbury to live with my grandfather, Ernest Tolliman. Having recently lost my dad, I was one angry and rebellious teen. And Granddad, known affectionately to everyone – including me – as Tollie, was also grieving.

Losing his son made him miss Grandma Nell even more. As time went on, I realised how disruptive my presence had been and that he'd put up with me out of sheer love for his, then wayward, granddaughter.

Eventually, an easy peace began to grow between us and over the years that has turned into admiration and mutual respect. We saw each other through the tough times and that is a special bond we feel blessed to share.

The highlight of the year for the little community of Aysbury, located in the picturesque Cotswolds, is without doubt the Santa Ahoy Christmas cruises run in aid of local charities. And this year is a special one indeed.

It's the tenth anniversary of something that has turned a group of friends into family, inspired by my granddad. Tollie is

Aysbury's very own Santa Claus. With myself as the chief elf and two helpers, Jade and Jude, my fiancé Gray Adams as the handsome captain, and a wider team beavering away in the background, the cruises kick-start everyone's Christmas.

The community is spread out over a wide area, but there is a small group of locals who live within walking distance of the Aysbury Junction Marina. The nature of a marina is that many of the boats moored there long-term have owners who appear infrequently throughout the year, however there are also a handful of permanent berths. Together with the families who run The Bullrush Inn and the Lockside Nurseries, there's always a helping hand on offer.

Tollie, who was the manager of the marina for twenty-five years, has a theory that Aysbury is a collection of waifs and strays, and he's proud to count himself amongst them. People have ended up here in desperate need of something. More often than not, without having a clue about what exactly that elusive something might be.

Perhaps it's a sense of community, the feeling of belonging somewhere, especially if that's never been true before, either because they don't have close family, or they've struggled to conform. People stay because they feel they can at last put down roots.

'Round pegs, square holes,' as Tollie often says. 'That's why we fit together so well and make a crackin' team. We're all in the same boat.'

We've learnt to respect the fact that one's past is not what defines you; the secrets people choose not to divulge are a private matter but whenever a problem arises there is always someone willing to listen. And it's the choices people make as each new day dawns that matter.

Shortly after last Christmas, Tollie moved into my former

home, a barn conversion known as The Retreat, which is in the garden of Lock Keeper's Cottage. Gray and I are making Tollie's dream come true to see the old cottage brought up to date and turned into a home of our own, but things are not going quite as smoothly as I'd hoped...

1

NO, NO, NO, NO, NO!

Leaning forward until my forehead is resting on the desktop in front of me, I let out an exasperated groan. My phone is still firmly grasped in my hand but, having read the message twice over, I can't even bring myself to respond.

Hi Immi, bad news I'm afraid. Mains water pipe has fractured. Give me an hour to get things under control and then could you pop in? Tollie has a spare room, right?

The message is from Reggie, the foreman in charge of the building works at the cottage, and he's obviously preparing me for the worst.

'Oops, so sorry. Um... are you feeling all right?'

The sound of an unfamiliar voice forces me to pull myself together quickly and I sit up, pushing back my shoulders in a determined way. Opening the drawer alongside me, I throw the phone inside and shut it with a snap.

'Yes. I'm fine. How can I help?' My smile as I turn is half-hearted, but it's the best I can do. A water problem at Lock Keeper's Cottage feels like the final straw today and it's only 11 a.m.

The kindly looking older man standing in front of me stares back hesitantly, looking as if he doesn't know whether to stay or go. He shifts from one foot to the other, uneasily.

'I'm... um, here to see Martin, but I'm a bit early, I'm afraid.'

The poor man looks so apologetic that I jump up, wondering what on earth he must think of my behaviour.

'Oh, of course! Patrick Hirst, isn't it?' I hold out my hand in a welcoming gesture. 'I'm Imogen Tolliman, but everyone calls me Immi. Please take a seat. Martin is running a little late, I'm afraid. I'll organise us a cup of tea, or coffee?'

It's the first time I've met Martin's business adviser, who, according to him, has taken a huge weight off his shoulders over the past year.

'Very nice to meet you at last, Immi. Martin talks about you all the time. I really don't want to put you out. It looks like you've had some bad news.'

'A fractured water main isn't the best text to get on a Monday morning, but I'm sure my builders will be able to sort it out.' It's not the fix I'm worried about, but the cost.

Patrick wrinkles his brow. 'Oh, dear. Now I understand. I'd be banging my head on the desk, too. If you're sure I'm not interrupting you, a cup of tea would be most welcome, thanks.'

I leave him to take a seat and head into the Lockside Nurseries' small kitchen. It's quiet in the back offices this morning as the delivery vans are doing their rounds, and everyone else is either on the shop floor or working in the greenhouses. When I head back to my office, the sign on the door still makes me smile. The decision to take on the newly created full-time position of Assistant Manager, in January of this year, was a big step for me. I don't regret giving up my other part-time job, working as Office

Administrator for the manager of Aysbury Marina. Everyone around here refers to him as Fisher as his surname is so apt. I'm closer to him than most – I regard him as family. But with another local resident, Valerie Price, now sitting at my old desk, I know that I've left him in good hands.

Nudging open the door with my foot, I step back inside my office, but Patrick isn't seated, he's studying the notice board.

'You start planning for Christmas early,' he remarks, pointing to the string of glittery white snowflakes.

'Yes, my granddad, Tollie, runs the Santa Ahoy cruises. It's the tenth anniversary this year and we're trying to raise enough money to build a children's playground.'

I pass Patrick a mug of tea, which he takes gratefully as he eases himself down onto the spare chair alongside the desk.

'Ah, I've heard something about that. Christmas has never been a big thing for my wife and I, um... soon-to-be ex-wife, that is; we always dine out on Christmas Day. Being just the two of us, it was easier,' he replies, rather soberly.

I don't quite know how to respond, as Christmas was always a magical time for me growing up and now, in adulthood, I keep that tradition going. Christmas isn't just for children, it's about surrounding yourself with the people you want to spend time with and it's sad to think of the fun that Patrick and his wife missed out on over the years.

He looks as if he's carrying a huge weight on his shoulders and his brow seems to be permanently furrowed. He's a troubled man and I can't help wondering what his story is.

'The tea is perfect, thank you, Immi. Do you live locally?'

'Yes. My fiancé, Gray, and I are renovating Lock Keeper's Cottage. It's the property set back from the towpath on the other side of the canal. This morning's news could be rather inconvenient, to say the least.'

Patrick places his mug down on the desk, shaking his head.

'I'm really sorry to hear that. It's a major work in progress, then?'

I manage a genuine smile this time. 'Yes. Gray works in London and I don't relish the thought of telling him that we might have to move out, or, rather, back into our former home for a while.'

'You're lucky to have that option.'

'It's a barn conversion built in the garden of the cottage, but Tollie lives there now.'

Patrick laughs. 'Ooh, tough one. You do get on with your granddad, I hope?'

'Oh, Tollie is the best. He took me in after my dad died and he put up with me through my tantrums and angst when I was the teenager from hell.'

'That can't have been easy for either of you. You don't get on with your mum?' Patrick enquires, his voice full of empathy.

'I lost contact with her early on in my life, but that's a long story. Now there's nowhere else I'd rather be. It just took me a while to realise how lucky I am.'

'You sound like a fighter, Immi, and I'm sure you'll get through this.' He tips his mug at me before taking a slurp. 'You're not the one getting married at Christmas, are you?'

'I am.'

'That's brave, considering the snowstorms we had last year.'

'Well, it was going to be a summer wedding,' I reply, 'but Gray composes music and he's involved in recording a film score. It's been all go, and what with the fundraising we've been doing, well, there aren't enough hours in the day and we had to move the date.'

Poor man, he's a good listener and I must sound like a real

whinger, but stress is now affecting the way I react to every little drama that arises, which isn't like me at all.

'Hey, where's that smile gone?' Patrick asks, giving me a wink. His genial attempt to lift my mood works, and the corners of my mouth instantly curl upwards.

'It's kind of you to listen to me wittering on like this, Patrick. I must sound like a crazy woman,' I reply, laughing.

'There are moments when we all need to let stuff out, Immi, so don't worry about it. It's been happening to me a fair bit lately, too. It isn't easy, but life goes on and somehow we manage to get through each little crisis.'

I catch a sudden movement out of the side of my eye, and the boss appears. Martin Williams is a good man to work for and he took me on as a Saturday helper at the tender age of sixteen. I had never touched a plant in my life at that point and he taught me everything I know. Understanding what happens out in the massive greenhouses really helps when you are the assistant manager, and now I run the office while Martin is out being the face of the company. He's a real family man and has a kind heart, which is why I love working for him.

'Oh, what I'd give for a cup of tea!' Martin comments as he steps forward to shake Patrick's hand. 'Sincere apologies for keeping you waiting, Patrick. I got stuck in a long queue of cars crawling along behind a tractor.'

'No problem at all. I was a bit early and it's great to finally meet Immi. Especially after I've heard so much about her. I can now see why business is booming.' Patrick glances at me, a hint of a smile easing his frown for a brief moment before his face settles back into serious mode.

'Convincing Immi to work here full-time was the best move I ever made. She's much more organised than I am when it comes to the paperwork, and things run without a hitch now. It's because of her that I can get out there and make new contacts. Anyway, I suppose we'd better start crunching numbers then Patrick.'

He gives Martin a nod, then turns back to face me. 'Thank you for the tea and the chat, Immi. Much appreciated. Hopefully, our paths will cross again before too long. With a bit of luck, the builders will get your problem sorted quickly.'

Martin screws up his face. 'Oh, no. Not another delay!' he declares.

'Yep. Just another Monday morning blip to start off the week, and it sounds like Reggie is preparing me for the worst.'

'Poor you,' Martin replies sadly. 'I'm here for the rest of the day, so if you need to make yourself scarce for a couple of hours, feel free, Immi. We'll catch up later.'

'Thanks, Martin, appreciated.'

As they head out of the office, I'm not sure what to do first. Jeez, I hope this week isn't going to go downhill from here, as I'm not sure I have the stamina right now. Why do I always take on too much? You would think I'd have learnt my lesson by now.

My phone pings and it's a message from my best friend, Sarah, at The Bullrush Inn.

Hi sweetie, any decisions yet on the final menu for the wedding buffet? xx

Sarah is right, of course, I do need to get my act together. Every time I sit down with the wedding folder something else crops up. I'm not usually so easily distracted, and the truth is that I need rescuing. Then an idea pops into my head. It's time to reach out to someone capable of pulling this together for me, and I think I know just the person to ask.

* * *

'Something must be up to see you on my doorstep at this time on a Monday. Come on in,' Val says as she swings open the door to Byre Cottage.

It always smells nice in here. A mixture of freshly baked goodies and a fragrance. Often, it's from the fresh flowers Val picks from the garden, but sometimes from the essential oils she uses in a small diffuser. Ziggy, Val's beautiful Bengal cat, comes running out of the study and begins to wind herself around my feet. She has an entire conversation with me as I bend to stroke her, and I give her a miaow back. Ziggy begins purring and tilts her head to let me stroke her chin; she is such a character.

'I'm sorry to disturb you as I know it's almost lunchtime, so it's just a quick visit, I promise.'

Val looks over my shoulder fleetingly, as if she's expecting someone.

'I'm... um... sure that Fisher would forgive me if I was running a little late because of you,' she responds, laughing. 'Anyway, the cheese and olive scones I'm baking have only just gone into the oven.'

'They smell delicious and if you take him one, he'll forgive you anything. Anyway... I wanted to talk to you about wedding stuff.'

Val shuts the door behind me and ushers me through to the sitting room.

'Have you eaten?' she asks. 'Can you stay for a quick lunch?'

'Thanks, but regrettably it has to be a no. I'm on my way back to Lock Keeper's Cottage as the water main has fractured.'

Val's reaction is one of dismay. 'Oh, Immi, I'm gutted for you. Just when it looked like the worst of the building work was behind you, that's devastating news. Is there anything I can do to help?'

Without thinking, I let out a huge sigh and she indicates for me to take a seat on the sofa.

'This wedding is beginning to feel like the final straw!' I blurt out and then realise how awful that sounds. Val looks at me, shocked, her expression pained. 'Oh, nothing's wrong, please don't think that. Gray and I are both fine and it's all wonderful, still. But who has time to fuss over flowers and menu choices and...?' I run out of steam, taking a moment to catch my breath.

'Just tell me what you want doing and I'll do it. You know that, Immi.' Val's voice is full of concern.

'I need an official wedding planner, someone who can make sense of what still needs to be done to make it all happen.'

She smiles sympathetically, gently lowering herself down onto the sofa opposite me. 'You want me to find someone for you?' she enquires, gently.

'Um. Not exactly. I was wondering whether *you* have time to take on the role.'

'You'd trust me to do that? But I've never been involved in planning a wedding before,' she replies. However, I can tell by the gleam in her eyes that she's pleased I'm reaching out to her.

'I'm desperate, Val. Everyone assumes a bride knows exactly what she wants, but I find it overwhelming. I don't want to disappoint Gray, but I have no idea what I'm doing. I need someone I can rely upon to draw up a master plan, or this wedding is going to be a total disaster.'

'The answer is yes, of course!' she replies, with real enthusiasm. 'It will be my pleasure.'

'The problem is that I don't even know where to start, Val, as I'm being pulled in so many different directions and that isn't going to ease up any time soon. You know me, I'm not one to let things slide and if I do it means I'm losing my grip. With Gray away during the week, the only quality time we get is at the weekend. And I'm taking on more and more at work to ease the pressure on Martin. Plus having to liaise with the builders and being chief organiser and treasurer for the Santa Ahoy anniversary fund, I'm like a headless chicken. We're halfway through the year and, as far as the wedding plans go, I've booked Aysbury village hall for the civil ceremony and the reception, with The Bullrush Inn doing the catering. But we don't even have a menu or a guest list yet, and Sarah texted me again this morning to give me a nudge.'

I sink back onto the sofa, feeling deflated and demoralised.

'Don't you worry about a thing, Immi. Give me whatever lists you have and, if we can take an hour one evening to sit down and talk through your vision, I'll get things moving.'

My chin wavers a little as I give her a look full of gratitude and relief.

'Hey, don't get upset. There are other people we can pull in to help once we have an action plan. But you will need to be on hand to make some firm decisions quite quickly. I'm sorry the original plan for a summer wedding hasn't been doable because of Gray's workload. I know you were both disappointed about that.'

I sit forward, shrugging my shoulders. 'This is his big break, and I wasn't about to make life difficult for him.' I sigh wearily. 'I wanted a simple service in a cornfield alongside the canal, with a small group of friends, and a big party for everyone in a marquee afterwards. The village hall is nice, but it's not quite the same, is it?'

Val chews her lip, deep in thought. 'And Gray definitely doesn't want to slip it back another six months to next summer?

There's so much going on and you're carrying a lot on your shoulders, Immi.'

'I know. But all we really want is a quiet little wedding, with close friends and neighbours. Gray feels guilty that I insisted on pushing back the date to take the pressure off him, but I'm totally in love with the idea of a Christmas wedding. After all, we did get engaged at Christmas and it is my favourite time of the year.' That makes us both burst out laughing.

'You did!' Val says, grinning at me. 'It wasn't quite the romantic occasion you'd hoped for, though, was it?'

'That's precisely why I need your help. My perfect plans went awry, didn't they? But,' I hold up my ring finger, proudly displaying Grandma's engagement ring, 'we pulled it off. A wedding, though, is an entirely different thing and I'm floundering. I want it to be a memory Gray and I will cherish forever, but at this rate it's going nowhere.'

'Have you at least thought about a wedding dress?'

I stare back at her miserably and Val sucks in a deep breath, shaking her head. 'Oh, Immi. We need to sort the basics as quickly as possible and then it's a case of attending to the finer details. I'll do some surfing online as there will be websites with lots of handy tips and checklists.'

'That would be amazing, Val. I can't thank you enough for coming to my rescue.'

'I'm excited to be involved,' she replies, sounding a little emotional. 'I'll give Rona a call, too, as we can't leave out Gray's mum. I think she'll be thrilled to be a part of it. What if the three of us meet up one evening this week to start the ball rolling?'

'Perfect, just let me know what works for you two and I'll bring along the wedding folder. There isn't a lot in there, I'm afraid, but the upside is that it won't take long to bring you up to speed.' I give her a sheepish look, but Val's smile doesn't waver.

'Well, that will make things easier. Once I've spoken with Rona, I'll text you. Right, off you go and don't give it another thought. Just focus on whatever's gone wrong today down at Lock Keeper's Cottage.'

We stand and I give her a grateful hug.

'Thank you for coming to my rescue. I know it sounds awful, as my wedding should be the main priority, but Tollie and the whole crew have worked so hard to make this tenth anniversary mean something. So many people are involved, and the money is coming in, but we have a long way to go with the fundraising if we're to meet our target. I really need to focus on it as there is still so much to be done to make it all happen.'

'I know, Immi, there's no need to explain. Just know that everyone appreciates what you're doing. Don't forget to rely more heavily on other members of the committee, though. You're shouldering way too much and there's no shame in delegating.'

A meaningful look passes between us. Tollie is eighty-seven years young and he's still spritely, but one thing life has taught both myself and Val is never to take anything for granted. We both know that's why I want to make sure everything goes smoothly.

'Well, you're a real star and Gray will be relieved to hear help is on hand.'

'It's quiet when Gray isn't around,' she muses. 'You must miss his constant tapping as a tune runs through his head, and the habit he has of humming when he's thinking is so endearing.'

'Oh, I do and it's one of the things I love about him, his passion for music. However, it's catching, and I often end up having the same little tune stuck inside my head, too. It can be very distracting at times. Anyway, I must go. I'm just about to break the news to Tollie that, unless there's a quick fix for this latest problem, Gray and I could well be knocking on his door and hoping he'll take pity on us.'

Val's eyes widen. 'Oh dear. It's not the best start to your week.'

'No, but it's not all bad news this morning, is it? Thanks to you.' The sense of relief I'm feeling is enough to lift my spirits and fortify me for what lies ahead.

2

I CAN FEEL A HEADACHE COMING ON

I head away from Byre Cottage. The Bullrush Inn is en route and it's unlikely I'll be able to sneak past without being seen, so I decide to pop in to reassure Sarah that a decision will be made about the menu by the beginning of next week. Sarah and Kurt, the owners of The Bullrush, and their twin daughters, Jade and Jude, will also be guests, which adds another complication to our planning. Aside from the summer season, Christmas is their busiest time of year and catering for a wedding is an additional pressure.

Pushing open the door and walking inside, the smells wafting out from the kitchen remind me how hungry I am. A low grumble from my stomach confirms that, but unfortunately this can only be a flying visit. I scan around but I can't see any familiar faces as it's still a little early for lunch. At this time of the day, the custom is usually made up of couples out for a walk along the canal, grateful to find a place that serves hearty, home-cooked food and the popular all-day breakfast. Sometimes, there are 'day-raters' around who have rented a berth for a night or two while they explore the surrounding area. It's always a bonus to be able to take a break from cooking on board and The Bullrush's reputation has travelled far and wide.

'Here she is, then,' Kurt calls out as he pushes through the swing doors, carrying a tray of condiments. 'How's it going, Immi? Are you here to eat, or are you looking for Sarah?'

Kurt and Sarah are one of the friendliest couples I know, and when they arrived in Aysbury the girls had just turned seven, now they're fourteen years old. It took Kurt and Sarah eighteen months to completely renovate the place and it wasn't an easy time, as they did the majority of the work themselves. While juggling the demands of two very lively little girls, they managed to keep the café open while the major building works were in progress. They succeeded in turning this place into the beating heart of our community. Jude and Jade are a credit to their hard-working parents, learning from a young age how a little help can go a long way.

A café and gift shop by day, every Friday, Saturday, and Sunday evening, between 6–10 p.m., The Bullrush is the haunt of the Aysbury Junction Marina Anchor Club members. With the celebrated Middle Norton Brewing Company just a short journey away, the variety of beers on offer has become quite an attraction. I suspect that some of the club members have never taken the helm of a boat as captain, but they all enjoy trips out on the waterways and canals. Everyone is welcome and it's good to see those familiar faces, despite the fact they don't all live on the doorstep. And whenever there's a litter-pick or work to be done that benefits the marina, they turn up to lend a hand. Now that's a club worth joining, in my book.

'I'm just popping in to let Sarah know that I'll email her by the end of the week once my wedding planner and I have had a chat.'

The look Kurt gives me is classic and he replies in a semi-hushed tone, 'Oh, you have a *wedding planner*.'

I nod enthusiastically. 'Well, hopefully two, as Val intends to enlist Rona's help to get things moving.'

Sarah appears behind him just in time to overhear our conversation. 'Thank goodness for that! You have way too much on your plate, Immi. It's about time you reached out for a little support. I'll email you a selection of menus we've used in the past. You can mix and match, or simply create your own buffet. It's entirely up to you. I know how busy you are, but it would be helpful if you could give me a firm number before too long.'

'I know,' I reply, hanging my head. 'My guest list is done, but I'll press Gray again when he turns up on Friday night.'

She gives me a knowing smile. 'Oh, don't pounce on him as soon as he arrives. I feel for you both. It hasn't been an easy first half of the year, has it? How are the renovations going?'

'Don't ask. Problem after problem, I'm afraid, and today is no different but I can't bear to talk about it. How are the girls?'

'Jade and Jude are fine. Sometimes I find myself staring at them and wondering how they got to be so grown-up. It's like having three women in the kitchen, now.'

'And fine young women they are, too. Right, I'm off. The builders are waiting to show me the latest disaster.'

Sarah rolls her eyes sympathetically.

'Hopefully it's something they can resolve without too much trouble. We'll see you and Gray on Friday night, if we don't see you before. I'll reserve your favourite table,' Kurt joins in amiably.

'Thank you. Friday feels like an eternity away right now,' I reply. Before Gray and I got engaged, Friday was our official date night. Sadly, there were times he couldn't get to Aysbury at all and then we'd video call instead. It was hard to keep our spirits up as being apart was agony. And now that we're finally living together, he's working in London again. It's like turning back the clock.

'Have a great day,' I call over my shoulder as I head for the door. I'm thankful to have such good friends, and once I'm out in the fresh air again the sunshine begins to lift my spirits.

There's a light breeze coming off the canal and I wish I'd worn a thicker jacket over my short-sleeved top. Picking up the pace, I turn left onto the towpath as a tidy-looking, fifty-seven-foot Delamere narrowboat chugs by, the couple onboard waving to me. I wave back with an acknowledging smile. They might be total strangers or people who have stopped here before whom I don't instantly recognise, but it doesn't matter. Boat owners who cruise the canals tend to be a laid-back, friendly bunch. That's another thing I love about living here and Gray feels the exact same way.

With a clear, forget-me-not-blue sky overhead and the usual hammering sounds echoing across the canal from the marina's workshop, it's a reminder of how lucky we all are to live here. June is my favourite month, when everything is green and luscious, with ever-burgeoning splashes of colour appearing in the hedgerows and borders to surprise and delight the walkers.

When I focus on breathing in, I can smell the sweetness of the grass and the freshness of the air as it filters through the leaves of the branches overhead. The birds fly in and out, chasing each other and having fun. Squabbling like children over the best perch, or the tastiest grub.

The only hint of the cornfields close by is as the breeze catches the growing stalks. There is a musical rustling in the air when the leaves flap around and the plants sway gently in waves, as if they are being orchestrated. It's easy enough to catch glimpses of the crops where the hedge thins. The ears of corn, with their tell-tale beards, have yet to become plump and sweet, but we've already had an exceptional number of sunny days on and off since the beginning of March, which bodes well for a good crop this year.

I'm about level with the far end of the car park situated next to The Bullrush when a raft of ducks, carried on the wake from the cruiser, decide to head for the bank. As they make their way up the slippery slope to my right, they begin squabbling. The older ones flop down, too intent on a preening session to care about the younger ducks, who are fighting to get ahead of each other. One of them waddles higher up the bank to settle down amongst a small patch of longer grass, close to the edge of the path. He doesn't even tilt his head to look in my direction, having sensed I'm no threat at all. However, the moment one of the other ducks decides to join him he becomes extremely vocal. Not all ducks quack, I've discovered, and this one has a raspy grunt. It makes me smile as it sounds as though he has a sore throat, but he makes enough noise to scare the interloper away.

The grass is all the same, no matter where they decide to settle, but I can see it's like a game and as two of the ducks begin to follow on behind me being extremely vocal, I chuckle away to myself. When my phone begins to buzz, I'm delighted to see that it's Gray.

'Ah, are you missing me already?' I enquire in a sultry tone.

'I always miss you when I'm away, of course, but actually I'm phoning to say that I left my toothbrush charging by mistake. It's tucked down at the side of the bed because I was using the shaving socket in the bathroom at the time, so you might not spot it. I'll have to go old school with a manual brush.' He chuckles to himself.

It's not exactly the romantic call I would have liked, but just the sound of Gray's voice is a tonic. He is the reason that everything in my little world is changing and it won't be long before these annoying little problems at the cottage will be done and dusted.

'I'm heading back there right now. That'll teach you to rush out the door.'

'Can I help it if you're way too much of a distraction? You just look so darned good with bed hair and sleep in your eyes. Monday mornings are tough, as it's hard to leave you.' He's laughing at me and yet I can feel that little undertone of sadness. It's not easy for either of us.

We spent so much time last year wishing away the days between his visits and now it feels like déjà vu. But then it was because he was looking after Rona, getting her back to full health. Gray was juggling work and being his mother's main support while working from home, so I'm not complaining, because now his mum is settled into a little cottage on the other side of the canal. And when he's not around, I'm here for her.

'Yes, well, that's the price you pay for being such a successful composer. I'm sorry to cut you short, honey, but I'll ring you tonight at nine, as usual. I'm off to see the builders before they break for lunch. Love you, mwah.' I blow him a noisy kiss and if I could see his face now, I'd be looking at that big, goofy grin of his.

'Love ya, babe. Bye for now.'

'Immi!'

I glance up to see Fisher, who took over management of the marina after Tollie retired. He's the man who, when I first came to live here, listened to a little upstart of a teenager going on and on about how my granddad Tollie didn't understand me. I thought I knew it all and what I wanted was more freedom to do as I pleased. Fisher managed to stop me from getting into trouble by being my sounding board. He didn't always say very much, but when he did, I listened. And now, with Val taking over my part-time job in the marina's office so that I can work full-time at the nurseries, I miss that daily contact with him. The ritual of making him two cups of strong coffee first thing in the morning in quick succession, and knowing not to disturb him until he drained the second one, always made me smile. I also miss the times we'd spend our lunch breaks together in The Bullrush, putting the world to rights, cementing that special bond between us.

I pick up the pace and as Fisher steps down onto the towpath I stride over to give him a hug.

'You smell nice!' I remark as he wraps me in his arms and rocks me back and forth on my feet playfully.

'Do I?' he replies cagily. I gaze up at him, shaking my head.

'You're off to Val's for lunch, aren't you?' I enquire, sounding the teensiest bit accusatory. 'You never used to let me slope off early at lunch time. I wondered why she wasn't in work.'

'Hmm... I can't recall you ever offering to make me lunch, darling girl,' he declares, smiling wickedly.

I'm still getting used to thinking of Fisher and Val as a couple. But they were both battling with loneliness and, since they've started dating, it's been lovely to see them getting on so well.

Fisher's ex-wife left him for a widower with two children of primary-school age. He was heartbroken, not just because they weren't blessed with a child, but because he thought they'd come to terms with that blow. They were working towards a plan for a different kind of future, one that could give them a level of freedom. Step one was to be mortgage-free but that meant working longer hours in the day jobs.

Fisher bought The Star Gazer, a fifty-seven-foot Colecraft narrowboat, spending every spare hour he had to strip her back to a shell and turn her into a pleasure cruiser. And then, with no warning at all, his world was turned upside down. Their stunning barn conversion was sold and now he lives in a modest little cottage in one of the winding lanes behind the marina. He takes little trips along the canal from time to time, but at Christmas The Star Gazer turns into The Santa Ahoy Special, which is when she really comes alive.

'And a good lunch it will be, I'm sure,' I muse, smiling at him.

His eyes light up and I can see that he feels he's been rumbled. 'I'm in need of some home-cooking today,' he replies, sounding sorry for himself, which is not like Fisher.

'What's up? Anything I can help with?'

'No. I'm just wrestling with the decision about whether or not to make the formal application to take early retirement the Christmas after next and start the ball rolling. As you know, it was a foregone conclusion. But... well, what was once a no-brainer now has question marks all over it.'

'If you want to come round to Lock Keeper's Cottage one evening for a quiet chat—' I stop short, remembering that, if this latest hiccough at the cottage is as bad as my gut instincts are warning me, I might be moving out for a while. 'On second thoughts, it would be easier if I come to you. All is not well back at the cottage, apparently, and there might not be a quick fix.'

Fisher shakes his head, sadly. 'That's disappointing to hear, Immi. It can't be easy juggling everything you have on your plate, with the constant upheaval going on around you. And thanks, I will be in touch, as I'd like to run a couple of things past you before I say anything to Val.'

* * *

'What on earth?' I stand with my mouth open, unable to believe the devastation.

'It looks a lot worse than it is, Immi,' Reggie calls out as he hurries over to me.

The beautiful, old flagstone patio to the rear of Lock Keeper's

Cottage is now little more than a mud pit and in the centre of it is a big hole.

'Has Tollie seen this?' I ask, hardly daring to think about his reaction.

'Yes, he heard the commotion when the pipe fractured. We calmed him down and he instructed us to remove the flagstones, which are now safely stacked in the outhouse, so don't worry.'

'Where is Tollie now?'

'He's in The Retreat, he umm... has a visitor.'

The original patio area is Tollie's pride and joy, and now it's just a muddy expanse.

'What happened?' It's hard to mask the anxiety I'm feeling. The sweeping border of perennial lady's mantle, with their soft round leaves, has been decimated and the spiky blue sea holly with the steely blue stems have all been flattened. The gush of water was obviously so fierce that it has also washed out much of the soil. It's a total mess.

'The pipes are old, Immi. Everything needs replacing and, having had a look, I'm afraid that includes the septic tank. I didn't like to ask Tollie the question, but why on earth wasn't all of this dug up when the work was done on The Retreat? It would have been easier to link the two together and get it all sorted in one go.' Reggie's frustration is clear.

'I know, and that makes perfect sense now, but it wasn't that simple at the time.' When I turned eighteen, I wanted to spread my wings a little. While I would never leave Tollie on his own, I wanted my privacy. The decision was made to use the legacy my dad left me to turn The Retreat from a basic rental property into my future home. The property was put in my name, but Tollie didn't want me to limit my options for the future in case I ever wanted to move away. 'It's a totally independent building and, if necessary, could be divided off and sold as a separate dwelling.'

Reggie scratches his head, staring at me as if that's a crazy idea. 'And now that Lock Keeper's Cottage is home for you and Gray, you're landed with an unexpected expense.'

'I know. It means a lot to Tollie that we turn the cottage into our forever home,' I explain. I couldn't see beyond the excitement of having my own place, at the time. Getting married, or even moving into the cottage, wasn't something I'd given any thought to whatsoever.

Reggie raises his eyebrows, a grim expression on his face. 'Well, this is the price you pay, I'm afraid. We'll have to run new pipes from the stopcock right through to where the supply feeds into the property, which is out on the towpath. The water pipe runs along the side of the cottage and around the back, as the stop tap is in the kitchen. When we dug up the footings for the extension on the other side, we didn't find any pipes at all. What I can't figure out is that, when we fitted the new kitchen, the pipework coming up through the concrete floor was fairly new, so this is a real shock looking into the hole and seeing the state of it.'

'The kitchen flooded a few years back and it was something to do with the water pipe under the sink. I remember the plumber drilling out a hole in the concrete floor and then cementing it back up afterwards,' I confirm. 'At the time it was simply an inconvenience as the water had seeped through into the sitting room and the carpet had to be replaced.'

I try hard not to sigh. The budget Gray and I allocated for the new extension includes the cost of the re-plumbing work so that part of it has already been spent. All we have left that isn't already earmarked is the contingency fund and some money we've set aside to buy new furniture.

'Can you give me a ball-park figure of the cost to put it right?'

'Well, a robust, low-maintenance sewage-treatment system

like a Bio-Pure is going to set you back probably three and a half grand alone.'

'And the cost of the labour involved to do both jobs?'

'Another couple of grand, at least. It depends on whether we hit any snags. It's going to add at least a couple of weeks, maybe a month to the deadline, Immi. I'll need to sort our schedule and see who I can free up to help out with the trench work. But in the meantime, there will be no facilities in the cottage whatsoever.'

The look of sympathy on Reggie's face is sincere.

'Well, I suppose I'm glad this happened now and not after the building work was completed. I'll pop in to have a word with Tollie next.'

'The office will email you a detailed breakdown of the costs as soon as the final figures are available. I hate to be the bearer of bad news, Immi, when the end was nearly in sight. If we'd been made aware of the age of those pipes it would have been the first thing we tackled.'

'It's not your fault, Reggie, and thanks for being diplomatic with Tollie. I've been on at him for the last ten years about letting things slide and I know he's going to feel guilty about it now. I suppose the upside is that everything will be new.'

As I turn and walk across to The Retreat, the figures are going around and around inside my head. We are definitely heading for a significant overspend and it's money Gray and I simply don't have. And, unfortunately, there isn't a penny spare in the wedding budget, which was modest to begin with. I won't break the news to Gray until he's back on Friday and by then, hopefully, I will have a better idea of what the bottom line will be.

3

THE SURPRISES KEEP ON COMING

'Well, this is rather pleasant,' Rona says, picking up her cup of Earl Grey tea and nestling back against the cushions on Val's sofa. She's obviously delighted to be involved in the wedding planning, and I don't know why I didn't think of it myself.

Ziggy appears and after making sure she gets a stroke from each of us, she runs back upstairs, no doubt to settle down under the bed.

Val has been baking and it doesn't take any encouragement at all to get me to tuck into one of her spiced-apple buns. 'Mmm...' I mumble as I savour the first mouthful. 'This is delicious and what a treat to perk me up. Wednesday is always a bit of a slump day for me. At least when tomorrow dawns I can say that Gray will be home the following day.'

Both Rona and Val look at me, their expressions tinged with sadness.

'It's such a pity that Gray is back working in London again.' I know that Rona misses her son as much as I do.

'Come on, ladies, let's not dwell on things we can't change.

Let's figure out where things stand so we can draw up an action plan. I was beginning to think this wedding was going to end up being postponed for a second time and we can't have that, can we?' Val states, matter-of-factly.

Having just picked up a second bun and taken a huge bite, I smile back at her, gratefully.

'It's so exciting,' Rona replies. 'After the disappointment of moving back into The Retreat, this will help to raise your spirits, Immi.'

I demolish what's left of the bun and quickly wipe my mouth. 'Talking of Tollie... do either of you know a woman named Daphne Harris?'

Val shakes her head, but Rona leans forward to place her empty cup on the coffee table and I notice she's pressing her lips together, as if deep in thought. 'Well, it might not be the same woman, but shortly after I moved to Aysbury I had a call from someone of that name. She lives at Middle Norton. Daphne runs the Women's Institute there and one of my old friends put us in touch. Why?'

'Tollie mentioned her name in passing,' I reply, trying to sound only mildly curious.

However, the two women look at each other, puzzled by my interest.

'She's not from Aysbury. I can't ever recall hearing her name before and Tollie immediately changed the subject. It just struck me as a little odd, that's all.'

'I expect it's something to do with fundraising,' Val offers.

'Yes, that's probably it,' Rona adds, sensing my unease.

'Well, let's keep this between ourselves, but if you hear anything about her, perhaps you could let me know. Tollie is saying nothing, which is unlike him. Besides, I'm the treasurer and if it's a new initiative then I can't see why they didn't involve me. I sincerely hope he doesn't feel that I'm not able to keep everything ticking over satisfactorily.'

Val looks at me, reaching over to squeeze my arm affectionately. 'Tollie is probably trying to give you a little space, Immi. He likes to feel he's pulling his weight and he's not one to sit around when we still have a long way to go to reach the target.'

I roll my eyes. 'I know. Now that the land has been fenced off, it's time to give thought to the timeline we should be working to in order to pay the deposit and meet the subsequent payments for the playground equipment. They begin building it six weeks before installation, but the deposit must be paid at least a month beforehand. That reminds me, I need to check with Tollie to see how it's going with the council and the transfer once it's all done.'

Val begins clearing the coffee table. 'Right, that's enough of that for now. Tonight, we focus on the task in hand. I'll just take this out to the kitchen, while Rona grabs our to-do list.'

I dive into my bag and grab copies of the menus Sarah emailed across. When Val returns, I hand them out.

'These are sample menus. I'll be going through them with Gray at the weekend, but as his eyes glaze over every time I begin to talk about the finer details, as he refers to them, I would really value your input.'

'Has he decided who he wants to invite, yet?' Rona enquires.

'No. And I've asked him so many times it's now becoming a bit of a thing between us.'

'Do you want me to have a word with him? I'm not making excuses, but when Gray has his head into his music it does tend to blot out everything else,' she replies empathetically.

I nod my head, as I know exactly what she means. Gray and I can be having a serious conversation and suddenly he jumps up to grab his iPad and disappears because inspiration is calling. Often, he's gone for ages, which can be rather inconvenient at times but I've grown accustomed to it.

'If you get a chance before Saturday, then that would be great. I'm going to take him off for a walk, so I can ensure that I have his full attention. I've no idea how many of his ex-colleagues in London he regards as friends, given that I've never met any of them in person; however, he talks about them often. Now he's self-employed, it's a different matter yet again. The London studio where he's working links up to the film studios in Los Angeles, apparently, where the film is being made. So, maybe there will be people there he'll want to invite. But in all honesty, all I want is a little gathering of the people who are closest to us both.'

'Leave it with us, Immi. You're snowed under and Gray needs to understand that. As busy as he is, you need him to step up and make a few decisions as well. If you intend to tackle him about the menu over the weekend, Val and I will pull together a couple of suggestions and email them over to you on Friday. It would be nice to get that sorted and off to Sarah on Monday. Now, let's whip down the tick list, in no particular order.'

Flowers, speeches, will there be an evening party after the lunchtime buffet... it's question after question but at least the ensuing discussions are productive. A plan is beginning to take shape, but there is still a long list of details to be thrashed out.

'Good, now we are finally getting somewhere, and it wasn't that bad, was it?' Val prompts, waiting for me to agree. When I don't reply, she stares at me, pointedly.

'I suppose that brings us back to the dress and the location again.'

'Immi, are you sure the village hall is the right place to hold the wedding and the reception?' Rona enquires delicately.

'It's the simplest solution,' I confirm.

'Yes, but,' Val continues, 'this is your wedding day we're talking about. You deserve something a little bit more romantic and inspiring. This is a day you will both remember forever and, hopefully, tell your children all about in the years to come.'

They're right, of course, and I wish I had this wonderful vision in my head that I could share with them. I often dream of Gray and I exchanging our vows, but it's always just the two of us, staring into each other's eyes.

'You're right. It's not what I want at all, but it's booked now. The fact that it's an approved premises in which to hold a civil wedding means we don't have to traipse between the church and the reception. Who wants to do that in winter?'

Both Rona and Val look at me, shocked.

'This is not the time to be practical, Immi, it's about making your dreams come true. That does it. We'll cancel it tomorrow,' Val declares adamantly.

'What do you really *want*?' Rona asks, pressing me.

I sit back and relax, closing my eyes as I conjure up the perfect setting. A rosy glow begins to wash over me.

'Gray and me on a boat, sailing down the canal as we say our vows to each other.' Then I open my eyes and reality kicks in. 'But that's impractical as my list of guests is already standing at a minimum of twenty-two people and if Gray comes up with a similar figure then the village hall is the only option.'

Val stares across at Rona, then back at me. 'Let's give this some consideration before we go any further,' she replies firmly.

Before I can respond, Val nods at Rona, who produces a stack of bridal magazines.

'Next on the list is the dress. This is the fun part,' Rona muses.

They aren't letting me off the hook and after an hour we earmark three as maybes, none of which really inspire me, but I did my best. Glancing at my watch, I see it's almost 9 p.m. and I make my excuses as Gray will be expecting a call.

Walking back to The Retreat, I do feel more hopeful about the arrangements. Just knowing that two women I admire so much have my back and are determined to deliver what seems to me to be little short of a miracle, given the timescale, is a blessing. But as for the dress... I simply can't visualise myself in any of them if I'm being totally honest. If Gray is expecting a vision of frothy white tulle, he's in for a bit of a shock, I'm afraid, and so are Rona and Val, but I didn't have the heart to tell them that yet. Even when I was small, I was never a girlie girl. I preferred having adventures to dressing up and Dad's idea of going clothes shopping was to buy the first thing that fitted. That was usually jeans and a top, not a dress.

* * *

'You're late, m'dear.' Tollie looks up when I walk into the room. He studies my face for a moment or two. 'How was it?'

'Good, actually. Easier than I thought, well, in some respects that is, but not in others. I rang Gray on the walk home. Just so you're aware, I haven't broken the news yet about what's been going on here. When he arrives on Friday, I'll suggest he goes straight to The Bullrush and I'll tell him over dinner.'

Tollie grimaces. 'Poor chap. He won't be expectin' to head back here to The Retreat. But it's only a couple of weeks and we'll muddle along.'

Hmm. Muddle along. That's an odd thing for Tollie to say, as usually he's delighted to have a bit of company. He looks tired tonight, though, so maybe he's been overdoing it again and that's why he seems a little down.

'You are feeling all right, Tollie, aren't you?' I ask, trying not to sound overly concerned.

'I'm good. Stop fussin' over me. I, um, wanted to say that this problem with the cottage is down to me, so I don't expect the two of you to pay for it. I let things slide and when we had the flood in the kitchen a few years back, the plumber did warn me that some major work was way overdue. It's just that you don't see what's out of sight, do you? And now I feel bad it's thrown the schedule out.'

I glance at him, shaking my head.

'You've paid for more than enough, Tollie. Gray and I have this, so don't give it another thought. How's that back of yours doing tonight?'

'It's okay.'

I can see by the way he's sitting awkwardly in his chair that it isn't and yet it's only been a month since he saw the chiropractor. 'You know, you really should think about getting a hot tub. Wes, up at Adler's farm, swears it's the best investment he's ever made. And you know how badly he's suffered with his back over the years, with all that lifting.'

'Hmm...' Tollie mutters, glancing back down at the newspaper in his hands. 'If you're about to put the kettle on, I'd love a cup of tea,' he continues, changing the subject.

'Why don't you pop up to see him and check it out? I'm sure he wouldn't mind,' I say casually as I turn and head off into the kitchen.

Tollie makes a grunting sound. I think he's tired because of the pain he's in and he might be due to take some more painkillers. The doctor says the problems with his back are only general wear and tear, and there isn't much they can do to help, unless it gets an awful lot worse. But as soon as the tea is made, Tollie takes the mug from me and disappears upstairs to run a hot bath. At least I've made him stop and think, which is a start.

I grab my laptop and snuggle up on the sofa, typing in 'alternative wedding dresses'. Goodness, two-thirds of them show way too much flesh for a winter wedding and I can quickly discount the black, dark red and purple options. There are a number of knee-length dresses that don't look too bad, but nothing jumps out at me. I type in 'winter wedding dresses' and to my dismay it's more or less the exact same pictures that come up, although there are a few with little satin jackets. That's going to make all the difference on a day when the frost doesn't melt until lunchtime, I mock. Do they expect brides to shiver and just put up with it?

Logging off, I lie back to drink my coffee. The problem with spending my teen years with no female influences around me is that buying clothes has never been a great experience for me. I shop when I need something, but it's never been a day out. The mere thought of window shopping is something I can't even get my head around. What a waste of time if you end up coming home with nothing. My wardrobe has several dresses in it, but they're all things that are easy to wear and not really posh frocks, because that's not who I am. Besides, I've never had an occasion that required me to really dress up, so I can only do smart casual.

What I need is some help and I need it from someone who has their feet firmly planted on the ground. I think that someone might be Sarah.

Heading up to bed, I stand outside the bathroom door. 'Goodnight, Tollie. And sorry for the disruption.'

'It's no bother. It's my silly fault, anyway, and I'm mightily sorry. Night, m'dear. Sleep well.'

'You, too.'

This is the first time I've ever slept in the guest bedroom and I wonder what Gray will make of it when I break the news to him on Friday. Reggie's guys have created a temporary pathway around the side of the cottage avoiding the mud pit, but Gray will need access to pack up some clothes before they dig out the front, too. Oh, this is such a nightmare!

I wander over to the window to look out over the fields, when suddenly a buzzing sound has me dashing to grab my bag. I told Gray there was no need to check that I got home safely, but I'm not surprised when I see it's him.

'I was just thinking about you,' I tell him, trying not to sound as sad as I feel.

'Ditto. I'm about to jump into bed and something made me pick up my phone. I hate Wednesdays.'

'Ah, me too.'

'Roll on Friday. Is our table booked?'

'Of course.'

'You sound distant. I mean, not the miles… just not quite your usual self. Is anything troubling you?'

Inwardly I suppress a groan. 'Only the usual. And the grilling tonight over the wedding stuff made me realise you and I need to have a serious talk at the weekend. It's decision-making time.'

'Uh oh,' Gray mutters grimly. 'I might have something to add to the agenda, but I won't know for sure until Friday afternoon. They're talking about a trip to Los Angeles to start working out the details of this new project, but I don't know when. They're still awaiting confirmation that the funding is in place.'

I know it's work, and I should be pleased for him, but the thought of even less time together is unsettling.

'Anyway,' he continues, 'don't worry about that now. You sound tired, so put it all out of your mind and get a good night's sleep. I forgot to ask how Tollie is.'

'His back is playing up again. It's time he paid another visit to the doctor.'

'Good luck with getting him to book an appointment, Immi, you know what he's like.'

'Anyway, I'm exhausted, so I'll say goodnight. Love you, Gray.' It's not that I want to cut him short, but if Tollie hears me talking and knocks on the door to check everything's okay, I'm not sure I can hide how down in the dumps I'm feeling.

'Love you more. Sweet dreams, Immi.'

4

EVERYTHING IS UNDER CONTROL

'It's Friday. Where's that spring in your step this morning, Immi? Usually, I don't need to look at the calendar to see what day it is,' Martin jests as he pours the hot water into the cups. He nods for me to take one.

'I don't even have the time to think about this evening until it's here. Have you seen my desk? And suddenly everyone is putting in their holiday forms, so that's going to be a juggling act to try to keep everyone happy.'

'You sound down. Is it having to move back into The Retreat temporarily?'

I shake my head, silently berating myself for being such a grouch this morning. 'Ignore me. Once I get stuck into my work, I'll soon clear everything. I didn't have a good night, that's all. It takes a while to get used to sleeping in a different bed.'

Martin takes a slurp of his coffee, then shoots me a look of commiseration.

'You've got too much going on, Immi, but it will get better. Oh, and I have some good news that will cheer you up. When I dropped off those trees at the Linden Hotel yesterday, the general manager, Harrison, came over and said they're thinking about running another fundraiser to help swell the anniversary fund. He asked whether you could spare the time to call in and have a chat sometime.'

It might be the caffeine kicking in, of course, but suddenly I'm wide awake and raring to go.

'I don't suppose he mentioned anything specific?' I ask hopefully.

'Well, no. I think he's hoping you'll come up with something.'

'Ah! Right.' Another task to add to my ever-growing list.

'But,' Martin jumps back in, 'Patrick mentioned he'd be more than willing to get involved in some way, so bear that in mind. He has plenty of time on his hands and he's also good with figures, as he started out as an accountant.' He beams at me.

'Hmm... good at figures, eh? That's useful to know,' I reply. 'It's kind of him to offer.'

'Look, I know he's not strictly a local, but he's had a tough time of it lately. His wife walked out a while back, having taken every penny she could get her hands on, which was the majority of their life savings. They're going through a messy divorce and, as it stands, she still owes him money.'

'How awful. Poor man.'

'Patrick keeps things pretty close to his chest, but I'm piecing together the few things he has told me and I feel sorry for the guy. Seriously, Immi, he'd be glad to have something to distract him and he's not that far away. Although, I think he's sold the house, so he'll be looking for something smaller. Patrick said it was much too big for the two of them and now he's on his own he can't wait to get out of there.'

'I can understand why. I'm sure I can find a way for him to get involved.'

'He could talk to Harrison, maybe?'

I don't want Martin to think I'm not taking Patrick's offer seriously, but he's not in the loop yet and so wouldn't be able to answer any specific questions that might come up.

'I think I ought to talk to Fisher, first off, as he's known Harrison for longer than I have.'

'Of course, why didn't I think of that? It makes perfect sense.'

'Thanks, anyway, and I'll give some thought to Patrick's offer, I promise. Where does he live?'

'North Charlton, just the other side of Middle Norton. I'll text you his phone number.'

As we part company, I'm well aware that delegating doesn't come easy to me, especially if it's to someone I don't really know. Another pair of hands would be helpful, but often it's about who you know, rather than what you know.

Suddenly, there's a loud crash and I start running in the direction of the ongoing commotion. Martin isn't far behind me and when we reach the yard, we see that the forklift truck has backed into a corner of one of the greenhouses, which has partially collapsed. It looks as if there's been an explosion, with metal, glass, shelving and tray upon tray of petunias, French marigolds and dahlias, crushed beneath the tangle. Obviously, it was an accident, and the driver is already inspecting the damage, looking acutely embarrassed. Martin stands surveying the scene, shaking his head in disbelief. At least half of yesterday's bulk delivery of plants are now written off.

'I'll do a re-order, Martin. Hopefully, we'll get it by the middle of next week.'

He gives me a brief nod. 'Thanks, Immi. I'll get onto the insurance company and find out what we need to do. We'll cordon it off for the time being and at least no one was hurt. Just in time for the weekend, though, which is bad timing.'

Weekends are busy throughout the spring and summer, but

that's only a part of the business as commercial contracts now far outweigh the customers purchasing through the tills.

'We'll make it up,' I reassure him. 'I'll place that order now.'

* * *

As Gray walks through the door of The Bullrush Inn, I head down the stairs two at a time. Rushing towards him, I throw myself into his arms and a cheer goes up. As Gray hugs me tightly, he turns me around so that we are facing the audience of fellow customers, who are all raising their glasses.

'Date night!' they chorus and we burst out laughing.

'We are so predictable,' Gray murmurs, his lips close to my ear.

'Did you have a good week, Gray?' Fisher calls out as Gray lowers his arms and we stand there holding hands.

'The project is almost done,' Gray replies, wearing a huge smile, and I can see that his week ended on a high.

'When will the film be in the cinemas?' Abe calls out, much to Ethel's annoyance.

'Leave them be, Abe. Go have a lovely dinner, you two, and ignore this lot,' Ethel adds warmly.

Abe and Ethel own a four-berth, forty-five-foot Admiral narrowboat named The Merry Robin and it's one of the handful of residential moorings here at the canal. Their lives revolve around our little community and our Christmas cruises wouldn't run as smoothly if they weren't involved. I think of Ethel as the quintessential Earth Mother and Abe as the Green Man, and I love them to bits. Nothing is ever too much trouble and they treat me like an adopted granddaughter.

I give them a little wave as Gray yanks on my hand and we head straight up to our usual table in front of the panoramic window overlooking the canal and the marina. But before we take our seats, Gray spins me around and plants a gentle kiss on my lips. I don't want to pull away, but the majority of the people seated up here are strangers and we're in danger of making a spectacle of ourselves.

'They're all a bit rowdy tonight,' Gray comments as I sink down onto the chair he pulls out for me.

Moments later, Karl appears with two menus and a lighter for the candle.

'Happy Friday, guys. Your man is home, Immi. What a week it's been.'

I glance straight up at Karl, who is renowned for saying the wrong thing at the wrong time. As we discovered last year, he just can't keep a secret. He let it slip to Tollie that we were planning a sit-down dinner to celebrate the tenth anniversary of the Santa Ahoy cruises but Tollie immediately threw that idea out of the window and we cancelled the big bash. Now we're raising money for the playground instead and are having a modest do at the village hall on Boxing Day, with everyone chipping in to pay for it.

'You're right, but the weekend is finally here,' I jump in brightly, and I can see from Karl's reaction that he got the message.

'I'll leave you guys to it, then, and I'll come back in a bit.'

He rushes off before Gray can begin quizzing him.

'Problems?' he enquires, pressing his lips together. Gray reaches out to place his hand over mine, and we intertwine our fingers.

'There was a bit of an accident at the Lockside Nurseries. No one was hurt, but one of the original greenhouses will need replacing.'

'Nightmare. I'm sorry to hear that, especially at this time of the year. Thank goodness for insurance policies. I'm starving, I don't know about you?'

We peruse the menu and, as usual, I can't make up my mind, so we order two different dishes. It's become our thing and we usually swap halfway through. Gray says it's endearing. The truth is that I can't eat a whole plate of the same thing, which tends to rule out pasta dishes for me. I love pasta, just not a massive portion of it and, luckily, Gray is always hungry.

'Are you ready to order?' Jade appears, looking very smart in her black dress and white apron. I notice she wears a little make-up now. The twins are both such sweet-natured girls and I know it's going to be tough for Karl once they start taking an even bigger interest in boys.

'We are,' I reply, smiling. 'Gray is going for the skillet pasta with mushrooms, pancetta and wilted greens, and I'll go for the summer salad with feta cheese, new potatoes and strawberries. Can we also have a dish of house fries, please, Jade?'

'Of course. And to drink?'

I look at Gray. 'The usual, please,' he says, winking at her. 'Immi only lets me drink beer at Christmas,' he says in a mock half-whisper.

'That is so not true!' I blurt out, offended. 'Jade, bring him a beer and I'll have a small carafe of the house rosé. Thanks so much.'

When she's out of earshot he leans in. 'I was only joking. You've had a bad week, haven't you? What aren't you telling me, Immi?'

I look around uneasily, but there's no one close enough to overhear our conversation. Gray is in happy mode and now I fear I might be about to spoil that for him.

'Well, do you want the good news first, or the bad news?' All I can do is try to lighten the moment, but Gray screws up his face, leaning closer.

'I knew something was up.' At that moment Kurt appears with our drinks and we spring apart.

'The food won't be long. Here you go, enjoy!' Kurt says amiably, totally unaware that Gray is sitting there anxious to hear what I have to say. He places the glasses down in front of us. Gray grabs his beer and takes a hefty swig.

Once Kurt has left, he sucks in a deep breath. 'Okay. Good news first.'

'A month, worst-case scenario.'

He peers at me, leaning in as he lowers his voice. 'Okay. That might not be the end of the world, depending on what comes next. And the bad news?'

'That's how long we're staying in the spare bedroom at The Retreat.' I can't even look at him right now.

'What?'

When I eventually do get up the courage to explain, he's holding onto the arms of the carver chair as if it's about to fly off somewhere.

'You're not kidding, are you? What on earth has gone wrong *now*?'

'The water main burst at the back of the cottage and all the pipework has to be replaced. When Reggie realised Tollie hadn't had it renewed when the work was done on The Retreat, he checked out the septic tank and that's had its day, too.'

Gray sits back in his chair, stunned. 'But he said the pipework going into the kitchen was probably less than ten years old.'

'And that's correct. There was a serious leak when the tap sheared off, but they only dug up and replaced the pipe coming into the kitchen.'

'And Tollie bought the place, what, fifty years ago?'

'Yes, Grandma and Tollie bought Lock Keeper's Cottage in 1969. He said there were no lead pipes or anything and apart from the one problem we had with the stopcock, everything has always worked.'

Gray's frown deepens, and I know what's coming next. 'And the cost?'

'Worst case is about ten grand, and Reggie said we could get a quote from a company who offer a trenchless solution, but he thinks it's cheaper to just dig it up and get it done. They have to dismantle the old septic tank and excavate a bigger hole for the new one, so I told him to go for it. He said if he can bring it in under that, he will, because he knows we don't have a budget for it.'

Gray picks up his beer once more, takes a hefty swig and then replaces it on the table before reaching out for my hand. He gives me a warm and gentle smile.

'Hey, it's only money, Immi. We'll sort it. Thank goodness it happened now and not a while down the line when all the work is finished. How did Tollie take the news?'

'He just felt guilty for not having sorted it out before. But it's a huge mess and I can understand why he let it slide. His "if it ain't broke, don't fix it" approach isn't always the best policy, though. It has destroyed the lovely borders and those old flagstones are now in the outbuilding. Tollie wanted to pay for the work, of course, but I told him straight that wasn't happening.'

'Quite right, too. So, we're going to be sleeping in Tollie's spare bedroom, then?'

'We are. I collected a few of your things, but tomorrow morning you'll probably want to go and pack a bag. There's no access at all at the rear of the cottage now and they'll be digging a trench along the front path early next week.'

Jade is heading in our direction, a plate in each hand and I stare at Gray, tilting my head slightly as I sit back.

'My, that looks good,' he declares. 'Thank you, Jade. This is going to be the best meal I've had all week.' She giggles as she walks off.

'So, we'd better keep the noise down, then, when we get back,' Gray says mischievously. One of the things I love about this man of mine is that whatever life throws at him, he can always raise a smile. He takes everything in his stride and he rarely moans about anything. When it's time to swap dishes, he doesn't immediately begin eating again.

'What's wrong? Aren't you enjoying the salad?' I ask.

'I'm sure it's fine. I just love watching you eat. You're so precise and neat,' he points out.

I look down at the plate and he's right, I never stab at the food in the centre, but instead I work around the outside.

'What other curious habits do I have that you've noticed?' I enquire, peering at him.

'Oh, *way* too many to trot them out now. Let's finish eating and head for home. Well, our temporary home for the next four weeks. I'm holding Reggie to that deadline,' he declares. 'So, you'd best warn him!'

5

IN A PERFECT WORLD…

After a leisurely brunch together, Tollie casually suggests that Gray and I go for a walk. As soon as we step outside, Gray looks at me, cocking an eyebrow.

'He's perky this morning,' he remarks.

'You noticed that, too, then? Last night he told me that he's going to see the chiropractor today. After his last visit he was able to stand upright from sitting without a single groan and he was almost back to his sprightly self for a while.'

'It means he listens to what you say, then, which—'

'Hmm. I have my suspicions. He refused my offer to drive him there and I seriously doubt he's capable of getting behind the wheel this morning. I think he's expecting a visitor because he couldn't have been more eager to push us out the door, could he?'

'It was a bit obvious,' Gray acknowledges.

'Did you notice that Tollie has trimmed his beard, too?'

Gray narrows his eyes. 'Am I supposed to be reading something into this?'

I shrug my shoulders. 'Who knows? But maybe I'm not the only one he's listening to, these days.'

'If the pain is getting him down, the chiropractor might suggest it's time to go back and have another chat with the doctor. Which would only be a good thing, Immi, as it's been stopping him from being his usual active self. Tollie isn't a fan of doctors, as we know. Just be pleased that he's doing something about it and relax.'

'When I popped back to collect my jacket at lunchtime on Wednesday, Tollie met me in the hallway. I spotted a woman in the background sitting on the sofa. When I got home later that day, I asked who she was and he told me her name was Daphne Harris. He brushed it off, almost as if they were old friends catching up, but I've never heard him mention her name before.'

Gray half-turns to look at me, hardly registering any surprise whatsoever. 'So Tollie has a lady friend, that's a good thing, isn't it?' His eyes crinkle up into a warm smile. 'You're not upset about that, surely?'

'Of course not,' I reply dismissively. I'm simply concerned as to why Tollie is hiding it from me.

Gray stares at me for a brief second before raising his eyes to the heavens.

'That accusatory look does you no favours,' I inform him. But to me Gray always looks good; with his floppy jet-black hair that is now almost touching his shoulders, he looks every inch the musician.

He draws close, slipping his arms around my waist. 'Stop worrying. If Tollie needs your help he'll ask for it. Have I told you recently how much I love you?' Gray asks, changing the subject.

'You have. And worrying is what I do.'

'Well, my sole purpose in life is to change all that. If Tollie thinks he's adding to your stress levels, do you think he'd be happy about that? No. He'd be mortified. So, cut him some slack and stop trying to be Superwoman.'

'Me, Superwoman? You're crazy, Gray, but I hear what you're saying.' Maybe he has a point. Tollie is entitled to his secrets, like everyone else, but I'd hate to see him get hurt.

I grab Gray's hand, and he leans in to softly kiss my lips before releasing me.

'Come on, let's head over to the copse. It's a beautiful day and I guess we'd better not hurry back. So, this Daphne is a bit of a mystery, then?'

'I asked Val and your mum if they knew her and guess what? Your mum said she runs the Women's Institute at Middle Norton.'

Gray helps me up over the stile and I jump down the other side, waiting for him.

'Oh, I remember Mum telling me that the WI were arranging for one of the locals to make contact with her. She misses her old group of friends, but now she's back to work she might not have time to get involved. Especially now she's helping to plan our wedding. Mum is so excited about it,' he adds, giving me a sideways glance as we head off across the open pastureland.

'You know what's coming next, then,' I retort.

'Yes. We need to sit down and have a proper chat, don't we?' he replies.

'We do, and I know just the place.'

I steer him over to the far side of the dense outcrop of trees, where last Christmas we came with our jute sacks to gather the foliage to decorate The Star Gazer and turn her into The Santa Ahoy Special. As usual, Gray never walks in a totally straight line, but he wanders here and there, easily distracted. In many ways the child within him has never left, or that sense of delight at the smallest of things. Perhaps it's the tunes he carries around inside his head, constantly distracting him. I'm surprised he hasn't already stopped to pull out his phone and hum a line or two of melody into one of his apps. A creative mind rarely succeeds in completely switching off.

We make a beeline for one of the trees that was toppled by the exceptionally strong winds we had last November. It's my favourite spot. It does make me feel a sense of loss, but in this natural setting it's a reminder that life goes full circle. As the years pass it will rot down and enrich the soil, from whence in years to come little seedlings will, no doubt, spring up.

'I'm waiting,' I call out, hauling myself up onto the tree trunk, but really I'm more than happy to sit here and enjoy the scenery. As the sun creeps higher in the sky, it filters through the trees and a subtle breeze disturbs the leaves overhead, sending out a cascade of little shards of light. The bluebells are beginning to die back, the blooms past their best. Clumps of wild garlic scattered around the forest floor are now starting to turn and add a pungent smell into the mix. But having trodden over the pine needles that are like a thick carpet in places, they release a powerful and pleasing fragrance that lingers in the air.

'It smells like Christmas!' I call out to Gray as he hurries over to join me.

'Can I ask you a question before you start quizzing me?' Gray says, settling himself down next to me.

'Fire away.'

'Forget about the cost, the problems and making everyone else happy – describe your perfect wedding day.'

I glance down at my hands, folded in my lap, and draw in a deep breath as I take a few moments to reflect.

'A wedding isn't just about the bride and the groom, Gray. Yes, I'd love to get married on The Star Gazer as we cruise along the canal, but how would we decide who to invite and who to leave off the list? We could make it simple, of course. You and me, standing in our tiny little parish church exchanging our vows, with Tollie, Rona, Fisher and Val as our witnesses.'

'No one else? And afterwards?'

I laugh. 'A big party. Relaxed, fun and no real pressure. How about you?'

'Hmm... it's more complicated than I appreciated, isn't it? Our friends are as close as family and I'd hate to leave anyone out.' Gray tips his head back, staring up as a little posse of birds swoop noisily in and out of the branches overhead. Their fluttering wings, as they move from branch to branch, shower us with little bits of debris. I brush them off my lap, smiling to myself.

After a stressful week, sitting here, I'm beginning to despair of finding the perfect solution.

Gray leans into me. 'Hold still,' he murmurs as he gently teases little pieces of dead twig out of my hair. Then his lips are on mine and I close my eyes, savouring the moment. We have each other and in times of need he is my rock, and I am his.

'I love you, Immi. More than anything else in the world. Life hasn't been easy for you and yet you give so much to other people. I just want to make you happy because you deserve it.'

My hand snakes up to brush away the hair that is now partially obscuring his face.

'I love your hair this length, it's so you...' The sincerity in Gray's eyes takes my breath away – the depth of his concern is touching. 'And I don't want to disappoint you, or the people who mean so much to us. I think we're safe in Rona and Val's hands, Gray. I was simply going around in circles and getting nowhere. I'm not making excuses, but Dad always said it was important to learn how to look after yourself and he encouraged me to spend more time outside the house than in. He taught me practical skills, for which I'm grateful. But when it comes to planning a wedding, I don't have a clue and that's the truth.'

As we pull back, Gray holds my hand in his.

'It was just you and your dad, and then it was you and Tollie, so I can understand that. Given his background, your dad was probably trying to make sure you could look after yourself.'

Gray is right.

'Dad took me off exploring and we did exciting things. We'd climb trees and wade through shallow streams as I shrieked at how cold the water was. He'd build little assault courses, just for fun. After spending his working week training naval officers, he'd come home and put me through my paces. And I loved it, but at school, I started to feel like the odd one out, and not just because I didn't have a mum.

'On one of our visits to Aysbury I must have said something to Grandma, because Dad's attitude started to change. If I went to a classmate's birthday party, he would paint my nails and help me to do something with my hair. Together we figured it out, but I came to realise that none of my friends were like me, so I faked it when I had to because that wasn't who I was. But I was no saint after Dad died, Gray. I gave everyone here, including Tollie, a hard time, because I was angry that an accident had robbed me of the person who was the centre of my world. But no one gave up on me and I'm simply repaying their kindness, and for the way they welcomed you into the fold.'

'I'm grateful for that, too. Having Mum here has taken a big worry off my shoulders. She's independent again, which is wonderful, but having her close by and knowing when I'm not here that she has you – well, it means a lot to me. I'm a happy man, Immi, because I have you by my side. And even when we aren't together, you're in my heart, always.'

'So, it was the right thing to do getting your mum and Val involved? You don't think badly of me because I'm not the quintessential bride, desperate to organise every little detail?'

'Heck, no! I'm the one who feels guilty not being here to help as much as I should, considering what you cope with every single day. Look, I've been remiss. I'm perfectly capable of liaising with our wedding planners,' he informs me enthusiastically. 'I'll sort the music, naturally, but as for the rest of the arrangements, together with Mum and Val, I'm sure the three of us can pull together and work it out. It will save them constantly dragging you away from more important things and I'm only a phone call away. Let me do this. Unless you don't trust me to get involved...'

Gray is offering to step up and is looking for reassurance. I know that working away from home is as much a sacrifice on his part as it is for me, and yet I can see he genuinely wants to do this.

'Our wedding is important to me, Gray, but I can't focus on it and keep everything else going. So, if you're sure you have time, then go for it! I'm way past refusing any help I can get.'

'What else is worrying you, Immi?'

Gray can always see through me.

'I'm worried that we won't hit the fundraising target to cover the costs for the playground in time for the tenth anniversary. Tollie will want to step in to make up the shortfall, and, with what he's already given to us to help with the renovations and the wedding, it's not fair he should put yet another dent in his savings. To get a real handle on where we stand, I'll begin by going through the figures in fine detail to give the committee a realistic update. Then I can set some target dates to focus everyone, but I'm afraid I've let things slip.'

'No, you haven't, Immi. You've just been pulled in too many different directions at once and I should have realised that. Anyway, what else is there to resolve on the wedding front before you leave me to liaise with our little team?'

'It's down to me to decide what colour scheme I want. Rona and Val are pressing me to decide on a dress and we've leafed through a number of bridal magazines, but nothing I've seen feels like me. You aren't expecting some vision in white, are you?' I ask, doing my best not to sound apprehensive.

Gray raises my fingertips to his lips and kisses them.

'I don't mind whether you come towards me wearing a princess dress, or your elf suit. Just make sure I know what the score is, so I don't get what I'm wearing totally wrong.'

'You want a Christmas-themed wedding?' I laugh, knowing he's not serious about dressing up.

'I don't really do the morning-suit thing,' he admits and now he's being serious. 'I'm not big on neck-ties, either, but if you insist then I'll do it. And I will write out my guest list, but I don't want to choose my best man until we can finally fit in that trip to London so you can meet everyone. I'm trying to fix the earliest date when everyone will be around and it isn't easy, but I want to show you off at long last.'

I don't really understand the ins and outs of Gray's job and the thought of meeting his friends for the first time is a little daunting. Not least because we've already cancelled a trip up to London twice in the last year, once because Rona wasn't very well and the second time because it was snowing. I can see from the expression on his face that this means a lot to him.

'Of course,' I reply breezily.

'Thank you, Immi. It doesn't feel right handing over a list of people who are just a bunch of strangers to you. Besides, my credibility is going to soar,' he declares, amused by that thought. 'I still can't believe someone as beautiful, kind and intelligent as you would put up with someone like me.'

'Like you?'

'Off-the-wall, a music nerd. Fortunately, most of my friends are the same.'

'On the meet-up, I'm not going to be walking into a room full of men wearing suits, then, with wives or girlfriends on their arms wearing posh frocks?'

Gray bursts out laughing. 'Hardly. Nathan has been wearing the same style of jeans since 1990. Reece is a night owl when it comes to work, much to the annoyance of his girlfriend, and rarely surfaces before 11 a.m. But he's in a band, as well as being a songwriter. They're a good crowd and they're gonna welcome you as warmly as I was made welcome here. When was the last time you visited London?' Gray looks at me quizzically. Because he works there, it's the last place we think of for a break away and, anyway, I prefer the country to the city.

'I've only been to London twice. The second trip was to celebrate my thirteenth birthday and Dad took me to Harrod's. We had afternoon tea in the café, and it was the first time I felt grown-up. I wore a dress that day because it was a special treat and I remember catching him looking at me and what I saw reflected on his face was pride.' A lump rises up in my throat, and I take a deep breath to compose myself.

'We could travel up on a Saturday and meet everyone for a drink, then come back the following day. What do you think?'

Gray doesn't ask for much so it's time to make this happen. I've noticed that on a number of occasions recently he's dropped into the conversation that his boss, Oliver, has asked when he will get to meet me. I'm wondering if Gray is going to ask him to be his best man.

'Sounds good, although I could take a Friday off as holiday and come up on the train. If I stay for the weekend, it will save you all that driving back and forth.'

'I'll fit in with whatever works best for you. And talking about little jaunts... we haven't discussed the honeymoon,' he adds. 'Not that there will be any money left in the bank after the overspend on the cottage.'

'I was thinking we could delay the honeymoon until next summer. It's not customary, I know, but in case we get a snowfall, I'd rather be here to keep an eye on things.'

This isn't just about Tollie, but last year the whole community had to gather together to get through what was a tough couple of days when a blizzard descended on Aysbury.

'The thought of simply being able to enjoy our new home over the festive period is rather inviting,' I continue. 'We can take some long walks and cosy up in the evenings, in front of the fire. There are a few day trips we've been talking about doing for ages, too. I rather like the idea of leisurely waking up each morning and seeing where the mood takes us.'

'Perfect. Once I'm working on the next contract, we can get something booked as I intend to fly you off to an exotic location then.'

'Things have sort of come to a head, haven't they? In a good way, I mean. I was beginning to panic but I didn't want to worry you, Gray. That's another reason why I didn't tell you on Monday about the burst pipe. There isn't anything you can do when you're not here and it's my fault that the contingency fund turned out to be hopelessly optimistic.'

'Hey, babe, it's no one's fault. These things happen. I'm only sorry that we had to slip the wedding date to December because of my workload.'

'Well, as it turns out, there's absolutely no way we could have had everything sorted in time. If it had all gone ahead, you know that we'd be looking at getting married a week from today? Imagine that and coping with moving back in with Tollie.'

Gray chuckles and I join in. 'That's a *no*. Anyway, Christmas is my favourite time of year,' he replies.

'Mine, too. It was obviously meant to be.' And I truly believe it was, so it will all come together... somehow.

'Will you do me one favour, though?' I can tell from Gray's expression that he's being serious. 'You're always talking about taking up yoga and I think it would do you good to have an evening off to do something fun.'

'I'll think about it,' I reply. It's not a bad suggestion, as, although I do a lot of walking, yoga would help tone my muscles. What bride doesn't want to look her best on her wedding day? And going to a gym isn't me, but yoga might also help me to relax a little. The truth is that I only really get a good night's sleep when Gray is lying next to me and everything in my world feels right.

6

OUR LITTLE CIRCLE

Today we're heading to The Bullrush for Sunday lunch. It's Fisher's birthday and he has booked the large table for the usual folk. As soon as Tollie, Gray and I step inside I hear that the atmosphere is buzzing. Tollie stops to talk to one of the guys who works in the boatyard and we leave him to it, waving to Jade and Jude in passing.

The noise coming from the conservatory is as loud as the main restaurant area and yet only seven guests have arrived so far, with Fisher at the head of the table.

'Hey, guys,' Gray says as he pulls out a chair for me to take a seat, but I'm already heading over to Fisher, who jumps up to greet me.

I throw my arms around him, and we hug. 'Happy birthday to you! Fifty-four... but who's counting?' I declare, and everyone begins to laugh.

'It's supposed to be a secret,' he replies.

'Oh, I assumed there would be a cake lurking somewhere and it's important they get the number of candles right.'

'What, and risk burning down our favourite eatery? Hi, Gray, thanks for coming.'

Gray and Fisher exchange a warm smile. 'One year closer to early retirement,' Gray comments and I shoot him a pointed look. My lovely man immediately changes the subject. 'It's been a while since we've had something to celebrate – who's missing?'

As Gray and I take our seats next to Rona, he leans in briefly to kiss her cheek. I notice Fisher turns to look at Val, and as their eyes meet it's obvious how happy he is; it's hard to believe how his life has changed over the past six months.

'Maggie is waitressing today as Sarah and Kurt are rushed off their feet, so sadly she can't join in,' Rona informs us. Maggie is one of our wider team of fundraisers and often reports back at committee meetings after recruiting new supporters.

Bernie and Yvonne are here. They live at Turnpike Cottage on the other side of the canal. Bernie runs the pop-up Christmas market and after he'd spent a couple of years cruising the water-ways following the death of his wife, Yvonne moved in with him just before last Christmas. They are now both heavily involved in the fundraising initiative and it's nice to have him back permanently. It's wonderful for Tollie, too, as their friendship goes way back.

I tune out as Ethel and Abe banter with Gray, asking where their wedding invitation is and, luckily, a hand suddenly appears on my shoulder. I turn around to see Martin and his wife, Ursula, who have just arrived, standing behind me. I get up to give Ursula a hug.

'It's been ages, Ursula. How are you? How are the kids?'

All eyes are on us, as their eldest, Olivia, who is twelve, has Crohn's disease and arthritis. She's been in and out of hospital over the last few years and has had two serious operations, one of which was recent. Ursula once told me that Olivia's courage and determination is an inspiration to them all. She said that when someone you love is living with a chronic illness, it makes you celebrate the good days and support each other through the bad ones. Life takes on a whole new perspective; you focus on what really matters and as a family they are closer because of it.

'Good. Olivia has bounced back well this time, although they're still adjusting her meds at the moment. Whenever they change anything it upsets her system, but she's a real trooper. And Katie is full of energy as usual and football mad. She managed to gain a place on the school's football team and she practices every chance she gets. They're with the grandparents today, being spoiled rotten, no doubt.' Martin and Ursula glance at each other affectionately. I'm sure that quality time alone together is at a premium.

'I have no idea where she gets her talent from. I was useless at sports, but Katie can certainly control the ball,' Martin says with pride.

'Well, we must catch up properly before too long,' I reply, as Martin makes his way to the seat opposite me. 'That's a gorgeous dress, Ursula.'

'Thanks, Immi. I made it myself,' she replies, before going to take her seat.

Maybe the person I should talk to about dresses, then, is Ursula. She always looks smart but in a casual way. I don't think I've ever seen her in jeans, but she's also never over-dressed.

'Lookin' good, Fisher,' Tollie's voice booms out as he steps into the conservatory to take his seat at the opposite end of the table. 'Happy birthday, my man. Another year older and closer to that early retirement. I've taken the liberty of ordering a couple of bottles of wine.'

I look at Fisher's face. It's clear he hasn't mentioned his doubts about retirement to anyone other than me, and I feel awkward on his behalf. He says nothing, but how I wish that I'd mentioned in passing to Tollie not to raise the subject.

'Here you go,' Kurt says as he places a wine bucket down on the table and a bottle of red next to it. He heads back to the bar, returning with a bottle of chilled white which he slips into the bucket.

Tollie indicates that he'll do the honours and pour the wine as Bernie gathers the glasses together. The girls are hot on Kurt's heels, handing out menus, and suddenly everyone is talking over each other and the madness of one of our little gatherings begins. We're a few people short, but that's par for the course. Fisher would have invited the entire committee, but we rarely manage to get everyone together in one place at the same time these days.

Out of sight below the table, Gray's hand seeks mine out as he leans in.

'If you want to avoid being quizzed about the wedding arrangements, it might be wise to make an announcement. Just saying.'

He's right, so after Tollie proposes a toast in honour of Fisher, as soon as it quietens down, Gray taps the table with his hand.

'Immi has a little announcement to make,' he explains.

'Gray and I have enlisted the help of two wedding planners. We'd like to raise our glasses to Rona and Val, to thank them for taking charge.'

Everyone joins in the toast and both Rona and Val look pleased with themselves.

'About time, too, Immi. You can't do everything yourself. If I can do anything to help, ladies, just let me know,' Ethel very kindly offers.

'And we'll sort the flowers,' Martin joins in. 'It's our present to Immi. You've bailed me out so many times in the past and I'll await my instructions from your wedding planners!'

'Aww, thank you, Martin and Ursula, that is so generous of you.' I turn to look at Gray, who is flashing them both one of his engaging smiles.

'Right, our waitresses are hovering, so it's make-your-mind-up time, folks,' Tollie says genially. Naturally, everyone plumps for a traditional roast because it's the best for miles around.

* * *

I was only half joking about a birthday cake, but just as Jude is taking the order for coffee a hush falls over the restaurant as Kurt staggers towards us carrying the largest cake I think I've ever seen. Val quickly makes room for it in front of Fisher, and as Kurt gingerly lowers it down onto the table, to everyone's delight we can now see that it's a replica of The Star Gazer in her beautiful, crimson livery. And, yes, there are so many candles they can't be far off the magic number.

'You'd better blow this out pretty quickly,' Sarah advises Fisher as she places a pile of plates and a cake knife on the table.

People are also crowding in from the restaurant, wondering what all the fuss is about. The rendition of 'Happy Birthday' ends up being raucous and totally out of tune. Fisher sucks in a deep breath and begins to blow out the candles.

'Thank you, everyone. I don't quite know what to say, except cake all round and who made this beauty?'

'That would be down to Val and Ethel,' Sarah confirms. 'Seriously, ladies, you did an amazing job. Now, Jade and Jude, I think we're going to need a lot more plates. Perhaps Fisher would do the honours?'

Sarah hands the cake knife to Fisher, who raises his eyebrows and hands it straight to Val. 'I think an expert is called for here and that isn't me, I'm afraid.'

My heart flutters in my chest as I watch their fingers making contact for the briefest of moments. True happiness radiates out of them, but Fisher's retirement plan has been his dream for a long time. I can't help wondering whether Val understands how serious he is about it, or how life-changing it promises to be.

Fisher's plan, before his wife left him, was to start a new business running luxury cruises on The Star Gazer. Will Fisher look to employ someone to assist him? I wonder. He'll be tied up at weekends and evenings throughout late spring, summer and possibly on into the early autumn. That could have a major impact on their relationship. Besides working for Fisher three days a week at the marina, Val teaches French online for Linguispeak. Having been on her own for a long time now, she's still adjusting to having a man in her life again. At a time when Fisher should be counting down the months to making his dream come true, he's suddenly facing an unexpected dilemma.

* * *

'This weekend has flown.' I sigh, snuggling into Gray. He snakes his arm around my shoulders, pulling me even closer.

'It always does, but it's been amazing, hasn't it?'

I roll onto my side so I can look at him in the gloom and I can see a little glint in his eyes. 'Hmm, amazing is one word for it! We're sleeping in the spare room in The Retreat and creeping around so that we don't disturb Tollie. He's pretending he doesn't have a lady friend and we have an expensive hole in the garden that is about to get a lot bigger.'

'I see your point. I think we should call Lock Keeper's Cottage the money pit from now on. But, hey – it has been great. And I've pulled together that list of names for the wedding invites, although I suggest we don't write them out until you've met the crew as one, or two, are a bit dodgy,' he jests.

The thought of heading up to London to meet Gray's inner circle makes me feel a little nervous, but I don't want him to see that. 'You're a nightmare at times, Gray, have I ever told you that?' I scold him, but his wicked sense of humour is a big part of his personality.

'Hey, the wedding is coming together, Fisher had a great birthday party and you'll soon whip up your helpers into a money-raising frenzy. Life seems pretty okay to me,' he replies firmly.

'Then why don't you sing or hum any more?' I remark.

'I've moved on to the more serious stuff now at work, Immi. Writing snappy little jingles for ads is fun, but it's not where my ambitions lie. You know how people complain that they stick in their heads? Well, it's the same when you're writing them. Now I dream bigger and what I hear in my head is a full orchestra with violins and cellos and wind instruments.'

'Is it ever likely you'd be able to work from home some of the time?'

Gray's face changes and the light in his eyes dims a little.

'Sorry, Gray. That was a stupid thing to say.'

He pauses for a moment and I hope I haven't upset him, but Sunday nights always make me want to cling onto him and I loathe Monday mornings when Gray leaves.

'It would be nice to be able to afford to set up my own studio. There will be space now we've extended the cottage, but the cost of kitting it out would be a stretch too far for now. Look, it's tough being apart four nights a week but I hope it won't be forever.'

'Any news about the trip to LA?'

'Ollie is still working on it; we just need to agree a date.'

'Oh, so it's imminent, then?'

'Yes. To sign off on the *The Columbus Adventure*, they've invited Ollie and me to go over for the screening of the final cut. I'm just working on the audio clips for a series of trailers to promote the film, and then we're done. The new project is with the same producers but involves working with an entirely different team. And, while we're there, Ollie has a couple of back-up options he wants to look into.'

'That's wonderful, Gray. And you'll get to see your name on the credits! What an achievement. You've worked so hard on this film and what you've earned has helped, not just us with the building work, but your mum, too. But why didn't you tell me sooner?'

'I didn't quite know how to broach the subject, to be honest, as I feel bad flying off on a jolly and leaving you all alone. But it's not just that. Sometimes I wonder if I made the right decision, insisting on helping Mum out financially when she moved here. My father knew that half of the proceeds of the house wasn't going to be enough to buy her a little cottage in the Cotswolds.'

'Rona means as much to me as she does to you, Gray, and I wouldn't have had it any other way.'

'That's because you have a good heart, Immi. I'm well aware that my father owes her, not least for the fact that she brought me up all on her own. But I knew Mum didn't feel it was right to take the extra money he offered her. I convinced her that it wasn't a problem, and I was more than happy to help her out, but we'd be well in the black if I'd let them sort it out between themselves. The truth is that I didn't want to give him the satisfaction of having to step up for Mum.'

Gray's paternal grandmother succeeded in splitting up his parents but, in the process, she lost all contact with her grandson when his father, Grayson, flew home to the States. When Grayson reached out to Rona and Gray last year, Gray had no idea they had never formalised their divorce. Or that the house in which she was living was still in their joint names. Gray was angry. Having given up work and moved back in with Rona when she was ill, he alone was her tower of strength.

'You wouldn't be the man I fell in love with, Gray, if you hadn't come to her rescue. Rona is free and she doesn't owe Grayson anything now because of you; she's working again and happy. We have a lifetime together to build up our savings. I know that taking on Lock Keeper's Cottage and having it renovated is a financial drain on us, but it means so much to Tollie and to me. He lived in that cottage with Grandma Nell for thirty-five happy years. It's the one place that Dad and I could come back to that was a constant when his job moved us from place to place. I think that makes you and me even, don't you?'

Gray reaches out to brush my cheek with his fingers.

'And incredibly lucky, when you look around at other couples starting from scratch. Imagine what life is going to be like next summer. We'll be able to enjoy our quality time at the weekends. It will be nice, though, when the money doesn't flow out quite as fast as it flows in, hey?'

I nod but it's a fight to keep my eyes open now. When I wake with a start a little while later, I ease Gray's arm from under me and lie watching him for a while. What I hate when he heads to London is that I'm not involved in his day-to-day activities, even though he talks about his musician friends all the time. Whereas here, at weekends, Gray is a real part of my life. What if his friends think I'm holding him back, expecting him to spend his downtime in a quiet little backwater of a place? I guess I'll find out before too long.

Lying back on my pillow, I wonder how on earth he can sleep

so soundly when Tollie has the volume on the TV up way too loud. He really should get his hearing checked. I turn over onto my side, bending the pillow to cover my ear. Three weeks and two days until we can move back into Lock Keeper's Cottage... but who's counting?

7

GETTING ORGANISED

In hindsight, I realise that last week I had hit a bit of a low point, but after talking it through with Gray things don't seem half as bad. When we kissed goodbye at 5 a.m., I decided that the time had come to put down on paper all the pressing issues that are crowding my mind.

Sitting at the table, I have a pen and a notebook alongside my breakfast plate and, intermittently, I add to the growing number of items. Tollie takes the seat opposite and keeps glancing across at me, anxiously. He's not a fan of lists, as he knows that when it gets to that point, look out world because I'm a woman on a mission.

'That looks worryin',' Tollie remarks.

'No, just time to get a few things sorted and see what else I can delegate. I need to make sure I can keep a close eye on the work here in case Reggie falls behind. I'll be popping back for lunch every day.'

'Can't, uh, I do that, m'dear?'

Tollie looks a bit down in the mouth.

'Reggie is a lovely man, but like all builders he has more than one job on the go at the same time. Have you noticed how he treats you and me very differently? Sometimes being a female is an advantage,' I reply and Tollie gives me a disapproving look.

'Well, I'm here and it would save you a bit of time. Lunch is for takin' a break and by the time you walk here and back, it's goin' to be a short one. If you change your mind, let me know.'

I can't tell if Tollie is put out because he's thinking about his visits from Daphne Harris. If anyone knows what's going on when I'm not here, it's going to be Reggie – maybe it's time I had a chat with him.

Armed with my list, I walk over to plant a kiss on Tollie's cheek. 'See you later. Have a fun morning.'

Stepping out onto the temporary path, I wave to the three men in the far corner leaning on their spades. 'Morning.' They all wave back, but there's no sign of Reggie. Out on the towpath, to my surprise, I see Bernie walking towards me.

'Has Tollie finished his breakfast?' he enquires as he draws closer.

'Yes. He's about to have a second cup of coffee. Problems?'

'No, just passing and wondering whether he'd like a bit of company,' he replies, sounding a little reticent.

Bernie isn't just passing, unless he was going for a long walk and has changed his mind. Lock Keeper's land abuts The Bull-rush's car park, which ends just beyond the bridge over to the marina. After the cottage, it's open fields right down to the next junction.

'I'm sure he would. I'd better speed up if I don't want to be late. Bye, Bernie.'

The parting look he gives me is an uneasy one, but this morning I'm going with the flow. My list will be a darn sight shorter by the end of the day and I dare anyone whose path I cross to add to it.

* * *

'Hi, Sarah, what a lovely lunch we had yesterday. Well done with the forest of candles on the cake. It can't have been easy!'

She stops wiping down the counter and straightens up.

'It wasn't, but it was worth singeing my hair to see the look on Fisher's face. I'm assuming you aren't here to eat?'

'Oh, no! Sorry to hear about the hair and I'm not, sadly. I'm on my way to see Val and Rona.'

'Ah,' she replies, lowering her voice, 'wedding planning!'

'Yep, but first I have the guest list at last, would you believe it?'

I hand it over to Sarah; she beams back at me. 'Forty, that's a perfect number for an intimate, cosy wedding.'

'Well, it's thirty-nine, but I rounded it up. That includes you, Karl, the girls, and Maggie. If you can liaise with my team,' I instruct her, trying to refrain from looking smug, 'they'll hire the waiting staff and someone to man the bar on the day.'

Sarah holds up her hand and we high-five. 'I'm glad you're cutting yourself a little slack, Immi. Between us all we won't miss a single thing, I promise you.'

'Thank you for your help, Sarah. I really do appreciate it – you're a good friend. Admin and figures are my thing, it's what I do best. But as for the minute details required to get this wedding sorted, well, I don't have a clue. I just want something simple, Christmassy and cosy.' I lean in, lowering my voice. 'That's not wrong of me, is it? Gray seems happy enough.'

She stares at me for a couple of seconds before reaching out to place a hand on my arm to give it a squeeze.

'Immi, it's time you realised that people do, actually, like to get involved and help. You'll end up with something magical, I'm sure, and it won't be over-the-top because we all know that's not you.'

I take a quick glance around; there's no one in earshot as there are only a handful of early-bird diners here before the evening rush begins in about an hour's time.

'And, um, while I'm here... would you consider being my maid of honour?'

Sarah's hand flies up to her mouth and she hurries around the counter to give me a hug.

'I'd be both thrilled and honoured, Immi. That means so much to me, my lovely friend. I've come to regard you as the sister I never had. Shopping for a dress isn't something I do very often, let alone for a maid of honour, so we're going to have to get our heads together on that!' she exclaims excitedly. I can see that Sarah is genuinely moved and I couldn't be happier.

'Oh, we will. I hope you're good at calming nerves because I'm going to be a total wreck on the day! I nearly forgot. Gray, Rona and Val will be figuring out the menu for the wedding buffet so you can expect to have that very shortly.'

'The ladies will make sure it's something special, then. I can guarantee it won't be sausage rolls and pizza.' She laughs.

I'm used to Gray humming as he walks along, but, as I say goodbye and set off, today I'm the one with a tune in my head. And it's the 'Bridal Chorus'. Gray is in total charge of the music and if he thinks this is me, then I will be a tad disappointed, I'm afraid, but it's in his hands. And that's a good feeling. If the best way to enjoy my own wedding is to rely upon the people I love to pull it together, that's better than any present they could get us.

'Immi, Immi!' I turn around and Rona is hurrying to catch up with me.

'Hi, Rona. How was your day?' I ask, giving her a hug.

'Good, thank you. Noisy, but then eight-year-olds are so full of energy, and I have a class of twenty-six of them.'

'Ooh, rather you than me,' I reply, grimacing.

'It's fun, you just need to keep them in line. There are one or two who like the sound of their own voices, but I watch them like a hawk. I'm a little late and I was worried I was going to keep you and Val waiting.'

'Ditto. I've just dropped the guest list into The Bullrush.'

'Oh, wonderful. You managed to pin Gray down, then,' Rona replies enthusiastically. She knows how hard it is sometimes to get her son to focus on things that, as he's given to say, make his brain ache.

As we pick up the pace I glance across at her, my mind ticking over.

'Gray has a trip to Los Angeles coming up. He doesn't have a firm date yet, but he thinks it will be quite soon.'

'Oh, thank goodness you know about it. Gray has been so worried about how stressed you've been lately, and he wasn't sure when to tell you. He wanted to pick the right time, although, given the week you'd had, I'm surprised he mentioned it at all this weekend.'

That's what I love about Rona: she never interferes between us, even when she doesn't necessarily agree with the way we're handling things. I'm beginning to wonder how long Gray has known about this upcoming trip.

'I'm pleased for him. It sounds thrilling. His first film score, and he gets to sit with the producer and the team for the screening of the final cut. I'm sad he felt awkward about telling me, because I wouldn't want to hold him back in any way, Rona.'

'I know, Immi. And Gray appreciates that, too. But it has been an unusually eventful time, hasn't it? And after last year's ups and downs, we were all hoping life would become a little less frenetic for you both.'

'It will, soon. I'm sure of it.'

'This trip he's making, I... um... well, Grayson lives in Santa Barbara and I don't know if I should say something to him.'

I feel guilty as Rona and Gray were due to fly out to meet up with his father just before the New Year. Gray changed his mind while he was at the airport and he returned home to me.

'To whom? Gray, or Grayson?

The sound she mutters is one of frustration. 'Mmm. Both. Like it or not, they will have to get together at some point, because Gray is the sole beneficiary in Grayson's will. There are papers to be signed that will make it easier when the time comes, which, I hope won't be for many years, but Grayson is anxious and would rather get it sorted sooner than later.'

'Rona, please don't take this the wrong way, but is that just an excuse for him to meet up with Gray in person?'

We arrive at Byre Cottage and as I put my hand up over the top of the gate to release the bolt, I pause for a moment to look directly at Rona.

'I do believe it is,' she replies sheepishly. 'But is that so wrong? And Gray is going to be within easy striking distance of his father when he's at the studios. It's a perfect opportunity to get it out of the way. As they have no direct contact, would it be so very wrong of me to make them both aware of that fact and then leave them to decide for themselves?'

Grayson returned to the States when Gray was not even five years old, after Grayson's mother gave him an ultimatum. The plan was for them all to go and live in her lavish home in Santa Barbara, but Rona knew that his mother intended to make her life so unbearable she would end up being the one to walk away. At the last-minute, Rona realised she had to choose between a husband she would love forever, or what was best for her son.

'I think you have to go with whatever your instincts are telling you is the right thing to do, but Gray doesn't want a reconciliation. It hurts him that you were rejected by Grayson's family. And he was shocked to discover you were still married and that the house he was brought up in didn't belong solely to you. It was a lot for him to take in.'

'I know, and I was glad in a way that Gray didn't accompany me on my visit. Grayson and I could talk openly. He is a lonely man, now his mother is gone.'

It's not my business to ask her about the divorce proceedings. When she returned, she simply told Gray that the house would be sold and she'd use the equity to move to Aysbury. Grayson didn't want what was due to him, not least because he doesn't need it, but Gray stepped in to help Rona out and she refused Grayson's offer. Oh, it's such a mess.

'Are you two coming in?' Val calls out as we step into the small, courtyard garden and make our way up to the front door.

'I'll just re-boil the kettle and make the tea. You ladies go through and settle yourselves down,' Val instructs us.

'Grayson doesn't know about the wedding, does he?' I whisper as we sit next to each other on one of the two sofas.

'No. I don't feel it's my place to tell him.'

I nod as Val appears in the doorway carrying a tray and I jump up to make room for it on the coffee table.

'I was telling Rona that I popped in to see Sarah on my way here. We now have a guest list and here's a copy for the file. Gray is going to be emailing you both to thrash out the details of the buffet.'

'Goodness, that's unexpected.' Rona looks surprised.

'He offered and I know you two will nudge him in the right direction. The guest list stands at thirty-nine, so we're catering for forty.'

Val is already pulling out her notebook and pen, as Rona pours the Earl Grey tea.

Ziggy suddenly appears from behind the TV unit in the corner, making her presence known with one of her drawn-out miaows. 'It's her favourite place.' Val laughs.

Ziggy stretches, straightening her legs and looking a bit like a robot as she begins inching forward. Then she arches her back and saunters off into the kitchen.

'We've disturbed her, poor thing,' I reply.

'Oh, she'll let us know if she's not happy. Sometimes I'm on the receiving end of a long and drawn-out conversation. Goodness knows what she's saying to me, but it's always amusing.'

It's surprising how fast the evening flies by as I share the highlights of the conversation I had with Gray, to give Val and Rona a feel for what we're hoping to achieve.

'We'll come up with a few suggestions for invitations, sticking with the cosy Christmas theme, and you can then take your pick,' Rona adds, at a point where I hope we're nearly done. My head is spinning with it all.

'We do need a steer on your choice of flowers. I thought it was rather lovely that Martin offered to do the honours. What a generous present from him and Ursula. I trust, though, that you won't be instrumental in making up the bouquet and the various floral displays,' Val adds.

'I doubt they'll even let me cross the threshold; I will be banned from the florist's area, I'm sure. As long as there's an abundance of greenery for the hall, with holly sporting red berries, ivy, the smell of pine... all the usual festive stuff, then I'll go with simple roses.'

'And the colour scheme?' Val asks as they both peer at me intently.

'I'm not sure yet.'

'You still haven't picked a dress, then?' Rona enquires gently. 'While we don't want to panic you, the style you choose will dictate the overall theme of the wedding. I've been emailing with Gray about suits, and we can't help him until we have a steer from you. It's not going to be a white wedding, then?'

I hate to disappoint them after flicking through the magazines last week and being shown brilliant white frothy ballgowns and sleek, lace mermaid dresses. But knowing what I don't want doesn't mean I know what I do want until I find the right one.

'No, but I'm handing out tasks left right and centre so that I can free up some time to find the perfect dress.'

I get the distinct feeling that they are a little disappointed. 'It might be a good idea to book an appointment at a bridal boutique and try on a few dresses. Just to help you rule things out,' Val says encouragingly.

Um, that's a firm *no*.

'I'm thinking of designing something myself. I'd like it to be unique. It won't be a ball gown, or a princess dress, but as soon as I have the design worked out I will be able to confirm the overall look and the colour scheme.'

Rona and Val smile across at each other so at least I've succeeded in reassuring them that I am taking this seriously.

'The most important thing about a wedding is that the bride and groom can look back on it in years to come and remember it as *their* day. It's not about pleasing anyone else, Immi. It is a lot to pull together given the timescale, but if you just focus on the dress, then leave the rest up to us. We'll liaise with Gray, and report back to him at every stage. As for the cake... well, Ethel and Val have offered to make something special for you, with a winter theme,' Rona informs me.

'Ah, that's so kind. I loved Fisher's cake. And all those candles – his face was a picture!'

The wedding budget isn't huge and we are grateful for the way people are stepping up for us because that means so much more than gifts we don't really need. We've been living together for the best part of six months now and, in all honesty, we have all the basics. Even if they are now packed up in boxes, stacked in one room of the cottage.

'We could head up the invitations with "A Winter Wedding Party". It sounds festive, without being too formal,' Val offers, breaking my chain of thought. 'And will you be pulling together a wedding-present list to give your guests a steer, so that you don't end up with a lifetime supply of toasters?'

'A list? I can't think of any small bits and pieces we need,' I answer truthfully.

'But you have some big items of furniture to buy, Immi,' Rona interjects. 'It's quite customary to suggest that, in lieu of a present, if anyone wants to make a small contribution towards a bigger purchase, it would be appreciated. What do you think?'

I look at Val and she nods her head.

'If that's acceptable, then it's fine by me,' I concur. 'Give me two weeks, tops, to get back to you with the information you need and then you can sort out Tollie, Gray, and his best man, once Gray has made up his mind who he wants to take on that role.'

Rona's eyes light up. 'A wedding is a special occasion, but a Christmas wedding has that extra touch of magic to it.'

It's wonderful to see how excited Val and Rona are, and how much fun they're having, I reflect as I walk home, leaving them to dot a few i's and cross some t's. Up until now, every time I thought about anything wedding-related, I didn't know which way to turn or what to tackle first. I was out of my depth and feeling inadequate.

On the way back to The Retreat, Gray texts to say he's having a drink with Ollie and it's likely to be a late one as it's work, not pleasure.

Just heading back home now after a couple of hours with our wedding planners. Enjoy your drink!

I finish off with a string of love hearts.

I know – Mum has already emailed me and I'm having a video chat tomorrow night with her and Val about the buffet. They certainly work fast! Night, babe, sleep well. Love you loads. x

Even though it's just after 9 p.m. people are still walking along the canal, enjoying the fine evening. Some of them will, no doubt, have eaten at The Bullrush and are heading towards the bridge over the canal. Once I get past that point there's only one couple further along the path, and when I hear hurried footsteps behind me my pulse quickens a little.

'Immi, Immi!'

I stop, turning around to see Patrick striding towards me. He's a little out of breath.

'I did call out, but you didn't hear me. Can I walk you down to your gate?'

He's such a gentleman.

'Thank you, Patrick, that's most kind. How are you?'

'Doing well, thanks,' he replies, sounding upbeat. 'Martin and I met up for a bite to eat in The Bullrush. I was grateful for the company. It gets a bit lonely, at times. Anyway, I just wanted to say that if you need any help with the fundraising, or the paperwork, my evenings and weekends are mainly free. So do call on me, as I'd love to get involved. I've asked Martin to pass on my contact details.'

'That's kind of you to offer. We'll sort something out.'

'It's my pleasure. This is Lock Keeper's Cottage, then,' he says, catching sight of the roofline and chimney above the high hedge that runs along the front of the property. 'I don't usually walk down this far, but it's a nice spot.'

'Yes. That area back there is where the new playground will go.'

'Oh, Martin mentioned that Tollie is donating the land. Does the orchard belong to the cottage, too?'

'Yes. Before we had this area cleared it was completely overgrown and full of stinging nettles and blackberry bushes. I never in my wildest dreams imagined it would come in useful.'

'Well, one thing I've learnt is that you never know what's around the corner. Anyway, I'd best get off. Thanks for the little chat, Immi. It's always a pleasure.'

'And I'll be in touch shortly, Patrick.'

I stand at the gate, watching as he walks back along the towpath and up to the car park. Patrick's shoulders are slightly slumped, and he looks like a man carrying the weight of the world on his shoulders. Maybe Aysbury's busy community activities can cheer him up a little and another pair of hands always comes in useful.

'Hey, babe. How was your day?' Gray sounds full of energy, even though his call is later than usual, which means he's still working and lost track of time.

I recline back on the bed cover, the window ajar. The sound of a tractor still hard at work filters through the window. As the early crops are harvested it involves long days before the ploughing begins all over again. But even the birds are still active tonight, and it seems no one is sleepy. In the sitting room below, the sounds of the film Tollie is watching generates a low rumble.

'Great. Busy as usual. You sound upbeat and wide-awake.'

'I've just finished a call with Mum and Val.'

'Uh, oh. How did it go?' I ask tentatively.

Gray replies with a throaty little chuckle. 'Good, actually.'

'Well, tell me all about it!' I demand.

'That's one of the things we talked about. You, delegating tasks and then not really letting go. They're going to consult you on the important decisions, like this colour thing, which is a biggie, they tell me. But other than that, I have a good idea what will make you happy and so we would appreciate it if you could put your trust in Mum, Val and me to conjure up a real Christmas fairy-tale surprise. Admittedly, I'm not sure why they want everything to match your dress, but I trust my crew and they say it's important.'

'Their faces fell when I broke the news that it won't be a white wedding. Unless it snows, of course!' Should I be taking this more seriously? I wonder.

'Our aim is to surprise and delight you, and we won't let you down, Immi. I want to start my married life with a happy wife, so there's a lot at stake but I'm up for the challenge.' Gray does sound excited.

'As long as you stick to a cosy, country, romantic, Christmassy feel-good vibe, then I'm happy. Having asked Sarah to be my maid of honour, that's two dresses to sort out. You, Val and Rona will need to sort out Tollie. His old suit still fits, but it's blue and—'

'I get the message. Colour coordination is important, Immi. And as for Tollie, leave that to us. Trying on dresses is supposed to be the best bit, isn't it? Why don't you go shopping with Sarah and have a little fun? You're bound to find something that feels right, surely?'

How can a man even begin to understand that all eyes are on the bride on her wedding day, and wearing something special requires a certain level of body confidence? If it's too fussy, the dress will look like it's wearing me, and I'll end up feeling self-conscious. 'You have absolutely no idea, Gray. Rona likes the princess look, Val thinks the mermaid style is elegant, and I just want to feel like me. But a dressed-up version of me. Not like the bride on the top of a wedding cake.'

'Okay, I'm way out of my depth here. All I'm saying is once you give them this one little piece of information, you'll be free to focus on the playground. When you have an up-to-date picture of where the fund stands, you can start cracking the whip and get the committee doubling their efforts, if necessary. I wish I could take some of that work off you, but I can't, so let me do this, babe. Think of it as one of my Christmas presents to you.'

'I love you, Gray. Thank you. I consider myself to be an extremely lucky woman and I am grateful. Anyway, come on, you have other news, I can tell.'

He clears his throat. 'We're still awaiting confirmation, but Ollie's assistant is organising the tickets to LA and it's looking likely to be the week after next, depending on availability.'

'Oh!' My surprise sounds slightly negative, and I hurry to correct myself. 'That's great news. How long will you be gone?'

'Eight days in total. We have a series of meetings at three different locations. I had hoped we'd have a little more notice, Immi, and I'm sorry to spring this on you.'

'It's fine, Gray. Not only do you get to see your first big project come to fruition, but there's a chance of even more work to come in the longer term, which is equally important. That's brilliant news and I'm excited for you!' My enthusiasm is genuine, but the thought of eight long days without seeing him makes my heart constrict in my chest.

'And have you thought any more about the other thing we talked about, a hobby for you?' Gray enquires encouragingly.

'You aren't going to let up, are you? Yes, I have and I'm going to talk to Ursula, as I'm pretty sure Martin said that she attends a yoga class.'

'Perfect! Together we got this, babe, and everything will be fine. You know you can always count on me, even if sometimes I need pointing in the right direction.'

'And the traditional "Wedding March" isn't my thing, just thought I'd throw that out there.'

'Immi Tolliman, it didn't even make the longlist,' he replies, so softly that I can almost envision him lying next to me on the bed.

This is the year my dream of having Gray slip that wedding ring on my finger is going to become a reality. I'm not going to fixate on the minute details, which, in the grand scheme of life, mean nothing at all when one's heart is full of love.

* * *

'Morning, Immi. An assessor is coming to look at the damage to the greenhouse today and take a few photographs. He'll be here around 11 a.m. It's unlikely I'll be back by then, so do you mind sorting him out for me?'

'No problem. And before I forget, can you text me Patrick's number, please? I bumped into him last night and we had a quick chat. I think he'd be a great addition to the committee.'

'Sorry, I thought I'd already done that. I'm glad you feel the same way and he has lots of ideas. I, um, don't like to ask how it's going—'

My smile begins to fade. 'Money is coming in, but it's mainly in small amounts, which is an admin nightmare. I'm preparing an overview ready for the next meeting. Once I can get a firm handle on where we are, it all depends on Fisher's negotiations with the manufacturers of the equipment and the timescale for the various staged payments.'

'If you need to take a little time off to work on that, Immi, we'll sort something out. Don't get overloaded.'

'That's kind of you, Martin, but I've decided to delegate a few things to allow me to catch back up, so it's not a problem. On another matter entirely, is Ursula still into yoga?'

Martin looks at me in surprise. 'Yes, why?'

'I'm thinking of taking it up.'

His eyes widen a little. 'Well, give her a ring. She'll be back from the school run and she's working on an order for some roman blinds today, so I know she'll be at home.'

'Thanks. I'll catch up with you after the deliveries, then, to let you know how the inspection goes.'

'I think they'll say it has to be pulled down. That means a hike in our premium next year, but that's what insurance is for, isn't it?'

I hope Martin isn't worried about money again, as business is booming. After the most successful Christmas he's ever had, we were banking on a busy spring and summer. If the decision is to demolish the greenhouse, that's a quarter of our retail space axed in one go and the solution isn't likely to be a speedy one.

* * *

'Hi, Ursula. Is it convenient to talk? I only have a quick question I wanted to ask.'

'Yes, I'm still getting set up, so I haven't made a start yet. How is everything going?'

'Well, a lot better this week than last, thankfully. It was lovely to see you at Fisher's birthday lunch on Sunday. We're a noisy bunch, aren't we?'

'You can say that again.' She laughs. 'But it was fun. Plus, I hadn't seen Gray for ages, so that was a bonus, too.'

'The reason I'm calling is to ask about yoga. I'm thinking of taking a class, but I wasn't sure if the one held in the village hall is still running.'

'It isn't, I'm afraid. The numbers kept declining. I drive over to Middle Norton as the church hall there holds a class on a Tuesday night. There are fourteen of us regulars and about half a dozen people who join in now and again. They're a great bunch and the woman who runs it has been holding classes for more than ten years.'

'Tuesdays are good for me. What time does it start?'

'Ooh, you're serious, then? It's seven thirty until nine. I could give you a lift. It would be lovely to have some company.'

'Why don't I drive us? The only time I have a chance to get behind the wheel these days is when I do the rounds of emptying the donation boxes,' I admit.

'That's the problem when you walk to work, isn't it? Working from home it's the same for me and, on top of that, I don't really see many people. Mainly customers when they call to collect their orders.'

'Exactly. Ursula, can I ask you one last thing... have you ever made a wedding dress?'

There's a slight pause. 'No. Prom dresses, yes, but working with tulle is an experience I've avoided.'

'Oh. Right. I don't blame you.'

'So, are you up for a class tonight?'

'What do I need? I have a foam rollup mat I use for sunbathing and I assume it's leggings and a simple T-shirt?'

'Oh, yes! It's very informal. No one comes in expensive designer wear. And we're all shapes and sizes. If you really don't mind driving, then shall we say 7 p.m.? Will that give you enough time to get home and have something light to eat first?'

'Perfect. Thanks, Ursula, I'm looking forward to it. See you later, then.'

As I put down the phone, it immediately kicks back into life, ringing in my hand.

'Fisher, good morning. Everything okay?'

'I wondered if we could meet up for lunch, Immi. I really need a listening ear.'

'Oh.' I pause, thrown by the edginess in his voice. 'Of course.

I'm going home for lunch every day in order to keep an eye on the progress at the cottage. If you meet me here at 1 p.m. we'll head to The Retreat and grab a sandwich. How does that sound?'

'That's fine. We can talk on the way, as I'd prefer to keep this just between us.'

Oh dear, he sounds fraught. Please don't let this be anything serious. What hurts Fisher hurts me too, because my life wouldn't have been the same without him in it.

9

A LISTENING EAR AND A HELPING HAND

'You look nice, Immi,' Fisher says as he leans in to give me a quick hug. When I'm stressed, I often rush out of the house with my hair still damp from the shower but now I'm taking a little more time each morning. Today I'm even wearing a touch of make-up. 'Sorry to spoil your lunch plans, but I can't even focus on work right now.'

'Why didn't you call me sooner? I'm always here for you, Fisher, you know that.'

Our pace slows as we step onto the towpath. It's no more than a ten-minute walk to the cottage and I have no idea if anyone is going to be home until I open the door to The Retreat.

'The pensions department has confirmed in writing that I can apply for early retirement and they've sent through an estimate of the actuarially reduced figures. On paper it all stacks up.'

'That's brilliant news, Fisher. You must be thrilled,' I enthuse.

'It is, but it's a big step to take.' His tone reflects a level of hesitancy and I can sense conflict deep within him.

'Financially, you mean?'

'Partly, although I will have a sizeable lump sum behind me if running pleasure cruises on The Star Gazer doesn't pan out quite as planned. Nothing is guaranteed, is it?'

'No, but you won't know for sure until you try. It's your dream, Fisher, and this is your opportunity. When's the cut-off date for making the decision?'

'By the end of December and my official leaving date would be the first of November next year.'

'I'm delighted for you, Fisher. It's been a long time coming.'

He gives me an acknowledging smile, but it's still lacking enthusiasm. 'It'll be a challenge setting everything up, of course.'

'It's never easy getting a new initiative off the ground,' I agree, 'but think about being able to spend time actually on board and not stuck in the office, glancing out enviously at the narrowboats cruising past. What would be on the agenda for The Star Gazer, then?'

'Cruises along the canal for birthdays, special occasions and corporate events. Everything from a luxurious evening cruise with champagne and canapés, to the leisurely afternoon cruise with a traditional cream tea. The Star Gazer is ready and waiting, Immi, and she's calling to me.'

'And this is crunch time. Getting cold feet?' I offer and he grins back at me.

'I guess so. It's hard to walk away from a job you love and the security that offers, to take a huge risk.' He lowers his gaze, staring at his feet.

We begin walking again in silence as I mull over his words. 'At least you have some time to think it through before you make the final decision. Come on, let's get something to eat. It's hard to think when my stomach is growling and I'm sure yours is, too.'

Swinging open the gate, I lead him around the side of Lock

Keeper's Cottage and I can see he's shocked as we step onto the temporary pathway.

'Goodness, Immi. I knew you had problems, but this is a right old mess. Just when everything inside was beginning to take shape. It's a nightmare you and Gray could have done without, for sure.'

'It's not quite as bad as it looks,' I concede. 'We'll have to redo the landscaping after the trenches have been filled in, but it's worse round the back.'

As soon as we turn the corner, what was once a beautiful, flagstone patio with traditional, English cottage garden borders is now an eyesore.

Fisher stops in his tracks. 'Strewth! This is total devastation!'

'Hi, Reggie. I see you have a few extra guys here today. Appreciated, thank you!' I call out. Turning to Fisher, I mumble, 'It doesn't do any harm to be seen checking up.'

Fisher's face is a picture as I hurry across to The Retreat, where Reggie is standing waiting for me.

'Is Tollie about?' I ask.

'No,' Reggie confirms. 'He left earlier this morning and I haven't seen him since. Hi, Fisher.'

'That's quite a job you have there, Reggie,' Fisher replies, having composed himself.

'Yep, but we're getting there.'

'And I'll report back to Gray tonight,' I inform Reggie, giving him one of my oh-so-appreciative smiles. 'When Tollie left was he on his own?'

Reggie looks at me, his expression one of alarm. 'Um... I'm um... not sure.'

That would be a *no*, then. 'Oh, not to worry. I just wondered whether I should make him some lunch.'

'I don't think he'll be back...' Reggie suddenly stops short, realising what he's giving away maybe. 'I could be wrong, of course. Anyway, I must get back to work. See you later.'

As Fisher and I step in through the front door, he turns to me.

'What's going on, then? What is it that Reggie doesn't want to get caught up in?'

'Tollie seems to have a lady friend and her name is Daphne Harris. But what I don't know is how they came to meet. It's clear that Reggie has been told to keep quiet about it. But Bernie was here early on Monday morning and dismayed to see that I hadn't already left for work. He looked uneasy and he's obviously been sworn to secrecy, too.'

'Oh.' Fisher begins to join the dots. 'You think Tollie has been seeing this lady while you've been at work?'

We walk through into the kitchen and I head straight to the sink to wash my hands. 'Well, I'm only guessing but it makes perfect sense. Why he feels the need to hide it, though, I don't know. Honestly, from what I'm seeing he's beginning to sort himself out after falling into a bit of a slump at the start of the year. It's a tough time for him anyway, as Grandma's birthday is in January. I take him to lay flowers on her grave, of course, but this year he couldn't shake off his sadness and I'm not sure why. And now he's suddenly perked back up again. Is cheese and tomato okay?' I call out as Fisher grabs two plates and pops the kettle on.

'Fine, thanks, Immi. Perhaps he feels a little awkward about it.'

'You mean he thinks I won't understand?'

'Hmm... no, Nell's been gone a long time, and he knows you only want what's best for him. But sometimes we all need a little privacy and living on each other's doorsteps makes it difficult for you both.'

'Well, it doesn't help that for the next couple of weeks Gray and I are living in the spare room,' I burst out and Fisher raises his eyebrows to the heavens.

'Oh, that's such bad timing!'

'Do you think I should say anything to him, Fisher?'

'Let him have his little secret, darling girl. If, and when, he's ready to talk about it he'll let you know. Perhaps it's his own sense of guilt he has to overcome. It's not easy to move on from the love of your life if that love never leaves your heart.'

'I don't want him to be lonely, Fisher. And I feel awful that he's creeping around as if he's doing something wrong.'

'In the same way that you did when you first met Gray?' Fisher points out.

Casting my mind back, I remember those early days, worrying what Tollie would think, and whether he'd approve of the man I knew from the very start I would be with forever.

'In the end it sorted itself out, but we had a rocky couple of months, didn't we?' I remark, grimacing. Gray had to work hard to prove himself before Tollie made him welcome.

'Precisely. All I'm saying is, be receptive when Tollie is ready to share his news. There is no way he'd want you staying anywhere else, so relax, Immi. Simply give him some space and see what happens.'

Cutting the sandwiches in half, I place them on the plates and carry them over to the dining table while Fisher makes the drinks.

'It's hard to stand here and not think about the night we camped out on the floor. That snow was something, wasn't it?' Fisher recalls and I wander over to the sliding glass doors.

As I stare out over the garden and the open fields beyond, it seems like a long time ago now and not just six months. But so much has happened since Gray and I got engaged.

'You don't regret honouring Tollie's wishes about taking over the cottage, do you?' Fisher asks, walking over to join me.

'No. It would have begun to fall down around him, and I know he couldn't face living through the disruption. At least inside The Retreat the noise doesn't really bother him and he spends a lot of time sitting here gazing out at the view.'

'But it wasn't the best way to kick off Gray's move to Aysbury, was it? Be truthful.'

'No. I can't deny that. We had two months of peace and quiet and now we're four months into this building work and the end still isn't in sight. Anyway, in a year's time this aggravation will be forgotten, and we'll have a truly stunning new home inside, outside and under the ground.'

'Ha! Ha! Ha! Only you could spin it like that, Immi. Come on, let's eat. Then I want your advice about my situation because I don't know what to do for the best.'

We both know this is about his relationship with Val. He's not good talking about his feelings at the best of times, but what he went through with his ex-wife made him totally clam up. I can see that the fear of being hurt all over again is paralysing him. As for Val, she's equally guarded about her feelings, so who knows what's going on inside her head? Or how honest they have been with each other? If all she's looking for is friendship, I don't think that will be enough for Fisher and it could break his heart all over again.

The only advice I can give him is to sit Val down and tell her exactly how he feels before he makes his decision. But Fisher isn't going to find that an easy thing to do when he can't even admit to himself that's what's holding him back.

* * *

'I didn't realise just how much I needed this yoga class. I was amongst the youngest and there were sixty-year-olds more flexible than me,' I moan, feeling ashamed of myself. 'Still, anything that will help tone and firm up my muscles is a bonus as I'm on a mission to look and feel my best.'

I indicate right, waiting to turn off the main road and begin the last leg of the journey down through the country lanes to the marina.

'Ah, this is in preparation for the big day, then. I'm glad you enjoyed it. I find it relaxing and I regard it as me time. Two-and-a-half hours in total without hearing the word mum, once! I'm just me and it's bliss. Does that sound selfish?' Ursula asks and I can feel her eyes on me, watching for my reaction.

'Not at all. I mean, I don't have kids, obviously, but sometimes I get sick of hearing my own name. And yet I'm my own worst enemy. I've always talked about trying yoga and Gray thought it might help me to unwind. He was right.'

'Ah, he's such a sweet guy. He reminds me of Jack Black when he was in that film... *The Holiday*. The character he played was always humming away to himself or tapping his fingers.'

That makes me smile. 'I love that film and you are so right. Gray is a cuddly, and cute, Jack Black.'

'By the way, I've been meaning to bring this up. You asked about wedding dresses. Are you having problems finding something?'

'Apart from leafing through a few magazines, I haven't even begun looking properly. The thought of trying on dresses gives me an instant headache if I'm being honest.'

Ursula tuts. 'It's supposed to be the best part,' she replies, sounding surprised by my jaded response.

'Not for me, it isn't. I grew up living in jeans and sweatshirts. I wear trousers to work. The number of times I slip into a dress on average over a year could be counted on the fingers of one hand. What do I know about dress shopping?'

'You've never been dress shopping? Ever?' The minute Ursula finishes speaking, even though I'm focused on the road ahead I can feel her tense up. 'Oh, Immi. I'm so sorry, I wasn't thinking. So, you only buy online?'

'Yes. And now I have a maid of honour's dress to sort out, too.'

'Do you know what you're looking for?'

Instinctively, I divert my gaze to look at her for one brief second and she looks back at me, stunned. 'Oh, Immi. You really are stressed out about this, aren't you?'

I'm embarrassed when my eyes well up, and I draw in a deep breath to calm myself as I focus on the road ahead. The lanes are narrow but at this time of night it's quiet and the only obstruction is likely to be a tractor making its way back to Adler's farm, which we've just passed.

'Sorry. I know it's ridiculous.'

'No, it's not, Immi,' Ursula says, the empathy in her tone very real. 'Okay. Let's start at the beginning. What *don't* you want?'

'Anything that makes me feel like I'm faking it.' My voice is barely a whisper.

'Faking what? You're the bride, it's your day to shine.'

I let out a huge sigh. 'And that's what everyone will be expecting. But that isn't me. I don't feel comfortable being the centre of attention in that way.'

Ursula's sigh is even bigger than mine. 'Okay. Take a few deep breaths to calm yourself down, Immi, because I don't want you driving into a ditch. If it doesn't involve a mountain of tulle, then I'm sure that between us we can design something you'll feel comfortable wearing. I have a huge file of magazine cuttings and if we can grab a couple of hours to sit down and go through them, I'm sure we'll come up with your perfect dress.'

'Really?'

'Yes. What's your colour scheme?'

It's crunch time, but feels like a lifeline, and the sense of relief that washes over me is unbelievable.

'I'd like my dress to be silver-grey.'

'Oh, that's perfect for the Christmas theme. Silver-grey, silver and can I suggest you add a little pop of colour?'

Colour? I cast around desperately, but my mind is a total blank.

'How about a soft heather?' she suggests.

'That's a colour?' I ask, way past worrying whether that's a silly question.

'It's a softer shade of purple, erring towards the pink side without being girly. I think it would go nicely with silver-grey fabric and silver decorations, to bring everything alive. And when it comes to flowers, there are some beautiful roses in that shade.'

Roses. It feels like an omen. Grandma Nell loved roses and they're my first choice, too.

'You may have just rescued me, Ursula, and you have no idea how grateful I am. I now have the colour theme and Rona and Val are going to be delighted.'

Ursula sits there quietly and I wonder if I've said something amiss, because when she begins talking, she sounds tearful.

'A few years ago, when Olivia had her first operation, she was very poorly indeed and the business wasn't doing so well. You stepped up for us, Immi. I have never forgotten that. You talked Fisher into letting you cover Martin's absences at the Lockside Nurseries. We know he let you take your work home and you did that in your own time. That was a kindness that Martin and I had no idea how we could repay. And this is that time.'

I pull over into the next layby because tears are now trickling down my face. As I turn off the engine, I can see that Ursula is crying, too.

'You were an angel, Immi, at a time when we thought we were going to lose our daughter. You kept our business going. This is the very least I can do, and Martin is going to be over the moon if I can make you the perfect dress to complement his flowers.'

JULY

10

FACING FACTS

'Oh, Immi, I so wish you were here with me. It's all so... amazing and unbelievable. Ollie and I are being ferried around in one of the studio's limousines. Tomorrow is the screening and tonight we have a dinner with one of the studio executives. Seriously, this is way beyond my wildest expectations and some.'

It's Friday and usually I'm counting down the hours until I'm in Gray's arms again. I'm feeling lost, while Gray sounds like an excited kid who has been let loose in a toy store. He's been gone three days and aside from some brief text messages back and forth, it's the first chance we've had to talk. Time is going to drag for me over the weekend without his company but I can't let my sadness spoil his trip because that wouldn't be fair of me.

'Just enjoy being pampered, you deserve it, but a limo for two is a bit over-the-top,' I reply jovially.

'I know. But it's how things work in LA. Did the landscapers turn up?'

'No. Their vehicle broke down, allegedly, but the excuses are beginning to wear thin. There isn't much Reggie can do about it, but he's constantly chasing them as he feels bad because it was his recommendation. Anyway,' drawing a line under the negative, I inject some positivity into my words, 'I'm going to spend the entire weekend cleaning the cottage. Reggie has two guys working on the final snagging issues in the extension today and if they finish, then I can start the big clean through. By the time you get home we should be able to move back in. We'll just have to take our shoes off until the outside work has been finished.'

'You mean properly? Not camping out in two rooms as we were before?'

'Yep. Time to begin unpacking all those boxes and arrange delivery of the new furniture.' I hear a loud groan and it sounds as if Gray is stretching. 'What time is it there?'

'Just after 6 a.m. and we have a full day ahead of us. Are you all ready for the committee meeting on Monday night?'

'There are a couple of unknowns, as Tollie is still waiting for information back from the solicitors and the local authority,' I say with a bit of a sigh. 'But the pressure is on and at least I know the exact size of the problem we face now. It's doable, but we'll need everyone to push really hard. If the meeting goes as I hope, it will be a bit of a rallying call to the troops, and it's not all bad news by any means.'

'And here I am swanning around as if I'm a VIP when I'm not. I'd be better off by your side trying to generate some fresh ideas. If I think of anything, I'll email you. Did you follow up that lead with Harrison, at the Linden Hotel?'

I tut. 'No, I delegated it, of course. This is the new me. Patrick has it in hand, and I've invited him along to the meeting.'

'Go, Immi! And do you intend to make it to yoga again next week?'

'Most certainly, and last night I went round to Ursula's for a coffee and she took about an hour taking measurements for the dress. All I need to do now is arrange for Sarah to pop in to be measured up and then hope neither of us gain any weight between now and the wedding.'

'I'm glad you mentioned that topic. Mum and Val think the invites should go out sooner, rather than later. They're back from the printers, so we can sign them when I get back.'

'Isn't it a little early?'

'I said the same thing, but we didn't send out "save the date" cards and, although everyone knows the date, as it's so close to Christmas they think it's necessary. And don't forget my motley crew are coming from London. Val is going to contact the Linden and see if she can arrange a special rate for a block booking. She said it makes sense for them to travel to and from the wedding in a minibus. That's why I asked about Harrison, in case you were seeing him.'

'Oh, great idea, but I can't really ask Patrick to raise the topic. It's probably best to leave that to Val. My goodness, our wedding planners have thought of everything, haven't they?'

The conversation lapses and I know we're both conscious that we parted having had a disagreement. It doesn't happen often and neither of us quite knows how to handle it.

'Are you going to raise the subject, or am I?' Gray's voice lacks his usual warmth and I know he's angry with me.

'I thought you didn't want to talk about it,' I offer gingerly.

'How can a man I was too young to even remember cause an argument between us, Immi? It makes no sense. I'm sorry I shut you down like that, it was unfair of me. Clearly it does affect you too, whether I like it or not.'

My heart feels so conflicted right now. 'Only because it's a loose end, Gray, and not one of your making, I know, but can't you do it for your mum's sake? It's a few papers to sign and then it's done.'

'Sounds easy, doesn't it, when you say it like that? But to even be in the same room as that man is unimaginable to me. If anyone tried to come between you and me, Immi, I'd fight for you until I took my last breath. He just gave up on Mum.'

Rona can speak more freely to me about the past than she can to Gray because it's the one subject that instantly riles him up every single time. What happened wasn't quite as simple as Grayson giving up on Rona. After the sudden death of his own father, Grayson's mother struggled to keep the family business afloat. In the end, going back to the States was inevitable for him, but Rona told me that he also knew his wife and son were better off out of reach of any interference.

'This is going to sound like emotional blackmail, Gray, but it isn't, because you know that's not what I do. But you meeting up with Grayson to sign those forms would make Rona happy, because you are his flesh and blood. Your parents see you inheriting as righting a wrong, the wrong that Grayson's mother inflicted on you all. Grayson suffered too, you know, because he lost a loving wife and his only child.'

The silence between us is heavy.

'I understand what you're saying, Immi, but I can't give you any guarantees. There's a lot planned over the next few days and just travelling from one side of LA to the other for a meeting can waste an hour and a half, more if the traffic is really heavy.'

His upbeat mood is now totally deflated and there's little point in making conversation for the sake of it.

'I miss you, Gray. Don't worry if it's not easy to find time to fit in a call, a text will do, just so I know you're safe. Virtual hugs from me and *have a nice day.*' I turn on my best impression of an American accent, which I hope raises a smile as we disconnect.

Twice now, Rona has asked me to do her a favour and both times it was to do with talking to Gray about his father. She's a strong lady who did an amazing job of bringing up Gray on her own, and, not only that, doing it on her own terms. She took nothing from Grayson other than the right to remain living in their marital home. She paid half of the mortgage each month until Gray left school. It was on Grayson's insistence that their arrangement continued and now even that link has been severed. But what Gray can't accept is that she never stopped loving his father. That's something he can't seem to forgive, but for some illogical reason his anger for that is directed at Grayson. Still, I've done all I can and it's up to Gray now.

* * *

On Monday evening I arrange to meet Patrick in The Bullrush car park so that we can walk over to the village hall together. I figured he might feel uncomfortable walking into the meeting on his own. Leaving a little early, I saunter along and when I get closer, I'm surprised to see he's already waiting for me.

'Good evening, Patrick. I wouldn't have strolled if I'd known you were already here. It's such a lovely evening and it's a shame we couldn't hold our meeting on the patio behind The Bullrush,' I remark wistfully, returning his welcoming smile.

'I'm early. It's in my nature. I've written a brief summary of what was discussed when I met up with Harrison. Would you like me to run through it with you before the meeting, Immi?' My goodness, Patrick doesn't hang around when you give him a job. No wonder Martin sings his praises.

'Why don't you read it out at the meeting? I know it's your first time and you won't know everyone, but they will make you very welcome. There's so much to do that any extra hands are a godsend,' I reply, not relishing the thought of having to tell the group that we're falling behind.

'It's not good news, then?' Patrick asks, his normally serious countenance looking even graver.

'A lot has been achieved, but the weeks are flying by and we're too committed now to make any changes.'

'Well, many hands make light work, as my wife says. Sorry, ex-wife, it's still a little... unreal.'

'Martin mentioned that you'll be moving soon. You live in North Charlton at the moment, is that right?'

'Yes. We're about to exchange contracts on the house and I'm hoping to agree at least a four-week completion date to give me time to find somewhere temporary to stay. I don't want to jump into buying again until my life is more settled.'

'It can't be easy, Patrick. Aside from Martin, do you have many clients in this area?'

'Some, but a large part of my business is helping start-up companies at the planning stage, so a lot of my work is online.'

It's less than a ten-minute walk across the footbridge to the stone-built village hall and while we walk Patrick tells me a little bit about his hobby, which is making model boats.

'The canal is a real attraction for you, then.'

'Oh, I love it here. I'd live on a narrowboat if I could, but permanent berths seldom come up.'

'Abe and Ethel were in the right place, at the right time, so you never know – you could get lucky. Maybe mention it to Fisher, as he has contacts all over and if he hears of anything, I'm sure he'd be delighted to let you know. Right, let's head inside and get this meeting under way.'

It seems that we're the last to arrive, even though we're early. The others are already seated at the extended table in the meeting room. The chatter dies down as we join them, but I notice that one person is missing.

'No Tollie yet?' I ask. 'He rang me earlier to say he'd meet me here and I had the impression he was with Bernie.' When I look in his direction, Bernie smiles back at me.

'I saw Tollie earlier on and he didn't say he was going to be delayed,' Bernie declares, shrugging his shoulders.

'Ha!' Tollie's voice booms out as he strides forward looking very nimble on his feet tonight. 'You lot are early, I'm not late.'

We all settle down and I point a finger in the air, leaning forward to catch Tollie's eye.

'Before we begin, can I quickly introduce Patrick Hirst? He's the charity's latest recruit and has already met with Harrison at the Linden Hotel, so he'll talk us through that meeting in the general round-up. If I can just work round the table by way of a brief introduction. Tollie is our chairman, Val sitting next to him is our secretary, then we have Fisher, Abe, Ethel, Martin, Kurt and Bernie. I'm the treasurer.' I turn to glance at Patrick to see if he's keeping up, and he gives me a nod. 'David has sent his apologies. You might know him, Patrick, as he and his brother run the Middle Norton Brewing Company. They hold a fundraiser for us every Christmas, and David is also our company secretary.'

'Hello, everyone. I recognise a few faces. Aysbury's great sense of community is inspired by the charitable works organised by this committee. That's quite a thing in this day and age, and I'm delighted to be here.'

It looks as though Patrick is going to fit in very well indeed, and a whole host of welcoming comments come back at him.

'If we can all quieten down now,' Tollie interrupts, 'we have a lot to get through this evenin'. The first item on the agenda is a quick update from me, so I'll just launch straight into it. As I confirmed at the last meetin', I've walked the parish councillors around the parcel of my land abuttin' The Bullrush Inn car park. It has now been cleared and fenced off, as agreed at that meetin'.' Tollie passes around a handout.

'This is a copy of the Land Registry title plan for Lock Keeper's Cottage. The bit of land in question is outlined in red.'

He gives everyone a few moments to study it.

'Once the playground has been installed and the technical support officer has signed it off, my solicitor will agree a date with the parish council for the land transfer to go through. Any questions?'

Fisher raises his hand. 'What sort of timescale do we need to build in for processing the paperwork, Tollie?'

I asked Tollie the same question only yesterday, but he wasn't expecting a reply in time for tonight's meeting.

'I had a call an hour ago, so even Immi isn't it aware of this latest news. We need to have the technical support officer's sign-off by the end of the first week of November, just in case of any last-minute hitches with the legal agreement and the transfer. If there are no other questions, that leads us on rather nicely to Fisher's update.'

I'm already scribbling away, trying to pull together some dates and figures.

'Most of you have had the pack from Charlton and Sons Playground Solutions with the detailed plans and their quotation...' Fisher rifles around in his folder, pulling out a copy and passing it along the table to Patrick. 'As I previously reported, the local authority is satisfied that the specification is fully compliant with the BS EN1176 and 1177 safety standards.'

'Did you resolve the query over the proposed surface?' Martin asks.

'Yes. In the end we went for something called wet pour. It's made up of a layer of impact cushioning with a rubberised finish on top. The effect on the bottom line was minimal and Immi is now liaising with them with regard to the payment schedule.'

Everyone is impressed and it's good to see the smiling faces, but I fear I might be about to make those fade a little.

'It seems things are really beginning to fall into place. Over to you, m'dear.' Tollie looks in my direction. My goodness, he's motoring tonight and at this rate we'll be done in an hour.

'Aside from giving us a discount of 10 per cent, they are donating two wooden benches and will waive the slight increase due to the change of surface, so the original quotation stands. Once the deposit of five thousand, two hundred and sixty-four pounds is paid, the job is added to their build programme. It's usually a ten-week period from that point to installation.'

Looking around, I can see it's beginning to hit home that time is running out and Patrick isn't the only one with a grave look on his face.

'As a family-run business they have been most understanding and, luckily, our reputation has put us in good standing with them. We have agreed that half of the remaining balance will be paid six weeks prior to installation, when they begin the build process.' There's a sucking in of breath as people do the maths in their head. 'Recognising that fundraising isn't a steady stream of money coming in, we have provisionally agreed that the final payment will be made within four weeks after installation. But there is a little flexibility, if we need it.'

The silence is eerie as the committee wait to find out exactly how much we have in the kitty. 'The balance at the bank, including another one hundred and eighty-seven pounds and fifty-three pence from the latest emptying of the collection boxes, stands at a whopping eleven thousand and forty-six pounds.'

It's a sound figure and I want everyone to realise that.

'I'm not good with figures off the top of me head, Immi. What do we still need to raise?' Abe asks the fateful question, always one to get straight to the point.

'Bottom line is we need another fifteen thousand, two hundred and seventy-four pounds.' As I glance around the table, jaws have dropped. 'Before everyone goes into panic-mode, let me explain two things. To make the deposit and the first part-payment in the middle of August, we need to raise just under five thousand pounds. We already have pledges for half of that, plus whatever updates on new initiatives anyone has for today's meeting. With things now gathering momentum, I'm confident we can do it.'

'But that last payment, it's daunting,' Martin replies.

Kurt unexpectedly speaks up and I'm grateful to sit back and listen to what he has to say. 'And it wasn't that long ago that the mention of just over twenty-six thousand pounds sent us into a tailspin and look how far we've come. We have until the end of December, it seems, to raise that final payment. Every year in December we beat the previous year's total and that's the way it's been for ten years now. How much did we raise last year, Immi?'

I have the figures in front of me ready to reel off, but I'm so grateful to Kurt as sometimes people's eyes glaze-over, but he's caught everyone's attention.

'The Santa Ahoy cruises, together with various local events in the lead-up to Christmas, plus the donations from the pop-up Christmas market run by Bernie, including the car-parking charges, raised two and a half thousand pounds.' I stop for a moment and let that sink in. 'And thanks to David, his brother, Kurt and Sarah, the Middle Norton Brewing Company raised a further three thousand pounds in three months from the sales of The Bullrush Christmas Brew.'

'And David has already confirmed we're planning an even bigger campaign this year,' Kurt informs us. 'Regard last year as the dummy run. We didn't start selling it until the start of December and I'm fully aware that their promo ran through until the end of February. However, this year the plan is to put The Bullrush Christmas Brew on sale at the start of October to bring it in line with our deadline. David and his brother are going to link it to a feature about Aysbury in their newsletter, too.'

'Thank you, Kurt, that's great news. I know that nothing is guaranteed until it hits the bank account, but I really do believe the target is achievable. It's time to begin thinking outside the box, as well as progressing what's in the pipeline.'

'Hear, hear, m'dear. Before we run-through the general updates, can I just ask for a quick vote of confidence? Hands in the air for those who are reassured that we are headin' in the right direction.'

All hands fly up in the air, except for Patrick, who isn't sure if he should join in, but I give him a nod and he raises his hand.

'Right, let's have your news, then. Every pound that comes rollin' in gets us closer to our target.'

We've climbed halfway up the mountain and it is hard not to keep looking up and thinking how far in the distance the summit appears to be. But if we stopped for one moment to look at how far we've come, we'd realise it's a real achievement. An achievement that is going to fuel us going forward.

11

ISN'T EVERY CLOUD SUPPOSED TO HAVE A SILVER LINING?

I leave Patrick deep in conversation with Fisher and Martin. It's obvious they are kicking around some ideas and I offer to walk Val back, so we can leave them to it. I'm sure they will end up in The Bullrush for a pint, but I've had enough for one day.

'I know it's not brilliant news,' Val acknowledges as soon as we're alone. 'But you were right, pointing out how well it's going. It's easy for us all to become a little complacent and I think tonight's meeting was enough of a push to re-energise us all.'

We saunter along the winding path that leads to the foot-bridge over the canal. I turn to look up at the viewing gallery, above the marina's offices.

'You miss working with Fisher, don't you, Immi?'

'I do. We had a lot of laughs and sometimes I'd grab us some sandwiches and we'd go up and spend our lunch break just watching the boats go by.'

'He misses you, too,' she replies softly. 'But I keep him out of mischief. Can't let him loose in the workshop until he's had his caffeine and is more approachable. He's a good man.'

The way she's speaking is enough to tell me that he hasn't said anything to her yet, so I decide it's best to change the subject.

'He is. Anyway, I'm glad what I said this evening didn't come across as negative, given how much effort everyone has put in already.'

'Well, there was a lot of enthusiasm in the room tonight, that's for sure. Patrick is keen to get started and he has joined us at just the right time. Often, a little fresh blood and a different perspective can stir things up a bit.'

'Hmm. I was thinking the same thing. Oh, by the way, Gray said something about the invitations being ready when we spoke earlier on.'

'Ah, yes. I was supposed to mention it to you. Do you want to part company here, or do you have time to collect them now?'

'There's no one home and it's a pleasant walk, so why not?'

'What time does Gray get back tomorrow?'

'The flight doesn't land until the early hours of Wednesday morning. I'm not expecting him to get here until at least 7 a.m. Later, if he stops off to have a nap in the car on the drive back.'

'And Rona tells me that you're still staying in The Retreat?'

'Yes. The paint bubbled up on one of the walls and the decorators were in over the weekend sanding them down and doing a repaint. I had planned to do a clean through, but when that plan went awry, I booked a local cleaning company to come in tomorrow to make it sparkle.'

When we find ourselves level with The Merry Robin, Abe and Ethel's forty-five-foot Admiral narrowboat, it's a joy to behold. Ethel is a colourful lady in all senses of the word, and the middle section of the cabin top is her garden. An array of pots bursting with summer colours makes every passer-by stop to admire the display.

'It must be lovely to lead a simpler life, living on the canal,' I ponder.

'Small can be beautiful and less of a burden, but it wouldn't do for me. I like to keep my feet firmly on the ground.'

'Is that why you don't ever come with us on the Santa Ahoy cruises? I did wonder.'

A little smile plays around her mouth. 'I'm happy standing at the end of the gangplank and clipping tickets.'

Poor Fisher. That's not something that's even crossed his mind. Inwardly I groan. Whenever he's behind the wheel of The Star Gazer, there's a look that comes over his face and it's of a man whose worries have all fallen away. Boating is in his blood and an integral part of him. I wonder if Val understands that, or whether she's happy enough living in Byre Cottage with Ziggy, knowing that Fisher is within walking distance. It is convenient for them both as it stands, but from the way Fisher is acting, I don't think that's going to be enough for him.

'And Gray's trip is going well?'

'He's had a wonderful time by the sound of it, but, with the time difference and meetings, most of our contact has been via text. He's taking a few days off this week and he's um... pressing me to go to London at the weekend to introduce me to his friends. I can understand that he wants me to meet them before the wedding, as our worlds are very different. It's only his boss, Ollie, and his wife, who have come into his life recently. The rest of them have known each other for almost ten years and have formed a real bond, one that I'm not a part of – yet.'

Val turns her head to look at me. 'I appreciate how it must feel, the thought of meeting such a closely knit group of people for the first time. Gray is a part of our community and he knows everyone you know, so your guest list is his, too. But that's not true the other way around. Take heart, though, Immi. Trust in the fact that his friends know how much Gray loves you, and, as he talks about them often, they aren't total strangers. There's no reason to expect they won't welcome you with open arms.'

Val's words touch my heart. It's the sort of thing that Grandma would have said to me if she were still alive.

'Thank you, Val. I guess I needed to hear that from someone I trust.'

Aside from Tollie, Fisher is my sounding board, but increasingly Val has become a voice of reason. Someone who can put things into perspective for me from a slightly different viewpoint and I appreciate that.

'It's lovely of you to say that, Immi. I'm always here if you want to talk. Now let's pick up our pace as the light will be fading soon and I don't want you walking back in the dark.'

* * *

It's unheard of for Sarah to take a night off. Miraculously, though, Ursula managed to talk her into coming to the yoga class and then going back to her place for the grand measuring ceremony.

'I refuse to feel guilty about having this glass of wine,' Sarah declares as we raise a toast. 'Um... what are we toasting?'

'A few hours of freedom.'

'Ah, yes,' Ursula joins in. 'Tonight, I'm not a mum, a wife, or a daughter, I'm just plain old me.'

'And I'm not mopping my brow in a hot kitchen, with three people trying to talk to me at the same time,' Sarah says candidly. They both turn to look at me.

'I'm not curled up on the sofa with a calculator next to me reworking figures and balancing budgets,' I join in, shrugging my shoulders.

'What a sad bunch we are!' Ursula replies, sounding a tad

exasperated. 'But isn't it refreshing to have a few hours to ourselves?'

'Are you thinking what I'm thinking?' Sarah asks, and we both nod in agreement.

'The classes are only once a week. The sky isn't going to fall in if we aren't around. And if it saves our sanity...' Ursula replies enthusiastically.

'Then it's a necessity,' I state as we chink glasses. 'But won't it leave Kurt with a problem?'

'Maggie will fill in for me. She's always happy to do an extra shift. When it's quiet, Kurt will go sit and have a drink with one of the club members, but if I'm not cooking, plating up, or serving, I tend to clean. The girls slope off to do their homework, or play online with their friends, while I scrub the grill and start prepping for the next day.'

'Working in the hospitality industry is a hard life,' Ursula replies with a frown. 'Don't you ever get bored of the constant demands, Sarah?'

'No. We're grateful as a family to be able to build our business and work as a team. The girls love helping whenever they can, but things will change when they leave school and that's only a few years away. That's the point at which we'll all sit down and decide how we move forward. Maybe I'll end up running a team of part-timers and taking more of a back seat, but we'll see. I suppose working from home is the only option for you, Ursula,' Sarah remarks.

'Yes, and it's going to be like that for the foreseeable future. Olivia has good days and bad days, fortunately more good ones than bad. But if she's taken poorly at school, I'm only a phone call away and I love being my own boss.'

They turn to look at me. 'Will things change when you are Mrs Immi Adams?' Ursula enquires, peering at me with interest.

'Oh, that sounds funny. Imogen Adams... that sounds like someone else!'

'Does Tollie have any brothers to carry on the Tolliman name?' Ursula asks.

'No. Sadly he lost one sibling at an early age, but it was a girl, I think. Tollie already regards Gray as his son, though. But beyond the wedding, I have no idea what's going to happen. Hopefully, we'll settle down in our spanking new cottage with everything in working order. I would like Gray to work from home sometimes, just to save him that awful drive. And the loneliness of being apart, of course. But in all honesty, unless he can afford to buy a few more expensive pieces of kit, he doesn't have a choice.'

'Aww. That's a shame. Still, life isn't meant to be easy, according to my mother-in-law,' Ursula declares. 'It's meant to build character.'

We burst out laughing in unison.

'I don't know about the two of you, but I feel like I've already learnt enough lessons to last a lifetime and I'm waiting to get to the stage where life begins to even out!' I declare with passion.

'Well, that's when you and Gray will begin talking about starting a family. You swap one set of highs and lows for another. Life is just one big circle, but each time you go around it, the circumstances change slightly. Anyway, are we going to let Sarah have a peek at the designs?' Ursula asks, leaving me to ponder the fact that we all have challenges even if they're very different.

As Ursula goes off to grab her design pad, Sarah and I take a seat on the sofa.

'If you like the sketches, then it's simply a case of choosing the colour. My dress is going to be silver-grey, with a hint of silver and a little pop of soft heather,' I inform her.

'Here we are, this is Immi's dress.' Ursula waits for a moment before flipping over the page. 'And we came up with two designs for you, Sarah, that we can play with. I've drawn them both as full-length dresses, but I think they'd work equally well if you prefer a shorter version. What do you think?'

Sarah is glowing and I don't think it's from all that stretching we did earlier on. 'Wow. They're stunning and that dress is so you, Immi. Gray is going to fall in love with you all over again, as if he's seeing you for the very first time.'

Now that is worthy of a toast, a toast to all those wonderful Tuesday nights to come. We've known each other for a long time, but, as busy people, it's nice to take time out for ourselves. It's not that any of us want to change our lives, but it's fun to relax in the company of friends with whom you feel safe to let down your hair and have a laugh, and a moan, if necessary.

12

TOGETHERNESS

Gray stands behind me, his whole body melting into mine as I'm drawn into his arms. He rests his chin on the top of my head as we stare out at the view from the new extension.

'It's wonderful, isn't it?' he mutters, still a little breathless from spinning me around as we danced across the empty space.

'What, the view, or the fact that there isn't a builder in sight?'

'Just everything. Being here with you, the fact that we can finally set up home properly. And—'

A sharp tap on the front door sees us reluctantly draw apart. 'Are you expecting anyone?' Gray asks.

'Not at seven thirty in the morning, unless it's the postman and he's under the impression that we've already moved back in. I'll go check.' I leave Gray to wander around. Seeing the extension completely finished without a speck of dust, and glass panels you can actually see through for a change, it's finally sinking in. The worst is over, and it won't take long to make the cottage ours.

Striding out into the hallway, I swing open the front door to see a burly young man with a clipboard.

'Morning. Arbour Landscaping?'

At last! 'Good morning to you. I'm Immi Tolliman.'

'I'm Pete,' he says, thrusting out his hand, and we shake. 'Reggie says the flagstones are stacked in an outbuilding? If you can point me in the right direction, we'll start work.'

'Of course.'

Gray walks up behind me, snaking an arm around my waist and leaning into me. 'Do you mind if I slope off? I'm shattered.'

I half turn to plant a kiss firmly on his lips as I smile up into his eyes.

'Go on, get your head down. Tollie is out most of today and I'll be back at 5 p.m. Right, Pete, let me show you the way.'

Gray disappears and I step out onto the front path, pulling the door shut behind me.

'We're going to make a bit of noise,' Pete informs me apologetically.

'Don't worry, Gray is so tired he'll sleep through anything. He's just back from a ten-hour flight and a three-hour drive.'

'Ah, I see. We're parked up by The Bullrush, but Reggie said there's a back entrance?'

'Yes. There's a lane that runs along behind the car park and where it ends there is a double gate that leads into our orchard. There's a gravelled area for parking. Reggie said it will take two to three days to complete the landscaping?'

'Pretty much. Although I have an extra guy on board, given that we're a few days late starting the job. Last week seems to have been jinxed for some reason and everything that could go wrong, did. So, please accept our apologies, as we hate letting anyone down.'

'Don't worry,' I reply genially. 'That's something with which I can identify.'

But when you're over the hump things just keep on getting

better and better, or so it seems, and today everything in my life is rather sparkly for a change.

* * *

'He's back, then?' Martin remarks the moment I step into his office.

'Is it that obvious?' I reply, but I can't wipe the satisfied little smile off my face.

'You're glowing. I've had an email from the insurers and the greenhouse isn't safe. But it's not all doom and gloom – there will be disruption, but, in the meantime, Patrick thinks it's worth investing in some polytunnels.'

'But isn't that a cost you won't get back?'

'True, but they come in all shapes and sizes, and the basic ones are just a couple of hundred pounds. If we had, I don't know – maybe a dozen of them, erected where we have the compost heap and the recycle bins, we could empty the second greenhouse. It could become our temporary replacement retail unit for the public, until the new one is built. The bonus is that we can utilise the polytunnels for bringing plants on in the future, to free up the second greenhouse permanently.'

'To what purpose?'

'Well, we're considering expanding the floristry section. We already cater for our commercial clients and the natural extension is to take on a driver and small van to do home deliveries.'

I'm a little thrown, as this is the first I've heard of these plans, and yet it sounds as if the wheels are already in motion. 'That's... ambitious,' I point out.

'Patrick has done the figures and we have the green light. We'll also take on another florist, part-time of course until we've built things up a little. I'm arranging for a leaflet drop and some ads in the local papers covering a twenty-mile radius for starters. I'd like you to take the lead on that, but it can wait until next week. You'll be wanting to square up your desk today ready for your couple of days off.'

At least that's not in jeopardy, but I'm worried. Martin already has enough to juggle during the peak summer period and so I'm rather surprised about this new development.

My work phone starts to vibrate and it's a text. 'Sorry, Martin, I need to head up to the customer services desk.'

I walk briskly, hoping that no one stops me on the way. There are certainly a lot of customers milling around already this morning. It's heartening, as two years ago we were lucky to see anyone before mid-morning. The Lockside Nurseries is now a popular destination, not just for the small on-site café where people can enjoy a slice of cake and coffee, but because the gift shop is also a big draw.

'Hello, Rona, how can I help?'

She often pops in, but today Rona is standing by the customer services desk looking uneasy.

'I hope I'm not being a bother, but I'm here to buy some roses for the garden and I wondered if you'd mind helping me choose a few?'

Something is up, but I play along.

'Of course. Let's go grab a trolley.'

As soon as we are out of earshot, I glance at Rona and she looks back at me uneasily.

'I do need a few roses, but that's not the main reason I'm here. Grayson emailed me to say that the papers have been signed. Has Gray said anything?'

That stops me in my tracks. 'Signed? No, he hasn't said a thing. Did this happen just before Gray flew back? We spoke briefly this morning and he's asleep now.'

'No. Apparently, it was a few days ago. Gray drove to the house and Grayson's solicitor, they call them attorneys over there, talked them both through the paperwork. Since my trip at new year, Grayson's emails have been chatty, but this one was different. It was to the point but it's what he didn't tell me that left me feeling that the meeting didn't go well. Gray texted me when he landed in the early hours and said he'd give me a call once he'd caught up on some sleep. Did he appear to be unsettled about anything to you?'

'No, he was simply glad to be home as he was tired out. I'm sure he'll sit down and tell you all about it once he surfaces and has had something to eat.'

'Come on, I don't want anyone to think there's something amiss. Let's grab some pots and put them in the trolley. I think it's best we don't mention it to him and see what happens. Grayson and I were talking about me taking another trip over to see him, but I assumed that was because he thought Gray might come with me. Now that won't be necessary, of course, and Grayson didn't make any further mention of it.'

The disappointment in Rona's voice is tangible. As we head out to The Plantarium she looks agitated and I find myself wondering whether she did, in fact, sign those divorce papers while she was in LA.

* * *

'Our last night in this old, rickety bed, assuming we can afford to pay for the new one, that is,' Gray throws out there, very aware that we haven't yet talked about money.

Tollie took two items of furniture with him when he moved across into The Retreat and, aside from the double bed in the spare room, the rest went to a charitable organisation. Gray and I bought a small sofa, so that we could turn the former master bedroom of the cottage into a makeshift sitting room, and that's how we've been living. When the entire ground floor was ripped apart, we had no cooking facilities at all. We either ate with Tollie, or had takeaway from The Bullrush during those dark, wintery weekends when all we wanted to do was to snuggle up together in front of the TV.

But now we have an entire cottage to furnish and tomorrow the deliveries we've delayed for so many weeks will begin arriving. We agreed that I would arrange an overdraft facility of eight thousand pounds, but I've yet to break the news to Gray that we're going to use every single penny of it. From now on we're living off our monthly income and that will include repaying the debt.

'Let's not spoil your first night back, Gray.' He's obviously not sleepy, even though he only slept for five hours in an attempt to kick-start his body clock.

'Let's get it out the way. Come on, I know it's bad.'

'We'll use it all, even the overdraft,' I confirm.

'Hmm. And how's the wedding fund looking?'

I swallow hard. 'I have a pile of receipts that need tallying up, but when we set the budget, I was thinking *small*, and with forty people to cater for it isn't really small, is it?'

'You have a point there. What if I could magic some money out of thin air?'

I roll onto my side, trying to make out his features in the shadowy darkness.

'Then that would be like pulling a rabbit out of a hat.' I laugh, loving his hopeless optimism. 'Your contract is done, though. Are you thinking of taking up a part-time job until you sign something else?'

'No. But the thing with a contract is that it contains clauses,' he replies, matter-of-factly, his eyes gleaming.

'Tell me, then.'

'Obviously, we were working to a strict deadline and, as you know, I made it with time to spare. On the flight back Ollie dropped into the conversation that he's chasing the end-of-contract bonus. I thought that was a part of the final payment I've already received, but apparently not.'

I'm stunned. 'Did he mention how much it's likely to be?'

'No. I just acted really cool, as I didn't want him to think I was a total idiot. But the contract is packed away in one of those boxes and all I focused on was making sure I didn't miss that all-important date. However much it is, it's on the way so let's add it to the wedding fund, eh? And talking of that, things are easing off for me a little, although I will be pulling together a few ideas for some potential new projects I might end up pitching for. But as I'm now an official member of the wedding-planning team, I thought I'd take over sorting out paying the bills, too. You've got enough of a headache keeping tabs on our bank account and the fundraiser. What do you think?'

Snuggling closer, I lay my head down on Gray's chest, listening to the strong but erratic beat of his heart.

'Your heart is pounding and it's all over the place!' I declare.

'That's what you do to me,' he murmurs, nuzzling his face into my hair.

I trail my fingers across his chest and down his side; he squirms, ever the ticklish one. 'As long as you promise to count the pennies and don't go mad.'

'Do you think Mum and Val would let me go crazy? I like being involved. I never thought I'd hear myself say that, but I do.'

We lay quietly for a little while. 'I know it's a bit scary with the periods in between when you aren't earning. Especially given that we have almost zero savings, but I'm earning more now that I'm the full-time assistant manager at the nurseries and business is doing well. And unlike many people, we don't have a mortgage to pay, so we can cover the overheads and chip away at what we owe.'

'Thanks, babe. And I have high hopes of getting another project before too long. We'll soon sort out our finances again and accrue another little nest egg.'

'Do you have any regrets, Gray?' I ask tentatively.

'I wouldn't change a single thing. The cottage needed gutting anyway and now we have our forever home, with all the space we need. Come with me. Come on.'

Gray swings his legs over the side of the bed and I follow him out of the bedroom door and down the stairs. Even in the gloom, the hallway is bright with the panelled glass of the new front door and the pale limestone tiles running through into the vast new open space, making it feel light and airy.

Gray catches up my hand in his, giving it a squeeze as he leads me into the heart of our home.

'Turn to look at the new limestone fireplace. What do you see?'

'I see my beautiful, cast-iron stag standing there, on guard. And it reminds me of the day we got engaged,' I reply, feeling emotional.

'And what else, Immi?'

My head instinctively turns to the right, as I envision Tollie, sitting in his old armchair, and then to my left as I see Grandma sitting in her chair, a blanket over her legs as she stares at the flickering flames in the fireplace. They're still here, the memories, even though it now looks completely different, and I understand what Gray is trying to tell me.

'It's our turn, isn't it?' I whisper as he pulls me closer, his lips softly touching mine.

'Yes. Those memories are still here and they're still inside you. What do you think your grandma would have thought of this view?'

He leads me over to the sliding wall of glass doors at the far end of the room, and I can just about make out the meadow on the other side of the low hedge, stretching out almost endlessly, and on the horizon the dark outline of the copse breaks up the flat landscape.

'She would have been wowed to have been standing here, looking out at the countryside she dearly loved.'

Gray pulls my hand up to kiss the tips of my fingers.

'You carry her genes, Immi. So, a part of her *is* standing here with you tonight and, sometime in the future maybe we'll both be standing here with a child of our own. Who knows? The thing is, we're building our future and every penny we've spent has been for the right reason.'

'I love you, Gray,' I say as we hold each other. My heart is full and yet it's also breaking, as sadness threatens to overwhelm me. To have Dad and Grandma here for my wedding day would have made everything feel complete and yet that wasn't meant to be. Somehow, Gray seems to understand how important it is to me to cling onto the things I treasure the most and, though the cottage might look different now, he's right. The changes are immaterial; they don't take away those precious memories which are forever locked inside my head and my heart.

13

THINGS ARE SHAPING UP NICELY

This morning we were both up bright and early, eager to head out to the supermarket to stock up our smart new fridge and freezer. When Gray swung open the doors and found them virtually empty, after a week of trying as many breakfast items as possible from an American menu, toast and marmalade didn't do it for him.

On the drive back to the cottage Gray tells me more about his trip and admits that he was anxious sitting in a screening room with four of the studio executives and the two scriptwriters. At the end, they all stood up and clapped, and it was then that it hit him what an achievement this project was, and he said he felt proud to be a part of it.

'So you should. Even writing jingles you always hit the mark. Whenever I wash my hair, I catch myself humming the one you wrote for that shampoo, and I don't even use that brand. The *zingy fresh* one.'

Naturally, Gray instantly begins to sing it to me and it makes me laugh. He's so happy and yet he still hasn't mentioned meeting up with Grayson. His phone kicks into life and he puts it up to his ear, still singing. '*Hi, Ma, good morning and how are you today?* Yes, I fully intend to come round and see you in a bit. We're heading back from the supermarket and I'll grab some breakfast, then head over to yours, okay? Right, see you soon.'

As I ease the car through the gates, Gray suggests I park on the far side to give the landscapers enough room to access a pallet stacked with rolls of turf.

'How about I whip you up some brioche French toast with maple syrup?' he offers as I park up and we head around to the boot. 'Darn it, I should have bought some streaky bacon, but I suspect ours is cut too thick to make it really crispy, anyway.'

'I'll eat anything, you know me.'

Walking through the orchard with our hands full of carrier bags, when the back of the cottage comes into view we see that Pete and his team of two are already hard at work.

'There you go. I reckon they'll have that patio laid by the end of the day. Then it's a case of re-planting the borders, a bit of levelling here and there, then turfing the trampled areas. They didn't bring any plants – are you getting them from work?'

I nod. 'Yes. They're lined up around the side of the outhouse. I had the pick of this week's delivery on Monday. We'd better head for the front door to save disturbing them.'

As we walk around the side of the cottage, a man is just opening the front gate.

'I'm assuming I have the right place,' he says, checking the sheet in his hand. 'Mrs Tolliman?'

Glancing across at Gray, I can't resist a little smirk. 'Yes.'

'We have a king-size bed and some flat-pack wardrobes. It says here "alternative access", so we can't get round the back?'

I indicate for Gray to dump the shopping bags by the front door, so he can deal with our delivery man.

'You can, but unfortunately you can't trolley anything heavy across because the parking area is gravel and then there's a large orchard with uneven ground, before you can access the pathway to the cottage,' Gray informs him.

'I did explain the problem when I placed the order and we paid an additional charge on top of the standard delivery cost,' I point out, but the guy doesn't look happy.

'Are you parked up in the public car park next to The Bull-rush?' Gray interrupts.

The man nods.

'Right, come and have a look around the back, but the best bet is to use the towpath.'

The man rolls his eyes, but he cheers up a little when he sees Tollie's contraption purpose-built for times like this – two men can move anything with that, no matter how heavy.

Leaving them to it, I take the bags through into the kitchen and as I look out Tollie appears. There's a short conversation before he leads the lorry driver and Gray over to the big shed.

I put the food away as quickly as I can and then jump online to find out how to cook French toast. I didn't even know you could make it with brioche. Perhaps I should consider attending some cookery classes. Out of mere curiosity, I type in a general query and our post code and begin scanning down the list. The first hit is a manor house near Stroud, which runs a luxury weekend retreat with a cookery class each morning and, in the afternoons, there is a choice of attending a talk with a vintner and wine-making team, or relaxing with yoga, or a spa session. What a lovely wedding present to give Gray in lieu of a honeymoon. It's something we can do together, and his new wife may well be inspired to be more adventurous in the kitchen!

* * *

Gray is late leaving for Rona's and is gone quite a while, so I'm hoping they are having a frank and honest chat. In the meantime, I've ironed the new bedding and made up the bed. There is nothing more luxurious than the feel of a crisp, new sheet on the mattress and a pristine duvet cover. The next job is to begin unpacking the boxes of china. As I trek up and down stairs, every single movement seems to echo around me. There are so many small jobs to be done to make the cottage feel more homely and give it some substance.

'I'm back and we have company,' Gray's voice filters up the stairs as I'm about to grab yet another box that has 'glassware' written on it.

'And we have takeaway pizza with us,' Fisher calls out, seconds later.

When I walk into the kitchen Fisher is poking around in the cutlery drawer as I place the box carefully on the worktop.

'Do you have a pizza wheel?' he asks.

'Somewhere. But it might still be packed. I just kept the basics to hand. Anyway, what are you doing out and about on a Thursday lunchtime?'

The two guys look at each other, guiltily.

'What's going on?' I ask, peering from one to the other.

'I'm taking a couple of days off and I wondered if Gray wanted a hand getting things set up.'

I can feel tears start to prickle in the corner of my eyes and Fisher puts down the knife in his hand to wrap his arms around me.

'Hey, I wanted to help out. Don't be getting all weepy on us. Val runs the office anyway, you know that. You're the one who taught her.'

'And don't blame me,' Gray adds. 'It wasn't my idea. Anyway, let's eat that pizza and then we can make a start. We don't need plates, do we?'

We stand at the countertop munching away and Fisher scans around the empty room. 'This is quite a space to fill,' he remarks.

'Hopefully by the end of the day we'll have a table, six chairs and a couple of sofas.'

'Bet the delivery men aren't too pleased.'

Gray frowns. 'I ended up giving the two men a hand with the bed and the flat-packed wardrobes. One of them was a bit of a jobsworth, but Tollie's flatbed trolley works a treat. It just took a few trips as there seems to be an enormous stack of boxes.'

'Well, I'm pretty handy with a drill,' Fisher replies keenly. Having stripped out and rebuilt the interior of The Star Gazer, he loves getting hands-on.

'Tollie helped me sort out a box of tools earlier and they're in the spare bedroom,' Gray confirms.

It doesn't take long for the three of us to demolish the pizza and as I put the kettle on, the guys head upstairs. When I take the tray of drinks up to them, they're in the bedroom, Gray hunched over an instruction booklet that is as thick as a magazine. Fisher is busy sorting screws, dowels and angular bits of metal into neat piles.

'That looks daunting,' I remark. 'I'll just put this on the windowsill and leave you to it. Shout if you want anything.' They barely raise their heads in acknowledgement, and I make a quick exit. It's going to be a long afternoon.

* * *

An hour later the sofas arrive and this time the delivery guys couldn't be more helpful and cheery.

'Lovely place,' one of them says as they manoeuvre the first sofa through the hallway. 'And what a location.'

'Yes, it's a beautiful spot.'

'Amazing looking out at the view,' the other man joins in.

As they walk back up to the car park to trolley down the other sofa, I go in search of my handbag. I know we paid extra for delivery, but they deserve a little something for getting on with it and not making a fuss.

When they return, before I even have time to offer the ten-pound note, the younger man says, 'Do you want us to unpack them and take the rubbish away? It's no trouble.'

'That would be a real help, thank you so much.' My phone begins ringing and before I rush off to grab it, I offer him the note. He looks surprised. 'You earnt a drink for that,' I reply.

'Thanks, lady, appreciated!'

When I lift the phone to my ear, Val's voice is on the other end and I walk out into the hallway. The landscapers are using a machine that compacts the soil and there's a loud thumping sound in the background that is shaking the ground beneath my feet.

'Hi, Immi. I don't know if Fisher mentioned it, but as soon as I close up the office I'm coming round. So, save a few jobs for me.'

That makes me laugh out loud. 'I think there are enough jobs to last a week, but thank you, Val.'

'I'm happy to make dinner. I can pop back to Byre as I have a steak and ale pie I made last night, if you like.'

'No, just come straight here. We did a big shop this morning and I'll rustle something up.' If I can figure out how to use the new oven, then I'm halfway there.

'Okay, if you're sure. See you later, then.'

There's a loud thump from upstairs and the sound of drilling.

Then another loud thump. I hope it's going well. As I stand at the bottom of the stairs and look up, a voice breaks my reverie.

'All done.' The two delivery guys approach, their arms full of packaging. 'We did a once-over, and both sofas are in good order. We screwed the legs in, too, and left a sheet of information on the side. Thanks for the tip, missus.'

'My pleasure. Let me get the door for you.'

After seeing them out, I hurry back to take a look. The lime-green sofas are perfect, and the colour lifts the room and seems to give it a glow. But they do look insignificant in the open space, even though the sofas are generously proportioned. I was expecting them to dominate the room and although they are fabulous, I'm a little disappointed. A light tap on the glass doors attracts my attention and Pete indicates yet more delivery men who seemed to have found their way around the back.

I've only opened the doors once and they're still rather stiff, so I put up my hand, pointing to the front door. We meet at the side of the house.

'We thought we'd see if we could get down the lane as we only have a Transit van,' the older of the two men informs me. 'We'd best not trample on your lovely patio, though, so we'll carry the boxes around to the front.'

'Oh, fine, if that's doable. Would you like a cup of tea, or coffee?'

Two smiley faces look back at me gratefully. 'Thanks very much. Two teas, strong as you can make it and only one with sugar, one spoonful.'

As I head back inside, leaving the door ajar, there's a loud bang and an expletive. I guess a cup of tea might not go amiss right now for my crew beavering away upstairs and it's going to be biscuits all round, to show my appreciation.

14

THE BEST THINGS IN LIFE ARE FREE

Poring over the instruction manual for the cooker, I'd hoped it would be fairly simple to operate the oven. But no. When the two knobs spring out and I turn it onto fan-assisted mode, three icons light up on the panel. It also goes into countdown, starting at ten-minutes. As you are supposed to run it for at least thirty minutes to remove any residue from the inside surfaces, I stab at the plus and minus icons on the touch pad, but nothing I do seems to make a difference. I'm going to have to reset it twice over, and the manual advises to ventilate the room to diffuse the fumes, so I open the kitchen window a little wider.

Sauntering across to stare out at the beautiful flagstones now back in situ and looking better for having had a light brushing, I can see it won't take long for the gaps to age a little to match the surface. The borders have been dug over and compost added, ready and waiting for the plants to go in tomorrow. Only one of the old climbers survived the digging out of the foundations and the trenches for the new pipes. It's a prolific pink rose and, while I am sad about what has been lost, I can't wait to see all the new plants begin to flourish in the ground. I turn my attention back to the doors, as the smell wafting over from the oven is very unpleasant. I turn the key in the lock but instead of the doors concertinaing back, I can't even move the first one. The brochure said it was effortless, but I just can't get it to shift.

Beep, beep, beep. The timer is going off and, in desperation, I walk over to switch off the oven and turn it back on again.

There's a tap on the front door and I glance up at the clock. It's just after six and I suspect it will be Val, but when I open the door both Rona and Val are standing in front of me carrying larges dishes wrapped in foil.

'Come in, come in,' I greet them, delighted to have visitors.

'We met up on the towpath,' Rona explains. 'I thought you might like something you can just pop in the oven tonight.'

'Ah, that's very kind of you, Rona,' I reply, thinking that's assuming I can get the oven to work properly. I hope Val isn't upset that I turned down her generous offer earlier on, but, as it happens, I couldn't be more grateful right now.

'And Sarah sent an apple pie,' Val chimes in.

'That's one big pie,' I exclaim. 'Come on through. Sorry about the smell. I'm having problems opening the glass doors.'

They both wrinkle their noses the closer they get.

'Let me take those from you. And that's so kind of Sarah. I'll just pop these down here and have another go on the doors.'

'What a difference!' Val utters and I realise it's the first time she's set foot inside the cottage since the new year.

'And the furniture arrived on time, I see,' Rona adds.

'Gray hasn't seen it yet – they're still upstairs assembling the wardrobes. I don't think it's as straightforward a job as they'd anticipated, so I decided to leave them to it.'

As I'm fiddling with the key and puzzling over whether it's the lock that isn't working properly, a shadow falls in front of me and I look up to see Tollie. I put up both my hands and shrug my shoulders. He tilts his head to the right and disappears around the side.

'Can you let Tollie in, please? I'll just have one more go.'

'I'll do it,' Rona says as Val crouches down to look at the touchpad on the oven.

'The instructions are just inside the first wall unit. The timer won't switch off. And these doors won't shift!' I declare, starting to run out of patience now.

'Hi, ladies. Shall I take a quick look, Immi? There might be a knack to that lock as it's new. It shouldn't need any pressure to slide the doors back. It's lookin' grand in here now.'

Val and Rona are both kneeling on the floor and suddenly Val pipes up. 'We got it. The third icon was the lock mode. It's still very smelly, so I think we should leave it on for a while longer.'

Rona leans over the sink to push the window open as far as it will go. Tollie isn't having any luck, so he asks for the key for the other set of sliding doors on the far side of the room. 'My goodness, this is a view and a half, Immi.'

Within less than a minute he slides them back with apparent ease and we turn to look at each other, perplexed. He closes them up. 'You have a try, now.'

Feeling a little sceptical, I'm shocked when they slide back so smoothly it takes no effort at all.

'The other side needs adjustin',' he says. 'The first door is probably touchin' a bit on the bottom. It'll be a five-minute fix, but you need the right tool.'

Val and Rona come over to stand with us, admiring the fact that the garden to the side now feels like a natural extension to the cottage.

'Once you get that temporary path taken up and the new turf goes down, it'll soon bring it back to life,' Tollie remarks.

'I know and patience is a virtue,' I say over my shoulder as I head back to the kitchen area to begin preparing a salad. 'One that I don't possess, it seems. At least the smell isn't quite so overpowering now and, with the new sofas too, it's nice to air the room.'

'Shall I venture upstairs and see how it's going?' Rona offers. 'It won't take long to get rid of that acrid smell and then why don't you heat up the lasagne I made? That and a salad will make a meal.'

'Great idea. I'll pop in some part-baked ciabattas and there will be plenty for all of us.'

Rona looks at me hesitantly. 'Oh, I didn't intend staying.'

'I insist. It's lovely to have everyone here. Another forty minutes and the food will be on the table, barring any accidents, of course.'

Rona scrunches up her face, making me smile. 'It'll be fine.'

'Oh, Val. I only have two plates unpacked. Some of these boxes are marked china, but I'm not sure which one has the plates in it. Would you mind doing some digging? I've already washed up the glassware and put it in the unit.'

'I'll pop back to The Retreat and grab a couple of bottles of wine and a few beers,' Tollie offers.

'We have red, so just bring a bottle of white. I didn't think to get beer, thanks, Tollie.'

I turn to rinse the lettuce leaves and Tollie appears behind me, placing his hands on my shoulders to give them a squeeze.

'It's good to see the place with some furniture in it. You made it yours, m'dear, and that makes me very happy,' he whispers.

'It's our forever home and I'm lucky to have a man who feels the same way as I do. Thank you, Tollie, for the money you gave us. I wanted something timeless that would last forever, and the stunning oak table and chairs are simply beautiful. And now we're about to christen them with our first meal together.'

'And the best thing of all is that I'm not the one doing the cookin',' he roars, putting his head back and belly laughing. 'It makes me so happy to be witnessin' this day, m'dear.'

* * *

'There's some more lasagne if anyone wants seconds,' I interrupt and both Gray and Fisher jump up from the table, plates in hand.

Tollie, Rona and Val are talking about this year's Santa Ahoy Special cruises and how many we're going to run, given that it's a landmark year.

'I'm thinkin' we should kick it off in the last week of November to give us an extra weekend. What do you think?' Tollie throws the idea out there.

'The extra ticket sales would be most welcome,' I acknowledge. 'If everyone is in agreement, then let's do that. And I'm thinking about approaching the local schools. Do they still do those non-uniform days, does anyone know? The playground is going to benefit all the local children and I wondered if it was worth approaching them to be a part of the fundraising.'

'Little Hampton primary school hold one a couple of times a year. Usually, it's organised by the Parent Teacher Association and sometimes it's to buy equipment or subsidise school trips. I think it would be worth approaching all the primary schools within a reasonable distance and see if they'd like to take part,' Rona confirms.

'And the children love an excuse to dress up – you only have to look at World Book Day for a prime example of that,' Rona continues. 'I could ask the school secretary to get a list of contact names and addresses, if you're willing to draft a letter, Immi.'

Gray jumps up to grab the wine bottle and top up everyone's glasses.

'Another beer, Fisher? Tollie?'

'Not for me, I'm watchin' my waistline,' Tollie replies, but Fisher nods enthusiastically. Since when did Tollie worry about a little bit of weight? Normally I can read him like a veritable book, but these days I have no idea what's going on inside that head of his.

Gray places his hand on my shoulder as he leans forward to top up my glass. 'Thank you.' The look we exchange is one of pure contentment. We're christening our new home at last – it's been a long time coming.

'So, is everyone in agreement about starting the cruises a little earlier? It's two extra days' work so I will check with Abe and Ethel, as we couldn't do it without them. And, Immi, I'm not sure about Jude and Jade, so you might be on your own. What do you think?' Tollie enquires, looking around the table at the nodding heads.

'We'll work something out.' I smile, knowing full well the girls will be up for it.

'Good! Let's toast, then. Here's to a bumper year for the kiddies. They put joy in our hearts and remind us that it's the adults who make life so unbearably complicated at times. It's a humblin' reminder never to let go of our inner child.'

As our glasses come together and the light begins to dim, it feels to me that a miracle is unfolding around us. The chaos of the last six months is finally dying down and what seemed at one point like an impossible list of tasks is becoming a little less daunting with each passing day. My dad used to quote a man named Norman Vincent Peale, 'Shoot for the moon. Even if you miss, you'll land amongst the stars,' but it took me a while to realise what it meant.

As an eight-year-old I puzzled over the image of a rocket setting off and running out of fuel before it got to its destination. There it was for a brief moment, surrounded by the heavenly stars before it fell back to earth. It wasn't until I was all grown up that I got it. The quote is trying to explain that you don't always have to take the easy path through life, and accept what comes your way, but instead we can dare to be the master of our own destiny. I waited for the right man to come along and Dad would have been proud of me. It's been a tough three-plus years since I first met Gray and nothing has gone smoothly, or so it has seemed. It's been one obstacle after another, but here we are – surrounded by family, and some of our closest friends, and I have no regrets at all. Perhaps my patience isn't quite as thin as I imagine it to be. Just one last push towards the end goal and then we will be kicking off the new year as husband and wife.

* * *

Gray locks the front door and wanders back into the family room. I'm gazing out into the gathering gloom, straining my eyes to seek out the well-trodden path across the meadow. I think back to the day when Gray dropped down onto one knee in the snow and asked me to marry him. Last Christmas was supposed to be perfect, but it didn't quite go as planned. This year is going to be the stuff that dreams are truly made of and I can feel that with every fibre of my being.

'What a great day it turned out to be,' Gray half whispers as he comes to stand alongside me. 'I will admit that The Retreat never felt like home for me. I know it was yours, always was, but I was merely a lodger when I arrived each weekend to spend time with you. The cottage, well, it feels like ours now, even though we've only just begun unpacking and getting everything sorted. We've invested our time and money into making it the best it can be. I know we have a way to go, but you don't have regrets, do you?'

I turn to face him, then glance back at the fireplace. It was formerly the heart of Lock Keeper's Cottage, but in the new layout it's off to the side of the kitchen area.

'None whatsoever, and Bert looks regal, standing guard in the corner.' Gray, too, regards Bert as one of the family – the engagement present that everyone we know contributed to because he's special. Made of cast iron, he stands proudly displaying his antlers. I fell in love with the stag when I began working at the nurseries part-time. I never walked out of the premises without saying goodbye to him, whether he was in The Plantarium, or the stockroom when the Christmas trees took over his spot.

'He does. And he approves. But the fireplace looks a little lost, don't you think? What we need are two comfy wingback chairs. Something colourful, contemporary, but cosy so we can light the fire and toast marshmallows and roast chestnuts in winter, as I always did with Tollie and Grandma Nell.'

'Then we will make that happen, my darling Immi.'

'You and Fisher did a great job of assembling the wardrobes. I can't wait to get shot of those temporary clothes racks that make the third bedroom look like a shop.'

'We had a handful of metal bits left over, but the cupboards are sturdy. If we spend all day tomorrow working flat out, how about we take that run up to London we've been talking about on Saturday afternoon? Just very relaxed, and we'll catch up with whoever happens to be around to grab a drink together. We can stay overnight, then head back on Sunday morning. What do you think?'

Feeling as happy as I do tonight, my anxiety has melted away. When life threatens to overwhelm me, everything becomes an issue, but now it doesn't seem such a big deal.

'I'd love to meet them, Gray. And tomorrow morning as soon as we've had breakfast, we must write out those wedding invitations and pop them up to the post box.'

'The wedding is beginning to feel very real, isn't it?'

'Yes. Very real. Thanks to you, Rona and Val.'

Gray begins to hum as he wraps an arm around my waist. 'Bi-ba-bi-ba doo bah doo...' he croons softly. It's not a tune I recognise, and I wonder if he's in composing mode. The fact that this is the first time he's done that since he arrived back means everything in his world is fine, and I can't ask for any more than that. It's not how much money you have in the bank that matters, but how many people you have around you who are there whenever you need a helping hand. And our Aysbury family are always there for each other.

15

OUT OF THE BLUE

I leave Gray chatting to Reggie and a guy he brought along to sort out the problem with the sliding glass doors. As soon as I appear from around the side of the cottage, Pete calls out to me.

'Morning, Immi. If we start carrying the plants over, can you spare a few minutes to decide where you want them to go?'

My face instantly lights up. 'You bet! This is the exciting bit. I'll give you a hand.'

We traipse across to the rear of the brick outbuilding and Pete glances up at the sky. 'Looks like we're gonna get some rain. I hope it holds off until this afternoon. As soon as we get these planted, we're going to start work on the re-turfing. No point having that stunning view when you're looking out onto an eyesore,' he informs me.

'That's wonderful news. When do you think you'll be finished?'

'Hopefully by the end of tomorrow.'

'Gray and I are away this weekend, but Tollie will be around if you need anything. I'll let him know when I pop in shortly, Pete.

It's already looking so much better, and I hope the rain doesn't hamper you.'

He grins at me. 'Actually, rain is a good thing, but not while we're planting, or scabbing off the surface of the old, patchy grass. After that if we get a good downpour it would save us setting up the sprinklers.'

We dump the first lot of pots, and he indicates for me to stay behind and begin positioning them on the bare soil. The other side of the glass doors, Gray is smiling away as he watches me. It takes a while to move the pots around, as the guys keep them coming. Some are best planted in clusters, and others need space to grow as they will turn into bushes. Every now and again I stand back to check the overall look and every time I happen to catch Gray watching me, he has a huge grin on his face. Without warning, the glass doors slide back with ease and the three men stand there looking pleased with themselves.

'Just a bit of plastic from the packing caught in the bottom runner,' Reggie confirms. 'That's all looking good, Immi.'

Pete and his mate carry across the last of the shrubs and perennials, the latter designed to add that wonderful pop of colour in spring and summer to brighten the evergreens.

'There, I think that will do.' I stand back to admire my handiwork. The day is young, but the clouds in the sky aren't the white fluffy sort and are beginning to gather on the horizon.

Leaving them to it, I tap on the door to The Retreat. When it swings open, Tollie greets me with a, 'Good mornin', m'dear. It wasn't locked. Oh, that's a vast improvement to my view already!' He glances over my shoulder and from this viewpoint he now looks out over a tidy patio area again, with enough greenery to pretty it up.

'It's not quite as lovely as it was, but the plants will soon begin to bush out and the lavenders will get those bees buzzin' around again.'

I follow him inside, my stomach beginning to grumble as a delicious smell wafts around the hallway.

'What are you baking?' The aroma tells me it's probably a cake.

'A Victoria sandwich. I have company comin' later this mornin',' he replies, a tad gingerly.

'That's nice. I won't stop you, then. I just wanted to call in and tell you that Gray and I are heading up to London tomorrow. We'll be staying overnight, and we should be back early Sunday afternoon. The landscapers will probably be around tomorrow, assuming the rain doesn't stop play. But the end is in sight and I think they'll be keen to finish up if at all possible.'

'I'm here if they need anythin'. I'm glad you popped in on your own,' Tollie says. 'While you're here, there's somethin' I've been meanin' to mention to you.'

His tone is growing serious as he leads me over to the sofa, and a sensation of anxiety hits me square in the solar plexus.

'I'm goin' to get this problem with my back sorted out properly. Now, don't look at me like that, it's not a big deal. It's just a pinched nerve due to a bone spur and a little operation should do the trick.'

Tollie is talking in medical terms, which must mean he hasn't just been seeing his chiropractor. 'Back surgery is serious, Tollie. There are all sorts of risks to consider. Aren't there any other options?' I'm trying not to panic, but I can't believe he hasn't involved me in making this decision.

'Look, Immi, I know you're bound to be a bit concerned but with everythin' you've had on your plate, I didn't want you worryin' over this. They tried steroid injections and it hasn't made much of a difference. The consultant I've been seein' says there is an 80 per cent chance that within six months of the op I could be pain-free. I have a friend who has been accompanyin' me to the appointments and she has a lot of medical knowledge.'

I'm stunned. I open my mouth to begin talking, but Tollie puts up his hand to stop me.

'Her name is Daphne Harris. We see a fair bit of each other, and she's been a great help.'

My head is full of questions, but I know I can't bombard Tollie. However, the fact that he's been keeping this from me is worrying. You hear so much about older people being conned these days and although Tollie is not a fool, he misses Grandma's company. 'How exactly did you meet this Daphne?'

'She's a friend of Bernie and Yvonne's and they invited her along one evenin' when we were playin' cards. You'll like her, Immi. She retired from nursin' five years ago and was a clinical ward nurse leader. She knows her stuff and knew exactly the right questions to ask. You know me, I just sat there noddin' me head and thinkin' let's get on with it, then.'

'I assume there's a waiting list?' My first thought is that I have no idea what exactly this operation entails. Until I read up on it, of course I'm going to panic. Tollie has just dropped a bombshell on me and if it were the other way around, he'd be reeling, too.

'There is, but I'm going private. They're doin' it the week after next.'

My jaw drops. 'But, but... there's aftercare and all sorts of things to consider.' Without understanding what the procedure involves, I have no idea what he'll need. How long will it take for him to recover?

'This is precisely why I've been puttin' off tellin' you. Daphne is going to come and stay here for a while, so that she can be on hand after I'm discharged. Like a live-in nurse,' he replies, as if it's no big deal.

'Move in here?'

'Daphne is confident I'll be up and around without too much fuss. Because my symptoms have been quite severe, the nerve pain may linger for a while and there will be a bit of discomfort from the surgery, but it'll just be a case of pain management. Daphne knows what she's doing, so she'll keep me on the straight and narrow,' he informs me, as if he's merely employing a nurse to look after him. Is that what he's doing?

'Right, um... so... what can I do?' I ask, trying not to sound as anxious as I feel that someone who is a stranger to me has been so involved in Tollie's plans.

'Just rest assured I'll be in good hands. My consultant says if it all works out as expected, then I'll feel like a new man. The almost constant pain is making my life unbearable at times, Immi. I intend to be back to the old me by the time I slip into my Santa suit again. All I need from you is to stop worrying and when you meet Daphne, which I'll arrange very soon, that should put your mind at rest. Now, off you go. You have a lot to do today what with goin' away for the weekend. It's about time you met Gray's friends, and I hoped he'd take you up there before the weddin'. Anyway, I have a cake to get out of the oven.'

I feel as if I'm being dismissed, and I stand, watching Tollie gently easing himself up off the sofa, and I force myself not to tear-up. 'Well,' I say, swallowing hard to push down the huge lump that is rising up in my throat, 'the thought of you being pain-free again is wonderful.'

'I'll soon be back mowing the grass.' He chuckles, stepping forward to give me a reassuring hug. I hold on for a few seconds longer than necessary, because Tollie means everything to me, and him cutting me out like this in his time of need hurts.

I head straight back to the cottage to jump online and do some research, leaving Gray to battle with hanging the roman blinds that Ursula made for the bedrooms. It isn't long before he calls out, requesting my assistance.

'That looks lovely,' I remark, even though the blind is a bit askew. Gray looks down at me from his position high up on the ladder, one eyebrow raised.

'Yes, it does, but is it straight? I've checked the piece of wood with a spirit-level, but when it comes to attaching the blind with the Velcro it's a bit fiddly.'

'Do you want me to have a look?'

I can see the relief on his face. 'I feel guilty pulling you away from your Internet surfing.'

'I think I've found out as much as I can without talking to an actual surgeon. Tollie is right, they can't guarantee it will be a success, but it works for at least 80 per cent of the patients undergoing surgery.'

As Gray descends the ladder he gives me a quick peck on the cheek.

'Please don't take this the wrong way, Immi, as I know you're struggling to understand why Tollie chose not to involve you in his plans. It probably feels like you are being pushed to one side, and he's taking advice from a stranger, but it's obvious Tollie and Daphne have come to know each other quite well. He's not the sort of man to be talked into anything. It's time to step back a little.'

'And abandon him?' I reply, annoyed that Gray is showing no signs of concern whatsoever.

'See what I mean? It's his decision and you're cross because he didn't involve you. Instead, he sought the advice of a... friend. How many decisions have you and I made since we've been together? Decisions that affect our lives going forward. When I appeared on the scene, don't you think it was a period of adjustment for Tollie as he stepped back to allow me into your life? He didn't know me, and it was a while until we felt relaxed around each other. If Daphne is going to be a part of Tollie's future, as their friendship develops, you'll go through a similar period of adjustment too. It's only natural.'

I grab the corner of the roman blind and pull. The ripping sound that the Velcro makes as it detaches sounds as angry as I feel. Gray turns, picks up the drill and walks over to the side window. With his back to me, he places it on the floor and begins unpacking the second blind as I mull over his words.

'Yes, well, maybe you're right but I won't know how I feel until I meet her face to face.' And if that doesn't happen very soon, then I'll find out where she lives and pay this Daphne a visit.

16

THE CRAZINESS IS ABOUT TO BEGIN

When we finally jump in the car and set off for London, I think Gray is genuinely glad of the drive ahead of us. His do-it-yourself skills have been tested to the limit over the past two days and it's time for a change.

'You seem a lot more relaxed this morning,' Gray reflects as he pulls away.

'I texted Tollie last night to remind him that I will be at my yoga class on Tuesday.'

Gray starts chuckling. 'A not-so-subtle hint, then, that you expect to meet Daphne next week and that's the one night you're not available?'

'Yes, and if it doesn't happen, then I'll know something isn't quite right.'

Gray grimaces while focusing on passing through the gate to turn into the lane as ahead of us is a tractor. He drums his fingers on the steering wheel as we crawl along.

'Is there a melody going around inside that head of yours?' I enquire, breaking out into a smile.

'There is and I will be honest – as fun as doing the house has been, I'm itching to do some real work.'

'Oh, and putting up wardrobes and blinds isn't work?'

'Let's just say that I'm glad it's done, and I don't know how I would have managed without Fisher's help. But you know what I mean. I'm eager to pull together a few ideas that keep bombarding me and I won't get any peace until I can get it all down on paper.'

The tractor pulls into a layby to allow us to pass and we both wave out, recognising one of the lads from Adler's farm.

Gray is concerned, not knowing when he'll be earning again. We can just about manage on one income, but I fully understand him wanting to press ahead and act whenever inspiration strikes.

'I'm eager to get back to work on Monday, too. I've been emailing back and forth with Patrick. He's offered to take on the role of treasurer to free up some of my time. We're generating fundraising ideas quicker than I can find people to take on the tasks and there are a few things that are best if I drive them forward. What we need is a couple of extra pairs of hands, people who live here and already have the contacts, as that's half the battle.'

'Ah, I see what you mean. But Patrick impressed Harrison over at the Linden Hotel, according to Val. She mentioned it when she gave me the leaflets to pass out to everyone with the details of the hotel and the minibus. Harrison told her that Patrick came up with a couple of good ideas. One was to invite their customers to add a discretionary amount to their bill in support of the fund. The other was to hold a ticket-only dinner, with ten pounds per head being donated. I thought that was a rather novel idea.'

'Yes, Harrison ran it past me afterwards and I was of the same opinion. If it goes ahead, we're going to print off some sheets showing the artist's impression of the plans for the playground, and someone will go along to the dinner to do a short talk. I was hoping Tollie would be up for that, but maybe Fisher will step in if necessary. It depends on the timing.'

I turn to stare out of the window, my mind ticking over. 'I'm pretty sure we can raise enough money in the timescale,' I say firmly. 'Patrick came along at just the right time to make a difference. I intend to get more hands-on now to drive things forward and with the cottage shaping up nicely, it's amazing what a difference that makes. After living on a building site for weeks on end, suddenly those horrors are behind us. All I need now is for Tollie's operation to go well and life will be good again. I hate seeing him in pain and I know how frustrated he's been.'

Gray nods his head in agreement. 'He's fit and strong for a man his age, but his bad back has knocked his confidence a bit. Honestly, Immi, I don't know how long he's been seeing Daphne, but he's changed over this last couple of months, despite the pain he's had to endure. I think Daphne has made a huge difference to the way Tollie is coping, so don't be too hard on her.'

Was Tollie hard on Gray at first? I wonder. Thinking back, I'm sure Tollie only had my best interests at heart, if that were the case. Surely, he will understand if the same is true for me?

* * *

'How do I look?' I ask, peering at Gray and trying to judge his initial reaction as I walk back into the bedroom of our hotel room.

'Wow. Just wow!'

'Yes, but is it too much?' I smooth the dress down over my hips feeling self-conscious. Both Sarah and Ursula said it was the right thing to wear, not too dressy but summery.

'Sorry, it's just that I don't see you in a dress very often and you look lovely. Simply lovely.'

I roll my eyes at him. 'You're supposed to be looking at this from the viewpoint of a bunch of people I've never met before. Not through the eyes of a love-sick man who thinks everything I wear is perfect,' I groan. It's not that I'm ungrateful, but whatever I wear Gray thinks I look cute.

'Okay. You look, cool, confident and... gorgeous. Every guy in the room is going to wish they were standing next to you. Will that do?'

I throw my hands up in the air. 'You're impossible, do you know that?' But I'm laughing and he closes in to waltz me around the room. Suddenly, I no longer care as it's clear I'm going to have to look in the mirror and decide for myself.

What I see is someone who looks happy. I swing from left to right, letting the knee-length fabric sway a little, and I feel confident. The sleeveless, A-line cut of the silky fabric gives it a life of its own. The turquoise blue reminds me of forget-me-knots, which grow like weeds in the meadow we look out onto from the cottage. With a U-shaped neckline, I've added a simple silver pendant and matching leaf earrings. It's the sort of dress, Ursula informed me, that transitions from day to night. Just as well, as we're meeting up at four in the afternoon.

'Well?' Gray asks, and I swear he's holding his breath.

'I'll do. I'm as ready as I will ever be.'

But as he ushers me out of the door, he leans in to whisper in my ear, 'I love you, Immi, and my friends are going to love you too.'

* * *

'Immi, this is Ollie and his wife, Sylvia.' I'm greeted with warm smiles and am surprised when both Sylvia and then Ollie lean in to give me a welcoming hug.

'It's a real pleasure to finally meet you, Immi, and thank you both for the wedding invitation,' Sylvia replies warmly.

To my relief, Sylvia is also wearing a summery dress, which immediately makes me feel more at ease.

'I was beginning to wonder whether you were a figment of Gray's imagination,' Ollie jokes and Gray immediately bursts out laughing. 'You must be a very patient woman indeed to put up with this man. How do you ever get him to focus on anything other than music?'

Gray can see that I'm not sure how to respond to that and he immediately cuts in.

'Immi is my muse, plus she has the patience of a saint. Although I've just spent the last two days assembling furniture and putting up blinds, so I know how to keep my woman happy!' Gray places his arm around my waist, pulling me closer, and when I look at him his face is lit up.

'Well, I can't wait to visit Aysbury. The Cotswolds is such a lovely area. And how are the wedding plans going?' Sylvia enquires.

Gray and I look at each other for a brief moment. 'Yes, how are they going, Gray?' I ask.

'As one of the team of three wedding planners, I can confidently say that everything is moving along quite smoothly.'

Both Ollie's and Sylvia's faces reflect surprise. 'You're letting Gray help organise the wedding?' Ollie asks, sounding stunned.

'It seemed like a good idea at the time,' I declare, pulling away from Gray a little to stare at him with a frown. 'You don't think that was a mistake, do you?'

Ollie and Sylvia begin to laugh incredulously. 'You're a brave woman, for sure,' Ollie replies.

'Hey, guys, thanks for the vote of confidence,' Gray responds. 'There's more to me than you think. Just you wait and see.'

The banter is fun and, even though it's packed in the bar area, I'm beginning to feel as though I fit in, which is something that doesn't always happen when I'm away from my own environment.

'Why don't you ladies find our table before someone tries to pinch it and we'll order some drinks?' Ollie encourages.

Sylvia leads the way. 'Come on,' she calls out over her shoulder. 'We're out on the terrace.'

It's a smart wine bar, the sort that has an industrial look, although it was probably refitted fairly recently, as everything looks pristine.

Surprisingly, the patio area is colourful with an array of pots burgeoning with flowers. Sylvia makes her way over to a long table with a reserved sign on it. Around us, most of the other tables are for four or six people.

'We're the first to arrive, then. What a lovely outside area,' I remark, pulling out a chair to sit next to Sylvia.

'I suggested to Ollie that the four of us meet up a little earlier. He wanted to have a quick chat with Gray about work anyway and it's not quite so daunting if people arrive in small groups, is it?'

'That was very thoughtful of you, Sylvia. I appreciate that. I am a little nervous not knowing anyone at all.'

'Well, Ollie and I are fairly new to the group, too, but they welcomed us.'

'What exactly is Ollie's role?' I ask, genuinely keen to know a little more about the set-up.

'Ollie has contacts throughout the music and film industry.

When a project comes along it's his job to find suitable candidates to put forward. It's up to the company concerned to make a final decision.'

'Hmm... so he's like an agent?'

'Yes, you could say that as he then negotiates the contract. But normally an agent represents his client exclusively, whereas Gray isn't tied to just looking at projects Ollie is able to put in front of him. A few of the other guys in the group are now involved with projects Ollie has put together and he's really pleased with the results.'

'It's nice to gain a little understanding, as I'd hate to say the wrong thing to anyone.'

Sylvia nods her head, and I can see she understands. 'It's a competitive industry but talent always rises to the top. Ollie can't speak highly enough about Gray, and I don't know if he told you, but we invited him to dinner at our house a couple of weeks ago. After we'd eaten, Ollie and Gray went through the itinerary for the trip to LA. Gray mentioned in passing that he intended to talk you into a quick trip to meet everyone. They are a... noisy bunch, but that's because they spark off each other. Just relax and go with the flow as, believe me, they will do all the talking.'

'Who will do all the talking?' Ollie's voice looms up behind us.

'I was just telling Immi that musicians are a fun bunch of people to be around,' Sylvia replies.

'That's one way to put it,' Gray quickly interjects before Ollie can answer.

They are each carrying a tray of assorted tapas dishes and following on behind are two waiters with wine coolers.

'We're just in time!' A loud voice booms out and we all turn around to see half a dozen people sauntering in. 'Were you about to start without us?'

Gray immediately walks back around the table and there's a lot of handshakes, back-slapping and hugs going on, interspersed with outbursts of raucous laughter.

'You didn't bring us anything back from LA, then?' The loudest of the guys pretends to check around, as if he were expecting to see gifts. 'I knew it would go to your head and the minute we were out of sight we'd be out of mind.'

'Never!' Rather dramatically, Gray throws his hands up in the air. The response is hilarious, as all five of the people standing around him start humming while the tall, thin guy pretends to be conducting them. It's the opening bars of the title music Gray wrote for the film.

What's weird for me is watching them all interact as if they are family and yet I'm on the outside looking in on a part of Gray's life that I don't get to see.

'Immi, come on over. I'd better introduce you before things start to get out of hand.'

My nerves begin to jangle as everyone turns to look at me and I rise up out of my seat. I desperately need to think of something funny to say to break the ice. My mind goes into overdrive as Gray grabs my hand to draw me into the centre of the group.

'They're not all here yet, but in no particular order this is Nathan. You notice he has the loudest voice of us all and he's the first one you spot in a crowd.'

Nathan steps forward and he's at least six foot six and over a foot taller than me. I look up at him, not sure whether to offer my hand, but he leans forward to give me a bear hug that almost takes my breath away.

'How on earth did someone like Gray snag someone like you? That's what I'd like to know!' Nathan releases me and everyone is waiting for my response.

'I'm a sucker for a jingle,' I reply and that does the trick.

Gray begins to hum the tune he wrote for the hair-shampoo commercial, and they all join in. The ice has been broken.

'You'll probably need reminding who is who, but Chrissy is Nathan's wife, and this is Reece and his partner, Leanne. At the back is Phil – where's Katie?' Gray asks as I move from one person to the next.

'Hi, Immi, lovely to meet you.' Phil squeezes through to give me a quick hug. 'She's working and sends her apologies.' He turns to Gray, poking him playfully in the ribs. 'I've missed my running buddy. I'm never going to get you into shape if you keep taking time off.'

I look on, hardly daring to believe my ears. Gray running?

'It was work and a man is entitled to take a few days off to keep his fiancée happy, isn't he?' Gray throws back at him, but I can see he's a little embarrassed by the revelation. So, my man is really prepping for the wedding, but I love him just the way he is.

'Sorry we're late, but you haven't started drinking yet and there's food!' Another four people appear, and we're all crowded in a narrow gangway now. As the others begin to take their seats Gray steers me forward.

'This is Dharma and her boyfriend, Grif. And, Immi, grab what you can eat before we let Dharma near the table. She's always hungry and she can eat her own weight in food and more. Finally, this is Kerrin and her fiancé, Mark. They're going to be tying the knot next year.'

As Kerrin steps forward she gives me a beaming smile. 'Hi, Immi, welcome to the crazy gang. Mark and I are hoping to pick up some tips from your wedding,' she adds.

It is a little overwhelming, I will admit, but they are such a happy bunch of people and Gray is clearly in his element. When Sylvia said they spark off each other, she was spot on, and Gray was right when he said I had nothing at all to worry about. Like attracts like, and his friends are as supportive and genuine as our friends and family in Aysbury. By the end of the evening my cheeks ache and I can't recall the last time I laughed this much. And everyone is looking forward to coming to Aysbury for the wedding. The excitement is beginning to build!

17

LETTING GO IS SELDOM EASY

'Thanks for popping round, Patrick. I don't want to spoil the whole of your Thursday evening so I'm sure we can work through this in an hour, tops.'

'Oh, don't worry, Immi. It's a pleasure to be able to make myself useful. Goodness, what a beautiful job you've done of renovating the cottage. From the towpath it looks like any other traditional stone building, and yet stepping inside it's so light and bright.'

'Thank you. It's still early days and there are a few things left to sort out, but we're pleased with how the renovation has turned out. Anyway, I've spread everything out on the table if you'd like to take a seat. Tea, or coffee?'

'Tea, please. One sugar.'

'If you want to read through that two-page document on the top of the pile, there's pretty much all the information you'll need there. I had confirmation this morning that you are now an official signatory on the bank account, and you should receive a pack in the next day or two.'

'Good. So, it's just the handover and then I'm all ready to take

the reins. Hopefully that's one pressure less on your shoulders.'
Patrick is a star stepping up like this and Martin says it's given
him a new lease of life.

I carry the tray across to the table but Patrick declines the
biscuits.

'I've put on a bit of weight as I'm living on takeaways these
days and it's time to start afresh. Can't let myself slip, can I?'

I give Patrick an encouraging look. 'You'll soon settle into a
new routine, I'm sure. Anyway, let's go through this from the top.
I'm conscious that we've only had time to do one run to empty the
collection boxes. They won't need doing for at least three weeks,
but if you want me to do the next one with you, then please don't
hesitate to let me know. There's a list of addresses somewhere...
ah, here it is.'

'I should be fine, and the list will make sure I don't miss
anyone out.'

'Right, what's next? Ah, yes, Fisher has offered to be the official collection point for ad-hoc cheques any of our team receive.
It saves them the extra walk down to the cottage anyway, but it's
also a reminder that I'm stepping back from the role. I've added
Fisher's telephone number at the bottom and I've passed him
yours.'

It's satisfying as I make my way down the list, ticking off item
after item.

'Last, but not least, I will email you the income and expendi-
ture spreadsheet. I'll go through that with you in detail once
we've finished our tea. You will note that there's an extra tab to
record every individual donation. We do like to put the names of
our supporters on the Santa Ahoy website. David usually does
that for me. Have you ever met him in person?'

Patrick shakes his head. 'Well, next time you're passing the
brewery do pop in and introduce yourself. He'd be delighted.

David usually only attends two or three of our meetings each year, but he's a very astute businessman, and busy. It's good of him to take the time to be our company secretary.'

'I'll do that as soon as I get a chance.'

'And here are the dates of the forthcoming meetings. Let's go through that spreadsheet and then I think that's about it, unless you have any questions.'

Patrick looks at me, briefly glancing down at the documents in his hands. 'No. I think you've covered everything, Immi. I'm impressed at how organised you are.'

That makes me smile. There are others who might use a different word, like methodical, or worse. It is true that I like things done in a certain way, but the time has come to step back a little and put my trust in other people.

'I'm so grateful to you, Patrick. Now I can refocus my attention on making sure we hit those targets.'

'I needed something like this, Immi, you don't know quite how much. I can't wait to get stuck in.'

* * *

Gray looks at me. 'Are you going to knock? Or shall I?'

We're standing at the front door to The Retreat and normally at this time on a Friday night, Gray and I would be holding hands across the table at The Bullrush. Instead, we're meeting Daphne for the first time. I ring the bell instead of my usual tap on the glass and Gray looks at me, his face dropping.

'Lighten up, it'll be fine,' he whispers as the door opens and Tollie ushers us inside.

'This is like old times,' Tollie jokes, leaning forward to plant a fleeting kiss on my cheek. As he straightens, he lets out a groan. 'Damn back! Anyway, go on in.'

Old times? Hardly. Today there are four of us.

I step into the open-plan area and a woman I presume is Daphne is standing in front of the hob, stirring a saucepan.

She looks up, a pleasant smile on her face. 'Forgive me, but this sauce will go lumpy if I don't keep stirring. Tollie, if you can sort the drinks, I'll only be a few minutes and then I can dish up.'

Being treated like a guest in what was my home until six months ago sets me on edge. Gray gives me one of his looks as we stand awkwardly, while Tollie does as he's told.

'Red sky at night, shepherd's delight,' Gray says jovially, tilting his head to encourage me to go and stand by the patio doors and look out. When I join him, I can just about make out the word, 'Relax,' as he says it so quietly, his mouth barely moves.

'Yes, it's a beautiful view, isn't it?' Daphne speaks up, to my mind acting as if she's the lady of the house.

'Red or white?' Tollie calls out.

Gray looks at me and I nod. 'Two for red, please.'

There's another awkward pause, and while Tollie and Daphne have their backs to us, Gray nudges me in the side, tilting his head in the direction of the kitchen.

'Is there um... anything I can do to help?' I call out.

'Oh, no,' Daphne instantly responds. 'It's all in hand, thank you, Immi. You can take your places at the table, though.'

Can we? How kind. I give myself a mental rap on the knuckles. Why am I acting like a... a... a moody teenager? I'm a grown woman and should know better. My ridiculous reaction makes me laugh and both Gray, who is now over by the table, and Tollie turn to look in my direction.

'What's funny?' Tollie enquires, frowning at me.

'Oh... I was just thinking about something Patrick said when I did the handover yesterday evening. He said I was organised.'

Tollie begins to belly-laugh, but Gray's face doesn't alter.

'That's one word for it, m'dear,' Tollie declares. 'I hope he sticks to the rules. My granddaughter is very particular, Daphne,' he adds.

She turns around to look at me. 'And so am I. Great minds think alike, Immi.'

I'm speechless. Did this woman just give me a warning that I might have met my match? Gritting my teeth, I join them at the table.

Tollie and Gray don't know how to react, and I have an awful feeling that things aren't about to get any better.

* * *

'Seriously, Immi, what is your problem?' Gray asks the minute we step through our own front door. 'This isn't like you, at all.'

'I'm sorry, were we listening to a totally different narrative?' I ask sarcastically.

Gray looks stunned. 'Narrative?'

'Daphne was laying down the law. What right has the woman to do that?'

Gray puts up both of his hands to stop me saying anything more.

'Whoa. This is in danger of getting out of hand, Immi. She was nervous, you were nervous... Heck, Tollie didn't know which way to turn. And I—'

'Sat there letting Tollie constantly refill your glass, because it was in your hand every other second, it seemed.'

'Immi, that's not fair. There was a point at which Tollie looked at me and we both wished we weren't there.'

'Fine. If you aren't going to take my side, then I'm sleeping in the spare bedroom. I will see you in the morning.'

'But... but... it isn't about taking sides...'

I leave Gray floundering, feeling too angry to even say goodnight.

At one point, Gray left the table to go to the bathroom and Tollie went in search of another bottle of wine. Daphne waited until they were out of earshot before she began speaking.

'It's always wisest to leave a patient's aftercare to the professionals, don't you think, Immi? Family mean well, of course, but they are often a hindrance. I'm sure I'll have Tollie up and about in no time at all. As long as he doesn't get a constant stream of visitors tiring him out, everything will be fine.'

The look she gave me couldn't have been more pointed.

Daphne has drawn the battle lines and if she thinks I'm going to roll over and let her have her own way, she's mistaken. This is war and there is no way that I'm going to let her dictate to Tollie, just because he's not himself and he's struggling. I'm here for him always, but he seems to have forgotten that and it's breaking my heart.

* * *

'What's wrong?' Fisher stares at me and I know the bags beneath my eyes are a giveaway I can't hide.

'Gray and I had a row last night. It's to do with Tollie.'

Fisher bites his lip. 'Tollie?'

'Well, Daphne and the hold she seems to be exerting over him.'

'Oh. It's officially a *thing*, then, is it?'

It's hard not to sound bitter when I feel that I'm being purposely pushed away. 'Tollie is having surgery on his back next week.'

'Surgery? On his back? My goodness, I didn't know things

were that bad. I'm sorry to hear that, Immi. If there's anything I can do to help, you only have to say.'

'Thanks, Fisher. But he doesn't need any help apparently because Daphne is moving in and will be taking care of him.'

'She's what?'

'I know. Gray and I were invited to dinner at The Retreat last night and I left feeling so angry that I thought I was going to explode. That's why Gray and I had a row, because he thinks I'm being unreasonable.'

Fisher frowns. 'And are you?'

I shrug my shoulders. 'Before Daphne retired she was in charge of a clinical ward. But Tollie never once mentioned that he was seeing a consultant and suddenly, out of nowhere, he informs me he's having an operation. What if it's Daphne who has talked him into this? If he'd at least discussed it with me beforehand and I was privy to what the consultant had told him, I wouldn't be quite so concerned. And last night I swear she was, ever so politely, making it clear that my help is not required. At all. Tollie and Gray were just sitting there, wishing they were somewhere else.'

Fisher clears his throat, looking uncomfortable. 'Um, don't take this the wrong way, Immi, but Tollie is no fool.'

'Not you, too!'

'Listen, you can't jump to conclusions until you know all the facts. And if Tollie isn't keeping you in the loop, that's his right. He hasn't even mentioned it to me, so perhaps it's not something he wants to talk about.'

'So, I leave him in this stranger's hands, as if he isn't one of the most important men in my life? I would never forgive myself if something went wrong, Fisher, and you know that. Tollie would be acting in the exact same way if the tables were turned. Even though he knows and loves Gray, if I had a problem, Tollie would be there every step of the way, making sure I had the right treatment. This is all wrong, Fisher, and I'm not going to bow out gracefully.'

We sit in silence while my words sink in and the pause feels like forever.

'You're right, my darling girl. But remember, pain does weird things to people and if he's on painkillers, there's a chance he isn't thinking straight. Do you want me to call in on him just in case he wants to have a chat? The two of us could always pop up to The Bullrush.'

'That would be perfect, thank you. All I want is for him to be healthy and happy. If he'd known this Daphne for a long time, it would be different, but I'm guessing they've only known each other for a couple of months, tops.'

'And now she's about to move into your old home.' Fisher's voice is full of sympathy.

'It's not about that, I promise. But she didn't seem bothered about getting me on her side. While being ever so polite, she went to great lengths to make it clear that plans have been made and it was none of my business.'

'She said that?' Fisher sucks in a deep breath.

'No. Of course she didn't. Fortunately, I've done my own research, so I know a little more about the procedure Tollie is undergoing, but everything has risks attached to it. Yes, I know that it's entirely his decision, but why can't I be involved in looking after him, too?'

'Let me pop in to see him and I'll report back. But in the meantime, unless he reaches out to ask for your opinion, you simply don't have a say in the matter.'

Fisher catches Kurt's attention. 'Another cappuccino for Immi, please, and a black coffee for me. Thanks.'

'Okay, that's enough about my problems. What's going on with you?'

I have never seen Fisher looking as uncomfortable as he does now. He shifts in his seat as his gaze wanders, focusing on someone walking past the window.

'I intend to ask Val if she would do me the honour of becoming my wife.'

My reaction is to freeze. His *wife*? I'm speechless.

'Please, Immi, don't mention this to anyone. You're the first person I've told, and I appreciate this might come as a bit of a shock.'

'You're not implying that this will come as a shock to Val, too, are you?' I ask tentatively and his reaction confirms my fears are correct.

'You know me, I'm not a soppy, wear-your-heart-on-your-sleeve type of man. Never was, never will be. But when I'm with her everything suddenly looks better, brighter and she makes me smile.'

'Is that your way of saying you love her?'

Fisher doesn't get anxious, but there's anxiety written all over his face.

'I suppose it is, if you want to put it like that.' His voice is deadpan.

Why are all the men in my life suddenly causing me problems?

'Fisher, you're going around in circles unsure of what to do about your future and you can't put this off any longer. Why are you talking to me about this, and not to Val? Stop making excuses. Seize the moment, now.'

'Now?' He sounds panicked.

'There's no time like the present. I'm heading home to sort

things out with Gray. You need to head off to Byre Cottage, because until you know how Val feels, your life is on hold.'

He nods, pursing his lips and frowning. 'Point taken. Good advice. Go and make it up with Gray. And I'll...'

'Get up out of your seat and start walking. It's time to man up. What have you got to lose?'

'You're right. Will do. And thanks, Immi, that was helpful.' However, Fisher does look a tad traumatised.

After a reassuring hug and a firm pat on the back, I leave him to drink his coffee and get mine to go. So much for a relaxing Saturday – I wish I'd stayed in bed!

18

LIFE LESSONS

One thing I've always loved about Gray is that, even though there are times when he's all wrapped up in his head, if something important crops up he's instantly there for me. I wonder if all artistic people are the same, living a part of their life in a world of their own.

Last night we both spoke our truth about the situation with Tollie and, whilst it wasn't easy for me to listen to his opinion, I understood that he was only trying to be neutral. My version, because I'm only human after all, comes straight from the heart, but he succeeded in convincing me that I should think carefully about how I handle the situation from here on in. He reminded me that going into hospital is a scary thing for anyone and Tollie will, naturally, be anxious. The question Gray asked me was: 'Are you making things better for him, or worse, by adding to his anxiety?'

I mulled it over for a while, but I know Gray is right. It's selfish of me to put my feelings first, when all that matters is Tollie's well-being. Maybe what I'm experiencing is similar to how a parent feels when their child grows up and becomes independent. Things I used to discuss with Tollie, I now discuss with Gray. And if my suspicions are correct and Daphne is going to play an increasing role in Tollie's life, I need to step back. What I didn't tell Gray was that when we walked into The Retreat the other night, for a split second before Daphne turned around, I thought it was Grandma Nell standing there. It made my heart ache and what Daphne saw on my face would have been a look of total disappointment. She didn't deserve that.

Switching off, I begin clearing the breakfast plates but Gray indicates for me to stop. He finishes off the last of his croissant, waggling a finger in the air.

'Leave it to me. You head off and have that chat with Val.'

'Are you trying to get rid of me?' I accuse, sounding miffed.

Gray shakes his head, laughing. 'No... but I suspect you will be gone a while, so I might as well get a little work done. And after that we can go for that run we keep talking about and never get around to.' I still pull his leg about Phil's revelation. It seems grooms, too, get a little self-conscious about the big day.

'Okay. I'll give you an hour, two at most, and then that's a date.'

'People are going to wonder what's going on when they see us out jogging, but it's time we got physical in more ways than one.' He grins at me. 'Anyway, what's so important that you're abandoning me to head off for a chat with Val?'

'We're talking flowers again,' I inform him, and he rolls his eyes.

'Oh, right. When Val asked me about it, I just shrugged my shoulders. That's one area in which I can't be of any help whatsoever. Have fun!'

I push back on my chair and Gray walks around the table to

give me a fleeting kiss. I can see his head is already in work mode and so I leave him to it.

I stroll along the towpath; there are a lot of families and people out walking their dogs today. The delicious smell of frying bacon wafts under my nose as I pass The Bullrush and, even though I've already eaten, my stomach rumbles. Ahead of me, I can see Ethel and Abe, busy watering the pots.

'Morning, another glorious one,' I call out.

Abe gives me a salute and Ethel turns around to face me. 'Nothing beats a bit of gardening on a Sunday morning,' she declares happily. 'Going for a walk without Gray? Did you leave him in bed?'

I smile, shaking my head. 'He's preparing for a meeting tomorrow with his agent, Ollie, and I'm off to see Val. You know what he's like. Now that his project is finished, he's keen to start something new and he's sifting through a list of potential options. He needs to narrow it down because each pitch is time-consuming to pull together. So, it's back to London again for Gray.'

'Ah, bless him. He works hard but he's like a tonic for us all whenever he's around,' Ethel replies. I know she has a soft spot for Gray, and he is a bit of a teddy bear. He's cuddly, affectionate and always makes everyone smile, traits that are hard to resist.

'And look who we have here – she's come looking for you, then, Immi.'

I turn around and Val is walking towards us.

'Am I late?' I call out, conscious that I'm not sure what time I eventually left the cottage.

'Not at all. I simply fancied a little fresh air and thought we could walk and talk. My goodness, you two, that is a stunning display this year. Congratulations on getting second place in the floral barge competition!'

'One year we'll get to that top spot,' Abe mutters, stroking his chin. 'The competition is fierce, though. We always give it our best and we aren't about to give up trying.'

'I didn't know the results were out,' I exclaim. 'That's brilliant news and well deserved!'

'We've been lucky with all the sun we've had. It only takes a heavy shower of rain to damage the more tender plants and spoil the show. But now we can relax and just enjoy the display,' Ethel points out.

'Well, it certainly raises my spirits every time I see it. Right,' Val says, glancing at me. 'Shall we talk about the wedding flowers?'

I nod and we say goodbye, but Val doesn't turn around, and instead continues straight ahead. I fall into step with her.

'Let's walk down to the junction, shall we?' she suggests.

'Perfect.' As we draw level with The Bullrush, I slow my pace and Val follows suit.

'What's up?' she asks.

I nod in the direction of the footbridge in front of the marina building. 'Daphne is just crossing the bridge. I suspect she's on her way to see Tollie. I'd rather not bump into her, if you don't mind.'

We stop for a couple of minutes, turning around to watch a stylish white Viking 24 with an electric blue flash making its way towards us.

'That's one of the boats which has a permanent mooring at the marina, although I don't know the owner. It is nice to see it in use, though. I always think it's sad seeing them all moored up. Boats are meant to be used,' I reflect.

'Well, funny you should say that. It's kind of what I wanted to talk to you about this morning. I hope you don't mind the subterfuge.'

'I did wonder. What's up?'

Turning around to see how far ahead Daphne is, Val touches my arm. 'Let's cross over the bridge, instead. You never know whether Tollie will take Daphne for a walk so it's better if we head in the opposite direction. Their friendship is common knowledge now, then, is it?'

We set off and I let out a sigh. 'Yes. Did you know that Tollie is having an operation on his back for a trapped nerve and Daphne is going to "manage his recuperation", as she put it?'

'Ah, I wasn't aware of that. And that was Tollie's decision?' Val checks, and I nod. 'Then you should be happy for him. Knowing Tollie, he won't make the best patient and sometimes it's tough on family members trying to nurse their relatives.'

Val is a practical woman and her past colours the way she looks at things. I wish I could be as objective as her, but my emotions rule my head.

'That's more or less what Gray said to me last night. Anyway, that's enough about my little trials and tribulations. I'm assuming this has something to do with Fisher?'

'Yes. He turned up unexpectedly at Byre Cottage and I could tell he had something on his mind. He kept pushing it away, but you know me, I don't believe in beating around the bush. I told him straight that it was time to get whatever it was off his chest.'

I try to imagine Fisher's reaction to that. 'And?'

Val draws to a halt halfway across the bridge, and we stop to watch the Viking as it makes its way down towards the junction.

'Come on, let's head for the bench alongside the marina's offices.'

Knowing what was on Fisher's mind, I'm a little dismayed to note from Val's demeanour that she's clearly in a quandary. We stroll along and it isn't until after we settle ourselves down that she begins talking again.

'Fisher has asked me to marry him, Immi.'

I'm not good at being fake, and while I'm trying to conjure up something suitable to say, Val turns to face me.

'But, of course, he's already talked to you about it.' She sounds accepting, rather than offended.

'He's like my second dad, Val. He was the one I ran to when Tollie and I were rowing all the time because I was being obnoxious and self-centred. It's only natural that he would turn to me, because you know he doesn't find it easy to share his feelings.'

She bows her head. 'He filled the gap for you, didn't he? And I'm grateful to him for that and also the fact that you are his support system, too.'

Val is my biological mother, but up until she revealed the truth to me last Christmas, she'd simply been a neighbour who lived a short walk away. She moved back to Aysbury five years before my dad died and when I came to live with Tollie she was his housekeeper for a while. Val had worked tirelessly to support the community here, but outside that she was a bit of a loner. Mainly because, by nature, she's a private person. Gradually, she has lowered her guard, and over the last year we've become friends because of her increasing involvement with the Santa Ahoy cruises.

Aside from Tollie and Grandma, Bernie was the only other person in Aysbury who was aware that Valerie Price was formerly Alison Tolliman. Out of love for me and respect for my dad, they continued to keep the secret. I'm not sure if I agree with Dad's decision that I should be kept in the dark, but it had been made very clear to Val that she wasn't to reveal her real identity. The fact that Val and Grandma were friends following her return, in hindsight tells me that Grandma believed her story. All I knew about my mum was that she disappeared a few months after I was born and that, according to my birth certificate, her name was Alison. I had no memories of her at all and Dad never, ever talked about her. Since last Christmas, when Val broke down and told me the truth, Gray, Fisher and Rona also know that she is my birth mother, but no one ever talks about it because for me it didn't change anything. Friendship doesn't miraculously turn into a mother/daughter bond because a buried truth is suddenly revealed. I wish it were that easy.

I swing my feet back and forth, my hands gripping the edge of the seat as I try to find the right words.

'Fisher was nervous, Val. I simply told him that he should be honest with you about how he feels and his hopes for the future.'

'He wasn't asking for your blessing, then?'

Why would she think that? 'No, of course not. He's a man who is guarded when it comes to the emotional stuff, that's all... and, well—'

'I'm the same,' Val interrupts. 'It wasn't an easy conversation, Immi, because I wasn't prepared for it, and he could see that. Fisher understands my hesitation and simply asked me to take some time to think over his proposal. I promised him that I would give him my answer tomorrow night. He's cooking us dinner at his place.'

'Oh, Val, you'll be sitting mere feet away from each other all day tomorrow in the office. That'll be agony.'

'No. I'm taking the day off. We decided it wasn't fair on either of us, for that exact reason. The thing is, Immi, I vowed I'd never marry again after my divorce from Liam's father. Two failed marriages feel like an omen. It seems as if I'm being punished for the pain I inflicted on you and your dad. Karma, if you like. And now I simply can't risk ruining Fisher's life, too.'

I know Val will never shed the guilt she feels so acutely for abandoning her baby daughter and her husband. Even though at the time she was mentally unwell and, as it turned out, unable to even take care of herself for a while. Discovering that it wasn't because she had rejected me meant everything. She eventually changed her name and began a new life, miles away from here, until she finally felt brave enough to return. But however much I understand, I still can't bring myself to call her Mum – it would feel like a betrayal to Dad.

Whenever we visited Aysbury, Grandma Nell was the female role model in my life and, although Dad knew Val was a stone's throw away, their paths never crossed. That, I was told, was his choice entirely. Val and I ended up becoming friends because, as much as she felt she had no right to grow close to me, she'd never stopped loving the daughter she'd walked away from. And although I appreciate having her in my life now, there is still a little awkwardness between us. Not least because of my bond with Fisher, who has been a big influence in my life ever since I came to Aysbury. There are times when Fisher and I are reminiscing about the past and Val goes very quiet. We quickly change the subject, because no one is standing in judgement here, but we can't change the past.

'Fisher is trying hard to leave behind the hurts of his past, Val. He's taking a huge risk opening up his heart to you, because it makes him feel vulnerable again. Doesn't that prove just how strong his feelings are for you?'

Val leans back against the bench, closing her eyes for a moment as she tilts her head up to face the sun. I gaze around, taking in the sounds of barking dogs and voices drifting on the breeze from a group of walkers on the opposite side of the canal. Then I see that it's the Aysbury Ramblers, out today with collection buckets on a ten-mile walk to raise funds. Kurt and Sarah organised it and are providing free bottles of water and energy bars to keep them going.

'What if I'm not capable of really loving someone, Immi?' Val turns her head away from me, swiping her eyes with the back of her hand, and my heart constricts inside my chest.

I swallow hard; the sadness I feel for the hand that life dealt Val leaves me feeling bereft on her behalf.

'Your love for your stepson, Liam, has never faltered, Val. Love is love. Liam turned up on your doorstep unannounced last Christmas because he wanted to see for himself that you were okay. When Liam and I were shovelling snow together, he told me that you were always there for him. He knew how hard you took it once he had his freedom, and his only concern was whether you had friends around you. He didn't know who I was, and I didn't quiz him. In fact, he sought me out because he wanted to know more about Fisher, once he knew you were working for him. You earnt Liam's love, Val, by treating him as if he were your own. When a child loses a mother, they need someone to step up and fill the void. You did that when his father chose to back away from him.'

She sniffs and I fear I'm making this worse, which is not my intention at all.

'And your father filled the void in your life, then Tollie and Fisher took on the role,' she admits sadly.

'My life was filled with love, when yours was falling apart, but that wasn't your fault. We've become great friends, Val, and there is no one I would trust more to be instrumental in planning my wedding than you. But...' I tail off, unable to explain that Dad did everything for me and I don't know if I'll ever be able to think of her in that way without feeling disloyal.

'There's no need to explain, Immi. I'm grateful to be that friend you trust and play a part in your life. I just don't want to hurt anyone. If I say *yes* to Fisher, what happens next? Everyone is aware of his intention to set up a little business, but the truth is that I can't be a part of it, no matter how strong my feelings are for him. I might put his dream in jeopardy, and I can't allow that to happen.'

'Everything in life is a risk, Val, but some risks are worth taking.'

I can see how difficult this is for her. Her arms are folded across her body, hands on elbows as if she's trying to hold herself together. 'In his dream Fisher probably sees us cruising down the canal together, side by side at the helm. Whenever I step on board anything that floats, the minute it begins moving I get sick to my stomach. I can't ask him to sacrifice his dream for me, can I?'

'But all that really matters is what's in your heart, Val. If friendship is all that you're seeking between the two of you, then you must be honest about that and put him out of his misery. But if that's not the case, dreams can, and do, change. What if Fisher's carefully made plans aren't supposed to work out and, instead, he'll be even happier remaining at the marina with his wife by his side?'

Val looks even more confused now. 'Can it be as simple as that, Immi? I don't know what I'm going to say to Fisher tomorrow. I can only hope that when my thoughts clear, the answer will suddenly present itself and when it does, it will be the right one.'

I reach out and squeeze her arm.

'I'll be thinking of you both, Val. I doubt either of you will get much sleep tonight.'

We stand to begin the walk back and I stop at the step up to the footbridge.

'I'll say goodbye here as I'm going to pop in to see Rona. If you want to give me a call after the two of you have spoken, no matter how late it is, phone me any time.'

We hug and go our separate ways. I hope I've said enough to stop Val walking away for all the wrong reasons. I think she's afraid to acknowledge how she feels about Fisher. Besides, no one really wants to face the future alone when they've finally found someone who lights up their life, do they?

19

A TURNING POINT

'Oh, how lovely!' Rona exclaims when she opens the door. 'Come on in. You're on your own?'

'Yes, Gray was eager to fit in a couple of hours on this presentation he's putting together for his agent tomorrow. So it's back to our old routine while they're working closely together to find the next big project. I wandered up to see Abe and Ethel's display and then had a chat with Val. The walkathon is on today, too, and I'd forgotten all about it.'

'Well, there's a lot happening, which is positive. Every little helps. I'll make a cup of tea and we can sit out in the garden. Go and make yourself comfortable.'

I love Rona's little cottage. It's classically cosy, and while none of the rooms are large, the stone mullion windows and square, leaded panes of glass make it light and airy. It has the prettiest little garden that wraps around the building, which stands on a small plot of land next to Aysbury's community-run library. Both buildings are of a similar age and style, originally tied cottages owned by the farm.

'The new rose bushes look lovely, Rona. Great choice. These

traditional, cottage-garden flowers really take me back. Grandma Nell told Tollie off once for pulling up her forget-me-knots. He thought they were weeds.' I laugh.

She places the tray on the little cast-iron bistro table before sitting down.

'And aren't the hollyhocks wonderful, too?' she adds.

'Glorious and so tall! You've settled in well, even though it was a big upheaval for you at the time.'

Rona begins pouring the tea. She knows why I'm here.

'It was, but life moves on. Immi, forgive me for cutting to the chase, but I'm assuming Gray still hasn't said anything to you, has he?' she enquires.

'No. How about you?'

'Not a word. It's the proverbial elephant in the room and I'm guessing Gray doesn't want to talk about it for fear of upsetting me.'

'What are you going to do?'

She passes me a cup of tea and I add a little milk.

'If their meeting had gone well, I'm sure one or the other would have told me all about it by now. I've decided I can't stress over it any longer, so I emailed Grayson the day before yesterday and kept it light. Just telling him a little about what's happening in Aysbury and letting him know that you and Gray are now settled back into Lock Keeper's Cottage. I didn't mention the wedding, as it's not my place.'

I raise my eyebrows, wondering how that went down.

'He has already responded,' she confirms. 'He replied in a similar vein and that suits me. I don't want to lose touch with him, Immi, and he feels the same way. I'd appreciate it if you didn't mention this to Gray, as my son has been through enough. You make him happy and that's all that matters to me. I am sad they couldn't put their differences aside, but I understand, and have to let it lie now for all our sakes. Life goes on, doesn't it?'

I can see that Rona is relieved to have reached a decision, but there's a sadness reflected in her eyes, even though she's putting on a brave face.

'Coming here was a fresh start for me, Immi, and I'm extremely grateful to you and Gray. Both for the help financially and in finding my new home. Now I'm back to work I fully intend putting a little aside every month to repay you.'

'Rona, we have everything we need. The fact that you're here makes us both happy. There is no way either of us would take any money from you.'

She smiles at me, shaking her head.

'But I'm allowed to give you a wedding present.' Her eyes are twinkling.

'Helping with the wedding arrangements is payment enough. Seriously, I was floundering and if you and Val hadn't stepped in when you did, everything would have ground to a halt. That's worth more than any present you could possibly give us. Gray is enjoying the new, relaxed me. And the yoga is beginning to pay off.'

'You must be nervous about the first fitting. When will Ursula have the dresses ready?'

'Mid-October. Enough time to shift a pound, or two, if Sarah and I have been comfort eating,' I reply with a grin.

'It's so exciting, Immi. There is such a lot to look forward to this Christmas and there's nowhere else I'd rather be.'

I wonder if Gray realises how much hinged on that meeting with his father. If they'd managed to at least part company on good terms, I believe that Rona and Grayson might have talked about a future together. How they would have made that work, I have no idea, given the physical distance between them, but if something is meant to be, then I truly believe that the impossible can happen. The alternative is to give up hope and that is just too depressing to contemplate.

After finishing my tea and saying goodbye to Rona, I hurry back to the cottage to change. Jogging along the footpath at midday isn't an option in this heat, so the quicker we set out, the better. But I'm glad to be doing something about my fitness – anything that will help boost my confidence on the day is very welcome. There are times when I pull up the sketch of the dress that Ursula has designed for me and it's hard to imagine myself slipping into it. I have never been in a situation where I will be the centre of everyone's attention and I still find the thought of it a little unnerving.

* * *

Mondays are seldom easy and today, with Gray back in his old routine, it seems to have dragged on forever. He texted earlier on to say that he's having a working dinner with Ollie and he won't get back to his room until late. I almost forgot myself and said I'd be up anyway in case Val calls, but fortunately I stopped myself just in time.

Normally I'd pop in to check on Tollie as I haven't seen him today, but it's awkward now. His operation is the day after tomorrow and I thought I'd text him in the morning to see if it's convenient to pop in after work. *Convenient.* I find myself shaking my head sadly. It's never been like that between the two of us, ever, not even when Gray first came into my life. Gray was extremely thoughtful being around Tollie when we first began seeing each other, but Daphne hasn't reached out to me at all, and the few times our paths have crossed, she's polite but distant.

If I were her, I'd be intent on making a friend of me, not an enemy.

I decide it's time to pop in a DVD, as I feel in need of something to stop me clock-watching, wondering how it's going with Val and Fisher. Lying back on the sofa, I press play on my laptop and as the music starts, instantly I'm transported to a forest. The camera pans around to reveal a camp with soldiers in red and white uniforms. Suddenly the face of Aidan Turner appears on the screen – his smile does it for me every single time. 'Take me to Cornwall,' I say, breathing out a gentle sigh. I want to hear the waves crashing on the beach and watch Demelza walking along the clifftops. How wonderful to be a heroine and as strong as the hero in your life.

I wince when the tip of a sword catches Ross's cheek, scarring him, and yet without that imperfection something would be missing. He wouldn't be the Ross Poldark we have come to know and love. I've watched this series so many times, but it doesn't matter, I still enjoy it every time.

Buzz. Buzz.

I jump up, press pause on the laptop and reach out for my phone.

'Immi, it's Val. This is just a quick call. Is it convenient to talk?'

'Yes. I was watching the *Poldark* series again for the umpteenth time.'

'Comfort food for the soul,' she replies, her voice low.

'How did it go?'

'I'm still here. I'm out in the garden while Fisher is making coffee. We're going to sit and have dessert on the patio. I knew you'd be on edge and I wanted you to know what we've decided. I'm going to move in with Fisher and I will give him my answer at Christmas.'

'Christmas?' I repeat, dully. But the real surprise is that they are going to be living together. That's something I didn't expect, and I don't quite know what to say.

'Yes. It's time enough for us to test our true feelings for each other,' she continues. 'I've agreed to taking a few little trips along the canal on The Star Gazer with him. I hinted, but he needs to discover for himself that I'm not a water lover. But I'll give it a go. Anyway, this is just between you and me. Act surprised when he breaks the news.'

'Oh, right, of course! And thank you for letting me know, Val. I've been on edge all evening. I'm glad you've come to an arrangement. Speak soon.'

To say I'm surprised is an understatement, but the more I think about it, the more I can see that it's actually a good idea. After all, you don't really know someone until you live with them 24/7, do you? I think it will come as a bit of a shock to quite a few people, as Val is rather... staid and Fisher, well, he's a real gentleman, so they're both cautious people. I'm delighted they're giving it a go, but jaws will drop when Val moves in for a trial period.

* * *

It's Friday, the best day of the week. I miss Gray even more now that we're settled and sometimes it feels a bit sad that, once again, we spend the first hour, or two, together simply catching up. He's back working in the studio complex he and his friends usually hire, busy recording some demo soundtracks.

There's a tapping sound and as I glance up, Patrick peers around the side of the door to my office. 'I'm glad I caught you. How's Tollie doing?'

'Good, thank you. I've only seen him twice since his operation, but he's moving around. It's too soon to say whether it has been successful, but the worst is over and each day should get a little easier.'

'I thought you'd be taking some time off work,' Patrick remarks.

'No. He has a live-in nurse.' Which I suppose is true... 'How are things with you?'

Patrick steps further inside. 'The contracts for the sale of the house have finally been exchanged and I had no option but to agree to a two-week completion. It's a total nightmare, to be honest.'

'Sorry to hear that, Patrick. Do you have anywhere lined up?'

'Not at present. I'm with a couple of rental agencies but the properties coming up aren't suitable. It's mostly one-bedroom flats, or three-bed houses. Still, I'll keep looking.'

'Um... I might know of a place if you're really stuck. It would mean renting it on a monthly basis, as it's only for a short term, possibly up to Christmas at the latest. Shall I enquire on your behalf?'

'Is it around here?'

'Yes. On the doorstep.'

'Then please do. I'm grateful for any leads I can get.'

'Leave it with me and I'll give you a call as soon as I can.' He's definitely looking a lot happier now things are moving forward and it's good to hear that he's being proactive and not burying his head in the sand.

'Magic. And the funds are rolling in. It's going to be a great summer, Immi.' The optimism in his voice is good to hear.

'Wonderful. That's music to my ears, Patrick!'

I immediately pick up the phone once Patrick has left, eager to strike while the iron is hot. 'Quick question, Fisher, can you talk?'

'Yep. I'm in the boatyard. What's up?'

'You know Val has been stressing about Ziggy, ever since she moved out of Byre Cottage, well, I was wondering if a live-in cat-sitter might be the answer. Someone who works from home most of the time and is looking for a short-term let? What do you think? It can't be easy for Val popping in first thing and at lunchtime to sort Ziggy out and relying upon a neighbour to feed her last thing at night.'

'Hmm. That's a thought. If it weren't for the dogs next door, Val could bring her here. But Ziggy is a bit of a princess, isn't she?' Fisher laughs because we all know it's true.

'Well, Patrick has to vacate his property in two weeks' time, and he hasn't found anything suitable to rent yet. It could solve a problem if Val would consider renting it to him a month at a time. Is it worth mentioning it to her?'

Now he's chuckling. 'You don't think she'll last the course with me until Christmas? I'm not that bad to live with,' he says emphatically.

'I wasn't trying to imply anything at all. I just thought it would ease her mind to know someone was there every night. Not just for Ziggy, but to look after Byre Cottage.'

'Okay. It's just Patrick, is it?'

'Yes, and I think he'd jump at it, to be honest with you. He's fitted in here so well already and he'd be able to walk home after our committee meetings.'

'And from The Bullrush,' Fisher jokes. 'Leave it with me and I'll get Val to think it over and give you a call back. Thanks, Immi.'

There's a pause. 'How... how's it going?' I ask tentatively.

'Aside from missing Ziggy, it's working out just fine. We take it in turns cooking. And this weekend we're taking The Star Gazer for a trip up to Wennington Lock tea gardens. I thought Val might enjoy a good, old-fashioned cream tea.'

I'm glad he can't see me screwing up my face. 'Oh, lovely. That sounds... perfect.'

'Yes, I'm really looking forward to it. Enjoy the rest of your day, Immi.'

Poor Fisher. That might not be the best surprise for someone who gets queasy at the slightest movement when they're not on dry land. Obviously, Val has skated over her little issue, but I guess she's right – Fisher's just going to have to find out for himself.

OCTOBER

20

SOGGY UMBRELLAS

After an exceptionally mild September, with a long run of unbelievably sunny days, October arrives with a marked downturn in the weather. After I've spent weeks watering the turf, it's now in danger of becoming waterlogged.

'That's a long face,' Gray whispers into my ear as he sidles up alongside me.

'Look at that sky again. We're moving the plants out of the polytunnels today and so it will be all hands on deck. We're going to get soaked, so I'd better take a change of clothes with me. I have a stack of paperwork to get through this afternoon and I don't intend sitting there feeling damp and miserable.'

'The weather might cheer up a little as the morning goes on,' Gray points out hopefully. 'Will you be home for lunch?'

'Sorry. I'll be grabbing a sandwich to eat at my desk. Don't forget that I'm up at the Linden tonight to do the talk after the fundraising dinner.'

'I thought you were going to ask Tollie if he wanted to do it, given that Fisher can't make it,' Gray reminds me.

Avoiding his gaze, I pull on my coat. 'It's okay, I don't mind.'

'You haven't even asked him, have you? This is getting silly, Immi.'

'I can't exactly text or call him out of the blue to ask a favour, can I? And whenever I pop over it's so awkward face to face. There's no chance for the two of us to sit down together and talk like we used to do. With Daphne constantly hovering, he's as subdued as I am. If Tollie wasn't happy with the way things are now, then he'd soon say something, wouldn't he?'

'Of course he would. But in the meantime, you're just going to let this fiasco continue, which means he's going to assume that you don't think he's up to it.'

'That's not true. He's almost back to his old self and, I will admit, he seems happy enough. Perhaps this is the new norm for us and I have no choice other than to accept that's the case. Isn't that what you suggested?' I know I'm putting it rather bluntly, but I'm simply paraphrasing what Gray said. However, my feelings are still hurt and I'm not going to hide that fact.

'Well, let's hope that when we start getting around the table to plan this year's Santa Ahoy cruises things will get a little easier.'

That's tantamount to Gray admitting that Daphne's presence is increasingly becoming a real issue and it isn't just my imagination.

'Right, I must go,' I reply, nipping this conversation in the bud. 'What's on your agenda, today?'

Gray gives me one of his wicked smiles, his eyes shining. 'Today is all about the chocolate. They're rebranding an old favourite of mine and I need to write a jingle to match the new image. I'm lucky to get this job as they want to steer clear of the trend to align themselves with current popular music. Think of a less sensual version of the old crumbly and flaky ad.'

I raise my eyebrows in surprise. 'Good luck with that, then.'

Standing on tiptoe, I plant a kiss on his forehead and work my way down to his mouth. 'If anyone can pull it off, it's you.'

Poor Gray. His next big project has been delayed yet again and he's taking whatever work he can in the meantime. That wonderful little windfall of a bonus he received covered the cost of two new pieces of electronic kit to allow him to turn the spare bedroom into his studio. The rest is helping to repay our overdraft, but it won't last forever. At least he's at home every night, which is a big positive and to me it's worth more than money in the bank.

Trudging along the towpath trying to keep the umbrella from blowing inside-out isn't easy. Keeping my waterproofs at work probably wasn't the best idea, but I have a backpack with a spare set of work cargo trousers and a sweatshirt. I've always enjoyed getting my hands dirty and some of my fondest memories are when I worked at the nurseries every Saturday, potting on the seedlings and deadheading the plants. While I'm grumbling about the weather, I know we're going to have a lot of fun getting hands-on this morning and it will be an enjoyable couple of hours.

'Hey, Immi. It's a real battle against this wind, isn't it?' Patrick calls out as I draw level with the footbridge. Hiding behind the umbrella for cover, I didn't know he was standing there waiting for me.

'It's slow going, that's for sure. I keep thinking my umbrella is about to be tugged out of my hands. I didn't know you were in the office today,' I say, having to raise my voice to be heard.

He turns to mount the steps and I follow behind him until we are on the bridge itself and then we walk side by side, wavering at times as the crosswind hits us in an intermittent blast.

'Martin and I are updating the business plan today. It will take a couple of hours, at most. Ziggy gets spooked when it's windy and so I left her hiding under the bed.'

'Ah, poor thing. She's really taken to you, which I know is such a comfort to Val.'

I can't see Patrick's face, but I know he's enjoying having Ziggy around too.

The canal is quiet today and I notice that the roller doors are still shut on all but one of the units in the boatyard. I'm not looking forward to going out if it's like this tonight, but someone has to do it.

* * *

'How did it go at the Linden Hotel last night?' Sarah asks as we pile into Ursula's hallway, having left our soggy umbrellas in the porch. Tonight, we're trying on our dresses for the first time and I'm nervous about it.

'It was a wonderful dinner but I do hope they broke even, as the five-course meal was amazing by the looks of it. Everyone was impressed when they saw the artist's impressions of the play-ground. It raised ten pounds per head for the fund, and the fifty tickets sold simply by word of mouth apparently. And for the last month they've offered diners the option of adding a donation when they get out their credit card to pay their bill. In total, Harrison says it will probably amount to a figure in excess of seven hundred pounds once it's all tallied up.'

'That's great news. A few more events like that wouldn't go amiss,' Sarah adds as she follows Ursula through into the sitting room. 'Coffee mornings are fine, but it takes an awful lot of them to raise that sort of money.'

'Hi, ladies,' Martin says, immediately getting up off the sofa. 'I'll put the kettle on and leave you to it.' He stops to give Ursula a

quick kiss on the cheek. 'The kids are asleep. Coffee?' We all nod
gratefully. My fingers are cold, even though my body is still
glowing from the yoga class.

'Tonight's the night, then,' he says, looking in my direction.

'Yes, it is,' I reply, trying not to sound excited, or unduly
anxious.

'Right, let me take your coats. Who is going first?' Ursula asks.
I look directly at Sarah, who is more than happy to volunteer.

'I've been looking forward to this all day,' she admits.

'Follow me, then, Sarah. I'll hang these up on the way to my
workroom.'

To pass the time I go in search of Martin. 'I bumped into
Patrick yesterday morning. He said you were updating the business plan. How did it go?'

Martin continues scooping coffee granules into the mug.
'Fine. The cash isn't rolling in quite as quickly as I'd like, but
we're marching ahead. Thanks for your help yesterday morning.
It was such a miserable day and I felt bad not being able to get
out and help.'

'Oh, it was fine. We had a few laughs. With the new greenhouse and those polytunnels, which were a brilliant idea of
Patrick's, we've got so much more retail space.'

'Yes, he's on the ball, is Patrick. It's going to be a bumper
Christmas and once the playground is open that's going to draw
even more families here. Aysbury is really putting its name on the
map. I had a pint with Fisher the other night and he said he's
thinking of running some evening trips along the canal in the
run-up to the festive period.'

'Really? He hasn't said anything to me.' Goodness, I wonder
what Val will think of that.

'Here you go. I'd best leave the other two mugs here if they're
in the fitting room,' Martin says, throwing me a wink. 'It's time I

made myself scarce. I'm off to watch an episode of *Dragon's Den*. Perhaps I should consider taking part and try to get a dragon or two onboard.' He laughs.

'Aysbury first, then watch out UK,' I say, laughing.

'Okay, time for the big reveal,' Ursula calls out. Martin hands me a tray and I place all three mugs on it before we head in opposite directions.

'Good luck.'

'Thanks,' I mutter. 'I'm going to need it.'

As I edge through the partially opened door to the garage conversion, which is Ursula's workroom, I see Sarah is standing in front of a full-length mirror. She looks stunning as she turns around to face me. The silver-grey chiffon material has a slight shimmer to it. Falling to just below her knee, the A-line dress has two ruched panels at the top, which cross over, hugging her torso, and below that the skirt hangs down over her hips in gentle folds.

'Isn't it gorgeous? And I love these little pleats in the front. I'll be able to eat whatever I want and not worry if I bloat up!' Sarah exclaims, her face beaming.

'I love the sheer illusion of the capped sleeves and the way it carries on across the neckline. You've done an amazing job, Ursula.' I watch as Sarah turns back around quite nimbly on the balls of her feet, the fabric gently swishing around her legs. How I wish I could emulate the confidence and gracefulness that Sarah embodies.

'Well, I can't ask for a better reaction than that,' Ursula replies happily. 'I will need to adjust that neckline a little, but I'll leave that until the second fitting, a month before the wedding.'

'Oh, don't worry – I'll be jumping on the scales regularly to check I don't put on, or lose, any weight. It's only eleven weeks to go now.'

A chill runs down my spine. Eleven weeks to the wedding and

just over twelve weeks in which to make sure there's enough in the kitty to pay the final invoice for the playground. I hope everything comes together at the right time.

'Your turn next,' Ursula says brightly. 'Then I have some gorgeous fabric samples to show you. It will be freezing, and you are going to need a jacket, or a warm wrap at the very least. We can't have you catching cold while you're posing for photos alongside the canal, can we?'

'We should talk about hairstyles, too,' Sarah chips in. 'You said you didn't want a veil, Immi, but most brides wear something in their hair.'

They both look at me expectantly. How I wish my enthusiasm were on a par with that of my two friends. They're having fun and excited about looking through yet another round of pictures of gorgeous models looking impossibly glam, for ideas. My dress is going to be fabulous – I know it is – but the question is whether I can carry it off on the day, or will I end up feeling that I'm trying to be someone I'm not?

* * *

When I park up I'm surprised to see the cottage is in total darkness. As if by magic, as I approach the light goes on in the sitting area and I walk up to the glass doors, to peer inside. Gray walks over to let me in, smiling. 'I didn't think anyone was home,' I comment as I step through the door.

'And where else would I be at this time of night?' Gray looks at me askance as he throws a hand towel down onto the floor. 'We must get a mat if you insist on not using the front door when you're dripping all over the place.'

My eyes travel over his face and his hair looks damp. 'Were you in the shower?'

'Yes, that's why the light wasn't on. Anyway, how did it go?'

'Yoga was fine. And the dress is lovely.'

He looks at me, his face falling. 'You aren't pleased?'

'No. It really is lovely. I just don't feel lovely in it.' I groan, feeling bad.

'What did Ursula and Sarah say?'

'Oh, they adored it. It's not the dress, it's me. I was just a bit hot and my hair is a mess as the rain makes it frizzy.'

Gray steps forward, wrapping his arms around me.

'Look, Immi, it's important you feel comfortable. This is about what will make you happy on the day.'

'It'll be fine. It's just that... well, the constant rain is getting me down. There's only eleven weeks to go and decisions still need to be made about the jackets Sarah and I are going to wear, and I haven't even given any thought to our hair. We spent ages looking at magazines tonight. It's one decision after another and what looks good on a model won't necessarily look good on me!' My exasperation is impossible to hide.

'Hey.' He pulls me even closer to him. 'You have two choices. Either sit down and just choose something, or let Sarah and Ursula guide you. There is no wrong decision here because it's all about you. So what if in years to come you look back and say, "Did I really wear a tiara?" It doesn't matter. I'm not making light of what you're going through, but we're tying the knot and that's the important bit.'

'I know. But people come to a wedding with expectations and I don't want to let you down.'

Gray sighs. 'Oh, Immi, like that's going to happen. Whatever you wear, to me you are going to look gorgeous. If you don't feel comfortable in the dress, then I'm sure Ursula will understand. Just be honest with her.'

'But she's giving her precious time for free, Gray. And the cost of that and the fabric would be wasted. No, I'm being ridiculous and you're right. Neither Sarah, nor Ursula, are going to steer me wrong and it's silly to get this upset over a blooming dress.'

'I do believe they call it a wedding gown,' he prompts, making me laugh.

'See? I didn't even know that!'

'There's still time to make it a Christmas-themed wedding, you know. You could wear your elf outfit. You look damned cute in that.'

I lean back, staring up at him. 'That's a definite *no*. It's a wedding and not a pantomime! Even I know better than that.'

21

MONEY, MONEY, MONEY

'Right, folks, let's get started, shall we?' Tollie booms out, quietening everyone down. We booked the conservatory at The Bullrush because the Aysbury drama club are holding a dress rehearsal for their Christmas play in the village hall. As they are donating 50 per cent of the funds raised to the playground, we were more than happy to make alternative arrangements. 'Fisher, would you be kind enough to close the doors, please?'

It's wonderful to see Tollie looking so well. He's on good form tonight and, being able to sit back and watch as he's interacting with everyone, I feel as if I have my granddad back again. Gone is that strained look from the months and months of increasing pain and taking tablets just to get through each day.

'I think we should let Fisher kick off the meetin' as he has some news,' Tollie informs us, sitting back in his chair as we all turn to look at Fisher.

'That's right. We have a date for the work to start, and it's a little earlier than expected. Now don't panic, Immi, the target date for that last payment remains as agreed, by the end of December. But the work will commence a week on Monday.'

There's a sharp intake of breath from most of the people sitting around the table.

'The team will aim to have the job completed within five working days and that gives Tollie two full weeks to arrange for the technical support officer to carry out his inspection. The end is in sight.' Fisher, like Tollie, is positively beaming.

'I'm assured that all they will need is forty-eight hours' notice,' Tollie confirms, 'and I'll get back onto the solicitors to give them fair warnin'. It looks likely that even startin' the Santa Ahoy cruises a week early, the playground will be open, too.'

There's a little round of applause. This is the first meeting for a while where the full committee is in attendance and it's a landmark moment. Everyone is now looking in my direction.

'Before I talk about what's in the pipeline for our final push, I will hand over to Patrick, as our treasurer, to give us an update.'

It's the first time Patrick has joined us in his official capacity but he's more than earnt his place.

'Certainly, Immi. Well, I can confirm that 50 per cent of the outstanding balance was paid in mid-August, as agreed. The bank account balance currently stands at two thousand two hundred and forty-three pounds. That doesn't include this week's emptying of the collection boxes.'

It could be more, but it's not terrible.

'Thank you, Patrick. Right,' I begin. 'With the last payment of ten thousand five hundred and twenty-eight pounds as our goal, I'll run down the list of events already held where the money hasn't yet hit the bank. I don't know if everyone is aware that the Linden Hotel raised around seven hundred pounds from the charity dinner and discretionary donations. As far as I'm aware, that isn't included in the running total,' I pause, and look at Patrick, who nods in agreement. 'Five local primary schools will be holding a non-uniform day, thanks to Rona's contacts. Then there is a packed schedule through to the end of the third week in December in terms of small groups doing the rounds of church hall fairs et cetera, with collection buckets. And Adler's farm have already sold an amazing eighty-three tickets, at ten pounds a head, for the Winter Barn Dance. All proceeds from the ticket sales will be donated as Wes and his wife are footing the bill for the buffet.'

'That's very generous of them,' Tollie interrupts. 'I'll take a walk up and express our sincere thanks.'

Heads nod in agreement.

'And we're running a bar up at Adler's farm,' David joins in. 'Sales of The Bullrush Christmas Brew have already begun, and we will have a big display of it at the dance. We're able to donate 20 per cent this year due to increased production levels and we hope to far outdo the three grand we raised last year.'

Scribbling down the figures, I can feel people watching me anxiously. 'Obviously, it's not wise to count money until it's in the bank, but that alone, excluding the weekly collections, could swell the fund to close to seven thousand-pounds. With the proceeds from the Santa Ahoy cruises, Bernie's pop-up market and the car-parking charge we levy, we're not far off the magic figure.'

The relief around the table is tangible.

'If we pull this off, we will have succeeded in raising a whopping twenty-six thousand pounds in just under a year. It's amazing, truly amazing. Well done, everyone.'

Kurt stands. 'This deserves a drink on the house. Give me a moment and we'll make a toast.'

'No,' Tollie calls out. 'This is on me, Kurt. You were all plannin' a posh dinner in my honour and I talked you into this. I knew it was a lot to ask – well, I'd hoped the figure would be a bit smaller – but we pulled together. I'm very grateful to you all for the hard work, and the new playground is a fittin' way to mark the tenth anniversary of the Santa Ahoy.'

'It is that,' Kurt replies, giving Tollie a nod as he heads off to the bar.

Everyone begins talking at once, as we're all in high spirits. It would have been a bitter blow not to have been able to have the playground up and running in time so it just goes to show what a small group of people can achieve. This is Tollie's legacy and I couldn't be happier that he's about to see it come to fruition.

* * *

As the evening winds down, I start to pull on my coat, when I notice Fisher heading straight towards me.

'You're not going yet, are you? I was hoping to run something past you and Tollie.'

'Oh, um, okay. It's just that Gray is home alone.'

David is saying his goodbyes, which will leave just Fisher, Val, Tollie and me. I slip my coat over the back of the chair as Fisher indicates for us to join Val and Tollie, at the other end of the table.

'Val and I had a bit of an idea. Just in case the fund needs topping up, as we know that if it pours down with rain the pop-up Christmas market has in the past been cancelled. We were thinking of advertising evening cruises on The Star Gazer in November and December. There are a few things I'd need to sort first, like the insurance, but, as long as we cover the costs, any profit we make we'll happily donate to the cause.'

I glance at Val, who immediately turns to look at Tollie, totally avoiding my gaze.

'That's a great idea. Get in a bit of practice and see how it goes, eh? Gearin' up for retirement!'

Oh, Tollie. I wish you hadn't said that.

'Well, the idea might not turn out to be viable. But I needed to raise the subject tonight because I suspect Immi will be designing the flyers soon and thinking about advertising.'

'Yes. It's top of my list now. How soon will you be in a position to provide me with the dates and the full details?'

'Give me two days and I'll get them to you. It'll be Thursday and Friday evenings, I think. The only downside is making sure we leave the boat pristine for Santa and his elves to take over the next morning,' he says, smiling at me.

'It won't be a problem,' Val joins in. 'They'll just be sedate trips along the canal with a glass or two of wine and a selection of canapés,' she explains.

'Sounds a bit posh there, Val. Very upmarket,' Tollie remarks. 'I'll have to buy a ticket for Daphne and me.'

My stomach turns over. Daphne isn't going anywhere, then.

'Sounds like a plan,' Fisher says, turning to Val. I can see how excited he is and it's obvious she's doing this for him. Let's just hope it turns out well.

'I'd best get off, as Gray will wonder where I am.'

Fisher and Val give me a hug, then I walk around to Tollie. He stands and wraps his arms around me as he used to do, lingering for a while.

'You kept us all on our toes, m'dear, and we'll have you to thank when we hit that target. I've not been as active as I'd hoped, but from now on I'm back to normal.'

I leave them all chatting and as I walk home I can't help but wonder what normal means going forward when it comes to my relationship with Tollie. The trouble is that I can't see anything changing if Daphne is going to be a permanent feature in his life. Will I learn to become more accepting of the way things are, I wonder, or will the divide between us continue to grow? And as for the wedding, well, there's an awkwardness whenever Daphne is around, and if it doesn't go away then I fear it might spoil everything.

As I turn the key in the front door, it strikes me as a little odd that only the hall light is on. After hanging up my coat, I make my way upstairs, poking my head around the door of Gray's studio. He has his headset on and he's rocking from side to side as he fiddles with the massive panel of switches, knobs and sliders. I tentatively approach him; he spots the movement out of the side of his eye and slips off his headset.

'I didn't realise it was this late. How did it go?'

'Good news all round. Work begins on the playground a week on Monday and we're on target to hit that final payment if everything goes according to plan. Tollie paid for a round of drinks to celebrate.'

'That was generous of him. Did you two get to talk?'

'Not really. Anyway, I'm tired. Don't stay up too late,' I say as he stands to give me a kiss.

'It will get better, you know. Just give it a little time. And the pressure is easing a bit, then?'

I nod. 'Sort of, but it's time to get into Christmas mode. I'm going to be busy sorting schedules and arranging the advertising.'

'But once the last cruise is done and that final payment is made, you can then relax for a couple of days and get into wedding mode.' Gray looks at me and I see his expression change in an instant as it begins to sink in. 'Goodness, that clock really is ticking, isn't it? But... it's all under control.'

Did I detect a hint of hesitation in his voice?

'And your best man?'

Gray looks flustered. 'I'm still giving it some thought,' he replies cagily. 'I was going to ask Phil, but then I kinda thought, maybe I should ask Fisher?'

'That's a kind thought, but it's entirely up to you, Gray. Just don't leave it too long because if you're hiring suits you need to get that sorted.'

'I know. Rona and Val keep chasing me about it, as if I'm likely to forget. I'll sleep on it and make my mind up in the morning, I promise. Night, babe.'

Heading into the master bedroom, I don't turn on the light but make my way over to the window. Looking out across the patio, I see the lights are on in The Retreat. I remember all the nights when I slept there on my own. I didn't notice how lonely an existence it was, until I met Gray and he began staying over at weekends. Did Tollie feel as though he rattled around over there when he first moved in, too? After all, he's spent the last fifty years living in what was a two-bed, cosy little cottage.

'Oh, Grandma,' I whisper to myself. 'How am I going to get through this?' Staring around the new bedroom above the extension, I know this represents a fresh start for me. And, because Tollie has never lived in The Retreat, that's his fresh start. But even though we're still on each other's doorsteps, we might as well be miles apart. My heart aches because it feels as if that special bond between Tollie and me has been broken. Maybe forever. And there is nothing at all I can do about it.

22

AS THE AUTUMN LEAVES FALL, MY SPIRITS RISE

We return to a spell of sunny, dry days, but a sharp chill in the air overnight sees the leaves on the trees quickly changing hue. From the vibrant greens, which were beginning to fade, suddenly come the golds, oranges and yellows. Leafy mounds appear everywhere, whipped up by some strong winds to delight both children and dogs when out walking. The Cotswolds is beautiful in every season, but autumn is a truly glorious time. Usually I'd be outside, enjoying as many long walks as possible, but a sense of sadness seems to hover over me. My family is split, or that's how it's beginning to feel.

Gray flew off to LA again yesterday and will be gone for the remainder of the week. His new project is finally up and running, and while he was loath to leave me, knowing that I'm feeling down, we both knew there was nothing he could do. As I walk to work this morning, I tell myself that it's just a normal Monday and we're back in the old routine. But as I scan the trees, I don't take in their beauty, what I see is the starkness of winter looming. Days will get shorter and nights longer. Nights when, even when Gray's back from his trip, he'll be up in London and I'll be on my own again. Those were the times when Tollie would cook for us both and I'd do the washing up. Sometimes we'd watch a film together, or sit and chat in front of the fire. Simple things, but it meant a lot to me, to us both.

I stop in my tracks, staring up at the sky for a moment before I scan around. It's crisp this morning and as I breathe out it creates a little misty cloud of white. There is beauty all around; every day nature creates a new little miracle and the fact that I'm not seeing it is a red flag. I turn around and begin the walk back to the cottage, yanking the phone out of my pocket.

'Hi, Martin. Sorry to spring this on you, but could you possibly manage without me if I take an unscheduled day's leave?'

'Morning, Immi. Of course. You're not sick, are you?'

'No. Just running behind on the plans for the Christmas advertising and I'd really like to get it all wrapped up today.'

There's a pause. 'Fair enough. Gray got off all right, then?'

Martin is checking that I'm okay about it and I appreciate the thought.

'Yes. It's quite a relief to know that his project is finally about to gather momentum,' I reply contentedly.

'When's he due back?'

'He'll be home in the early hours of Saturday morning and he's taking the following Monday off.'

'Oh, good. I'll book a day's leave for you then, too, shall I?'

'Hmm... it's a busy time, Martin.'

'Don't worry about that. There isn't anything that can't wait. And if you need anything, Immi, you know where to come.'

I thank him, making a huge effort to sound upbeat, but Martin can clearly read between the lines. If I don't shake off this gloom quickly, I'm going to flounder, and there is no way I'm going to let anyone down. There's only one simple remedy and it's time for action.

* * *

I turn down the music while I make a quick call to Val.

'Morning. Sorry to bother you at the office, but I'm working on schedules today for the cruises. I was just wondering if you could give me an idea of how many silver tickets, plus guests, will be handed out this year, so I can calculate the number of trips to factor in.'

Val has contacts throughout the wider community with local charities, churches and schools identifying families with children who are true little stars – either because they have stepped up in troubled times, lost loved ones, or faced personal battles. She pulls together lists and for those nominated we issue silver tickets and run Santa Ahoy Little Stars Specials.

'If I give you a figure now, off the top of my head, I'd only be guessing. Sorry, Immi, I appreciate that it's a high priority, but I've had a few distractions recently. Do you need it right now, or can I email you the information tonight?'

Now would have been convenient but, given that Val is juggling so many things at the moment, I know she's doing her best. Working at the marina, keeping the wedding plans moving forward, her fundraising work, moving in with Fisher... there's a lot going on.

'Tonight will be fine, thank you. It's an extended programme this year anyway, so I'm sure we'll fit everyone in. Say hi to Fisher for me.'

'He's missing his gym buddy.' She laughs.

'Gym buddy?'

'Gray. Their Tuesday and Thursday night jaunts. Fisher is

determined to continue, though. He says it's giving him more energy. He was thrilled when Gray asked him to be his best man and at first he went along to support Gray, but now Fisher is really enjoying it.'

I'm shocked. Gray has been going to the gym?

'Well, that's a surprise which they kept very quiet. How funny! Anyway, take care, Val, and we'll speak soon.'

I push back on my chair, in need of another cup of coffee. Naturally, I've noticed the change in Gray's body shape, but I had no idea how much effort he was putting into it. And then I twig. Tuesdays I'm at yoga so he must have been rushing to get back here before me. That's why his hair was wet the other week. Thursdays he's been meeting up with Fisher for a pint at The Bullrush, except that's not what they've been doing. So the wedding madness is getting to him, which is a little sad as I love him exactly the way he is... And then it hits me – he loves me exactly the way *I* am, no matter what I wear. Gray tells me that all the time, but how often do I say it to him? Obviously not often enough.

As I wait for the kettle to boil I turn the music back up. My mood has shifted, and the dark cloud that has been hovering over me for a while now has been banished. Dancing around in my tracksuit bottoms and sloppy jumper to Slade's 'Merry Christmas Everybody' fills me with a sense of exhilaration. Magical things happen during the festive period because it brings out the best in most people. Those wintery nights are going to be fun when Gray is here *and* when he isn't. I'm going to keep myself busy, and watch and re-watch films that make me laugh, like *Home Alone* and *The Holiday*.

There's a sharp rap on the front door and I hope it's the gifts I've ordered for Sarah and Ursula, to hand out on the twenty-second of December. I must remind Gray to choose something for Fisher, and we still need to decide what to give Rona and Val. Flowers are lovely, but I'd rather we gave them a keepsake, I reflect as I swing open the door.

'Val? I thought you were at work,' I exclaim.

'I was, but Fisher suggested I pop in and get this sorted. He knows it's been on my mind and I feel remiss having let it slip. Is that Christmas music you're playing?'

'It is, it cheers me up! Come in. The kettle's on. Let me take your coat.'

'Sometimes living with the boss has its perks.' She smiles and I look at her, stifling a chuckle. This lady in front of me has changed so much in this last year and it's wonderful to see.

'While you're here could I ask for your opinion on something?'

'Of course!'

Val follows me inside and her eyes light up as the track changes and a choir begins singing 'O Come, All Ye Faithful'. 'This was one of my mother's favourite hymns.'

As her words sink in I realise with a jolt that she's talking about the grandmother I never knew.

'It is a beautiful song. I wish I'd known her.'

'Oh, Immi, that was tactless of me. I'm so sorry. It just popped into my head and I didn't stop to think.' Val looks mortified.

'No, no. Don't worry. Let me make some tea and we can sit down and have a chat before we sort out those dates.'

Val hesitates and I indicate for her to take a seat at the table. Turning down the volume on the music before I quickly make her an Earl Grey tea, I glance out of the corner of my eye as I watch her unpack her bag. She pulls out her iPad, a notebook and pen.

With my back to her, I begin talking. 'I was surprised but

delighted when Gray made the decision to ask Fisher to be his best man.'

'Oh, I assumed you were in on that,' she remarks.

When I turn around to carry the mugs over to the table, Val is watching me intently, and her sense of unease is obvious.

'No. But it made me think about our situation.'

Val begins fussing around to find something to use as a coaster, anything rather than look up at me.

'They're probably under that pile of paperwork,' I indicate, nodding my head, and she retrieves two of them as I continue. 'It feels wrong that you will be standing by Fisher's side and yet less than half a dozen people will know who you really are. And I'm not sure I feel comfortable about that any more.'

As I ease myself down on the chair opposite Val, she looks directly at me.

'Why?'

I take a deep breath. I didn't plan on having this conversation, even though the idea has been floating around inside my head for a while now. How does anyone know when they are ready to truly let go of the past? But I'm surprised to realise it feels right.

'Because when I introduce you to Gray's friends it's only right that I acknowledge you as my mother. And how can I do that, if our wider circle of friends is still in the dark?'

Val fiddles nervously with her hair and I can see she doesn't know how to respond.

'You're afraid that they won't understand?' I ask her, but I continue before she has a chance to answer. 'Rona knows what happened and she doesn't judge you. Neither do I. And Grandma and Tollie didn't either, once they knew how you'd suffered.'

There's sadness in her eyes, which is hard to bear.

'But your dad never forgave me, Immi, and I don't deserve... I mean... I don't believe that it's the right thing to do. I'm not thinking about myself here, because I hope by now you know exactly how much I love you and always have, since the moment you were born. But my illness caused me to abandon you and what if it's you people question, as they struggle to understand what happened? I can't put you through that.'

'I think the time has come to call you Mum and so that's going to be a bit of a giveaway, isn't it?'

Val's face visibly pales as we look at each other. 'Drink your tea. We can do this, Mum. Everything is going to be fine.'

* * *

'Hi, Daphne. I thought you might like these. It's the last of the rosebuds on the climber and their perfume is so gorgeous, it's a shame not to bring them indoors to be enjoyed.'

'Thank you, Immi,' she replies, taking them from me. Tollie appears behind her.

'Are you coming in?' he calls, over her shoulder.

'Only if it's convenient. You aren't about to go out, or anything?' I respond, hoping he'll say no.

'We're just sorting through the Christmas trimmings, actually. Come on in.'

As I follow Tollie inside, Daphne shuts the door behind us and disappears into the utility room.

'Goodness, it seems we're both having a Christmas fest today. I've been doing the schedule for the cruises.'

'How's it lookin'?' Tollie asks.

'Good. Packed and we're going to factor in three Little Stars cruises.'

'Amazin'. The toys for the kiddies are starting to come in and we're storin' them in the attic for the time bein'. It's goin' to be a bumper year by the look of it. That's why Daphne and I are sortin'' through these boxes to try to condense them and free up some space.'

I stand idly by, not sure where to sit, and Daphne breezes into the room with a small jug containing the roses.

'Are you staying?' she asks, looking directly at me. 'If you are, I'll make a drink.'

'No. It's just a quick visit.'

Tollie looks directly at me. 'There's news? What's goin' on?'

Oh dear. Maybe this isn't such a good idea, after all. I glance at Daphne and Tollie follows my gaze.

'Come on, Immi. I can tell from your face that you've got somethin' to say. What's said between these four walls goes no further,' he states firmly. I can see Tollie wants Daphne to stay, and I have no choice but to respect his wishes.

Tollie needs to hear this directly from me before word gets out.

'Val and I have decided it's time to share the secret.' His face doesn't alter, he simply extends his hand, indicating for me to take a seat on the sofa, but I continue standing. 'Really, I can't stop as I need to forewarn a few people before it becomes general knowledge.'

'I see. Well, the choice is yours, Immi. It'll be a shock, but you know that.' He sounds hesitant and I can understand his apprehension.

'It's bound to come out at some point and I'd rather it was before the wedding. As it's family and close friends only, Val... I mean, Mum, has had a key role in planning the wedding together with Rona, and it's only right to acknowledge how close we've become.'

He shrugs his shoulders. 'There'll be no goin' back once it's done.'

Daphne stands by, silently watching, but I notice that her face doesn't register even a hint of surprise. Has Tollie already talked to her about this?

'I wasn't sure I would ever get to this point, but I'm ready. And so is Mum. Gray will be in touch as you, him and Fisher will need to sort out the suits for the wedding.' I turn to face Daphne. 'The general colour theme is silver, grey and soft heather, as I'm not going for the traditional white. It won't be a big frothy dress and morning suit affair,' I offer, trying to engage her in the conversation.

'Daphne isn't coming to the wedding,' Tollie informs me and I turn around to look at him.

'I think it's for the best,' she adds. When I turn back around, she's wearing a pleasant smile as if she hasn't just dropped a bombshell. 'It sounds like it's going to be a wonderful event.' With that she places the jug of roses on the coffee table and heads for the door.

I feel as if I've just been slapped in the face. 'I'd... um... better go. Lots to do.'

As Tollie sees me out he stoops to place a quick kiss on my cheek. I can't help feeling he's disappointed by my decision about Mum, and that has thrown me. I thought after all these years he'd be glad to know that finally I'm acknowledging my mother, and I'm somewhat bewildered by his reaction.

NOVEMBER

23

A CEREMONY WITHOUT THE POMP

The excitement is building and the last month has flown by. Jade, Jude and I have dusted off our Christmas elf costumes and they are freshly pressed and waiting. The cruises begin tomorrow morning and we're doing two trips a day, every Saturday and Sunday through until Christmas, with three additional specials for our Little Stars silver ticket holders.

The padlock is still firmly attached to the gates of Aysbury's new playground, but this evening, as soon as Gray arrives, a small group of committee members will be gathering to affix a commemorative plaque to one of the benches.

'I'm nearly home, Immi,' Gray says the moment I pick up his call. 'I'm just driving past Adler's farm. The traffic was awful. Give me twenty minutes tops and I'll be there.'

'Listen, take care when you go through the avenue of trees. It's a little icy out there tonight. I'll start making up the thermos flasks. Love ya, honey.'

I immediately give Fisher a call. 'He's on his way. If you can let everyone know and get them to head down to the playground in about half an hour, that would be perfect. Thanks, and I'll see you in a bit.'

Mum is stirring the large pan of mulled wine and I'm heating hot chocolate in another one that Kurt kindly lent us.

'Is this looking chocolatey enough?' I ask her and she peers in.

'Hmm... it's a bit pale. Give it a taste.'

Pulling out a teaspoon, I gingerly take a sip. 'It's hot but it's too milky.' I add a whole heaped dessertspoonful of powder and give it a stir, but Mum looks at me encouragingly and I add another one.

'That's more like it.'

I turn the heat onto low and go in search of the disposable paper hot cups and lids, then pack them into one of the two wicker baskets.

'I wish Tollie had agreed to having his name on the plaque,' I murmur, thinking out aloud.

'I know, but he's just happy it's done, and tonight's little ceremony was a great idea of yours. He's not one for being the centre of attention, is he? Just like you.'

That thought makes me smile. A flicker of light flashes over the table and I look up, knowing that my man has just pulled up in his car and I can relax.

'Right, let's get pouring. I hope the others remember to bring the lanterns.'

By the time Gray rushes into the room we're all ready to go and he stands there beaming. Striding across, he throws his arms around my waist, lifting me off the floor.

'You're all coat,' he moans as it bunches up around me.

He lifted me with ease and when he puts me down, I poke him playfully in the rib area, although he's equally well wrapped up.

'I think it's more to do with that six-pack of yours,' I joke. He's lost his cuddliness now and I'm still trying to get used to the new, toned Gray.

'Don't sound so disapproving. How do you feel about me cutting my hair?'

I look at him aghast. 'Why?'

'For the wedding, remember? It's coming up.'

He walks over to Mum to give her a hug. 'How are you doing, Val?'

'Great, thank you, Gray.'

'Please don't cut your hair. I love it.' That shoulder-length, floppy jet-black mop of his really suits him. 'I won't recognise the man standing beside me when we say "I do" at this rate.' I'm only half-joking as I pick up the last of the thermos flasks and pack it into one of the baskets.

'Well, you need fattening up a bit, Immi. You've been working far too hard in my opinion and pre-wedding nerves tend to add yet another stress factor,' Mum joins in, a frown creasing her brow.

I catch her and Gray exchanging a brief look of concern. It's true that I've lost a fair few pounds recently, but that's probably down to the yoga classes and eating a little less due to tiredness. Winter makes me want to curl up in bed and sleep, not sit on the couch and munch away. I certainly am not lacking in body fat, that's for sure.

'Here,' he says, 'I'll take those. You ladies lead the way. It's a firm *no* to the trip to the barbers, then? I thought I'd try something more up to date, you know, shaved up the back and longer on the top.'

'If you're doing it for me, then please don't. You are perfect just as you are. But if you fancy a change, go for it. Who knows? It might feel like I have a new man in my life.'

We continue the banter as we walk along the towpath. The icy blast doesn't bode well for the temperatures overnight. We've already had a couple of hard frosts, and I always worry about black ice. Not only is it dangerous, but if people can't get to Aysbury through the narrow lanes, then our bountiful Christmas celebrations could fall flat. Think positive, Immi, I tell myself sternly. Adler's farm has extra staff on call this year and, as usual, they are more than prepared to make us proud if the snow begins to fall.

'Did you remember to bring the plaque?' Gray enquires when we're literally only a few paces away from the playground.

'I did. It's in my pocket and Tollie is bringing a drill, and some screws. Ah, don't the lanterns look wonderful?' I exclaim as Gray swings open the gates and we step through.

Waving across to Kurt, Fisher, Rona, Abe, Ethel, Martin and Patrick, who are standing in a huddle, I can see that they are in good spirits and the laughter is raucous.

'It's all official now,' Tollie calls over his shoulder. 'My solicitor confirmed this morning that the legal agreement with the parish council for the transfer of the playground, and the land, is now complete.'

'Well, better late than never. And it'll be open tomorrow, which will make all the hard work worthwhile.'

'Can you hold that lantern a bit higher?' Tollie instructs Fisher, a screw now tucked between his lips. How many times have I warned Tollie about doing that? Old habits never die.

'Here's the plaque.' I hold it out, stepping forward, and Tollie turns to look at me, taking the screw out of his mouth.

'I'm just doin' the guide holes. Nearly there.' He takes the little package from me and as we look at each other it's a special moment. 'It's goin' to look grand on this bench,' he adds softly.

While the others help to pour out the drinks, Fisher and I

stand watching Tollie finishing off drilling the holes and then screwing the plaque in place. In the golden hue from the lantern, it sparkles.

'We're ready, folks,' Tollie says, straightening, and I can't help but reflect that this task would have been impossible for him six months ago. The old Tollie is back. 'Gather around. I feel a speech comin' on.'

'Mulled wine, or hot chocolate, Tollie?' Mum asks.

'Hot chocolate, please, Val. That will go down a treat.' He takes the cup from her with a genuine smile.

'My goodness, this day has finally come and it's humblin'. Ten years ago, I had this crazy idea and all my friends and family jumped on board with me, literally.' Tollie pauses and there's a groan, followed by laughter. 'How many children and parents have joined us on The Santa Ahoy Special is almost impossible to count, but, when all is said and done, we've brought smiles to faces and succeeded in spreadin' the Christmas joy. This toast isn't just to us, but to every single person who made this play-ground a reality.'

'Read what it says on the plaque, Tollie,' Kurt prompts him.

Tollie turns to begin reading, as Fisher raises up the lantern to illuminate it:

> To commemorate the 10th anniversary
> of The Santa Ahoy Special
> and everyone who sailed in her.

'Your name isn't on there?' Abe points out, as if it's something we've overlooked.

'No, it isn't. If you want to put my name on somethin', then when I'm dead and gone you can stick it on the other bench. But I ain't dead yet and I hope I have a good few years left in me!' With that he bursts out laughing and we all join in.

'To Aysbury and the children whose voices will fill the air with their laughter as they revel in using this playground, and to you all, for your sterlin' efforts.'

We raise our cardboard cups and there isn't a dry eye amongst us.

* * *

It's going to be a long night, but I don't care. A little group of us are aboard The Star Gazer and it's time to turn it into The Santa Ahoy Special.

'It's so kind of Kurt to let us use one of his lock-up garages to store the presents, and bits and pieces for the trips,' Mum remarks as we clear the kitchen area.

'How are the *Cruise in Style* evenings going?' I ask tentatively. The fact that she hasn't mentioned them at all, and they've been going for three weeks now, is probably telling.

Mum looks around, anxiously, to see if anyone is within earshot, but Abe is busy adding more wood to the stove, while Fisher and Tollie are checking the lights for the three small Christmas trees. There's some head-scratching going on and only one set is working, which is par for the course and happens every year like clockwork!

'It was awful at first, Immi. Those first couple of trips were a nightmare. I tried everything – ginger capsules, some herbal tablets and even patches I bought at the chemist and nothing worked.'

'Why didn't you just tell Fisher? How are you going to get through this next round of trips?'

She shakes her head. 'To see his face when he's on board tells me how important it is to him. Anyway,' she eases back the sleeve of her jumper, 'acupressure helped, so I bought these bands. They have a small plastic bead sewn into them and you simply slip them on and make sure the plastic ball is about two finger widths away from the wrist.' She looks pleased with herself.

'And it works?'

'Yes. Mostly. Towards the end of the evening I sometimes feel a bit wobbly, but it's okay. If I can survive until Christmas, then I will have proved to myself I can do it.'

Poor Mum, she's trying so hard. Fisher is totally oblivious to what she's putting herself through because she's determined to overcome her issues with nausea and dizziness, rather than disappoint him.

'Have you thought about hypnotherapy?' I suggest. 'There's a woman in Stroud who practices various holistic therapies, but she began as a hypnotherapist. I only know of her because one of the guys who used to work in the boatyard was telling me about his wife. She had a fear of spiders and I mean a debilitating fear. If she saw one in the house she'd begin screaming and, even after he took it outside, she could barely sleep for a week as she'd imagine it crawling between the sheets on her bed.'

'That's awful.'

'I know. He said this lady traced it back to a prank that his wife's brother had played on her as a child when he put a plastic spider under her pillow. But after three sessions with the hypnotist, while she still doesn't like spiders, she doesn't freak out any more. And she can even put a glass over one, slide a piece of paper underneath and release it into the garden herself.'

'Hmm. That might be worth a try.'

'I'll get the number for you. There's no point suffering in silence if there's something that can be done about it. Although, you could just be honest with Fisher, as it's not your fault.'

Mum looks down in the mouth. 'I do enjoy being on the boat, I just don't like what the constant movement does to my stomach and my head. It's lots better if I'm wearing the bands and if I start to feel really nauseous, then there are other pressure points that give almost instant relief.'

'Is this wedding talk I'm interrupting?' Neither of us were aware that Abe was heading in our direction.

'Of course,' I reply jovially. 'We were wondering if you were going to turn up in your penguin onesie.'

He grins at me. 'Nope. That's for the kids only. Anyway, this year I'm coming as a Christmas pudding.'

Both Mum and I burst out laughing as I place my hand on his arm, giving it a squeeze. 'Oh, Abe, I can't wait to see that! Did you know that we're having a fairy this year, too? The twins are going to take it in turns as we only have the one costume. I think there's something special about a magic wand, isn't there?'

'Ah, the little ones are going to love that. Anyway, the stove is pumping out the heat – what do you want me to do next?'

'Well, we're nearly finished clearing up here, so if you'd like to dig out the boxes of baubles for the trees, Mum and I can begin unpacking them. How are the lights going?' I whisper, leaning in close.

'Not well. You know what it's like checking every single bulb, and it's always the one you miss!'

Abe heads off to the lock-up and as Val wipes down the kitchen worktops Ethel calls out, 'I've got the pinecones, Immi. Shall I leave the basket on one of the tables?'

'Perfect, thank you, Ethel.'

'I assume we're not going to trim up the outside in the dark, so is it an early start tomorrow?' she asks.

'Eight thirty. That gives us two and a half hours until it all kicks off, which should allow time for Tollie, Gray and me to change into our outfits.'

'Great, I'll see you in the morning. I'm off to bake the cupcakes and gingerbread men, then. Sleep well, all.' Ethel heads off for what promises to be hours of non-stop baking.

'Have you picked the greenery?' Mum asks.

'No. Gray and I are getting up tomorrow at six thirty to head over to the copse. Last year we were a little more organised.'

'Make sure you both wrap up well and wear some gloves.'

It's funny, but Val would never have said that to me, but my mum is beginning to open up and show her true nature. I always wondered why I was such a worrier and now I guess I know. It's in my genes.

When the alarm goes off, Gray throws his arm around me and snuggles in. The heat of his body is comforting and in such contrast to the empty longing I feel whenever he's away. I'm always a little on edge until he's back here with me, as if he's the last piece in the jigsaw puzzle that is my life and it's not complete without him.

'It's time to get up,' I whisper, trying to sound enthusiastic. 'We need to go foraging.' I am excited, but the thought of going out into the cold makes me pull the duvet up over my head.

Gray follows suit and we lie, side by side, in the darkness.

'How are we going to be able to see what we're cutting?' he points out.

'By the time we've had a cup of coffee and a slice of toast, showered, thrown on our clothes and traipsed over there, it's going to be seven thirty. The sun will be waking up and we'll get to savour the magic of a brand-new morning. Aren't we lucky?'

'If you say so. Does that mean we can have another five minutes?'

'No. Come on. Everyone is going to be waiting for us at eight thirty sharp, as there's a lot to be done. Stir your lazy bones,' I instruct him as I hop out of bed.

'Is the heating on? It's f... freezing!'

Gray pulls the pillow over his head as I yank on my dressing gown and go downstairs to check the thermostat.

'It's on eighteen degrees,' I call out, scandalised.

'Well, it was hot last night lying on a blanket in front of the log burner. You said you were sweating, and that's why I turned it down.'

I ramp it up and head off to make breakfast. Gray is not a morning person, whereas the moment I open my eyes I want to get up and get started. Twenty minutes later he appears and joins me, as I stand looking out into the gloom.

'I told you it would be too dark.'

'It's getting lighter by the minute,' I point out, my eyes glued to the horizon. The narrow band of opaque sky is beginning to grow, and it looks as if it's going to be a bright day. Hopefully the sun will quickly melt the frost, as it climbs in the sky. But for now, it's going to mean layers of clothes and padded coats if we don't want to freeze our socks off.

'You love it, don't you?' Gray turns to look at me, his hands wrapped around his coffee.

'Every second of it. From picking the greenery, to decorating the trees, to seeing Abe announcing that Santa has arrived. What's not to love?'

'There's a little kid inside each of us, but sometimes we forget that,' he murmurs, leaning in to kiss my lips and lingering for a moment. 'Come on. This is going to be fun.'

As we scurry around getting ready, Gray demolishes an entire pile of toast while I start my day with just a coffee as food is the last thing on my mind. I know I'll probably be ravenous by eleven, which will spoil my lunch if I then start snacking; I really do need to get back into a proper routine. Tollie wouldn't have let me get away with it, and I miss his eagle-eyed, razor-sharp reproaches.

'Here are your boots. I'm wearing two pairs of socks,' Gray warns, looking down at my ankle-length trainer socks.

'Don't worry, I'm not wearing these. Give me a minute. The jute sacks and the secateurs are under the stairs if you can dig them out.'

There's something magical about stepping out into a frosty, bright morning when your body, head and toes are toasty and only your face is exposed to the chill. We stop for a moment to adjust each other's scarves, to cover our mouths. Gray winds mine around me like I'm a bobbin and as it's one of Ethel's never-ending, hand-knitted ones, he finds it amusing. It is a bit claustrophobic, but it's a gift I treasure and enjoy wearing.

'Don't make fun of me,' I whisper as we head out through the gate.

There are no lights on in The Retreat, I notice. There aren't even any dog walkers, which is unusual. A few of the regulars are usually out and about this time of the morning, even on a Saturday.

As Gray helps me over the stile, I jump down the other side and take the sacks and the tools from him. Looking around, I notice there's a grey mist, which is threaded like a ribbon through the large oak trees at the far end of the meadow, where the cultivated fields begin.

'You're right, it was worth getting out of bed to see this,' Gray comments as we stand in awe of the myriad colours reflecting off the rays of the watery sun. With the panel of pale grey sky now turning a muted gold, it's like a little line of fire far off in the distance. 'Let's do this.'

The grass beneath our feet crunches and we leave a trail of

footprints as we trample over it. The wild summer flowers are long gone, but dried stems poke up out of the earth like straw-coloured sticks and, here and there, clusters of dried wild thistles sparkle where the frost has settled on the spiky heads.

'Do you hear it?' Gray turns to look at me, pulling his scarf away from his mouth.

'What?'

'The sound of peace and quiet, of stillness. Well, if you strain your ears, I can hear something rustling over in the hedges, but it's probably a bird. But no cars, no voices, no planes, no tractors.'

'Everyone's in bed. Except for us.'

'They don't know what they're missing.' He leans forward and I begin to loosen my scarf until it slips down around my neck. Tilting my chin upwards with his fingertips, Gray smiles down at me. 'I love you, Immi Tolliman, soon to be Mrs Immi Adams, or maybe you'd prefer Mrs Immi Tolliman-Adams,' Gray remarks, frowning as he considers it.

'Maybe I'll change back to Imogen once I'm married. Mrs Imogen Adams sounds rather posh, doesn't it?'

He shakes his head. 'You'll always be my Immi – Imogen just isn't you!'

I push my hands against him, urging him to walk on. 'Come on, we don't have a lot of time. I want some of these feathery branches, but don't cut them all from the same bough,' I instruct him, reaching out to snag one and pull it closer. 'The fragrance these pine needles give off is simply beautiful.'

'Hold still.' Gray begins snipping and when he moves on, I quickly scoop them into one of the sacks. It doesn't take long to fill it to the brim, with long trails of ivy, clippings from a cluster of overgrown laurel bushes and a few cuttings from a blue spruce.

'We need some holly,' I remind him.

'Hand me the sack and I'll hang it from this branch. We'll pick it up on the way back.' It might take a while to find some with a decent number of berries on it, so we'd better start walking a little faster.'

I follow on behind him, revelling in the way the sun's low rays filter like little orbs of light between the leaves and boughs of the trees around us. You can almost feel nature waking up and the silence is now broken with the raucous calls of blackbirds squabbling and the snapping of twigs, no doubt by rabbits scurrying away as we approach.

When we were here foraging last Christmas, we were looking forward to our engagement, and now the wedding is almost upon us. I will no longer be a Tolliman, and it will truly be the end of an era for me, and for my family. I wonder if that thought has occurred to Tollie.

* * *

The atmosphere on board The Star Gazer is one of frenetic activity. Ethel, Rona and Mum are inside sorting out the little snack boxes for the children and I'm outside with Fisher and Tollie, tying on the greenery to make the magical transformation from The Star Gazer into The Santa Ahoy Special. Gray has gone off to fetch the toy sacks to store them temporarily in the lock-up.

'She looks a treat every year, doesn't she?' Tollie says to Fisher.

'I like to take good care of her,' he says with pride.

'The decorations won't get in your way for your evening jaunts up and down the lock?' Tollie remarks.

'We could rig it differently so it will come off in long lengths. It wouldn't take long to whip them off and put them back on again in the morning,' I offer, feeling remiss that I didn't even give that a thought.

'It's fine, perfect, in fact. Gives it a bit of atmosphere and Val will want to be adding mince pies to the savoury platters, no doubt,' Fisher replies. 'Every trip is a bit of a learning curve for us both.'

I bet it is. 'Right, would you guys mind if I head back to shower and change? Mum has kindly offered to help in The Bullrush whenever the girls are here. They're busy already and the car park is full. Is there anything either of you need?'

'No, we're fine m'dear. Get off and have a warm-up.' I stand on tiptoe to kiss Tollie's cheek and he seems amenable.

'I'll finish up here with Tollie, then stoke up the log-burner as Santa will be wanting to get himself ready.' Fisher and I exchange smiles.

'See you in a bit, guys.'

Pulling my bobble hat down over my ears and yanking the gloves out of my pocket, I step off onto the towpath and stand for a moment looking at our handiwork. She's a proud vessel and immaculate. Fisher spends hours and hours polishing the brass rails and is constantly touching up her paintwork. And now, decked in her Christmas finery, she looks like a floating sleigh. Once the gangplank is in place and the lock-side Christmas tree is standing alongside her, the only thing missing will be Mum dressed in her fake white fur coat and jaunty red beret, taking the tickets. She always looks like a cross between Mother Christmas and a polar bear, which the kids love.

I turn and hurry back in the direction of Lock Keeper's Cottage when Patrick falls in beside me.

'I won't stop you as I know you're busy, but I was expecting a cheque from Harrison and it still hasn't arrived.'

'Oh. That's strange. Check with Fisher. I don't suppose the Linden Hotel paid it directly into our account? They have the details because they did an afternoon tea fundraiser back in the summer.'

'Ah, right. No problem, I'll double-check. Is everything all set up? It certainly looks the business.'

We're weaving in and out of people, as word has spread that the playground is open and everyone seems eager to check it out.

'Thanks, it's hard work, but worth it.'

'I'll leave you to it, but if you need anything, you only have to shout. Maybe see you later at The Bullrush, then. Bye for now.'

It's such a relief knowing that Patrick has his finger on the pulse.

'Oh,' he says, turning back around. 'The non-uniform day raised a total of four hundred and twenty-two pounds. The teachers dressed up, as well.'

'Ah, that's wonderful, Patrick. Thanks for letting me know.'

My toes are tingling with cold as I stride off, and all I can think of is standing in the shower under that flow of warm water and grabbing a hot chocolate, before I transform myself into Santa's chief elf.

* * *

This moment always makes my heart sing and I'll never tire of savouring these precious memories. Mum is standing next to The Santa Ahoy Special, beaming from ear to ear, as she begins to work her way along the queue, clipping tickets and handing them back. The children grasp them in their hands as if they won't be allowed on board if they lose theirs, and even the children-in-arms reach out with glee, not wanting to be left out.

Mum is the warm-up act and when her task is done, she addresses the small crowd of children and their parents.

'Good morning, everyone! We're so excited as we're expecting some special visitors this morning.' She moves closer, lowering her voice just enough to make the children draw nearer. 'But to get on board, we need to ask the captain's permission first and I can't see him anywhere.'

Eager eyes search around and even the adults turn their heads.

'Oh dear! Do you think he's fallen asleep? We must wake him up immediately!' Heads start to nod. 'After the count of three, repeat after me, as loud as you can – "Wake up Captain Gray!" One... two... three!'

The chorus of voices is wonderful to hear and suddenly the doors to The Santa Ahoy Special swing open and Gray appears.

He looks so official in his navy-blue uniform, decorated with gold buttons imprinted with an anchor, and four bright yellow stripes embroidered onto the cuffs. The white cap really suits him with its navy peak, gold braid and anchor badge, but my face drops. While he does look every inch a seafaring captain, where is that long, curly hair of his? I have never known Gray to tie it up and I glance at Mum, frowning. She simply shrugs her shoulders rather guiltily. He's standing at the entrance to the gangplank now, with his legs firmly planted on the towpath and arms linked behind his back.

I hurry forward to the head of the queue, sporting my bright-green fitted tunic and woollen trousers, black belt, red and white striped hat, holding a clipboard firmly in one hand.

'Permission to come aboard, Captain!' I boom out, theatrically, trying not to look as though I'm fixating on the lack of hair around his shoulders.

'Permission granted,' he replies, saluting me, and as I encourage the children to filter inside he salutes each and every one of our arrivals in true nautical fashion. The kids are absolutely loving it.

Next, they are greeted by Jude. Today Jude is on the elf team, wearing a green elf dress with a red pointy collar and a red bobble hat. Kurt and the girls made them last year and, while it was knee-length back then, she's grown a good couple of inches in twelve months. Her red and white striped leggings are reminiscent of candy canes and she offers everyone a warm welcome. She ushers us all inside quickly to keep in the heat, taking coats and handing them to Ethel to hang up in the stern.

'This is Jude, everyone,' I call out. 'My assistant. We work very closely with Santa. Now slip off your coats and make yourselves comfortable.'

All but two of the children sit down on the handmade rug donated by Ethel and Abe. It took them two winters to make it, using small strips of fabric pulled through the base material, which is a heavyweight hessian. It's seven feet by eleven, and the kids love the textures. I often spot them running their fingers back and forth against the various fabrics as they sit watching Santa. It covers the open area in front of Santa's bench seat.

Ethel steers the parents over to the banquette seating booths, so that the tiny ones can run up and down in the gangway if they get restless. Gray turns to shut the doors and keep the heat in and my jaw drops for a moment. So it's true – his lovely hair is gone and the back has been shaved, right up to his cap. Only a few curls show beneath the peak as he turns back around. He does look achingly handsome, but my heart is pounding as I turn back to face my audience.

The soundtrack kicks in on cue, as Ethel get things started, and this year Gray has recorded some magical-sounding riffs. A soft tinkling gradually gets louder and louder, until suddenly Jade appears in her fairy costume waving a magic wand.

'Hello, everyone. Are we ready to have some fun?' Heads turn as the children follow her every movement. She looks like a ballerina in her pale blue dress with a long, chiffon skirt and pale blue satin slippers. Her wings are just big enough to poke up above her shoulders an inch or two, and on her head is a twinkling tiara. But it's her magic wand as she waves it gently back and forth that fascinates them all.

Making her way along the gangway, she walks around the edge of the rug to join me. 'This is Jade, and she's come to sprinkle a little fairy dust around for us today—'

'Hush!' Gray puts a finger to his closed lips, looking wide-eyed at his excited audience. 'I heard a noise up on deck.'

The silence is immediate as everyone stops talking to hold their breath and listen. Suddenly there's a sharp rap on the door, which prompts a little chorus of excited shrieks.

Gray waits a moment or two longer, until the backing track changes and suddenly the cabin is filled with the sound of sleigh bells jingling. A few moments later, he swings open the double doors, letting in a blast of chilly air. Santa looms up, stooping as he steps inside and letting out a jolly, 'Ho! Ho! Ho! Merry Christmas, everyone!'

One of the littlest ones throws her hands up to her cheeks, her jaw dropping as she stares in wonderment. Tollie makes the most amazing Santa, even though it's mostly padding. His naturally white moustache and beard, topped off by a very realistic curly white wig, is the image I remember from my own childhood. Rosy-cheeked and with an expression of pure joy on his face, he doesn't just look good, he looks real.

'I'm thrilled you could all come to see me today. And how colourful you look. We have jumpers with snowflakes on them and even one with my face on it! What's your name?' Tollie asks, indicating for the little boy to stand up and show everyone.

'Toby, Santa. And my grandma knitted this jumper.'

Bless him, he's probably four years old, at most, and his eyes are shining.

'Well, tell your grandma from me that Santa says she did an

amazing job, will you?' His baritone voice is both gentle and jovial as the little boy sits down, crossing his legs, his face the picture of happiness.

'My chief elf, Immi, will be writing down your requests ready to take back to the North Pole,' Santa informs them. 'And her helpers, Jude and Jade, are here to make sure everyone has a really good time. Shall we ask Captain Gray to up anchor and cast off?'

Everyone is still, following Santa's gaze at he looks towards the doors and Gray, who is standing in front of them. There's a little excited chatter until Gray cups his hand around his right ear. 'Did you hear that?' he asks in a semi-hushed tone, stabbing his index finger up towards the cabin-top. Everyone falls silent once more. Something scrapes along the top of the cabin, followed by a succession of hollow tapping sounds, and eyes open wide in wonderment. Jade and Jude are now on the mat alongside the children, egging them on.

'Do you think it's Rudolph and the sleigh?' Jude asks, and the children's eyes widen even further in anticipation.

Santa claps his hands. 'I wondered when my friend Rudolph would arrive with the presents. Captain Gray, can you do the honours, please?'

Gray swings open the doors to the cabin once more and Abe, dressed in his Christmas pudding onesie, with a knitted green hat and a large sprig of holly on the top, waves at the children, before handing Gray the first sack.

'Sorry we're late, Santa. It's a long journey and we had to stop for a snack, as the reindeers were hungry. Rudolph sends his apologies. Hi, girls and boys.'

There's a chorus of 'Hi' back as Gray lifts the sacks over the children's heads to stack them alongside Santa's bench seat. We're full to capacity and there isn't an inch spare, but no one's complaining.

'Right, it's time to get under way,' Gray declares as he disappears out of view.

I change the backing track to fill in the time it takes for Abe to pull up the anchor and cast off, while Gray heads out to take up his position at the tiller.

Jude and Jade hand out printed lyric sheets and glow sticks to the parents and children, as the first of the Christmas songs begins to play.

'Who's going to sing along?' I ask.

Hands fly up into the air as the opening strains of 'Rudolph the Red-Nosed Reindeer' fill the air.

There's a lot of arm waving, much wriggling about and – most importantly of all – a sea of smiling faces. The drone as the engine kicks into life signals the start of our little forty-minute cruise up past the marina to the junction and back.

I leave Jade doing a wonderful job of taking the children up to talk to Santa one at a time, to share what's on their Christmas wish list. Jude, wearing her serious face, diligently makes notes on my special clipboard.

Tollie is doing what he does best and it warms my heart. Our real-life Father Christmas jokes and laughs out loud in genuine merriment. He's just a big kid at heart and his rotund belly jiggles as if it really is a part of him. He was made for this role and the kids and adults alike are enthralled – and not a single electronic device in sight! Even the parents have switched off their phones and are content to sit back and enjoy the trip.

Ethel and I begin handing out the snack boxes and I wish Mum were here, rather than heading to The Bullrush to help Rona do some waitressing while the girls take part. At least she has her two feet planted very firmly on solid ground, but she's missing out on the fun and I know she'd love this. I hope Mum uses that number I texted her, as anything is worth a shot. The atmosphere on board is magical and we didn't need fairy dust to make that happen. It just bubbled up naturally in the hearts of each and every child here. As adults we're transported back to our own childhoods and, hopefully, golden memories of equally wonderful moments.

DECEMBER

25

TRIMMING THE TREE AND DRESSING UP

I survey the pile of boxes Gray and I just carried down from the attic. Then I look across at the naked blue spruce tree standing in the centre of the glass doors which look out over the patio to the rear of the cottage.

'Are you sure you have the energy to trim up tonight?' he asks, and I can tell that he's half hoping I'll say no.

'Gray! It's the sixth of December already and we're getting married on the twenty-second. With the next two weekends taken up with cruises, unless you expect me to do it all myself while you're in London, this is it. I want it to look special, because this is the one Christmas we can lock ourselves away, and it will be just you and me. Besides, I have way more decorations than you, and we need to whittle them down.'

I find myself staring longingly at the fireplace, which looks like a sad gaping hole.

'You want me to light it again, don't you?'

Even Bert the stag, standing on guard, looks a little dismayed. 'I do and he needs some holly, or something,' I say, pointing in Bert's direction.

We bought a plush rug to place in front of the hearth and the last couple of Friday evenings we've scattered the cushions around, to lie in front of it and watch the flames. With the new open-plan layout, it's not quite the same cosy setting as when the sitting room was separate and Grandma and Tollie would sit in their armchairs either side of the fire. But it's festive and the glow and warmth of the flames cheer a dark winter's evening.

'I'll turn off the heating and you do the honours. Then we'll make a start.'

When I return to the room Gray is already on his hands and knees. Lighting fires is an art and he's getting better at it, but it's still a bit hit and miss at times.

I begin opening the boxes and think back to last year. I remember only too well how the pressure was on. Our closest family and friends were coming to The Retreat for a Christmas dinner that doubled as our engagement party. Hanging fresh bunches of greenery from the large oak beams and having a floor-to-ceiling Christmas tree made it special but I'm a little at a loss about what will look right in here. The furniture is still rather sparse, as, although Gray has had the upfront payment for his current project, we used a part of it to pay off the overdraft.

As I ponder the best way to decorate this large space, I realise I may still be in shock after the way Gray surprised me yesterday, without any forewarning whatsoever. He suddenly appeared with my coat in his arms, saying we had an appointment and we needed to hurry. We were still dressed in our Santa Ahoy costumes, and he whisked me off to see our parish vicar, Mr Golding, and a solicitor, to swear an oath and sign an affidavit. My dream of getting married in Aysbury's little parish church, St James's, is going to come true!

'How did you know you could apply for a special licence at

such short notice?' I'd asked, looking at Gray questioningly. He'd turned to grin at me.

'I didn't. I was talking to Val, saying that it didn't feel right having the ceremony at the village hall. She felt the same way, so she rang the vicar. Mr Golding confirmed that the banns need to be read over three consecutive Sundays and we only have two left, but when she told him that your heart wasn't really in the civil ceremony, he asked to talk to me. He explained the process, and I think you must have a fan there, Immi, because he really did make it all happen. Val and Mum sent our guests a little note to make them aware of the change of venue and the whole thing turned out to be a lot simpler than either your mum, or I, imagined.'

It made me realise that I'm not the only one who's a bit of a traditionalist, and that Gray feels the exact same way. He heads over to stand behind me, wrapping me in his arms, and I stop what I'm doing as he peers inside the open box at my feet.

'Oh... not the dreaded lights. Tollie sorted those last year.'

'You're the man of the house now,' I inform him with a wicked grin.

'Guess I am.'

'I'm thinking less is more this year. It's not a cop-out, but, until we manage to get all the bits and pieces we want to make the cottage more homely, I think we should focus on the tree, the table and some sort of big, green extravaganza over there in the corner. It looks so empty at the far end of the room, doesn't it? The problem is that the entire wall of glass turns into a mirror at night, and there isn't a lot in the reflection, is there?'

'My darling Immi. I promise that when this project is done, and the rest of the money comes in, we will go shopping. Or, at least, you'll generate a list of items online and we'll place those orders.' He gives me one of his goofy grins and I stare at him. 'What?'

'Your hair still comes as a bit of a shock,' I reply, making a sad face. 'It takes a lot of getting used to.'

The top is still a mass of curls that flop down over his forehead a little, but the back is very short. He does look handsome and cute, but it's a different sort of cute.

'It's my new image. I'm not that guy who scribbles tunes on paper napkins any more, Immi. Once the film hits the cinemas my name is going to be out there. And, most importantly of all, I'm about to become a husband. Our life is changing, and good things are coming.'

Well, at least the new haircut isn't just a silly thing he did for the wedding, as that would have been crazy.

'I know,' I murmur, pushing back against him. 'It's time to take control of the Christmas lights then!'

He groans as I pass him the first box. 'There are another two of those, but thankfully we'll only need two sets of lights for that tree. Why did you buy such a big one?'

Gray looks at me timidly. 'It's a guy thing. Who wants to be seen carrying off a little tree, when you can strap a monster onto the roof of your car and pretend you don't look like a total idiot?'

That makes me laugh. 'If you're an idiot, at least you're *my* idiot,' I declare lovingly. 'If we sort the tree and the table tonight, then we can laze in front of the fire for an hour or two. I'll find something to brighten up that corner during the week.'

'Don't you have a dress fitting?' Gray asks, frowning.

'Tuesday, after yoga.' When I know Ursula will be telling me off. I had to make yet another hole in my elf belt as my waist just seems to be getting smaller. I'm on the go all the time but it's mince pie season and, hopefully, I'm about to begin putting a little of what I've lost back on.

Once Gray has finished untangling the lights and checking that they're all in working order, he carries in the tall stepladder. As I feed the string of bulbs to him, I keep up a constant narrative.

'The section you just wound around the top is coming undone,' I warn him, 'and don't overstretch!'

There is a little moaning along the way when sharp ends of the little needles catch him unawares, but eventually we stand back, and as the little white lights twinkle we're beaming. Last year Gray missed out on this Christmas ritual because he was caught up in the snow, doing his best to get himself and Rona to Aysbury in the worst snow we'd had for many years.

'Right, let's sit on the floor and decide which decorations we're going to use,' Gray says with gusto and I glance at him, surprised at this sudden spurt of enthusiasm. 'Goodness knows what's in the box Mum gave us, but she said not to feel guilty if none of the items "see the light of day", as she so quaintly put it.'

As I make myself comfortable Gray chooses one of our favourite Christmas CDs, a mixture of carols and classic oldies. With the fire now burning brightly, just the smell of the woodsmoke is enough to transport me back to my childhood. As I open the box from Rona and peer inside, my face breaks out into an instant smile.

'Ah, a Santa Claus made from a cardboard tube!'

Gray settles himself down next to me as I hand it to him. 'Not bad for a four-year-old, is it?' he says with pride. 'Okay, the face is a little lopsided, but I did that on purpose as it makes him rather endearing,' he banters.

I sit back, letting him discover the contents for himself, happy to watch and listen as he shares some festive moments from his childhood.

'Oh, we gotta use these! I made them in woodworking class, and I even signed the backs!' he exclaims, holding up some decorations – quavers and treble clefs – cut from thin plywood and hanging from lengths of narrow red ribbon.

'It's so kind of your mum, but won't she miss having these things on her own tree?'

Gray stops for a moment, his mind elsewhere as he places them on the floor in front of us. 'I doubt it. Mum has kept every single thing I made, wrote, or drew – including all of my school exercise books. Besides, her tree in the new place is going to sit on top of the TV unit, but I bet most of the decorations will hark back to my childhood.'

Rona, too, is experiencing her first Christmas in her new home and it's a time of change and adjustment for us all.

'You and Tollie must have gone through this when you moved out of Lock Keeper's Cottage, Immi,' Gray reflects.

I nod. 'We did. He's not overly sentimental about *things* – he says his memories are all that he needs to keep the past alive. I kept everything he gave me, but when I decorated my first tree after moving out of Lock Keeper's Cottage, I went on a shopping spree. I wanted baubles and decorations that reminded me of nature – hence the silver stag heads, the white resin acorns and the wooden snowflakes. I love bells, too,' I point out and he laughs.

'Yes, I had noticed.'

I pull out an old sweet tin from the days when they contained enough sweets to last well beyond Christmas, not the modern plastic version that seems to get smaller with each passing year.

'This is my memory tin,' I explain. 'Every year I choose three things to put on the tree, for fear of anything breaking. Some of them are very delicate, as Grandma loved glass baubles. Others are home-made, like this one.' I hold up my version of a Christmas cracker and Gray's face puckers up.

'Aww...'

'I know. Grandma and I spent hours making a dozen of these little beauties and eleven of them ended up being shredded by Grandad's Labrador, Bessie. She was the best and usually sweet-natured, but keeping her away from the Christmas tree was an impossible task.'

With a cardboard toilet-roll tube as the core, we covered them in red paper and tied the ends with gold thread. On the front is a small picture of a robin that I still remember painting. 'This one is very special,' I add, holding up a small silver cardboard box about three inches square. On the front is the letter I emblazoned in red felt. 'Dad hung this on the tree every year and I was allowed to open it on Christmas Eve. As far as I can remember, it began when I was about five years old. It always contained a little keepsake – a ring, a bracelet, and then one year a beautiful little ceramic robin. I loved it and after that I started collecting the whole range. They're all in here.'

I dig out my box of treasures, taking off the lid and pulling out one of the screws of tissue paper. Gingerly unwrapping it, I hold up a hedgehog that would comfortably fit onto a two-pound coin. A sense of nostalgia sweeps over me, momentarily taking my breath away.

'You know, Dad always said, "You can't live in the past, every day is a chance to create a new and exciting memory," and he was right. But I think I'll keep these in my drawer in the bedroom, instead of in the box up in the attic.' I'm talking to myself, of course, and Gray says nothing, but I can feel his eyes on me.

There is nothing wrong with new, or different, but sometimes it's good for the soul to take a little time out to enjoy those old memories. Tonight is one of those times, and Gray and I sharing the little things that are never forgotten, but seldom spoken about, is a special moment for us both. He reaches out for my hand and, instead of sadness, what I feel is a huge buzz of excitement. And as we gaze at each other, I can see that mirrored in Gray's eyes, too.

* * *

Tuesday is bitingly cold, and I awaken to the first hoar frost of the season. It's beautiful when I stand looking out over the fields at the shrubs and the trees, but how I wish Gray were here beside me to see it. It is a veritable winter wonderland, and it looks as if Jack Frost has visited every single branch, leaf and dried twig to transform it into a scene from the North Pole. We even had snow forecast yesterday but it didn't come to anything other than some disappointing sleet.

At the nurseries we're rushed off our feet and both outside and inside are heaving with stock. We have everything, from Christmas trimmings to toys, and the new greenhouse is full of dwarf Alberta spruces, Christmas cacti, vibrant poinsettias and beautiful orchids. The tills are ringing constantly, and business is good. Martin is usually out visiting customers or assisting with special deliveries, but we have five temporary staff helping to keep things ticking over while our regular crew focus on the commercial contracts.

At lunchtime I saunter out to do a little shopping of my own, quickly filling my trolley with a sizeable lemon cypress, one of those gorgeous lime-green potted trees that can be used both indoors and out, and a Christmas cactus. None of the standard bays on show are big enough for the space I have to fill, but I know that a new delivery arrived this morning, together with some potted lemon trees, which are yet to be unpacked. I seek out a stack of silver-coloured metal planters made out of zinc that I've admired since the day the first order arrived. Choosing five of them in varying sizes, I stack them up and pile them into the trolley.

Making my way over to the customer services desk, I ask them to put a call out to my favourite guy, Leonard.

'What's up, Immi?'

As I explain exactly what I'm looking for, he gives me a thumbs-up. 'Leave it with me. I'll go and dig out two fine specimens for you now and get these repotted. If you want this lot delivered, I could drop it off in the pickup on my way home.'

I was rather hoping he'd offer to do that.

'Awesome, Leonard, thank you so much. You know Lock Keeper's Cottage and there's parking at the rear. The first lane past the entrance to The Bullrush. I'll be there from twenty to six onwards.'

Kelly says she'll phone me when she's ready to ring up the transaction and I head back to work. Even with my staff discount, it's a bit of an indulgence, but it is going to make the family room look stunning. And I know that Gray won't begrudge me a penny of it.

As I'm walking back to my office, the phone begins to ring and I see that it's Ursula.

'Yoga is cancelled. A pipe has burst in the ladies' toilets and it has flooded the entire ground floor. I doubt it will reopen until after New Year.'

'Oh, no! That's such a pity.'

'Sarah's still up to come along for the fitting, though.'

'How about popping down to Lock Keeper's Cottage tonight instead, then? And why don't I invite Rona and Mum, too? They keep asking me to describe the dress and, given how much work they've put into planning the wedding, it seems only fair.'

'Excellent idea. Is there anything I can bring?'

'Just Sarah, the dresses and yourself,' I reply, laughing. 'And some pins,' I add. 'Half past seven?'

'Perfect.'

* * *

When Leonard taps on the glass doors at the back, I can see the lights from his vehicle shining across the orchard. Pulling on my coat, I go out to help him.

'Thank you for going out of your way to do this for me, Leonard. It's much appreciated.'

'My pleasure, Immi. First time I've been here. It's a nice spot.'

The door to The Retreat opens and Tollie appears.

'Everythin' all right?' he asks.

'Fine, thanks, Tollie. Just a delivery of plants for the cottage.'

'Hi, Leonard, how are you doin'?'

'Good, thanks. How's the back?'

'Champion. I'll pull on my coat and give you a hand.'

Leonard drives one of the nurseries' open-backed pickup trucks and, as he doesn't have his own transport, Martin lets him use it outside work. Leonard more than repays him in loyalty to the company and always makes himself available, even when he's off duty.

'Take the Christmas cactus, Immi, as it's the most delicate of them all.'

Leonard wraps his arms around the bay, which stands very tall in the pot and I suspect it was the biggest one he could find.

'Here I am,' Tollie calls out, stepping up to lift the dwarf lemon tree out of the back. He manages with ease, I'm pleased to see, and as we tramp across the frozen ground he asks Leonard if he's ready for Christmas.

'You know what it's like, Tollie. We won't know until the shops are shut and my mother suddenly discovers there's something she's forgotten.'

Tollie laughs. 'That'll be a tradition, then, Leonard. Treasure it!'

Tollie is right. It's the little things we remember that make us laugh every time. Grandma's infamous turkey soup to use up the leftovers, for instance. No one liked it, but we still ate it.

As I slide open the glass doors and step inside, the guys put their pots down on the patio and head back to the pick-up truck for one more trip. By the time they return, I've laid some old sheets on the floor and they lift the pots inside for me.

'I could slip off my shoes and carry them over for you,' Leonard offers.

'That's very kind, but I can slide them across on the sheets. Thank you both for your help. And this is for you, Leonard.' I hand him a carrier bag with a bottle of wine and a large box of chocolates.

He smiles gratefully. 'Merry Christmas, Immi! It's going to be a wonderful one for you and Gray!'

'Thanks, Leonard. I am looking forward to taking some time off after the wedding and simply relaxing.'

Leonard looks in Tollie's direction, giving him a nod, before walking back to the pickup.

'Do you want to come in for tea or coffee?' I ask Tollie.

'I'd best not. We're in the middle of watchin' a film. It's yoga night for you, isn't it?'

'Yes, but it's cancelled. So, it's girls' night and the final fitting for the dresses.'

'Oh, I'd best make myself scarce, then. Whatever you wear you'll look amazin', m'dear,' he says as he turns and trudges back across to The Retreat. Tollie has only been inside the cottage once since it was finished. I know we've been distant, but I can't help wondering whether he can't reconcile the changes Gray and I have made with the memories the cottage holds for him.

There isn't time to ponder further though as it's almost 7 p.m. and I need to pop some frozen nibbles into the oven once I've sorted these plants. Closing the doors, I slide the first pot over, pulling it with ease and manoeuvring it into the far corner. It doesn't take long to move them all across, although arranging them requires a bit of shuffling around. I begin by pushing the tallest to the back and the smallest to the front, but the two middle-sized pots don't look right sitting side by side, as the trees contained within are different heights. Instead, I create a small semicircle, tall, medium then tall, with the smaller of the two medium pots in front and the vibrant red Christmas cactus nestled at the foot of the group.

Standing back to admire my handiwork, I immediately notice that the plants have already succeeded in dampening the hollow sound within the room. Packed quite tightly together, the pop of different greens, yellow and red works well – it's like being in a conservatory. I add a small string of battery-operated, crystal-clear snowflakes, each containing a small white light and it looks very festive indeed.

Before I have time to unwrap the selection of Christmas nibbles to heat them up, a light tap on the glass doors attracts my attention. Sarah and Ursula are staring inside, their arms full of bags.

'Come in, come in. Here, let me help.'

'Thanks, Immi. Rona just texted me to say she's picking up your mum, so they won't be far behind us,' Ursula confirms.

It still sounds a little odd, hearing everyone referring to Val as my mum now, and it makes me smile to myself. There is a mound of navy-blue dress bags and a medium-sized suitcase as we pile everything onto one of the sofas.

'Goodness, what a lot of stuff.'

'I brought the jackets, too. I thought we'd have a full dress-rehearsal tonight.' I look at Ursula and she scowls at me. 'You're amongst friends, relax.'

I leave them to take everything upstairs to hang up in the guest bedroom, while I pop two trays of bite-sized festive fare in the oven, discreetly dispensing with the boxes.

The sound of someone rattling the front door knocker sends me hurrying through into the hallway, wiping my hands on a tea towel.

'I left the car up at The Bullrush car park and we walked down together,' Rona says as I let her and Mum in, giving each of them a swift hug. 'The back lane is a bit narrow for me and it's not that far.'

'This is exciting,' Mum says, her eyes bright. I take their coats and hang them up, before walking Mum and Rona into the kitchen area so they can warm up.

'Shall Rona and I sort the drinks?' Mum asks and I nod, stopping to pull out five plates. I hunt around for some napkins and carry a few things over to the table.

'Sarah and Ursula are upstairs, I presume?' Rona asks.

'Yes. Shout up, they're just hanging up the dresses.'

The consensus of opinion is to plump for hot chocolate and, foraging around in the cupboard, I find some miniature marshmallows. It doesn't take long until the table looks rather grand, with some freshly cut greenery from the garden and a small bowl filled with Christmas roses that I found in the border underneath the hedge to the side of the cottage.

'This is all very festive and pretty,' Sarah remarks as we gather around the table. 'I love how green everything is in here, Immi. And that tree is stunning.'

I remember Gray, moaning as we struggled to space the decorations out evenly over the tree. This is our first year of setting our own traditions and you have to start somewhere. Next year I'm going to propose that we have three smaller Christmas trees in a line. It's a little different, fun, and will be a lot easier when it comes to trimming up.

'Right, time for some nibbles.' I carry the platter across and place it on the wooden block in the centre of the table. 'Tuck in.'

'Who's going first for their fitting?' Ursula asks as we stand around eating.

'Not me,' I reply instantly. 'I'm working myself up to it.'

'Oh, Immi,' Mum says sympathetically. 'There's no need to be on edge.' But I notice Ursula glancing across at her and Mum bites her lip. She's nervous on my behalf.

It isn't until Sarah appears and stands in front of the Christmas tree doing a twirl that the butterflies really begin fluttering around inside my stomach.

'I love that little jacket,' Rona exclaims, 'and the colour is perfect! What is it?'

'Soft heather,' Ursula confirms proudly. And she should be proud because Sarah looks stunning. The fabric falls just perfectly, swirling around her legs as she moves, and the cropped, long-sleeve jacket ends just below her bust, ensuring that the pleated detail on the front of her dress isn't hidden.

'The jackets need to be warm for when you're outside, but I didn't want to use too heavy a fabric. It's a lightweight wool mix, but it's also lined. Immi wasn't a fan of the heavy satin, were you?'

'Goodness, no! I don't like shiny anything when it comes to clothes,' I declare firmly.

'Well, I agree with you, Immi,' Rona responds, 'and this is a wonderful alternative. The style reminds me of the little cropped jackets they used to wear back in the early eighteen hundreds.'

'Oh, yes. With those peak bonnets!' I'd better be careful what I say here, or Ursula will be rethinking our simple hair decorations.

Reluctantly, I leave them to finish off their hot chocolate and wend my way upstairs. I'm perplexed to find two navy dress bags hanging on the back of the door and as I slide down the zip of the first bag, the dress inside isn't one I recognise. There's a soft tapping sound and I call out, 'Come in.'

Mum pops her head around the door and then gingerly pushes it open.

'Don't be cross, Immi. Your first dress is in the other bag. Gray came to see me and he was stressing because he said you weren't happy. It is beautiful, I've seen it, but Ursula and I put our heads together and came up with an alternative. Even if you don't feel comfortable in it, we thought it might help to put the other dress into perspective.'

I don't know what to say as I ease it out of the bag and hang it up on the hook.

'It's gorgeous, but the other one looked wonderful until I tried it on. It simply wasn't me...'

'When you're ready, come down in whichever one feels right for you.' Mum turns, shutting the door behind her.

It's a dress, Immi, I tell myself. *It's only a dress. You'll wear it for one afternoon and an evening.* Ursula has spent hours in her workroom just to make sure I'm happy and that means more to me than anything else.

The new dress is fitted at the waist, the folds of the silver-grey taffeta hang down to mid-calf level. As I turn, the natural movement in the fabric makes me want to spin around to show it off. It's absolutely perfect.

Even so, it takes me a while before I can pluck up the courage to make my way downstairs. When I walk into the room everyone falls silent.

'Is this the one?' Ursula asks nervously, holding her breath.

'It's the one,' I reply and suddenly she's able to breathe again.

'Result!'

26

CHRISTMAS CAROLLERS, HOT MULLED WINE AND FEELING
JOYFUL!

'I can't believe how much it's warmed up,' I complain to Gray,
after getting excited about the dusting of snow on Thursday,
which he missed. Today the skies are blue and, while that's good
for Aysbury's Christmas market and the crowds are out, walking
around the stalls in between cruises in my elf costume, I need to
unzip my coat. Or risk overheating.

'What I can't fathom is how you're happy enough to dress up
as an overgrown elf, and yet you turn into a drama queen over a
posh frock.'

Gray's getting his own back because I told him off for what I
felt was breaking a confidence. I didn't mean for Mum to get
pulled into my dress dilemma, or to put Ursula to the trouble of
making a second dress. Admittedly, she told me not to worry,
because she was sure she would be able to find a buyer for the
first one, which is amazing even if it isn't right for me.

'I'm wearing a costume, Gray, everyone knows that I'm not
really an elf,' I reply, laying on the sarcasm, still a little cross with
him. 'What if I'd told you that I wanted the men dressed in black,

satin-collared tuxedos, with wing-tipped white dress shirts and proper bow ties?'

Gray stops walking and turns to face me. 'Was that what you really wanted?'

'No, of course not. But would you have felt comfortable?'

We link arms and continue strolling around to look at the stalls.

'Point taken, but that's precisely why I spoke to Val. You weren't happy and now you are. That's all I want for you, Immi.'

I know he's right, but I still feel guilty. As we walk past the stall selling mince pies, spicy mulled wine and hot toddies, the air is filled with a rich and festive fragrance. It's so tempting to stop, but I keep on going.

'Oh, look at these tea-light holders, aren't they lovely?' I let go of Gray's arm to pick up one of the silver metal snowflakes. 'How much are these?'

'Four pounds fifty. Immi, isn't it?'

'Yes,' I reply, smiling.

'I'm Joanne's daughter, from The Candle Emporium.'

I look at the sign hanging from the back of the stall. 'Oh, of course! I thought I recognised the face.'

'They're pretty, aren't they?'

I look at Gray. 'Yes, they are.'

'Guess we'd better have one, then,' he replies, and I stare at him intently. 'Perhaps you'd better make that two.'

The young woman is smiling as she wraps them for me.

'Mum asked me to ring Patrick yesterday as our collection box is full. I tried twice, but there was no reply. Could you let him know for us, please, Immi? Trade is brisk right now, and we're using a small tub, but Mum prefers the sealed boxes.'

'Of course. Leave it with me. It's so good of you. Please let your mum know that we've almost hit the target. Have you popped down to have a look at the new playground?'

'I have and it's wonderful. Elves get a 50p discount, by the way,' she says as Gray offers her a ten-pound note.

As we walk away I turn to look at Gray, wrinkling up my nose. 'See, being in costume has its advantages.'

He shakes his head. 'I will never figure you out, not completely, will I?'

'If you did, you'd be running in the opposite direction.' I laugh, glancing at my watch. 'At least you, my dashing captain, are turning the heads of every woman we pass, whereas all I'm getting are broad smiles and high-fives from the kiddies. Anyway, if you can take this little package and stow it on board, I'll just pop round to see if Patrick is in and see if he needs any help – in case he's struggling and doesn't like to ask for help. I won't be long.'

Gray steps forward to give me a quick kiss, just as Bernie is approaching.

'Have you two been at the mulled wine already?' Bernie jokes as we turn to look at him.

'That's a pound in the fundraising bucket, Captain Gray. Elves don't give kisses away for free!' he chortles.

I leave the two of them chatting and walk briskly along the lane. It's so busy today that a couple of times I step back into one of the lay-bys when there is a steady stream of traffic in both directions. The stalls are laid out in the public car park next to The Bullrush and it's a tradition that's been upheld for as long as I can remember.

Thankfully, Aysbury Manor allows the use of a large, gravelled courtyard the other side of the lane as a visitors' parking area. There are a few old farm buildings that are no longer in regular use, but store farm machinery that hasn't been moved in a long time. Most of the manor's farmland is now leased, and worked, by Adler's farm, but we charge two pounds a car for parking and it soon adds up.

I turn into the Saint Nicholas's Well complex, walking past the side window and the tall wall that surrounds the pretty courtyard garden to Byre Cottage. As it backs onto the lane, there is only one entrance via the tall wooden gates. It's a perfect little property for a person living on their own as it's very secure with the cluster of larger barn conversions abutting what was formerly a farmyard. Standing on tiptoe to reach over the top of the gate, I undo the sliding bolt and step into the garden, pulling the gate shut behind me.

Tapping on the stable door that leads directly into the kitchen, I stand back but there's no sign of movement at all. To my right is the sitting room and I walk over to peer in through the patio doors, but everything looks normal. Ziggy has a chair of her own and her cushion is there, but she's nowhere to be seen Patrick could be out Christmas shopping, of course, and I know Ziggy has numerous little spots in which to curl up and sleep.

I decide to try his mobile, but when I do it goes straight answerphone. As I'm walking out of the gate and about to rea over to slide the bolt shut, a voice calls out. 'Hang on, Immi, do overstretch. We can't risk Aysbury's number one elf pulling muscle.' It's Cameron who, along with his wife, Lizzie, lives Meadow Barn on the far side of the complex.

'There you go,' he says, giving me a broad smile. 'We did F er's booze cruise last night and had a whale of a time. I hope the start of an annual tradition.'

'Booze cruise, is it? I was told it was wine and canapé laugh as he looks at me mischievously.

'Well, it's a nice little addition to the Christmas jollity, is and this year's market is the biggest I've seen.'

'Yes, Bernie said he didn't have enough pitches to meet the demand. Have you seen Patrick this morning?'

'No. Not since yesterday, actually. I bumped into him on his way to the vet's. Poor Ziggy was in her carrier and she was a little vocal, to say the least. Val has the same problem every year when she takes her for the jab.'

'But he was here last night?'

'No, I don't think so. Whether he dropped Ziggy back a bit later, and then went off, I don't know, as we weren't around. The car wasn't parked up when we arrived back just after eleven last night. We stayed behind and sat chatting with Fisher and your mum for a while. It was an enjoyable evening.'

That's strange. I hope Ziggy is all right.

'Thanks, Cameron. Well, if you do bump into Patrick can you let him know that I was looking for him?'

'Will do.'

'I'd best get off, as our second Little Stars Special cruise sets sail in half an hour,' I reply, looking at my watch.

'And I hear that the fund has almost reached its target. That's quite a feat, Immi. I take my hat off to the committee. Tollie is walking around with a permanent smile on his face these days!'

He's right about that and it seems that everyone is noticing it.

* * *

Tollie is talking to a little boy named Joshua. His younger sister was killed in a tragic car accident only six months ago and the family are still in pieces. They are facing their first Christmas without her there beside them. It's hard not to tear-up as I look across at his mum, sitting at one of the tables, her eyes unnaturally bright as she tries to hide her emotions. It was Joshua's father who emailed Mum to put his son's name forward for a silver ticket:

We are all broken and there have been times when the only thing keeping us going is Joshua's attempts to make us smile. He talks about Kaitlin every single day and, at first, we found that hard to deal with. There were times my wife and I just changed the subject. It was too heart-breaking and there was no normality to our lives. We were going through the motions of getting up each day and trying to cope as best we could.

But Joshua was strong, despite his tears, and he made us realise that a child's view of death is different from an adult's. He understood that Kaitlin will never be here in the physical with us again, but he'd sit and talk to her, anyway. Telling her what had happened at school and even just how much he missed her. When we noticed Kaitlin's favourite teddy had disappeared, we found it next to his pillow and that has been a comfort to him. So now we talk to her, too. And while it's going to be the hardest thing we've ever done, this Christmas we are going to celebrate it as a family in the way Kaitlin would have wanted us to. There will be tears, we know that, but her Boo Bear will be sitting on the dining table next to Joshua as I carve the turkey.

Kaitlin would want us to make Joshua's Christmas as special as possible under the circumstances. It's not about the presents, of course, which is why I'm writing to you. Last year was Kaitlin's and Joshua's third trip on The Santa Ahoy Special and it was a magical experience for them both. This year we'd love for our little star, Joshua, to get a silver ticket. In the last six months he has kept us going and while the pain will never go away, without him I don't know how we would have kept going. That's a testament to the strength of a six-year-old boy who has taught us to count our blessings and to treasure our memories.

God bless for all you do, and for the joy you bring!

Will and Jessica Beaumont

Reading the email broke all our hearts and reminded us why we do what we do.

For the Little Stars cruises, Mum liaises with the family to find a meaningful gift for the child concerned, and often their siblings too, when the trauma extends to the whole family. I remember that last year Mum managed to get a bridal company to donate a stunning crystal tiara for a little girl named Laura. She wanted to be a ballerina when she grew up and her eyes sparkled when she opened her gift. Laura's mum is diabetic, and she collapsed at home. This plucky five-year-old dialled 999 and stayed at her mum's side until the paramedics arrived. Joshua's dad is right, it is humbling how selfless and brave children can be. What shreds my heart as I watch Joshua taking his very special gift from Santa is that tucked beneath his arm is a teddy bear and I wipe away a tear with the sleeve of my elf jacket.

Turning to gaze out of the window, I take a moment to compose myself. In front of The Bullrush Inn, the Aysbury Christmas carollers are in full flow, attracting an ever-growing audience. Two men walk around with buckets as the children happily throw in coins and then rush back to their parents to ask for more. Christmas is a time that reminds us of the fact that the pleasure is in the giving, not the receiving.

'Right,' Santa booms out with gusto. 'It's time for a bit of a sing-song again before I tell you one of my favourite stories!' Tollie signals for me to change the backing track and I make my way to the galley.

'What story, Santa?' a little girl calls out, clasping her new stuffed reindeer in both arms. Since opening her present, she hasn't put it down once.

'Well, it's all about the time when Rudolph single-handedly

rescued everyone's Christmas,' he replies, a serious expression making him wrinkle his brow.

'But how?' she asks, impatient for the story to begin.

Tollie puts back his head and laughs. 'You'll have to wait a little bit longer, but it begins with one snowy Christmas Eve when I couldn't even see my hand in front of my face. We were about to get lost, very lost indeed!' Tollie instinctively knows which stories are right for each group of children.

Seconds later, the opening chords to Wizzard's iconic 'I Wish It Could Be Christmas Everyday' strike up and Jude and Jade's voices encourage the little ones to join in, while the adults sitting at the banquettes are raising the roof. Moments like this are priceless.

Jude is today's fairy, and she stands alongside Santa's seat, using her magic wand to conduct the singing. Jade makes sure everyone has a glow stick and those who are too shy to sing wave their arms in the air. Before the last chord is struck, I notice that everyone has joined in, in one way or another, and Ethel, bless her, is also having a whale of a time.

'Come on, girls, I'll walk you back to The Bullrush. Thank you so much for making it yet another wonderful cruise,' I say as we walk back arm in arm. Even though we're wearing our thick coats, there's no disguising our costumes and we attract a lot of attention, but everyone smiles back at us.

The carollers are still on fine form and I'd love to stop for a while and listen, but I'm a little worried about Patrick. If Ziggy isn't well, what if he feels that he can't tell Mum about it? I could be wrong, of course, and my thoughts go off in a totally different direction, sending a shiver down my spine. Christmas is a tough time for some people and it's his first Christmas on his own. Patrick wouldn't do anything silly, I hope.

'Let's go in through the back door,' I suggest to Jade and Jude, as it's so crowded at the front. Inside isn't any better; it's heaving with people. Small children are running between the tables and it's total chaos, but everyone is good-natured. I give the girls a goodbye hug, and then go in search of Mum, who is in the kitchen, loading dishes into the dishwasher.

'Hi, everyone,' I call out, waving to Sarah as she turns away from the hob to smile at me. 'The girls are back and have gone to change.'

I walk over to Mum as she closes the cabinet door. 'That's all done. Anything else I can do before I go, Sarah?'

'No, it's fine. The girls will be down shortly. Many thanks for helping, Val.'

'My pleasure, Sarah.' Mum turns to look at me. 'Is everything all right, Immi?'

I nod. 'Yes. I'll hang on while you get your coat.'

Mum gives me a questioning glance before we make our way out to the rear hallway.

'Problems?' she asks, once we're out of earshot.

'Has Patrick said anything to you?'

'About what?'

'Ziggy, maybe?'

'She's okay, isn't she?'

I don't want to alarm Mum, but my unease is growing.

'He's not answering his phone, which is unlike him. He mentioned to Cameron that Ziggy was off her food and he was taking her to see the vet yesterday. I popped round earlier on, and his car wasn't there. I peered in through the patio doors and couldn't see Ziggy, either.'

Mum frowns. 'She wasn't on her cushion?'

'No.'

'Something's not right, then. Come on, let's head round there now. I have a key in my bag if we can't get a reply.'

I can see Mum is visibly shaken.

'She was fine when I last called in a couple of days ago, Immi. You know what she's like – if she's not in the mood for whatever food you put down for her, then she'll go straight to her biscuits. There's nothing unusual in that.' But Mum isn't really talking to me, she's trying to reassure herself.

'How did your session go with the hypnotherapist?' I enquire to distract her.

'It was interesting, actually. We spent an hour talking through my most memorable childhood stories. It seems the travel sickness might be down to a ride I had on a waltzer at the fair, of all things. Do you remember those rides?'

'I do. Yes, they go round quite fast, and can be ever so disorientating.'

'Well, I don't know exactly how old I was, but this boy jumped on the back and was spinning the individual little carriages around by hand. I think he was the son of the owner and he might have been trying to impress me. The moment I got off the ride my head was spinning and I was violently sick in front of everyone. It was so embarrassing. After that I never went on a ride again. Anyway, the hypnotist relaxed me and I can't really remember the last bit of the session, but it has helped. I'm going back to see her again next week.'

I'm glad it wasn't a waste of time and at least Mum is no longer frowning.

When we turn into the complex and Patrick's car still isn't there, I start to worry again.

'I wouldn't normally let myself in, but I need to know that Ziggy is fine. But I'm also wondering what's happening with

Patrick, Immi, not to have said anything to me. I do hope he's all right.'

The look we exchange is one of concern.

Mum turns the key in the lock, swinging open the door and calling out, 'Anyone home? It's Val.'

I follow her inside.

'Ziggy, Ziggy?' Mum's voice wavers as she calls her beloved cat's name, turning to look at me anxiously. 'She's obviously not here. Everything looks in order, so it's not as if Patrick rushed out. There are no dishes in the sink. Oh, where are Ziggy's food bowls?' Mum's face drops as she looks at the little rubber mat where the three bowls are usually lined up.

'Stay here and I'll check around,' I reply, my stomach beginning to churn.

Making a huge effort to remain calm, I leave Mum leaning against the countertop, trying to figure out what's going on. The sitting room is immaculate, the cushions on the sofas plumped and not a single thing out of place. Warily I head towards the staircase that leads up to the bathroom and the galleried bedroom. The bathroom door is ajar, and I gently ease it back. The shelf below the mirror is empty, not even a ring on it from toiletries, or splashes of toothpaste. The bar of soap on the hand-basin is dry, the taps polished.

I go back out into the bedroom. The blind on the Velux window overhead is closed, but the light is pouring in through the main window, which looks out over the courtyard garden. The bed is made up and nothing looks out of place. I walk over to the wall of wardrobes and ease open one of the doors. It's empty. And the second one is empty too.

'Mum, you'd better come and take a look.'

Patrick is gone and so is Ziggy.

27

DESPERATE TIMES

As Fisher, Mum, Rona, David, Gray and I sit around the table in Fisher's cottage, the news I have is even worse than we feared.

'Okay. Here we go. I've been online and the fund's bank balance stands at zero. The remainder of the money was drawn out the day before yesterday.'

A collective gasp goes around the table.

'It's been a tough day, knowing that the news was likely to get even worse as the enquiries began, but with three cruises to get through, I had to leave it all in Martin's hands.'

I stare down at the papers in front of me, having scrawled some notes while Martin filled me in.

'Martin's first reaction, when I told him that Patrick has disappeared, was disbelief. When I told him about the missing funds, he went into panic mode. He is devastated as he recommended Patrick to us. While it seems that Patrick hasn't taken money from the Lockside Nurseries, Martin was horrified to discover that several of the contracts Patrick negotiated on his behalf involved him levying a charge as a broker. That's something Martin was never informed about. He rang me about an hour ago with an update, having succeeded in tracking down Patrick's ex-wife.'

I pause to let the news sink in. When I glance across at Fisher his face is ashen and I steel myself for what's coming next.

'The truth is that their house was repossessed, and Patrick's wife is divorcing him because he has a gambling addiction. The debt became overwhelming, and she decided she'd had enough. She hasn't spoken to him for several months and had no idea he was living in Aysbury. Martin was discreet and didn't mention any details, only that he was expecting him at the nurseries on Friday but Patrick isn't answering his phone.'

'But messages have been left?' David asks, struggling to comprehend what has happened, which is understandable.

'Yes. Up until about lunchtime today, when Martin texted to inform me the number is now unobtainable.'

David mutters an expletive under his breath and we're all sitting in silence and total shock. I keep thinking this can't be happening. The silence is chilling, and I shuffle the papers in front of me into a pile, then stare across at Fisher, dreading what he's going to reveal. Please, please don't let it be any worse than it is already.

Fisher clears his throat, letting go of Mum's hand and resting his elbows on the table, his hands so tightly clasped together that his fingertips begin to turn white. 'There is no easy way to say this, guys, but I rang Charlton and Sons to explain what has happened and ask for an extension beyond the end of the month. Immi and I did a quick calculation and with the money from the cruises, the Christmas market and the car-parking charges, the barn dance and the sale of The Bullrush Brew, that should bring in around six and a half thousand pounds—'

'Well, that's something,' David cuts in. 'The final target is ten thousand something, isn't it, Immi?'

'Ten thousand five hundred and twenty-eight pounds,' I confirm, wondering how long it will take to raise yet another four grand.

Fisher sits back in his chair, looking grim. 'It's worse than that,' he mutters as our eyes meet. And then I know what he's trying to tell us, but he hasn't the heart to do it.

'Patrick didn't make that first payment, did he?'

Rona's hands fly up to her face as she gasps and Mum, I notice, is crying.

'No. Only the initial deposit has been paid, which you arranged, Immi. Patrick convinced them that it was just a case of waiting for the money that had already been raised to come in and they had no reason to disbelieve him. It was agreed that the remaining twenty-one thousand and fifty-six pounds would be paid by the thirty-first of December.'

That's why Patrick was so diligent about keeping track of what was coming in and what was outstanding. He needed every penny he could get his hands on to take him as far away from Aysbury as possible.

Fisher puts his arms around Mum's shoulders, hugging her close.

'I'm sure I'm speaking for everyone when I say we are all really sorry to hear about Ziggy, Val,' Gray offers empathetically. She wipes her eyes, sniffs, and pushes back her shoulders resolutely.

'Thank you. Ziggy liked Patrick, no doubt sensing how troubled he was, and if she wasn't happy around him, then she would have bolted. Maybe his need is greater than mine.' She sighs. 'Animals sense things and he must have been desperate to take that money because he knows how hard everyone has worked towards our goal. He has that on his conscience forever and I can only hope that burden makes him mend his ways. He was always good to her and at least that shows he does have a heart. If Patrick can beat his addiction, then this could be his fresh start. I wish none of this had happened, but if he needed a companion who wouldn't judge him, then I understand why he was driven to take my lovely Ziggy with him.'

My goodness, Mum's words of kindness and understanding make me feel ashamed of myself. I was sitting here with uncharitable thoughts running through my head, but it's easy to sit in judgement of other people, isn't it?

'When do we tell the others?' Gray's question is on the tip of everyone's tongue.

'It will break Tollie,' I reply firmly. 'The fewer people who know, the better, until we can establish a way forward, at least. Fisher, is there any leeway or have we lost all credibility with Charlton and Sons?'

The mood is shifting as people realise what we need is an action plan.

'They were as horrified to hear about this as we are, believe me,' Fisher confirms. 'Obviously, I've informed the police and they will be in touch for some more details, Immi, but Patrick is an intelligent man and I've no doubt he'll hide his tracks and start somewhere afresh. January is a quiet month, John Charlton explained to me, and whatever cash we can get to them will help to pay the wages, but at least they're being understanding. I know it's hard, but perhaps we should gather the whole committee together and tell them what has happened.'

Mum puts her hand on Fisher's arm affectionately. 'Let's not act in haste. Tollie, Abe, Ethel, Kurt and Bernie will take it hard, as we have. There are enough heads gathered here today to brainstorm our next steps. What does everyone think?'

'I can't even imagine how Tollie will react and I think Mum is right. Let's go away and let it all sink in before we get everyone together. There are ways to raise money quickly, but Charlton and Sons shouldn't suffer because of this,' I immediately wade in. 'Raise your hand if you're in favour of reconvening this meeting tomorrow night.' Gray places his arm around my shoulders, giving me a reassuring squeeze as I watch all five hands go up in the air, before raising my own.

It's time to start thinking outside the box. I have no intention of letting this ruin everyone's Christmas.

* * *

The following evening, as we trudge along the snowy towpath towards Fisher's cottage, Gray and I walk arm in arm.

'Are you sure about this, Immi?' he asks. I know he's fully on board with my idea, but he's fearful of what Tollie would say if he knew.

'Never been surer of anything in my life before. We are not going to let this defeat us.'

'Fair enough, I'm with you – you know that. But...'

I stop walking, waiting for Gray to turn around and face me.

'I have an idea of my own, too. Let's not hang around and prolong the agony. Besides, we might not be the only ones to have come up with a plan.'

He stoops to gather up the saddest-looking snowball I have ever seen in my life, but it still makes me run off. What we need now is a real Christmas miracle, the sort that even Santa can't deliver. When I slow down, beginning to overheat in my padded coat, scarf and bobble hat, Gray strides towards me.

'Let's keep this on a need-to-know basis for the time being. Between us we'll sort something, don't you worry.'

I stare up into the sky and the flakes are coming fast and furious, but they're too small to come to anything. Although the sky is that ominous opaque white colour, tinged with grey, the temperature has warmed a couple of degrees at least and that's enough to make everything start melting before it can really pitch. We were motoring towards the festive holidays with such positivity and now everyone in the know is feeling dispirited. And what sort of a mood is that for a wedding three days before Christmas?

We hold hands and Gray starts to swing his arm as if we are little kids. Then he begins singing 'The Holly and the Ivy'. The pitch is a little high for him, but his voice is clear and comforting. As we swing open the gate to Fisher's cottage, a voice calls out behind us. It's Martin, and he has Kurt with him. I thought we were keeping this quiet for the time being?

'Hey, guys. Are we ready for this?' Gray throws out there.

'Yep,' Karl replies firmly. 'We aren't going to let a little weasel like Patrick defeat us.'

He's in a fighting mood and I wish Martin hadn't pulled him in. Kurt and Sarah have their hands full during their second busiest season of the year. With the big Christmas lunch coming up and our wedding to cater for, the last thing they need is to get pulled into this mess.

Mum opens the door for us, and we hang our coats in the hallway, slipping off our wet shoes.

'I don't know who ordered this snow,' Martin grumbles, 'but it isn't much fun.'

The quicker we sit down and thrash out a solution, the better, before it ends up spoiling what's left of the most wonderful time of the year. That would be a travesty.

'Go on through,' Mum encourages us, bringing up the rear. She looks more like her old self tonight, I'm glad to see. The loss of Ziggy isn't easy to bear, as she's been Mum's little companion for the last four years. Renting out Byre Cottage seemed like a great way to help both Patrick and Mum, while she decides where her future lies, but now I'm regretting the day I trusted the man who succeeded in fooling us all.

'Hi, Kurt, what are you doing here?' Fisher remarks, genuinely surprised to see him.

'I heard a rumour about Patrick and—'

'Kurt asked the question in confidence and I wasn't going to lie,' Martin admits.

'Fair enough,' Fisher replies. 'Does anyone else know outside the people here tonight?'

Kurt shakes his head. 'I didn't mention it to anyone, not even to Sarah. It's too unbelievable. Tonight's meeting is to come up with a plan, then?'

'Yes,' Fisher confirms. 'The police are now in possession of all the facts and a case number has been assigned. It could be a long-winded process and if they succeed in tracking him down the money could well be gone by then, anyway.'

We take our seats around the table, as Mum dispenses tea and coffee as if it's a café, before joining us.

'Can I kick off with our idea?' I ask, looking at Gray for a nod of approval.

'Go ahead, Immi.' I watch as Fisher picks up his pen, ready to make notes. Usually, that's Mum's job but she seems happy to leave it to him.

'It's a fair chunk of money to find and, let's be honest, there is no way we can raise that in time. The playground is up and working and it's not fair to expect Charlton and Sons to wait beyond the original deadline. So, my proposal is that I take out a loan. Whatever we manage to get in, cash-wise, can go towards paying it off and that will lower the repayments. Whatever the shortfall is, I will cover it.'

Martin immediately leans forward. 'It's not fair that you take the brunt of this, Immi. I was the one who put Patrick forward. Sadly, I can't stump up the full amount as I'm consulting a solicitor about repaying the back-handers Patrick inveigled out of my customers. However, I'll see what I can get my hands on and then we can take it from there.'

'Sarah and I can throw in maybe two thousand pounds,' Kurt joins in.

Fisher looks at Mum. 'I have money set aside for having the hull of The Star Gazer overhauled and a new paint job prior to my retirement. I'm more than happy to put that in the kitty. She can last another year or two as she is.'

I put up my hand to stop them before it goes any further, but Gray cuts in.

'Can I jump in here? I'm working with some big clients now and they sponsor all manner of charitable events around the world. Sums of money like this are a tax write-off for them, but for us it's money no one really has lying around spare. I know you just want to get this sorted quickly, Immi, but what harm will it do to wait a day or two? I'll make a few calls as soon I'm back in the studios tomorrow morning.'

Fisher rests his hand on his chin, deep in thought. 'We have some expensive boats moored up in the marina, owned by some wealthy people. Okay, they might only appear a couple of times a year to travel the canals, but when they do come here, they really appreciate the surroundings. I could put out some feelers because Gray is right, it would be merely a tax write-off to a lot of them.'

'How about approaching Aysbury Manor?' Kurt interjects.

'It's usually only the estate manager around these days,' Fisher points out.

'Yes, but they sent three of their groundsmen to help shift the snow from the towpaths and around The Bullrush last Christmas, didn't they?' Martin points out.

I look at Mum and she stares back at me, pointedly. 'That's a good idea,' she replies. 'I know the estate manager and I'll pop along and have a chat with him to find out where the family are staying. If they're still in Spain, it might be difficult to get hold of anyone, but you never know!'

'So, we have a sort of plan, then,' Fisher declares. 'Immi, hang fire, darling girl. This isn't your burden to shoulder, or Gray's either. In fact, the same goes for us all. Let's agree to meet back here on, say, Wednesday evening, and see if anyone has come up with any promising leads. Agreed?'

Hands are raised in the air, but mine remain in my lap.

'What?' Fisher asks, his eyes scanning my face.

'On the proviso that no one speaks of this to Tollie, or anyone else, until it's all resolved – after Christmas, if possible. I don't want Patrick's actions taking the shine off the anniversary celebrations and that's precisely what will happen if word gets out before the Christmas party. It's gone from a triumph to what feels like a disaster and do we really want other people feeling as miserable as we do about it? The playground has already become a popular attraction and is drawing even bigger crowds to support our local businesses. But I know how Tollie will look at it – that if he'd just accepted the posh dinner we'd originally planned in his honour, none of this would have happened. He would be wrong. It has pulled us all together and made us stronger.'

Gray reaches out to clasp my hand. 'We'll sort something out, Immi, don't you worry.'

'Okay. Everyone in agreement?' I ask.

There is a chorus of hmms, and yeses. 'And I'll make enquiries tomorrow morning, as soon as I get to the studios,' Gray states firmly. 'If we want to part people from their money, Christmas is the season of goodwill!'

They all mean well, but time is of the essence. This problem isn't going to go away and the quicker we pay the outstanding amount, the less likely there are to be rumours. Tollie will be cross with me when he eventually finds out, but it will be a done deal by then, hopefully. I was the one who gave Patrick unfettered access to the money and I didn't think to check up on him. No one has pointed that out, but it's the truth. We wouldn't be in this position now if I'd shown due diligence and my naivety allowed this to happen, so the onus is on me.

28

Even though I promised I'd wait until this evening's meeting before doing anything, yesterday morning I spent some time at the police station and then paid a visit to the bank. They'd already withdrawn Patrick's access to the account but, as it stands, the shortfall will be in the region of fourteen and a half thousand pounds and we discussed the possibility of a personal loan to cover that amount. It will take about a week to set up and get the funds through into my personal account, but it was surprisingly hassle-free. I walked away with the application forms and a decision to make regarding the term of the repayment.

I pop back to the cottage for lunch to await a call from Gray; my phone rings and I see that it's Mum.

'Immi, I thought I'd let you know that I spent the morning at Byre Cottage giving it a clean through. I knocked on Cameron's door to let him know that I'm no longer renting it out and that Ziggy wasn't going to be around. I was vague and I think he assumed that she's with Fisher and me for the time being. Fisher is going to pop round tonight to change the locks and put the side light in the sitting room on a timer. It all looks a little less suspicious then, doesn't it?'

It's horrible having to cover up Patrick's tracks like this.

'Thanks, Mum. And thank Fisher, too. This is the right thing we're doing, isn't it?'

She expels a long, slow breath. 'Things seem to be ticking over as usual in Aysbury for the moment and it's not as if we're ignoring the problem. I agree with you though that there isn't any point in ruining everyone's Christmas. Whether we will be able to keep a lid on it for that long, who knows, but for the moment it's still contained. Anyway, I'll see you tonight. Try not to worry, Immi. We're all in this together.'

I know what Mum is thinking – that if the local papers hear so much as a whisper about this, it will make the front page. People gave their hard-earned money in good faith and now most of it is gone.

There's a tap on the patio doors and I glance up to see Tollie looking at me, no doubt wondering why I'm sitting on the sofa, staring into thin air. I jump up, plastering on a smile to mask how jaded I'm feeling.

'Mornin', m'dear. I'm off to the wholesalers with Kurt to do me usual pre-Christmas top-up. Anythin' in particular I can pick up for you?'

The last thing on my mind today is toilet roll, kitchen towel and trays of baked beans and soup in case we get snowed in, but it's kind of him.

'No, we're good, thanks, Tollie.'

'Everythin' all right?' He peers at me and, although it is upsetting keeping him in the dark like this, I know he'd be totally horrified if he knew the truth.

'It's all good. Just taking advantage of a little peace and quiet until I can be bothered to make myself some lunch.'

'Oh, well, I'm sure Daphne would be glad of a bit of company and she's just about to make a sandwich. I'll pop back inside and let her know you're coming.'

This is the last thing I needed, today of all days, but I suspect Tollie wouldn't be suggesting this unless he feels there's something Daphne and I need to thrash out when he's not within earshot.

'Fine, thanks. I have a phone call to make first, and then I'll head over. Enjoy your little trip out with Kurt.'

'Oh, I will,' Tollie replies, sounding pleased with himself, while I'm trying my best not to groan out loud.

I press speed dial and Gray immediately answers. 'I was just about to call you!' he exclaims.

'I've been summoned to lunch with Daphne, so I thought I'd best ring you now. It was Tollie's idea.'

'Oh, poor you,' Gray commiserates. 'Just make some light conversation. She'll know you only get an hour. Anyway, good news. I mean *really* good news. We have a taker. Fifteen thousand pounds ready to be donated, and I was totally upfront about the situation.'

I flop back down onto the sofa, holding the phone tightly to my ear.

'You're joking! OMG! But what if we succeed in getting any money back, or the outstanding funds due in take us over the final payment for the playground?'

'Then the donor is happy for it to go back into the general charity fund. As I said, tax write-offs are just that, and as long as we have an invoice covering that amount, which we do, it's fine.'

'It's fine,' I repeat, dazed. 'And you told them about Patrick?'

'Like I said, I was honest about it and told them that the fund was defrauded. If you let me have the bank details and sort code, the money will be transferred within a few days. I called in a favour, Immi, that's all.'

My head is buzzing as it sinks in. 'We're sorted, then?'

'Yes. Relax. Now go and make friends with Daphne, because that will put a smile on Tollie's face. If I can just point out one thing though, and don't bite my head off... I suspect she's feeling left out. Think about that and how you'd feel coming into such a tight-knit group. Anyway, I'd better get back to work.'

'Love you, Gray, and thank you, thank you so much. That can't have been an easy conversation to have. Miss you, and roll on Friday night!'

* * *

'Ah, Immi, come in. Tollie said you were all alone and looking a bit down.'

Did he, now?

'It's just been crazily busy, lately. How are you?'

'I'm well, thank you. I've made ham sandwiches and there's a quiche, too. Let me take your coat and I'll pop the kettle on.'

Things feel a little stilted and as Daphne indicates for me to take a seat at the table, I'm struggling to find something suitable to say to break the ice.

'Well,' Daphne says, beating me to it. 'This is rather nice.'

'Is it?' I ask truthfully.

There's a pause as Daphne turns around to face me. 'Oh, so this was Tollie's idea. He gave me the impression you were looking for some company.' She raises her eyebrows and laughs. 'Men, eh?'

'I am sorry to be foisted upon you, but you know what he's like when he gets an idea in his head.'

'Oh, you don't have to tell me about that. He can be stubborn all right,' Daphne admits. 'Please help yourself as I know you don't get a long break. Tea, or coffee?'

'Coffee would be great, thank you. And I skipped breakfast this morning, so this is very welcome.'

She joins me and suddenly the atmosphere between us is more congenial. After the traumatic events of the last few days, I'm wondering why I haven't been more understanding. Gray is right and it's time for me to do something about it.

'You know, Daphne, I would love for you to come to the wedding. Not just for Tollie's sake, but for mine and Gray's, too.'

She seems pleased as I fill my plate and begin eating.

'Really? You're not just saying that? I completely understand how... difficult this is for you, Immi. I warned Tollie things were moving along a little too quickly and his operation only succeeded in bringing things forward, I'm afraid. It wasn't planned.'

I stop eating to look at her intently. 'Can I ask how long you and Tollie have been seeing each other?'

Her eyes meet mine as she answers me. 'A little over a year. We first met when Tollie was helping Bernie and Yvonne move back into Turnpike Cottage. Shortly after that we started meeting up for coffee and our relationship grew from there.'

'I had no idea,' I admit.

'Tollie wanted to be discreet because one never knows how a friendship is going to develop, does one? There's no point in upsetting people if that's all it's meant to be.'

'You mean me, I presume.'

'Oh dear, I really don't want to make things any worse than they are now, Immi.'

'It's fine. I think I'm beginning to understand.'

'I do hope so, because as time went on Tollie and I realised that to find someone to share your life with at our age is a true blessing. Tollie was nervous about the fact that this was your former home and concerned about how you would feel if I moved in with him. It happened a lot quicker than we'd envisaged, of course, because of his operation, and that's the problem. Neither of you were ready, but he wasn't going to add to your problems.'

That makes me sad. 'But looking after him wouldn't have been a problem at all,' I state emphatically. 'We've always been close and Tollie has been there for me through some very troubled times. I wouldn't have begrudged anything I could do to help him.'

Daphne looks at me, a pinched expression on her face. 'And I told him that. But he said you were so overloaded already and he knew the signs.'

I let her words sink in.

'He risked us falling out in order not to be a burden to me?'

'That's about the size of it. But I was happy to be there for him, and please understand that he was happy for me to be here too. He still is, although personally I think the price of risking losing you is too high. You are the most important thing in his life, and you always will be. That's why I won't come to the wedding, because I'm not family, Immi, and we're not even friends. It's your day and I don't want to spoil it in any way.'

I sit back in my chair, waves of guilt washing over me.

'I'm sorry. I was stressed, it was true, and everything seemed like the final straw. It hurt, because I felt he was pushing me away. And I was wrong to take that out on you, because that's what I ended up doing. You make him happy and now he's fully recovered it's taken ten years off him. The old Tollie is back and I have you to thank for that, Daphne.'

'That's very generous of you to say that, Immi, and it means more to me than you can possibly know.'

'And the wedding?'

'Well, if you really mean it, then I'd be delighted to accompany Tollie and be a part of your celebrations. Let's not tell Tollie exactly what we've spoken of today. It's enough to tell him that we've made friends. He's not good with the emotional stuff, is he?'

That makes me laugh. 'No, he isn't, but he has a heart of gold.'

'And I'll take great care of him, Immi, of that you can be very sure.'

* * *

'That's incredible, Immi.' Fisher's tone is one of relief and shock. As I look around the assembled group, they're all mirroring his reaction.

'I know. Gray called in a favour and he explained that the money had been stolen. If we manage to get any of it back, or we end up raising more than we need for that final invoice, they are happy for it to go into the general charity fund. I thought I'd type up an official thank-you letter to let them know which local charities we support. We could end up with a little money left over to distribute as we normally do, which, as we all know, will be greatly appreciated as they weren't expecting anything at all this year.'

'It's a pity Gray's not here, but tell him well done, and I'll buy him a pint on Friday,' Martin joins in.

'Me too,' adds Fisher. 'He was right when he said there's something about Christmas that encourages people to dig deep, because Val has some news, too.'

We all turn to look at Mum. 'I spoke to Seth, the estate manager at Aysbury Manor yesterday, to pass on my telephone number. I explained that, as a courtesy, the family might be interested to know more about the proposed new playground. It worked and earlier this evening I had a phone call from Stephen Harrington-Forbes himself. He will be instructing his son, Anthony, to set up an annual donation to Aysbury's fundraising initiatives for the sum of five thousand pounds. Given that we are celebrating the tenth anniversary of the Santa Ahoy cruises, Stephen will be sending a personal cheque for one thousand pounds to foot the bill for the party. He wanted to express his thanks and acknowledge the sterling work that has been carried out by the community.'

I'm speechless, but Martin is quick to reply. 'It's about time they put their hands in their pockets. As the biggest landowners around here, even though that son of theirs is seldom in residence these days, as the heir he's a key employer hereabouts. No doubt they make big profits off the back of that and it doesn't hurt for them to be reminded of it. Kudos to you, Val, because it's quite something to get the old man on the line. Calling from his villa in Spain, was he?'

Mum nods her head, looking a little flushed, and I interrupt. 'It's not what you know, it's who you know, eh? The estate manager has always been supportive when it comes to letting us use the old farmyard opposite as parking every Christmas. I'm not even sure the family know about that. Well, what a turnaround!'

'I think we should crack open a bottle, Fisher,' Mum responds, giving me a jubilant smile.

Everyone is talking at once, the relief tangible, and I can't wait to tell Gray. But first, Mum looks at me, inclining her head, and I follow her into the sitting room.

'Mum, it's not what I think it is, is it?'

She looks at me, shrugging her shoulders.

'I gave Seth my number and told him that while doing some research of the area, I stumbled upon some photographs of Stephen Harrington-Forbes's grandfather, Joseph, and his brother Henry. Which is true. You gave them to me yourself, do you remember? They were amongst that pile of albums Martin picked up at the table-top sale for you last year, when he noticed a photo of Lock Keeper's Cottage amongst them.'

My heart is racing. When I lent them to her, I had no idea she was my mother, and I thought her interest was purely historical.

'But getting money out of him... isn't that blackmail?' I whisper.

'No, Immi. All I said was that my grandmother was the nurse who took up residence in Lock Keeper's Cottage back in 1936, to look after Henry's ailing wife. There was no need to say any more than that. My mother always suspected that the family knew my grandmother left her position because she was having a baby and Henry was the father. As it turned out, Henry left no official heirs, which suited them perfectly, as everything went to Stephen in the end. Stephen is in his seventies now and there's no point in raking up the past after all these years. I then told him all about the Santa Ahoy cruises and the new children's playground and asked if he would like to make a donation. The choice was his entirely.'

I can't believe Mum put herself in that position. When she finally sat me down and told me who she was, I also learnt about the family connection to the Forbeses. Mum had no interest in it, other than she longed to see a photo of her biological grandfather. Ironically, it was looking through that pile of old photos and albums with her as we talked about the history of Aysbury over a year ago that was the turning point for us both. We'd been acquaintances, rather than friends, up to that point. But our interest in history, mine in particular about Lock Keeper's Cottage, turned out to be a bonding experience.

'It was a big risk, Mum. And one you needn't have taken as it turns out,' I declare, shaking my head sorrowfully.

'As it turns out, you're right, Immi. But I believe in karma. It doesn't right the wrong that was done, but Henry's life was a sad one. He lost his wife and the woman with whom he sought comfort – my grandmother and your great-grandmother. Even if their backgrounds hadn't been worlds apart, I don't believe they would have made a life together. It was a different time, where everyone knew their place and Henry was already a broken man at the point. You forgave me, my lovely Immi, and my mother and grandmother forgave Henry for his wrongdoing. It's as simple as that. But it doesn't do that family any harm to acknowledge the charity work being done on their doorstep to support the local community.'

At the end of the evening Fisher walks me back to Lock Keeper's Cottage and before we part, he gives me the biggest of hugs.

'Sleep well, darling girl. Let it all go now and start getting that head of yours around the fact that in six days' time you'll be tying the knot with Gray.'

As I get ready for bed, a sense of calm envelops me. When I woke up this morning I didn't leap out of bed as usual, but instead I pulled the duvet up over my head and groaned at the thought of what lay ahead. Now, here I am, feeling that somehow the impossible has happened. Someone up there is looking after me and I wonder if it's Grandma Nell. She loved it when a wrong was righted, and maybe this miracle is her doing...

'Sunday evenings don't get any better than this, Gray. Everything is right in our little world and it's about to get even better.'

Gray is lying on the rug in front of the fire, propped up with a mound of pillows and watching me toasting marshmallows. 'I think you're right,' he replies contentedly.'

I hand him a stick with a melting lump of goo precariously perched on the end, looking as if it might be on the move. 'Careful, it's hot.'

'Is that a burnt bit?' He screws up his face and I shake my head at him.

'Have this one, then.'

We swap and I lie down next to him, waving my sweet treat around to cool it down.

'Grandma preferred roasting chestnuts and Tollie enjoyed white sliced bread. Toast doesn't taste any better than when it has that hint of smokiness to it.'

It's the twentieth of December and Gray doesn't go back to work until the second week of January. The last of the Santa Ahoy cruises are done, our wedding is the day after tomorrow, and on

Boxing Day everyone will be attending the tenth anniversary party at the village hall.

'Remember last year? You were frazzled and panicking about a little engagement party.' He smiles to himself, then chuckles.

'Ah, the good old days,' I reply as Gray starts to hum the tune to 'Let It Snow'.

When my phone begins to ring, he places a hand on my arm. 'Don't answer it. Whatever it is can wait.' Of course, I ignore him and jump straight up to grab it off the new coffee table.

'Hey, Mum. No, you're not disturbing us,' I reply as Gray stares at me, rolling his eyes.

'We're on our way to a police station in Norfolk to collect Ziggy. We have no idea what time we'll be back, but we wanted you to know the good news. Patrick has handed himself in!'

'Really? Oh, Mum, that's brilliant news! Ziggy must be really missing you and I'm so glad Patrick finally did the right thing.'

Gray is already on his feet and walking towards me. Well, dancing towards me as he hums is a more accurate description.

'Me too, Immi. I said that any person who is capable of loving and caring for an animal can't be all bad. The police officer assured me she was fine and being extremely vocal, so that tells me she's okay, bless her.'

'She's not in a cell, is she?' I ask, horrified to think of Ziggy locked up, and Gray stops in his tracks.

'Oh, no, they've all been fussing over her. One of the policemen even went out and bought her a litter tray. Now, how thoughtful is that? I bet she was really stressing, needing to pop outside, and she wouldn't have her bearings. We might never have seen her again if they hadn't been so thoughtful.'

'Well, thanks for letting me know and drive safely. See you tomorrow!'

Gray comes closer. 'They found Ziggy?'

'Yes. Patrick walked into a police station in Norfolk to hand himself in and Ziggy is with him. Mum and Fisher are heading there now to collect her.'

Money can be, and has been, replaced. Ziggy, however, is unique and life hasn't been quite the same without her in it.

* * *

Normally, at this hour on a Sunday evening my spirits begin to dip at the thought of waving Gray off in the morning, so it feels wonderfully decadent as we laze back on the sofa to watch a film. Gray loves musicals, obviously, and tonight I figured the choice was his. He picked *North by Northwest*, starring Cary Grant and directed by Alfred Hitchcock. It dates back to 1959 but Gray gives me a running commentary about how well the music score works to heighten the tension. It's a welcome distraction after all the angst over Patrick and Ziggy, until I glance up and see Tollie at the patio doors and I hurry over to slide them open.

'Come in, it's freezing out there.'

'Yep. Sure is. At least we won't be gettin' any snow by the looks of it. Can I have a quick word?'

'Come on through to the hallway. This is Gray's favourite bit,' I half whisper and he nods in Gray's direction.

'What's up?' I ask, frowning, as Tollie doesn't look happy.

'What's this I hear about Patrick?'

Oh, darn it. My face drops and I don't know quite what to say.

'I thought it was odd that he hasn't been around, and I just had a pint with Cameron at The Bullrush and he says Patrick is no longer rentin' Byre Cottage. Is this somethin' to worry about?'

'Let's pop up to Gray's studio,' I reply diplomatically.

Tollie follows me upstairs and when we walk through the door he whistles. 'Goodness, this is quite a set-up Gray has here.'

'Yes. He's hoping to work from home a lot more in the future. There's still some kit on his wish list, but every project gets him closer to his target. Anyway, take a seat.'

'Right. What's goin' on?'

I start at the beginning and don't stop until Tollie is aware of everything, including the fact that Patrick has now handed himself in. Naturally, he's in a state of shock. No one knows for sure what will happen next, or whether any of the money will ever be recovered.

'Why didn't you tell me what was goin' on?' His tone is accusatory, and I feared this would be his response.

'There were enough of us involved to sort it out and, to be honest, Granddad,' I use the term affectionately, so that he'll understand that I meant well, 'we didn't want it to bring everyone down when we'd all worked so hard.'

Tollie sits quietly, shaking his head. 'He must 'ave been desperate, Immi.' The compassion in Tollie's voice surprises me. I thought he'd be angry. 'Well, thanks for tellin' me the truth, even though you should have told me at the beginnin'. I understand why you didn't want word to get out, but nothin' fazes me at my time of life, Immi. And I can't believe how fast you acted to turn it around.'

'It wasn't down to me. Gray and Mum managed between them to get donations to cover the loss and more. It's going to be the best year ever, Tollie.'

Tollie's chin has sunk down onto his chest. 'Your grandma would have loved to see you and Gray here, in the cottage.' His voice breaks a little as he stands, pushing back his shoulders and swallowing hard.

'I know. And I think of her all the time.'

'Thanks for mendin' fences with Daphne. She's not in my life to replace Nell, but we're good company for each other. That's a comfort and it means a lot to me that you talked her into going to the weddin', m'dear. Anyway, I'm glad it all turned out well in the end. I hope Patrick has learnt his lesson. The sins we commit weigh heavy on our souls, but it's never too late to seek redemption. At least returnin' Ziggy to your mum is a comfort.'

As I follow Tollie downstairs, it strikes me that I've never heard him talk like that before. I hope he doesn't regard being with Daphne as a sin, as that wouldn't be right, or fair. If they bring each other a little happiness, they're hurting no one. He once told me that he was just waiting to be called to 'upstairs', as he termed it, and that made me panic. It would be wonderful to think that he might not be so eager to let go of his grasp on life now. He's fit and healthy again, and he's more active than a lot of people much younger than him.

I see him out, and when I turn around Gray is no longer watching his film.

'Tollie figured out that something was up, then? I can't say I'm surprised.'

'Yes. I told him everything and he took it well enough.'

'Good. Now come and sit next to me. There's something I need to tell you too.' Gray pats the cushion next to him and I can see he's uneasy. 'I have an admission to make and at first I thought it was a brilliant idea, then as the days have gone by I've begun to wonder whether I should have consulted you about it first.'

As I lower myself down next to him, Gray clasps my hand in his, and stares deep into my eyes as if he's apologising to me. 'Immi, don't be cross with me, but I changed my name by deed poll. I know we didn't really discuss it properly, but it was something I've given a lot of thought to, and it felt right at the time.'

Uh, oh. My mind goes into overdrive. *Do you, Immi Tolliman take Elvis Adams to be your lawfully wedded husband?* He wouldn't, would he? Oh, Gray, there are times when that weird and wonderful mind of yours isn't quite in touch with reality. I compose myself, fearing the worst.

'Okay. Who am I marrying?'

He licks his lips nervously. 'Gray Tolliman-Adams.'

I throw myself at him, my tears wetting the shoulder of his shirt. 'Oh, I love it! And Tollie will be so touched. I would gladly have taken your name as it was,' I sob, 'but this means so much to me. Gray, you are my rock, my hero.'

As Gray settles back to watch the remainder of the film, I grab my notebook and a pen. This time last year I wrote a heartfelt letter to Santa, after what had been a rather difficult year. There was only one thing that I wanted – to celebrate Christmas with the man I love, Gray, by my side. I can look back now and laugh, because I did get what I wanted, plus a few surprises I wasn't expecting.

This year will be different.

Dear Santa,

If ever I had any doubts that you could deliver, the events of last year made them all disappear. You gave me exactly what I asked for and more. It wasn't the most romantic of Christmases, it's true, but it was the best fun ever.

This year is the last time I will write to you and send my letter in wisps of smoke up the chimney. It's not that I've stopped believing, but my life feels complete in a way it never did before. And I've come to the realisation that the magic of Christmas is a gift that exists within us all if we choose to use it.

So, as Aysbury's chief elf, I will continue the tradition and inspire children to believe. I know that sometimes the impossible can happen because of the people who understand that giving is the most precious gift of all. And that, Santa, is down to you.

With much love,

Immi

'What are you burning?' Gray calls over to me.

'My letter to Santa.'

'Oh dear, am I in trouble? I thought we weren't giving each other gifts this year?'

'We're not. This is a goodbye letter.'

Gray's face drops. 'What? You're hanging up your elf suit?'

'No. Never. But this is one tradition I've carried on, simply because I couldn't let go of the past. But now it's time to move on.'

Gray gets up and pops in a CD, and as Christmas carols fill the air he reaches out for my hand and waltzes me over to the Christmas tree.

'And you didn't even ask for snow?' He checks, stopping for a moment to look down into my eyes, teasingly.

'I most definitely did not ask for snow. The last thing we want now is for our guests to get stranded on their way here.'

'And, I'm just checking, but we definitely aren't buying presents for each other?'

'Correct. I do have a wedding gift for you, but that's not the same thing.'

He peers at me, screwing up his face. 'Ah ha! I knew it! Luckily, I have something for you, too.'

'You do? What is it?'

'It's a surprise.'

'Along with the wedding arrangements...' I muse.

'You agreed to leave those in my capable hands. It's too late to change your mind now. Besides, my partners in crime did their best to keep my feet firmly planted on the ground.'

I sink into him, and Gray wraps his arms around me as if he's never going to let me go. The night before the wedding he's going to stay with Rona, who is inviting Fisher and Val around for the evening. Sarah is coming here and we plan to watch back-to-back feel-good films, in between applying face packs and doing our nails. We decided against hen and stag dos at the very beginning and, given all the excitement lately, it was so the right decision to make.

When you find your soulmate, everything falls into place and it fills you with a sense of peace. That was the one thing that was missing from my life and now I've finally found it.

30

HERE COMES THE BRIDE

When the doorbell sounds and I hear Sarah greeting Rona and Val, the hairdresser is still fussing with my French veil.

I've chosen a clip decorated with rhinestones, which secures a small veil that covers my eyes and hangs down over one cheek. Having curled my hair and pinned it back at the sides to allow a single ringlet to hang either side of my face, she's finding it tricky positioning it. I'm about to ask her to give up when she mutters a triumphant, 'Yes!'

'Thank goodness. I was about to suggest we give it a miss. Thank you so much, Claire, for your patience.'

'My pleasure. You and Sarah look lovely. Do you want me to help you on with your dress before I go?'

'No. It's fine, thank you. I'm going to need to calm my nerves a little first.'

'It's very pretty,' she comments, gazing at the hangers hooked over the wardrobe doors. 'It's classic, simple, but elegant. Anyway, have a fabulous time, Immi. I'll see myself out.'

'Would you ladies like a coffee, or a tea?' Sarah calls up from downstairs.

'Claire is just going and I'm good, thanks!'

After seeing Claire out, I sit back down and stare at myself in the mirror. The moment I tried on the second dress I knew it was the one, although it's a lot more bridal looking than I'd initially envisaged. But it's good to step outside your comfort zone occasionally and I smile back at myself, feeling content. There's a gentle tap on the door and it opens an inch or two.

'Should I close my eyes?' Mum asks before stepping inside.

'No. It's fine, come on in.'

'Oh, Immi, your hair and make-up is lovely. What an enchanting little veil – it really suits you!'

'Thanks. It took Claire about twenty minutes of fiddling around to get it in place, but I think it was worth the hassle.'

'There's no "I think" about it, it's perfect. Are you ready to put on your dress?'

'Almost. I just need a couple of minutes to compose myself.' Her face instantly falls a little. 'Could you pop back in five minutes?'

'Of course. Shout when you're ready.'

As soon as the door closes, I open the top drawer of the dressing table and pull out one of the old photo albums. Carefully turning the pages, I find a photo of Dad, Grandma and me, sitting around the table one Christmas. I was seven, maybe even eight years old. It was taken here, in Lock Keeper's Cottage. Dad is reading the jokes from the Christmas crackers and Grandma and I are laughing, while I'm playing with what looks like one of those plastic games with a tiny metal ball in it.

As I browse through the photographs, I realise how lucky I am. I had a wonderful childhood, and Dad and Grandma would love the idea of a Christmas wedding.

'It's not a day to start feeling nostalgic, Immi,' I say aloud by way of a reprimand. 'But that doesn't stop me from wishing you were both here. Mum is with me today and I thought you'd like to know that.' Running my fingers over the photograph, with my other hand I blow them both a kiss.

'Mum, I'm ready,' I call out and seconds later she appears. I wonder if she was standing outside on the landing and whether she heard what I said, but she's giving nothing away.

'Okay,' she says brightly. 'We need you to step into this dress so that we don't mess up your hair.'

Even in my wildest dreams I could never have envisioned myself slipping into a V-neck taffeta tea dress and feeling able to carry off the look with confidence. It has no decoration at all, but the cut and the fit make me feel tall and elegant. There's a hint of glamour to its simplicity and I can't wait to see Gray's reaction.

'Your waist is tiny, Immi. You look stunning,' Mum comments.

'I know I've lost a bit of weight recently, but it just accentuates my stomach. At least the folds hide that, or I'd look pregnant.' I laugh.

Mum smiles. 'Now isn't that a thought? Here, hold onto my arm while you slip on your shoes. They're so pretty.'

They're a kitten heel, Audrey Hepburn style, in a slightly darker shade of grey and with a single line of rhinestones running along the side. I turn around to open the little jewellery box, a present from Rona and Mum. I put in single pearl earrings, fastening them at the back.

'A touch of perfume and then it's time to go downstairs,' I declare.

'Shall I bring your jacket?' Mum offers and I step forward to put my arms around her.

'Yes, please. And thank you, Mum. Having you here means everything.'

She sniffs, and sucks in her cheeks.

'Right, deep breath,' she replies, determined to hold it together. 'We mustn't keep everyone waiting.'

As I step out onto the landing, I hear Tollie's voice and the sounds of laughter. Negotiating the stairs one at a time, my legs are shaking.

'Hold onto the rail and take a few slow, deep breaths as you go, Immi,' Mum says softly. At the bottom, we stand side by side for a moment and she gives me an affirming nod. 'It's time.'

As I walk into the kitchen and through into the sitting area the sound of my heels on the floor announces my arrival and everyone stops talking as they all turn around.

'My goodness, you all look so lovely. Anyone would think we were going to a wedding!' I exclaim.

'Beautiful, just beautiful,' Rona remarks, glassy-eyed.

'It's perfect, Immi, it really is,' Sarah adds.

Daphne is all smiles. 'You're glowing, Immi. Gray is going to be overwhelmed.'

Tollie is speechless as our eyes meet.

'No tears,' Mum states adamantly. 'We don't want to ruin Immi's make-up before the groom has seen her in all her glory.'

Tollie takes a deep breath, then walks towards me, smiling.

'This is a proud day for me, m'dear. Not just because you look amazin' in that dress, but because it's obvious how happy you are.' He looks distinguished in a new, pale grey suit, white shirt and heather-coloured tie.

I think he's about to lean in and hug me, but Mum steps between us. 'Mind the gown,' she fusses. 'Right, is the car here?'

Tollie walks over to the patio doors to check. 'Ready and waiting.'

'I'm not late, am I?'

'Five, maybe ten minutes, that's all. You don't want to appear too eager. Make him sweat,' Tollie replies, laughing.

'Oh, the flowers,' Sarah calls out, rushing off to the utility room to retrieve the box that one of the florists from the Lockside Nurseries dropped in first thing this morning.

It takes at least five minutes to get everyone sorted and then Mum helps me into my fitted, waist-length heather-coloured jacket. The wool blend is a fine weave and, being lined and with long sleeves, it's cosy. When I pull up the little collar it stands nicely against my neck and will stop any draughts.

The bouquet is a simple hand-tied cluster of heather-coloured roses with fronds of eucalyptus leaves. As we leave the cottage and I step out into what is a cold but bright afternoon, I don't know why I was stressed about today. The fun part is here at last and I'm going to enjoy every single moment.

A friend of Fisher's has a white Jaguar SJL and he kindly offered to be chauffeur for the day. I didn't like to refuse such a generous offer, but, in all honesty, I would have been equally happy jumping into Tollie's runaround. I stare out of the window, thinking how surreal this feels.

It's a smooth ride and when we pull into the car park of St James's church, which is just the other side of the marina, I couldn't be happier. Gray made the right choice because this church is very special to me. We always attended the evening Christmas carol services here when Grandma was alive.

'This is perfect, but we could have walked,' I comment, laughing.

'Brides don't walk, well, not along a canal.'

There's a luxury minibus already parked up, so Gray's friends have obviously arrived safely, and there are a variety of cars belonging to our other guests.

Rona parks on the other side of us, and I watch as Sarah, Daphne and Mum follow her into the church.

'Right, are you ready?' Tollie asks as I wait for my wonderful chauffeur to open the door.

'I am.' I turn in my seat to swing my legs out and stand up as our driver, Jeff, catches my hand.

'My goodness, Gray is one lucky man,' he comments, and I feel myself blushing. 'You'd better get used to the compliments, Immi, because you're going to get a lot of them!'

Tollie comes to my rescue, but not before I plant a kiss on Jeff's cheek. 'Thank you. I don't think I've ever had such a comfortable ride.'

Tollie links arms with me. 'Come on, there's fashionably late and there's *late* late. We'd best walk a bit quick.' Grandma would have found that comment hilarious.

The birds are singing in the trees, happy to bask in the sunshine, even though it's only warm enough to melt this morning's frost and the temperatures are icy. I'm glowing from head to toe and if we don't slow down a little, I'm in danger of breaking out into a sweat. Tollie eases up, seeing that I'm taking two steps to his one stride as I tread carefully in my new shoes. Thank goodness I didn't choose a long dress.

Fisher is standing just outside the church door and he waves, hurrying across to us.

'Everything all right? You're a sight for sore eyes, my darling girl. Rona and Val are inside, and Sarah is waiting in the vestibule. I'll warn you now, Gray is mightily nervous and emotional.'

'Oh, no! Poor Gray. Sorry we're late – there's no one to blame but me. I should have walked, it would have been quicker,' I half whisper, hoping Jeff is out of earshot.

Once inside, it's time to take a breath, unbutton my jacket and compose myself. Sarah comes over to turn down the collar and position it so that it falls perfectly. The smile she gives me is one of reassurance and I feel blessed to have such a wonderful friend.

Sarah looks amazing in her dress, complemented by the unusual cut of her jacket, but she does look a little chilly.

'Why don't you stand next to the radiator to warm up a bit?' I suggest as I move over to stand in the draught from the partially opened door, to cool down.

Tollie, on the other hand, looks flushed as Fisher comes over, lifting up my hand to place a kiss on the back of it before he heads inside. This is it. Sarah follows him to the double doors, peeping through to await the signal.

'Right, m'dear. There's no point askin' if you're sure, because I know the answer and I wouldn't be walkin' you down the aisle if I didn't think Gray was the man for you. But are you ready?'

'I am.' With that, Tollie plants a kiss very gently on my temple.

Sarah gives Fisher a discreet wave and seconds later the music begins. To my delight it's a piece I recognise. Gray wrote it for me a couple of months after we first met, but it's being played by string instruments and as we're walking down the aisle I realise the music is live. Off to one side, near the altar of this small parish church, are five musicians seated in a semicircle and the sound is heavenly. Each note touches my heart. Gray was so excited when he played it for me that first time and he said that it was the music he heard in his head whenever he was around me.

With almost forty guests in total, only the back two rows are empty, and I smile and nod, trying to remember to turn from side to side to catch as many people as I can. Rona's cheeks are rosy, and she looks so happy, it's wonderful to see.

Then my eyes are front and centre. I come to a halt alongside Gray and he turns around as I hand my bouquet to Sarah. Tears instantly fill his eyes and seconds later I'm looking at him and he's struggling to focus, too. It's like swimming under water and we start laughing, which makes it worse, because the tears start to overflow as his eyes crinkle up.

'Don't,' I half whisper. 'I sat still for nearly forty-five minutes having this make-up applied and I can't burst into tears!'

Churches have amazing acoustics, it seems, and a little ripple of laughter runs through the small gathering of relatives and friends.

Fisher hands Gray a tissue and he swipes it across his eyes. He looks so devastatingly handsome I just want to kiss him now. Standing there in his light grey suit, white shirt, and heather-coloured tie, which is slightly askew, that's my Gray. As I pull myself together, we turn to face the front.

When it's time to say our vows, the vicar begins. 'Repeat after me. I, Gray Tolliman-Adams, take you, Imogen Tolliman, to be my lawfully wedded wife.'

In the second or two it takes Gray to draw in a breath and begin speaking, I turn my head to look across at Tollie, who is standing next to Daphne. He gives me a huge smile, surreptitiously wiping his eyes. Then I turn back to look at Gray as he stumbles over the words and decides to start all over again. These are the moments I will remember in the years to come that will make me smile, not what I'm wearing, or how much money we spent on the wedding. These are the precious memories that will never fade.

31

MR AND MRS TOLLIMAN-ADAMS

'I know it was all change at the eleventh hour, but Val and I felt sure you'd regret having a civil ceremony. Did I do the right thing?' Gray enquires anxiously, the moment Jeff swings shut the door of the Jaguar. Having taken a countless number of photographs inside the church and a few in the grounds, we're all feeling the cold and conscious that our guests will be hungry.

My eyes are sparkling as I turn to my husband – my husband! 'The beautiful quintet, the flowers and the service, it was simply magical, Gray.'

His smile lights up his face. 'That's all I needed to hear.'

He clasps my hand, then raises it to his mouth. 'There are a couple of surprises yet to come, but I know they'll make you happy.'

I can't stop grinning as he plants a kiss on the back of my hand, before releasing it.

Jeff slides into the driver's seat, half turning to look at us. 'Shall we set off on our little mystery tour, then, Mr and Mrs Tolliman-Adams?'

'Mystery tour?' I thought we were going to the village hall, which is less than five-minutes away by car.

'Drive on,' Gray commands with a grin.

Jeff turns right when we leave the church car park and I'm totally confused. As our journey continues, it feels more as if we're out on a leisurely afternoon drive through the country lanes, rather than heading for a specific destination. Then I realise what he's doing.

'We've just gone in a full circle, Gray!' I declare. 'What's going on?'

Jeff pulls back into the church car park and all our guests' vehicles are still parked up. 'She's rumbled us,' Gray replies, laughing, and Jeff joins in.

As the car pulls to a halt directly in front of the church, I'm curious about where we're going. There is nothing immediately on the doorstep that will accommodate a wedding party and we surely aren't walking along the narrow lanes to the village hall on such a bitterly cold day.

'Do not worry, Immi, all will be revealed,' Gray says with gusto.

Jeff opens the door and helps me out.

Mystified, I go with the flow. 'Thank you, Jeff. It was a relaxing little drive and I did enjoy taking the scenic route,' I muse.

Gray joins me and, holding my hand, he steers me along the path that wends its way around to the rear of St James's. There are three huge oak trees on this side of the churchyard, and we follow the old lichen-covered path to the rear gate. In front of us is the marina and I'm surprised when we continue walking straight ahead.

'Are we going to The Bullrush Inn?' I query, thinking that I've discovered their secret plan, even though Sarah and Kurt would be crazy to shut it for the entire afternoon and evening so close to Christmas.

Gray says nothing, but seconds later, instead of going straight on towards the bridge, we take a left turn and then I spot a wreath of greenery, threaded with heather-coloured ribbon and white roses, pinned up on the marina's office door.

As Gray leads me inside and up the stairs to the viewing gallery, I'm speechless.

'Surprise!' Tollie's voice booms out. Everyone is holding a champagne flute and our guests raise their glasses as he continues. 'Please join me in wishin' a very warm welcome to Mr and Mrs Tolliman-Adams!'

In a daze, I glance around, taking in the beautiful decorations and the view out onto the canal from the panoramic windows. It feels as though we've stepped into a Christmas wonderland, with garlands of greenery hung from the ceiling. It's too much to take in all at once. In the background, the music changes and I realise that Gray has created a playlist of some of our favourite seasonal tracks.

Along the wall to one side, a buffet is laid out on a long line of tables covered in white linen tablecloths, and there are tiny silver snowflakes scattered in amongst the plates. Tall, silver candelabra with ivy wrapped around the bases and flickering tapered white candles, add a touch of elegance, as do the small bowls of heather-pink roses adding yet another fragrance to the air.

Gray puts his arm around my shoulders, resting his head against mine.

'Well, this is the first time my wife has been rendered totally speechless. I guess we did a great job of surprising her!' This breaks the silence, and everyone begins talking at the same time. I'm surrounded by a sea of smiling faces and I feel a little overwhelmed.

'I knew you'd love it,' Gray whispers into my ear. 'Your hands are cold, my darling. You need warming up.'

Mum and Fisher hurry over to us and at last we can hug properly. 'Oh, Immi. I can tell by your face how thrilled you are with how everything has turned out,' Mum says, delighted by my reaction.

'It's... beautiful. Stunning. It's everything I could have dreamt of and more. You've all worked so hard, and words aren't enough to express my thanks.' A lump rises in my throat as Mum stands back and Fisher closes in.

'No, you're beautiful and stunning, Immi. And I have never seen you looking as radiant as you do today.'

As he steps away I can see how choked up he is.

'Right. Our bride and groom need warming up. What can I get you both?'

'I'd love a hot chocolate, if it's not too much trouble.'

'Me, too,' Gray adds, and Mum claps her hands together, raising them to her chest as she gazes at us both.

'I'm so happy for you. Right, let's get these drinks sorted. Fisher, can you ask Tollie to announce the buffet is open, please? It will give Immi and Gray a little time to relax and um... catch up.'

Fisher gives Mum a little salute, then flashes me a rueful smile before they both walk off in different directions.

'Catch up?' I turn to look at Gray.

'Yes. There's someone you haven't had a chance to meet yet.'

Behind us, Tollie raises his voice to be heard up above the general chatter.

'If I can please have everyone's attention for a brief moment,' he asks, and the room quietens. 'Now that we're all beginnin' to warm up a little, please make your way over to the buffet. We can't have anyone faintin' from hunger and it's been a while since breakfast. Enjoy!' There's a little ripple of laughter. Tollie looks so proud and happy. I can't spot Daphne in the crowd, but I know she's somewhere around.

Gray gently yanks on my hand. 'This is the last surprise, I promise you.' He leans into me, his eyes so full of love it melts my heart, but I can see a momentary hesitation. As our lips touch, I close my eyes, savouring the moment. How did Gray know this place had a special meaning for me? Was it Fisher's idea? I wonder. Even the walls have had a fresh coat of white paint, I notice. That must have taken some organising and I can't believe how hard they've worked to pull this off. It's incredible.

When I open my eyes, Gray leads me over to the viewing area, where I've spent many a lunch break with Fisher sitting on the bank of seats, watching the boats cruising along. Today, garlands of greenery and little bunches of hand-tied roses decorate the handrail in front of the window, making a festive frame for one of my favourite views. It couldn't be more perfect.

Rona is deep in conversation with someone and as we approach, they draw apart.

'Immi, my dear.' She catches hold of my hand, placing an arm around my shoulder to give me a hug. 'Your fingers are freezing.'

'Yes, Mum is making us a hot chocolate. It's all so wonderful, Rona. It seems my wedding planners had a much clearer idea of what I wanted today than I did myself!' I declare happily.

Her cheeks are glowing and there's a lightness to her countenance that I haven't seen before as she turns to the man standing next to her. 'Using this room was Fisher's idea and it's such a unique setting, even if it did take a lot of preparation. Val, Gray and I were only responsible for the finishing touches, but I'm so glad you're happy with it. And now it's time to introduce you to Gray's father, Grayson.'

The man in front of me is tall and distinguished-looking.

Gray has the same chin and jaw line, but his eyes and hair are the same colour as Rona's. Grayson offers me his hand, and we shake, but as we do so he places his other hand over the top of mine and lingers for a second or two.

'It's a real pleasure to meet you at last, Immi. That was a lovely service,' he comments warmly.

This was the last thing I ever expected and I'm not sure what to say to him.

'It was, wasn't it? And yet I didn't really play any part in planning it. That's down to Gray, Rona and my mum.'

'Well, they did an awesome job of it!'

'I can't argue with that.' I smile warmly. 'Hopefully, your stay will be long enough for us to catch up properly, Grayson. And no doubt you will be doing a little sightseeing while you are here.' I'm guessing, of course, but Rona looks delighted.

'I'd appreciate that, Immi. Aysbury is a lovely little community and Rona certainly seems happy living here.' His words are sincere and I'm glad he's able to be a part of today.

Gray comes in search of me, giving his father an acknowledging smile before grasping my hand in his. 'Sorry to interrupt, but it's time to get my wife warmed-up a little,' he says apologetically. 'We'll leave you to enjoy the buffet.'

'Of course, and I will. It looks very festive indeed.'

Gray leads me out onto the landing to stand next to a radiator.

'Ah, here you go, guys,' Mum says, walking up the stairs with two hot chocolates on a tray. 'This should do the trick.'

'Thank you. My toes are already showing signs of life again, which is a good start,' I declare with some relief.

'I'll see you back inside, then.'

As soon as Mum is out of earshot, I turn to Gray. 'What is your father doing here?' I blurt out, unable to contain myself any longer.

'My father is the mystery donor I approached. He wasn't looking for anything in return, especially as he wasn't aware that we were getting married. Mum decided that it wasn't her place to share the news, given that I hadn't mentioned it when the two of us met up.'

'What made you reach out to him?'

Gray bows his head, staring down at the mug in his hands.

'Tollie's situation made me stop and reconsider my actions. After handing out advice to you, I was beginning to feel like a bit of a hypocrite, to be honest. I knew that my mum wanted my father to be here, although she never said as much. It was all last-minute and things are a bit... strained between us, but at least I won't have any regrets looking back on today. And I knew that it would make you happy, too.'

'Oh, Gray, I'm so glad you did that; if not for yourself, or for your father, for Rona's sake.'

'Hey, Christmas is a time of goodwill to all men, isn't that what they say? And it felt like the right thing to do. Anyway, let's finish our drinks and start circulating. It's time to show off my new wife.'

'Your forever wife,' I add with a sense of pride.

* * *

As we join the queue to grab some food, it seems like the most natural thing in the world to stand around chatting and it's wonderful to see everyone having a good time. The viewing gallery isn't a huge space, but it accommodates forty-one people with ease, while also giving it a cosy feel. There's just enough space for people to spread out a little, plenty of seating for those who want to enjoy the views, and it's easy to mingle.

I spot Daphne patrolling the room for empty glasses, tray in hand. I walk over to say thank you, and I give her a brief hug.

'It's so good of you to help and much appreciated,' I acknowledge.

'Oh, it's nothing, Immi. I like to keep busy. I can't keep up with Tollie, right now. He's talking to some of Gray's friends, telling them all about you when you first came to live at Aysbury. He says you were a firecracker.'

I shake my head, fearing the worst. 'No doubt he'll trot out the tale about when our housekeeper quit, as she soon tired of hearing us arguing all the time. I was so precocious! Tollie and I went for three weeks living under the same roof without talking to each other at one point.'

'You did? Was the housekeeper someone local?'

'My mum, Val. I didn't know she was my mum at the time, obviously.'

Daphne looks shocked. 'How did you get through it?'

'Tollie and I both dug in our heels and went on strike. Eventually we didn't have any clean clothes and I was fed up living on beans on toast, because that was all I could cook for myself. We called a truce and spent several days establishing some house rules and getting everything in order. Together we shared the cleaning and the laundry, Tollie cooked, and I washed up. Mum's plan worked and Tollie and I learnt a lot about each other at the same time.'

'It's funny how things work out, isn't it? Anyway, can I get you a drink?'

'I'd love a soft drink, something thirst-quenching, thank you, Daphne. Fruit juice would be great if we have it.'

'No problem.' She nods her head, indicating behind me.

'Oh, hi, Sylvia and Ollie – how are you both?'

Sylvia leans in to give me a hug, and Ollie follows on behind.

'Thrilled to be here, Immi. What a gorgeous dress – so unusual and perfect for a Christmas wedding. And this is delightful. We feel quite spoilt looking out onto such an incredible view,' Sylvia enthuses.

I draw them closer to the window. 'You see where the footbridge ends, on the other side of the towpath? If you scan along until you see the run of tall hedging, the chimney stack rising up behind it is Lock Keeper's Cottage.'

'Wow. That's some location,' Ollie remarks. 'We've often talked about taking a week to cruise the canals on a narrowboat and this trip has inspired us to finally do something about it.'

'It has, indeed,' Sylvia continues. 'It's time we stopped talking and booked something. Fisher was just telling us about some of the lovely places to stop off and he's going to put us in touch with one of the canalboat owners.'

'I hope you can arrange something. If you do, let us know and we can all meet up. If you fancy an overnight stay to break your journey, we have a guest bedroom.'

Sylvia looks delighted. 'That would be fun, thank you, Immi.'

Daphne returns with my drink, and I take it from her, introducing Sylvia and Ollie. Fisher joins us and after a few minutes I leave them chatting about the history of the area.

I notice Rona standing all alone, gazing out of the window, and head in her direction.

'Do you think we're going to get a white Christmas?' I ask.

'Maybe a light dusting, but there's nothing heavy forecast.' She falls silent, and I can see that she's not sure what to say to me.

'I'm glad Gray invited Grayson.' I check around, but neither of them is in sight. 'Did you have any warning of his arrival?'

'No. Grayson is staying at the Linden Hotel and he travelled to Aysbury by taxi yesterday afternoon to see me. When I answered the door I almost fainted.' She chuckles. 'I'm so glad that they can at least talk civilly to each other. It's a start,' she concedes.

'Do you really believe that?'

'I like to think so, but I really don't know for sure.'

'And as for you and Grayson?' I venture, keeping my voice low.

Her eyes brighten and I can see she's trying not to get her hopes up, but she can't hide the optimism leaping up within.

'I haven't given up,' she whispers back at me. 'He and Gray popped outside to get a little fresh air.' She smiles knowingly. 'Hmm, in this weather. So, who knows what will happen next?'

Tollie waves me over to the buffet table. 'I'm glad for you, Rona. I'd better see what Tollie wants. He really does scrub up well, my granddad.'

'And he has a little skip back in his step. I'd better top up of some of those plates on the buffet before my men get back,' she replies happily.

'Tollie, what's up?'

'Fisher and I need to make our speeches at some point and there's a cake to cut.'

We stand side by side, gazing down at it. It's a simple, white-iced rectangular cake and there isn't a bride and groom decoration in sight. On top you would think someone had picked a handful of fresh greenery and laid it out. There's even a sprig of holly with red berries and yet it's all made from icing sugar.

'This is all so me, isn't it?'

'It is that, m'dear. And the church ceremony made me very emotional, indeed. That was a huge surprise, the name thing. It means a lot.'

'To me, too, Tollie.'

I hear Gray burst out laughing behind me, and Tollie and I turn around to see what's going on. Gray is standing over in the far corner with some of his friends, Sarah, Kurt, Jude and Jade.

An impromptu performance breaks out, as Wham's 'Last Christmas' has just begun playing in the background and they all start to sing along. Gray takes each of the girls by the hand and they spin around when he raises their arms in the air.

Martin and Ursula appear next to me as the whole room begins to erupt. Those who aren't singing put an arm in the air and begin swaying.

Ursula nods in Abe's direction. He's holding Ethel's hand and as he watches her he's mesmerised; she has a lovely voice and who would have thought that she'd know every single word?

'Now this is what I call a good old-fashioned weddin' celebration,' Tollie says with great satisfaction. 'I think it's time we broke out the bottles of The Bullrush Christmas Brew and some champagne for the ladies, naturally!' The party, it seems, is only just getting started.

As I glance down at the plain white-gold band gracing my finger next to Grandma's beautiful engagement ring, I still can't take it all in. After a year of incredible highs and unforeseen dramas, that's all behind us now. Is this the rainbow moment after the rainstorm? I wonder. They do say that there is a silver lining inside every cloud.

As I instinctively run my hands down over the waist of my dress, carefully smoothing the folds before I go to join Gray, I can't help thinking that nothing that has happened leading up to today is a coincidence. All that worry and angst, when really all I had to do was to believe that life has a plan for me and Gray. And looking back, I realise that was obvious from day one.

32

'Merry Christmas, wife,' Gray's voice seeps into my consciousness.

'Merry Christmas, husband – what time is it?'

'Five thirty. Are you awake?'

I groan. 'No. Not really. If you'd stop talking, I'd actually still be asleep. I'm not used to staying up until the early hours of the morning.'

'That's no fun. I want to give you your wedding present.'

'The one you, Tollie and Daphne organised last night when you ordered me up to bed and then kept me awake with your chatter?'

'Yes. I'm too excited about it. I'm going to head downstairs, turn up the heating and put on the Christmas tree lights. I'll give you ten minutes and then you can come down for the unveiling.'

'Is it another stag? A friend for Bert?' I ask, perking up.

'No. There is only one Bert, you know that.'

I yawn and stretch as Gray jumps out of bed and disappears out of the door. Lying here in the dark I reflect that he's such a kid at times. I love his enthusiasm, though. Yawning again, I ease myself out of bed and decide to dig out my favourite snowflake jumper to throw on over my pjs, and I'd better run a brush through my hair, too. I hope Gray is happy with the wedding gifts I have for him.

As I pull on my jumper, I walk over to the window to gaze out. The Retreat is in darkness still and it looks cold outside, but there's no sign of any snow. I hope it was the right thing to do today, deciding to stay home alone. It's the first Christmas ever that I've not sat around the table with family. But tomorrow is the big party at the village hall and even though we've had two days to ourselves already, the time has flown. It's been fun lazing around, although both afternoons we've headed out for a long walk. And after looking on enviously at owners throwing balls and sticks for their dogs, Gray has now decided he wants one, too.

'I'm waiting,' Gray calls out expectantly.

'On my way.'

I saunter downstairs, an envelope in my hand, a big smile on my face, and a *huge* sparkly snowflake on my jumper.

The moment my foot lands on the last tread of the stairs, Gray comes hurrying towards me.

'Close your eyes and I'll guide you into the room,' he insists, and I do as I'm told.

Except that he doesn't take me by the hand but stands behind me and makes me walk like a robot, guiding my arms. 'And what's this in your hand?' he asks, over my shoulder.

'Never you mind.'

He manoeuvres me into position. 'You can open them now.'

I gasp. Either side of my lovely fireplace is a wingback chair in an oatmeal-coloured fabric with small black stag heads printed on it. I swear Bert has a bit of a smile on his face now, too.

'Oh, Gray, I love them!' I squeal, throwing my arms around his neck, and he dances me around.

'I wasn't sure whether you'd prefer plain green to match the sofas, but I did pick up two green scatter cushions. Well, I asked Mum to sort that for me.'

'They make this room, Gray, and now we can sit and enjoy the fire, rather than lie on the rug pretending that we're comfortable,' I confess.

'Yes. It wasn't the best, was it?'

'Right, now it's your turn,' I state, waggling a finger at him. 'Surprise number one, or surprise number two? The choice is yours.'

'Well, two armchairs are hard to beat, so the gauntlet has been thrown down. Surprise number one, I think.'

'Oh, I'm pretty confident I'll win this challenge,' I reply breezily, holding out the envelope.

'Let's take a seat.' Gray indicates for me to step forward. 'You go first.'

'This is going to be my chair. That was always Tollie's side of the fireplace,' I explain. 'Well, open it, then.'

He teases the envelope open and begins reading. 'A luxury cookery weekend? Oh, that's a surprise.'

'Read on. It's not just two classes we'll be attending together, but we get to indulge in a pamper session in the spa every afternoon. Or a yoga class, if you want to find out what I do every Tuesday evening. Or you can learn all about wine from a vintner and take part in a tasting. It's in that beautiful manor house in Stroud, not far from the canal.'

'Ooh, a posh weekend away, then. And fine dining, too. When is it?'

'The weekend after next.'

Gray sits, deep in contemplation. 'It's a brilliant gift and I love it. But does it beat two stag chairs? I mean, aren't they incredibly comfortable?'

He settles himself back, thinking he's won.

'Well, you might like my second surprise even more – Gray, we're pregnant.'

Staring at him, I wonder whether he heard me as he hasn't moved a muscle.

'I couldn't believe it either, and I know we weren't trying. But, apparently, it's the reason why I've not been eating as much as I usually do, because I'm off my food. The doctor said that's normal with some pregnancies. I know we were looking forward to a new year without any hassles so that we could get into a nice little routine, but these things happen, and I really hope you're as happy about it as I am.'

'Stop talking, woman.' Gray jumps up out of his chair, throwing the envelope and the sheets of paper on the floor. Then he extends his hands in my direction, pulling me upright and into his arms. 'I thought we'd start off with a dog, but a baby is so much better! I just didn't think you were ready.'

'I'm not,' I reply. 'I'm terrified and I still can't quite believe it's real. I couldn't leave it much longer to tell you, though, as it won't be long until you'll notice it for yourself.'

'And I can't wait for that day!' Gray replies, grinning. 'I was so convinced I had played the trump card with those chairs, but you've blown my gift out of the water!'

* * *

After a leisurely breakfast Gray insists that I head upstairs for a relaxing bath.

'You can trust me to lay the table and pop everything in the oven,' he says firmly. I suppose, having bought our entire Christmas dinner in a one-stop shop at Marks & Spencer, it's just a case of sliding in the small foil trays and getting the timings

right. No culinary panics as there were last year, which is a huge
relief, but it was rather fun.

'Yes, boss.'

'And put on something nice. It is Christmas Day, after all. I'll
pop up in a while and change. You have an hour and a half, at
least.'

'I'd have broken the news sooner if I'd realised that you'd wait
on me hand and foot.' I laugh, giving him a quick kiss and scanning around for the book I purchased last week.

It's nice to take an hour to pamper myself and let the news
really sink in. I'd suspected for a while, but thought at first I'd lost
my appetite due to stress. Then it became obvious what was
happening, and I felt a little overwhelmed. There was so much
going on and I couldn't deal with it. Now, though, I feel excited at
one moment and scared witless the next. What if I go through the
same thing that my mum did? I talked to the doctor about post-
partum depression, and he said cases like that get picked up very
quickly these days and he is always on hand to talk things
through if I have any concerns.

Anyway, it's Christmas and my number one favourite day of
the year. But, after all the excitement of the wedding, it somehow
doesn't feel like it. Whether that's due to the sun trying desperately to break through the clouds, rather than snow covering the
ground as it did last year, I'm not sure. Gray is setting the table for
two and it's quiet, so quiet that the cottage feels a little... empty.

* * *

When eventually I go downstairs looking cosy in a new cream
cable-knit jumper and black leggings, the door into the kitchen is
shut. As I turn the handle, a lovely smell wafts towards me, and
the sight that greets me brings tears to my eyes.

'Oh, Merry Christmas, everyone!'

Tollie, Grayson and Fisher are standing in front of the glass doors, looking out over the meadow, glasses in hand.

Gray, is arranging chairs around the table and Mum, Rona and Daphne are laying out plates on the countertop. There's a whole turkey sitting on a platter with a mesh dome over it, and four pans on the hob simmering away.

They turn around to look at me and I stare at Gray, who hurries across, a hesitant look on his face. 'Here she is, then!' He leans in to kiss my cheek, giving me a comforting hug.

'Thank you, Gray. This is truly what Christmas is all about,' I whisper, stepping back from him. I am feeling a little bewildered, but totally delighted while making a concerted effort to mask my surprise.

The atmosphere is both lively and jolly. I take a moment to gaze around. The blue spruce looks elegant, draped in a network of sparkly white lights and heavily laden with decorations. The greenery in the far corner helps to give the room a sense of connection with the garden outside and adds a wonderful freshness to the air. And the garland draped over the mantlepiece above the fire looks authentic, even though it isn't real. The small silver bells I incorporated into the design contrast beautifully with the rich and vibrant red of the holly berries – and the bonus is that it will look equally good next year.

'It's so kind of you and Gray to invite us, Immi,' Rona pipes up. 'It was a little quiet back at the cottage.'

'Same for us, over in The Retreat,' Tollie chimes in. 'Wasn't it, Daphne?'

She nods. 'Yes, and I always cook a whole turkey, anyway. Between us all, there's plenty to go around.'

Mum looks up at me and I can see she's delighted to be here. 'Fisher and I were just saying the exact same thing, before Gray called. After the excitement of the wedding, it seemed a little flat getting up this morning.'

'Love those stag armchairs,' Tollie says, coming over to try one out. 'They've been stacked in the utility room in The Retreat for the last week,' he owns up, smiling to himself.

'I did wonder what was going on down here last night,' I reply. 'I would never have guessed it was going to be some new chairs, though. I thought Bert might be gaining a friend.'

'Oh, you'd never find another like him, m'dear. He's a one-off, for sure. So, what did you give Gray?'

I glance across at Gray and he looks back at me, uneasily. I simply shrug my shoulders.

'A couple's cookery weekend in a luxury hotel with all the perks,' he confirms.

'What a lovely idea,' Mum acknowledges.

Tollie is trying not to laugh. 'Immi prefers washing up to cooking, but it's never too late to learn something new.'

'I'm not much better,' Gray admits. 'But that wasn't the only surprise I—'

'Somethin's burnin',' Tollie interrupts.

'Oh, the stuffing!' Mum yanks open the oven door as Rona moves the trivets around. 'I think we can begin dishing up. Is the table ready?'

I walk over to check and I can see that Gray has done his best. We have our six new oak chairs, and two from The Retreat, spaced evenly around the table. I ironed the tablecloth yesterday and he's put out the silver charger plates, the best crystal wine glasses and laid out the knives and forks. He's even picked two bowls of Christmas roses and cut a selection of greenery. It does look festive and homely.

'All we need are some paper napkins, but aside from that we're all set to go. I'll come and give you a hand.'

'No, you ladies take a seat. Us guys can serve the food, can't we?' Tollie, Fisher and Grayson look at Gray and they seem happy enough to take charge.

Tollie carves the turkey, while Fisher and Gray start plating up the vegetables. Grayson is tasked with sorting out the wine.

'Right, ladies, white or red?'

When he reaches me, I decline. 'I'm in the mood for a nice cold bottle of water from the fridge, if you don't mind, Grayson, thank you.'

'My pleasure, Immi. What a wonderful surprise to be invited into your home today. It will certainly make this Christmas a memorable one for me.'

His smile is genuine and I can see that he's not simply being polite.

'Oh, it's snowing!' Daphne points and we all stare out at the tiniest of flakes, still small, but there is a steady stream and the sky seems full of them. 'They did say we might get a light dusting today.'

With the guys toing and froing with plates and condiments, it takes a little while to get everything sorted. I manage to distract Grayson, leading him over to gaze out at the snowy scene as we talk about the renovation work. In the background, the general chatter and laughter is the perfect cover for me to talk openly to him.

'Gray told me about your generosity, Grayson. It was kind of you to come to our rescue.'

He shakes his head. 'It's only money, Immi, although now I'm here I'm beginning to realise just how devastating it must have been for everyone when the theft was discovered. And, although it was totally unexpected, I really do think that what I have received in return is little short of a miracle.'

His sincerity is touching and instinctively I reach out to place my hand on his arm. 'Well, it wouldn't have been the same without you, Grayson, and Gray knew that. I couldn't be happier and, looking across at Rona, it's made her Christmas, too.'

'Come on, Immi and Grayson, grab your seats – it's time to raise our glasses,' Fisher calls out. I look over at Gray, who looks set to do a toast, and Grayson and I hurry over to join them.

'Considering this was a last-minute decision, it's really wonderful to have you all here. Both Immi and I woke up this morning and felt that something was missing, and that was family. Merry Christmas, everyone, and may every year be as wonderful and special as this one!'

As glasses chink and the banter and laughter circulates around the table, I reflect that Gray knows me so well. Something really was missing and, yes, it's nice to have alone time, but special occasions are for sharing, and family is everything.

Tollie is sitting next to me and he leans in closer. 'It's the start of some new traditions for Lock Keeper's Cottage, then, m'dear. That's a thrilling thought and just the boost we all need. You were right. This place was in need of some serious fixin' up. Now it'll do you proud for many years to come.'

Next year promises to be different yet again, I think to myself. 'The old and the new, side by side. That thought makes me happy, Tollie. It really does.'

He turns to look at Gray, who is sitting opposite him.

'Sorry, Gray. You were about to say somethin' earlier on and I interrupted you,' Tollie suddenly remembers.

Gray puts down his knife and fork, looking nervously across at me.

'Oh, yes. Um... well, it's Immi's news, really.'

I stare back at him and he looks like a rabbit caught in the headlights of a car. It's still sinking in.

'We're going to have a baby,' I announce matter-of-factly.

Eyebrows go up and for three seconds no one makes a sound.

Then Mum flings her hands up to her face, 'Oh my! That's wonderful news!'

Rona can't even speak, and she looks as if she's about to burst into tears. Dinner was about finished anyway, which is just as well, as everyone gets up out of their seats and it's one round of hugs for both Gray and me. This is one surprise none of us were expecting and I can't even look at Grayson's expression, having thrust this news upon him.

'But you never said...' Mum begins, drawing to a halt.

'You've been losing weight...' Rona joins in.

They huddle around me as Gray tops up everyone's drinks. 'I know,' I reply, lowering my voice as we ferry the plates over to the kitchen area. 'I thought it was wedding nerves and stress upsetting my whole system. Believe me, I was as shocked as you all are when the doctor confirmed the home-testing kit was correct – I'm now eight weeks pregnant.'

'Eight weeks?' Rona repeats, her face a picture of happiness.

'Yes, and my appetite might not get back to normal for another month. He said I'm lucky the nausea only comes and goes in waves.'

'Well, what a Christmas present for us all!' Mum declares. 'Life just keeps getting better and better by the minute!'

Rona and I both turn to face her.

'You've given Fisher your answer?' I hold my breath, anxiously.

'I did. We're going to sell both cottages and buy a new place together. On the doorstep, of course, so if you hear of anything coming on the market let us know.'

'And The Star Gazer?' I ask.

'We're going to give it a go. We've proven that there is a

demand, and it was more fun than I thought it was going to be. But let Fisher be the one to tell you officially.'

Rona puts her hand on Mum's arm and gives it a little squeeze. 'That's marvellous news, Val. How is Ziggy settling in?'

'She's getting used to the dogs. I think after her little adventure she's just glad to be back in Aysbury. Is there any news about Patrick, Immi?'

They both turn to look at me. 'Patrick's wife gave me a call a few days ago and I wasn't sure quite when to pass on the message to everyone. She hasn't given up on him and he asked her to tell us how sorry he is for the crime he committed. He's out on bail, pending the hearing. Apparently, he's getting counselling for his gambling addiction, which should help when it comes to determining his sentence. It's also his first offence, so he might be lucky and avoid jail time. She's decided he deserves a second chance; his intention is to straighten himself out and eventually repay every penny he stole.'

'It helps knowing he has a conscience. Let's hope he doesn't let his wife, or himself, down.' Mum mirrors my exact thoughts, but only time will tell.

'And how are you and Grayson getting on?' I turn to Rona, tempted to cross my fingers.

'Now I'm working full-time at the school, I won't be able to visit LA until the summer holidays, but that doesn't stop Grayson flying over for the occasional visit.' The little sparkle in her eyes tells me that their story isn't over.

'This snow might last a while,' Tollie calls out and our heads turn in his direction. Seconds later, we're all standing in a line looking out at the side garden and the meadow beyond.

'I haven't seen snow since I was up in the mountains a few years ago,' Grayson comments. 'Do you normally get it as bad as this?'

We all begin to laugh. 'This is nothin', Grayson,' Tollie confirms. 'This time last year we were snowed in by a real winter blizzard. It's no more than a couple of inches, but I bet there will be a lot of kids out there buildin' snowmen while they can.'

'Well, it sure looks mightily pretty standing here looking out over the English countryside.'

Gray's hand finds mine. Last Christmas was full of unexpected surprises and this Christmas has been, too.

And now Gray and I are standing here, both trying to imagine what next Christmas will be like. The one thing of which we can both be very sure, though, is that whatever surprises are in store we'll face them together. It's the start of a new era in our lives and the best – as they say – is yet to come!

ACKNOWLEDGMENTS

The author is just one link in a long chain to take a manuscript from a draft and turn it into a polished novel. Grateful thanks go to my awesome editor and publishing director, Sarah Ritherdon, whose guidance ensures we end up with it in the best shape possible. A grateful hug to my wonderful copy editor, Sue, and to Candida, for her eagle eyes in making it sparkle.

My agent, Sara Keane, is also very instrumental in the process and an incredible support. Knowing there is someone only a phone call away, whenever I need to chat something through, is a blessing.

And to the wider Boldwood team – a truly awesome group of inspiring women I can't thank enough for their amazing support and encouragement. The sheer enthusiasm of everyone involved is so appreciated.

I'd also like to thank my family and friends who understand my erratic lifestyle as a compulsive writer. The person I am now is rather different to the person I was before I gave up the day job to write novels. It is hard to switch off when a story simply wants to be written and the characters fill my head with constant chatter. I tend to disappear for long periods, coming up for a breather in between to catch up on what's been going on around me. Fortunately, my husband – Lawrence – is always there to keep the herbal teas coming and make me take frequent breaks. He also helps me by researching locations to visit for upcoming stories and he is my rock!

As usual, no book is ever launched without there being an even longer list of people to thank for publicising it. The amazing kindness of my lovely author friends, readers and reviewers is truly humbling. You continue to delight, amaze, and astound me with your generosity and support.

Without your kindness in spreading the word about my latest release and your wonderful reviews to entice people to click and download, I wouldn't be able to indulge myself in my guilty pleasure – writing.

Feeling blessed and sending much love to you all for your treasured support and friendship.

Lucy x

MORE FROM LUCY COLEMAN

We hope you enjoyed reading *A Christmas Wedding in the Cotswolds*. If you did, please leave a review.

If you'd like to gift a copy, this book is also available as an ebook, digital audio download and audiobook CD.

Sign up to Lucy Coleman's mailing list for news, competitions and updates on future books:

http://bit.ly/LucyColemanNewsletter

Explore more glorious escapist reads from Lucy Coleman.

ABOUT THE AUTHOR

Lucy Coleman is a #1 bestselling romance writer, whose recent novels include *Summer in Provence* and *A Springtime to Remember*. She also writes under the name Linn B. Halton. She won the 2013 UK Festival of Romance: Innovation in Romantic Fiction award and lives in the Welsh Valleys.

Visit Lucy's website: www.lucycolemanromance.com

Follow Lucy on social media:

facebook.com/LucyColemanAuthor

twitter.com/LucyColemanAuth

instagram.com/lucycolemanauthor

bookbub.com/authors/lucy-coleman

ABOUT BOLDWOOD BOOKS

Boldwood Books is a fiction publishing company seeking out the best stories from around the world.

Find out more at www.boldwoodbooks.com

Sign up to the Book and Tonic newsletter for news, offers and competitions from Boldwood Books!

http://www.bit.ly/bookandtonic

We'd love to hear from you, follow us on social media:

facebook.com/BookandTonic

twitter.com/BoldwoodBooks

instagram.com/BookandTonic